The Yellowwood Tree

Rick Auterson

For information, or to order additional copies, please contact:

Beacon Publishing Group
P.O. Box 41573 Charleston, S.C. 29423
800.817.8480 | beaconpublishinggroup.com

Publisher's catalog available by request.

ISBN-13: 978-1-949472-96-7

ISBN-10: 1-949472-96-5

Published in 2019. New York, NY 10001.

First Edition. Printed in the USA.

Table of Contents

The Yellowwood Tree

Chapter One

The Spanish Flu effectively ended World War I. Waves of viral death decimated Germany and Austria before it crossed into France and England. From there, it reached every corner of the planet. It was wartime. The Allies censored the news. Governments prohibited the press from reporting the alarming numbers of casualties. Spain was not involved in the war, so the death toll there made it into the newspapers. As far as people could tell, it began in Spain.

A third of the world's population grew sick, and twenty percent of those died. Spanish Flu killed more people in a year than the Black Death killed in a century. It came in three waves, from 1917 through 1919, with the worst being in 1918. In every corner of the globe, one person in twenty perished.

An odd thing about the pandemic was that it killed those in the prime of life. Flu normally kills the very young or the very old. The Spanish Flu took those who were the fittest. A cruel killer, it took mothers and fathers, leaving only the very old and the very young.

***

It was the end of September 1918, and the weather was hot and dry. Emma Taylor ran along the wagon trail from her family's farm. Tears ran down her cheeks, and her blonde hair tangled in the breeze. It was half a mile along the wagon trail through thick forest from their farm to the nearest gravel road and miles more to the nearest house.

Emma was twelve years old and her idyllic little world was falling apart around her. Her mother was sick, sicker than Emma had ever seen before. The first symptoms appeared early in the morning, and now, only six hours later, she was struggling to breathe. Her face and fingernails had taken on a bluish cast and she was coughing up foamy blood. Emma left her little brother, Tommy, sitting at her bedside with a washbasin and a damp cloth. Tommy was only six. He could do very little, but she trusted he would stay there and wipe away the bloody foam from their mother's face.

Emma's lungs burned. The sickness struck her two weeks before, but she recovered. Tommy too had sickened and then recovered. He was not yet well, but it was less severe for him, he had not coughed up blood.

Her tears became desperate, and Emma slowed to a walk. She could not afford to walk, she had to run! She forced herself to run again, only to stop completely when a fit of coughing overwhelmed her. Her head was pounding. The dappled shade of the huge oak trees was disorienting. Black spots appeared before her eyes. She staggered off the trail and clung to the trunk of an oak tree until her vision cleared. Then she began to run again, as quickly as she could.

When she reached the gravel road, the forest gave way to prairie grass. Off in the distance was a harvested wheat field. Their nearest neighbor was Ike Pearson, although everybody called him Old Man Pearson. He lived alone. His wife died years ago. His oldest son married and moved into town, and the younger one was killed in the war. Old Man Pearson was sort of a curmudgeon. He did not take part in community activities like woodcutting or harvesting. Instead, he preferred to hire those things done and avoid the obligation to return favors.

Emma travelled this road often. During the school year, she walked this way to school. Once a month, her mother dressed up, and they hitched up the wagon to drive the eight miles to the mercantile, where they bought what they could not grow and picked up their mail. Her father was off in Europe, fighting in the war, but he wrote often. Every trip into town, they found his letters waiting for them and collected thirty dollars and change from the postmaster, his deferred pay. He earned an extra three dollars a month as a sharpshooter.

Her father always wrote to her and her mother separately. Emma felt grown up pride at receiving letters with her name on the envelopes. She kept them all and read them over and over. She read them to her mother then she read them to Tommy and lastly, she read them to their horses, Buck and Jane. Their milk cow paid little attention, so she gave up reading them to Susie.

Away from the shade of the forest, the sun beat down. She rubbed sweat and tears from her eyes as she ran. Her side ached, so she pressed her fingers under her ribs to ease the pain. She could see the Pearson place more than a mile away across the flat landscape. She has never really spoken to Ike Pearson, but he knew her name from casual encounters at church and the mercantile. She did not know what she wanted from him, only that she needed help. She needed an adult to take charge and tell her what should be done.

She kept putting one foot in front of the other, and with incredible slowness, she finally reached the dirt road that led to the Pearson's house. When she saw Old Man Pearson sitting on his front porch, she gasped in relief.

Staggering off the road into tall grass, she called out, "Mister Pearson!"

The old man stood up and shaded his eyes to see who shouted at him. He picked up the shotgun leaning against the house and ran out into his yard.

"Y'all stay right there. Don't come no closer!" he shouted.

Emma stopped, clutching her side and breathing

heavily. She shouted back, "It's me! Emma Taylor!"

The old man walked to within ten feet of Emma. He cradled his shotgun in his arms and asked, "You sick, child?"

"No sir. I was, but I'm better. Momma is real sick, she needs a doctor."

The old man glared at her. "Ain't no doctors, Doc died last week. Nearest doc is thirty miles away."

Two small boys came out of the door behind him, and he whirled around to shout, "Git back inside!"

They timidly backed up and turned to run into the house, but stopped to look through the screen door. They appeared to be not much older than Tommy.

Emma took two steps toward Mister Pearson. He swung the barrel of his shotgun around. She stopped—shocked that he would do such a thing.

"I'm sorry, child. These is hard times, people have to do hard things. Maybe even be the end of days."

Emma dropped to her knees in the tall grass and sobbed. "Please, Mister Pearson! Please help us!"

The old man swung the barrel of his gun away from her. Emma thought that he too had tears on his face.

"Go home, girl. I buried my boy and his wife two days ago. Them is his kids. Go home and bury your momma. We done had all the sickness we can bear."

Emma was enraged. She jumped to her feet. "No! You call yourself a Christian, you mean old man!"

He swung the barrel of his gun back at her. "I reckon not. I'll carry that burden and burn in Hell if it keeps my grandsons alive."

Emma stood, quaking with tears, and felt her soul leave her body. She saw herself as if from above, a frightened little girl begging for help from an equally frightened old man. What did she expect from him? The world has gone to war and this sickness was its shadow. Perhaps Old Man Pearson was right, and this was the end of days.

She felt sorry for Mister Pearson. He had lost his sons and daughter-in-law, and at more than sixty years of age, he would have to raise two small boys.

She wiped her tears on the back of her arm and said, "I'm sorry for you."

She turned on her heel and walked away, headed for home. She had no idea what to do when she got there, but there was nowhere else to turn. She hung her head and prayed for guidance.

***

Ike watched her walk away, a beautiful little girl in a blue and white checkered dress, her head down and the weight of the world on her shoulders. He knew for certain he just damned himself to an eternity in Hell. He turned and walked back to the house, leaned his shotgun against the wall, dropped down into his porch chair, and reached for the bottle sitting under it.

***

Emma staggered back home. She tried to run but could not. It was all she could do to walk. When she turned off the gravel road and began the climb up the dirt wagon trail, she could not hear the birds nor see the sun shining. She was marching off to war, just like everybody else.

She detested the war, although she actually knew little about it. She only knew what her father wrote in his letters, and he sheltered her from the horror, but she understood all too well that fathers and sons had been taken from their families and sent to impossibly faraway places to kill the fathers and sons of other families. She thought it no wonder the Almighty sent a pestilence to wipe the Earth clean of His cruel creations.

She emerged from the woods into the clearing of their farm and felt a small measure of comfort. She loved her home and her family. She has always been a good girl. She worked hard, said her prayers, and tried not to sin. According to a preacher she heard speak at a revival, nearly everything was sinful. He said that even a newborn baby carried the burden of sin. It bothered her greatly, until her mother told her that she could only try to do right by others, and if she ever committed an actual sin, she would feel it inside. In her heart, she forgave Old Man Pearson and hoped that God would ease his burden.

The Taylor's farm was eighty acres of gently rolling farmland, situated between wooded hilly areas. Although built from logs, their house was more than just a cabin. It was a grand house, two stories tall, with a stove or fireplace in nearly every room. Oak trees were felled, and then square-cut and notched before being fit together so tightly. All that was required to make an airtight seal was a layer of tar. Her father built the house and barn before he felt himself worthy of asking his sweetheart, Anna, to marry him. A stream ran through their property, emerging from a spring farther up on the hillside.

They intended to fill all those rooms with children, but six years separated Emma from her little brother. His birth was hard, and Anna came to realize that he would be their last child. They were not wealthy, but they were far from poor, and never went hungry. Emma lived a happy life, until the war came.

She had spent her whole life at her mother's side—they were inseparable. She looked just like her mother, and even had her unusual eyes. The irises were deep blue, but around the outer edges, a corona of gold radiated into the blue. Her eyes were so striking that when people looked closely at her for the first time, they were often rendered speechless.

Now that she could see her house, she managed to run the last fifty yards and threw open the screen door. She heard the familiar squeak and clap behind her as she quickly made her way to the back of the house to her mother's bedroom. She found Tommy, still at his post, holding a damp, bloody cloth.

He looked up at her through welling tears. "Ma ain't bleeding no more."

Emma's breath caught in her throat. It was the end of days for sure. Her mother had reclaimed her beauty. The hard lines of pain were gone. Her golden hair framed her face with soft curls—no longer wet with perspiration.

She put her arm around her little brother, and with tears streaming down her face, she said, "You did real good, Tommy."

She guided him outside under the big oak tree that shaded the house. A swing hung from a heavy rope tied to a branch. She sat down on it, and Tommy climbed into her lap. It was his favorite thing to do, to swing in their front yard on his big sister's lap.

Tommy felt like a rag doll in her arms. He hung his head and rocked with the motion of the swing. She held him close and sang softly through her tears—a hymn she learned at church.

They sat in the swing, holding on to each other until the sun dropped behind the trees. Emma could not recall for certain, but she did not think that Tommy had eaten all day. When she stirred, he looked up at her. His eyes were red, but he was cried out. He slid off her lap, and Emma stood up stiffly. She took his hand and led him back into the house through the kitchen door.

She made dinner for herself and Tommy. Thin slices of salt pork sputtered in a frying pan while two new potatoes boiled in a pot on their woodstove. His eyes followed her every step. He was uncharacteristically quiet. He did not want to ask and know for sure, and she did not want to say the words aloud. They picked at their dinner in silence by the light of a kerosene lamp. Then she washed him, dressed him in a nightshirt, and tucked him into bed. She knelt down at his bedside and silently prayed for their lost mother. In the darkness, she allowed her tears to fall.

Anna Taylor was a good woman, caring and gentle. She never spoke an unkind word. When she found herself in the company of those who said hurtful things, she would become visibly upset and excuse herself, leaving the gossips to consider the company they kept.

She graduated from high school sixty miles away in Clinton, the daughter of a coal miner. She moved to Owen County to teach in a one-room schoolhouse at the age of eighteen. She no longer taught at the school, but she passed on her love of literature to her daughter. There were two large bookcases in their parlor packed with books, Anna's entire inheritance from her mother. At age twelve, Emma could read and write better than most adults. Little wonder, their home contained far more books than any schoolhouse.

Emma ended her prayer by asking God to watch over their father. She had not seen him in almost a year, and she worried that her memory of his face was fading. She feared she would not recognize him when they met again. She was frightened out of her wits by her mother's death, struggling to think what to do. If it were not for Tommy, she would have just curled up into a ball and wept. Until her father's return, it was up to her to care for her little brother.

Stars and a half moon lit the night. Emma was bone tired and emotionally wrecked, but she could not allow the animals to go unfed. She struggled to her feet and walked out to the barn. She carried buckets of feed out to the pigs—they were waiting by the trough. Then she climbed up into the hayloft to fork down hay for the horses and their milk cow. It was nearly pitch black in the hayloft, but she had done this so many times it didn't matter.

She climbed down the ladder and dumped buckets of feed into the troughs for the horses and their cow. Buck, their big draft horse, loved Emma. He sensed that tragedy had befallen his home. Ignoring his feed, he stuck his head over the fence and nuzzled into her. She wrapped her arms around his long nose, ran her fingers through his mane, and cried her heart out. Buck was Emma's favorite animal on the farm, and she considered him to be a friend. He stayed at the fence long after she walked away.

Still dressed, she climbed into bed with Tommy. When she curled up next to him, she was not surprised to find tears on his face. He was awake, and in his own way, bravely coping with their mother's death. She stayed with him, waiting for him to fall asleep, and fell asleep herself.

***

Emma rolled out of Tommy's bed long before sunrise, careful not to wake him. She wandered through the dark, quiet house, stopping at her mother's door, but unable to go inside.

She washed in cold water and changed clothes in the early twilight of dawn. Then she tiptoed into the kitchen and took down her egg basket; Emma always gathered the eggs first thing in the morning. She stopped just outside the kitchen door, alarmed that she was simply going about her business as if nothing was wrong. Suddenly, the full weight of what happened yesterday crashed down upon her, knocking her to her knees. Time seemed to stop, trapping her in an unbearable moment of despair.

Emma did not know how long she had been there, when she felt a light touch on the top of her head. She looked up to find Old Man Pearson standing on her doorstep. The sun had barely risen. A soft yellow light silhouetted him from behind. She wrapped her arms around his long legs and cried.

He reached down and helped her to stand. "Forgive me, Emma. I'm here."

She threw her arms around him, and then realizing what she had done, she backed away. "Aren't you afraid?"

He looked into the sky and then into her eyes. "I was, but I ain't no more."

He lifted a bloody handkerchief to wipe at his nose. "I come to help you lay your momma to rest and to ask a favor I do not deserve."

He turned and walked away. Emma followed him around the house to find he had driven his Model T truck up the wagon trail and parked beside the barn. Only a handful of automobiles have ever managed that feat. In the back were five-gallon cans of kerosene, bags of salt, sugar, oats, and feed for the animals.

She looked up at him in confusion. "Why?"

He turned away and said, "I know your family. Y'all are good people. Your momma was the sweetest woman I ever met. Hope you be like she was."

He opened the passenger door of the truck and the two boys she saw yesterday climbed out. They were identical twins, not much older than Tommy, with identical brushes of blonde hair, identical green eyes, and identical terrified looks.

"This here is Clyde and Claude. I ain't never sure which is which, always have to ask."

Emma looked up at Mister Pearson. The fear in his eyes caused her heart to race. Did he expect her to care for his grandsons? Her mother was at the center of her world and now she was gone. The unthinkable has happened and she was lost. She began to cry again.

"I don't know what I'm going to do, Mister Pearson. We got nowhere to go, no relatives. Daddy is off in Europe somewhere. I don't know when he'll be home."

Mister Pearson bent over with his hands on his knees. He coughed weakly. Emma heard his chest rattle. She was unfamiliar with the smell of whiskey, and blamed that sour odor on his sickness.

"Emma, look at me," he said.

Emma turned slowly and stood looking at him with tears rolling down her cheeks.

"I have known your momma since she came here. I ain't never seen such a kind, God-fearing woman. You being her daughter, you got more in you than you know."

He stood up abruptly and took two steps before he doubled over in a fit of coughing. He spat bloody foam onto the ground. Emma was concerned for him. Her mother went through this. The bloody foam was a sign that the end was near.

Still bent over and facing away he said, "I'm begging you to take those boys and watch over them. They's a lot of orphans these days and they do not fare well. You got a nice place here. You stay put and wait for your daddy. Don't tell nobody you're alone up here. Tell 'em your momma is sick, but don't let on y'all are alone."

Emma wrapped her arms around herself. "I can't," she said softly.

Ike Pearson swung around to face her. She saw the telltale bluish tinge on his lips and realized he was just as alone as she was. He too had nowhere to turn. He was placing in her care the most precious things in his life, his two grandsons, because she was Anna Taylor's daughter.

He stood up straight, grimacing, took a spade from the back of his truck, and only glanced at Emma. She could not face him. She hung her head and walked away. He followed her up the hill to the edge of the woods. She stopped at a place she had chosen in her mind during the long fitful night.

There was a yellowwood tree, set out away from the big oaks, roughly forty feet tall. It did not flower every year, but when it did, it was a stunning sight. Foot-long clusters of fragrant white blooms would cascade from the branches. Yellowwood trees were rare this far north and only grew in Indiana in the forest that had been named for them. A few groves of yellowwoods grew deep in the forest, but this one stood alone. Before Emma was born, her mother saw this tree in bloom and took that name for their farm. The words Yellowwood Farm were painted on their red barn in big white letters.

Ike placed his hand on Emma's shoulder and said, "It's a fine spot. Wake your little one and feed those boys some breakfast."

Despite his shotgun, Old Man Pearson came down with the flu. Emma was glad she had not wished it on him. The legacy of her mother's kindness saved her from a grievous sin. She embraced Ike for just a moment and then walked back to the house to check on Tommy.

Ike leaned on his shovel and coughed. He awoke during the night with the first symptoms of flu, and it advanced quickly to a bloody nose. He was a deeply religious man and thought that this was God's retribution for the disgraceful way he turned Emma away. He looked up and squinted at the rising sun, still low behind the trees. The grave would face in that direction, if he could dig another grave without falling into it. This would be the fourth grave he had dug in three days, and he dug his own before sunrise—next to Martha's.

People in this part of the country were mostly Baptists—hellfire and damnation believing Christians. There was no law to speak of, and what little there was, existed more for the purpose of political appointments. Sheriffs and their deputies were untrained. Their primary function was to collect debts and ensure that certain people did not get arrested, while they carried out the more gentlemanly crimes of land grabs and fraud. Ike understood that if word got out, a twelve-year-old girl had little chance of hanging on to Yellowwood Farm. He had to convince Emma to hide the fact that only children lived here, until her father came back from the war.

Vigilante groups called Regulators kept the peace. Regulators filled a real need to maintain order, but operated more from scripture than the letter of the law. They were members of church congregations that looked out for their own under the guidance of a pastor, and provided assistance to those less fortunate, but they also punished wife beaters, thieves, and sinners of every sort. If word ever reached them that Old Man Pearson pointed a shotgun at Emma, he would be tied to a tree and whipped. That was what would have happened in normal times. Now, in these desperate times, the Regulators no longer met, and their leader, Pastor Williams, had died of the flu.

Emma stood quietly over Tommy, watching him sleep. She did not want to wake him; only heartache and loss awaited him. She left him asleep in his bed and walked away quietly to make his breakfast. She felt hollow, but even in all that emptiness, she found a warm corner filled with love for her little brother. Until their father returned, she was all he had.

She started a fire in the woodstove and put on a kettle to boil. She would make oats for the boys and take Mister Pearson a cup of hot tea to ease his breathing. In the meantime, there were eggs to gather, animals to feed, and the cow needed milking. It surprised her that she was even aware of such things. Her heart was broken.

Through the kitchen window, she saw Mister Pearson's grandsons still standing beside the truck. They appeared to be seven or eight years old, maybe a year or two older than Tommy. They stood where she left them, shoulder-to-shoulder, staring down at the ground. Emma's grief tore at her, urging her to lie down and mourn, but that was not what her mother would have done. She always made the most momentous decisions of her life by asking herself, *What would Momma do?*

She went quietly out the kitchen door, taking care not to let the screen door bang shut behind her and walked over to stand in front of the two young boys. She could not hold back her tears; they rolled down her cheeks. Sorrow shrouded the world in a thick fog. She struggled to make sense of her surroundings and figure out what to do. The breeze carried the sound of Ike's spade slicing into the ground. She asked herself again, *What would Momma do?*

She ushered the twins into the house and sat them down at the oak table. They watched her closely, not speaking. Emma saw in them what she herself felt—sadness and fear. They must have stood at their parents' graves only three days ago, and they were about to lose their grandfather—the last person who loved them.

Emma placed a hand on each boy's shoulder. The moment she made contact, they jumped up to throw their arms around her. Tears ran down their faces. She held onto them, still crying herself.

"Shush now, don't cry. My name is Emma and I will take care of you."

Chapter Two

On December 18, 1917, the Eighteenth Amendment to the U.S. Constitution was overwhelmingly passed by Congress. Three-fourths of the state legislatures would have to ratify the amendment before it became law. That process would take another two years.

The Eighteenth Amendment did not prohibit the private possession or consumption of alcohol. A person could make liquor for themselves, they just couldn't sell it. It also made allowances for consumption of alcohol for medicinal purposes or religious sacrament. Feeling that the Eighteenth Amendment was inadequate, some states enacted much more stringent laws. Indiana passed a "bone dry" law that took effect in April of 1918, prohibiting possession or consumption of alcohol for any reason. The Catholic practice of accepting the Holy Eucharist became punishable by law, and Catholics became the favored targets of the White Caps.

Prohibition was an attractive concept to a dwindling group of moral crusaders known as White Caps. They had been around for decades in Indiana and depending upon whether the governor at the time was a White Cap, they were alternately praised and reviled. In Owen County, White Caps took the place of Regulators, who ceased to exist when the churches were closed to stop the spread of the flu. White Caps met in secret and hid their faces, while Regulators introduced themselves, even to men they were about to whip.

***

Emma fitted Buck with a breast band harness, checking carefully to ensure she had not turned a strap. Buck was an experienced draft horse and did not require a bridle. She fitted him with a halter so that, if need be, he could graze. Emma was always kind to him, and he followed her around whenever she was in the pasture.

Yesterday, she stood at her mother's grave and wept, holding Tommy's hand. She tried to sing but could not. Instead, she whispered a prayer. She felt wounded—a raw weeping gash in her soul. She dared not give in to her grief. The boys needed her, and there were things that needed to be done.

Rising before the sun, she milked the cow and fed the chickens, horses, and pigs. At first light, she wrote a tearful, terrifying letter to her father, begging his forgiveness because she allowed her mother to die. Then she wiped away her tears and made breakfast for the boys. She took the twins into her heart late in the night, getting out of bed again and again to stand over them while they slept, watching for signs of sickness. They still have not spoken a word.

The twins slept in her grandmother's room. Her father's mother lived with them until her death two years ago, the last relative Emma was aware of. Her mother's brothers disappeared into the territories out west. Her father was an only child, or rather the only surviving child.

She hitched the harness to their wagon and went inside to get the boys. When Ike unloaded his truck, he told her he would return in the morning. And if he did not, then she should come to his house. As tough as that old man was, he could not bury himself. Emma had no way of knowing that all across the country, the mortuaries were full, the gravediggers overwhelmed, and families everywhere were forced to bury their own.

She found the boys still sitting at the breakfast table. Clyde and Claude had their heads down. Tommy watched them from the other end of the table.

Seeing Emma, he asked, "Can they talk?"

She said, "Not right now, Tommy."

"They're too sad to talk, ain't they?"

His understanding of the world often surprised Emma. She expected him to ask about their mother today—he has not. Yesterday at the graveside, he hung onto her tightly, cried when she cried, and mumbled a prayer. Then he walked back to the barn and climbed into the cob house to collect two baskets of corncobs to burn in the kitchen stove. He emptied them in the wood box and walked to the edge of the forest to collect acorns to mix with the feed for the pigs. He seldom did his chores without being asked, but he did his best on the worst day of his life. Emma admired him. She understood that he was doing his chores for his mother, and she could not do any less.

She dreaded taking the twins to their grandfather's farm, but they were too young to be left alone. She trembled every time she imagined herself walking uninvited into that house and seeking out his body.

***

Yesterday, after unloading his truck, Ike Pearson wearily sat on the ground with his back against the barn and called her to stand in front of him. He told her that he'd already dug his grave and asked that she shelter the boys from seeing his dead body. Then he begged her not to let on that they were alone. He told her the world was a hard place, and if she let on that only children were living on this farm, then men would come and take them away, claiming the land as their own.

The ways of the world terrified Emma: dishonesty, the war, and this horrible sickness. She gathered up the boys and led them outside to the wagon. Boosting them up one at a time, she checked to make certain she had her letter to her father before climbing up into the seat. She had driven the wagon by herself only a handful of times, but she and Buck had an arrangement—they were good to each other. She shook the reins, and he headed off for town. The Pearson place was on the way, so she would stop there. Depending upon what she found, she would continue on to the mercantile. She had to post the letter to her father as soon as possible.

The summer rains had been gentle, so the wagon trail through the woods was not rutted this year. The hill was steep in places, so Emma applied the brake to keep the wagon from creeping up on Buck. Once they reached the gravel road, the going was easier, and she could focus on her thoughts.

The Pearson place was only a mile or two away, so it was hard to judge on the wide flat plain. The twins stared off into the distance at their grandfather's farm. She knew what was on their minds.

Buck pulled their wagon along the road easily, and sooner than Emma wished, they arrived. They might be here for some time. She unhitched Buck and attached a long rope to the wagon so he could graze on the tall grass in the yard. She left the boys on the wooden seat and set the brake, terrified by what she was about to do.

The Pearson place was a small clapboard house once whitewashed, but now a dingy gray. She stepped up onto the rickety boards of the small front porch and knocked on the door. She waited, knocked again, and fought to control her runaway heartbeat. She prayed that Mister Pearson would answer the door. He did not. Unwilling and afraid, she opened the door. The inside of the house was dark and dusty.

"Mister Pearson!"

There was no reply. She looked at the boys in the wagon. They looked back with identical little frowns. She steeled her resolve, took a deep breath, and went inside.

The house was filthy, a thick layer of dust lay over everything. What little furniture there was appeared to be about to collapse. The Pearson farm was profitable, the animals healthy, and the crops abundant. Mister Pearson was the only farmer Emma knew who owned a truck. He might be prosperous, but he did not live well. His wife died years ago, so perhaps he did not care.

She called out for him again, "Mister Pearson! It's Emma!"

No answer. She peeked into the next room, the kitchen. It was in worse shape than the parlor. There were dishes overflowing from the bathtub-size sink and piled on the table. A mouse scurried for cover. Empty whiskey bottles crowded together on the table and littered the floor. She went back to the living room, opened a door, and found a bedroom. Blood stained the sheets, but the room was empty.

There was only one door left. Reluctantly, she opened it and peered into the gloom. Ike Pearson lay on the bed, dressed in his Sunday best. Emma's heart caught in her throat. She expected this but prayed for it not to happen. She stood for a moment, looking closely. He was motionless. His hands were folded over his chest, and beneath them was an empty bottle.

What would Momma do?

Trembling, she knelt down on the dirty floor beside that filthy bed and began to pray. "O Jesus, by your resurrection, death no longer has dominion over those who die. So we ask, take Mister Pearson into Heaven…"

Something touched the top of her head. "That's real pretty."

Emma screamed and flew out of that house. She ran for the wagon, still screaming. Seeing her coming at them wailing, the boys jumped down and ran off across the road into a harvested wheat field. Buck paused from cropping grass long enough to watch Emma fly past the wagon and follow the boys into the wheat stubble. When she stopped running, the boys converged on her and clung to her dress.

Her heart hammered in her chest. She bounced up and down on tiptoe. She managed to stop running, but her body was still thrumming with the need for speed. Ike appeared in the doorway some hundred yards away. Emma shaded her eyes from the sun and stared hard at the first ghost she ever encountered, but he looked real enough.

Mister Pearson stepped outside and sat down on his porch. He beckoned to Emma with a wave. After a moment's hesitation, she dragged the boys forward. They held onto her as far as the wagon and then stayed behind it, peeking around as she crept forward alone. She stopped in front of Mister Pearson, still trembling, and waited. His head was down. He had yet to look at her.

"I ain't dead yet, but death will not be long in coming," he said.

Emma believed him. His gray hair was uncombed and his suit wrinkled. The bluish tinge had left his face, replaced by a gray pallor.

She knew what her mother would have done. It was not something she wanted to do, but she had no choice. Sometimes it was hard being Anna Taylor's daughter. She turned around and beckoned to the boys. They disappeared behind the wagon. She called out to them, "Clyde! Claude! Tommy!"

She could see their legs under the wagon. Tommy leaned over to peek under it, then stood back up when his eyes met Emma's. She walked around the wagon and shooed them toward the house, right past Mister Pearson, through the filthy parlor and into the kitchen.

She lined them up. "Boys, we are going to clean this house from top to bottom."

They looked around the room, looked at each other, and then back at Emma. They did not appear to believe her. She clapped her hands, making them jump. "Clyde! Claude! Empty that sink. Tommy! You find a broom." Still, they just stood looking at her. She leaned forward and shouted, "Now, boys!"

They scattered.

Emma lit a fire in the woodstove and carried buckets of water from the hand pump over the sink to fill the reservoir. She needed hot water, lots of it. Once she had a kettle boiling, she opened a canister labeled tea, and had to chip a dark clump from the bottom with a spoon. It smelled like tea and was not moldy, so she placed it in an infuser and poured boiling water over it. It fell apart and became recognizable as tea.

She carried the hot tea out to the front porch, but Mister Pearson was no longer there. He was nowhere in sight, so she reasoned that he had to be in the barn.

She found him feeding his pigs and noticed acorns mixed with the chopped corn and cob. They did that, too.

"Mister Pearson, I made you some tea. It will do you good to get a hot drink down you."

It was strange to see him working in the pigpen wearing his suit. He stepped over the low fence, tripped, and nearly ran Emma over. He stood up swaying and took the warm cup from her hands. "Thank you, child."

Emma thought he looked terrible: unshaven, unkempt, and pale. He had a sour smell about him that she blamed on the sickness. In sharp contrast to the house, his barn was clean and tidy. He staggered back to lean against the fence and drank his tea.

He handed Emma the empty cup and said, "I should not be alive. For certain, I won't last the night."

Emma thought he looked some better and asked, "Have you eaten today?"

He shook his head and said, "Don't waste no food on me, girl. And tell them boys to leave the house alone. Ain't no sense cleaning it."

Emma looked him over. He was less dead than he seemed to think. She decided to make him some lunch, turned and walked away, leaving him to his chores. It was a shame to muddy up his suit that way.

She found the boys hard at work. Tommy had swept the kitchen clean and was working on the parlor, while Clyde and Claude washed dishes. She had found a big bottle of Palmolive and hoped they would not run out. Soaping a rag in the sink, she wiped down the cupboards so they would have a place for the clean dishes.

Tommy lined up all the empty bottles on the back porch. Emma knew what they were only because she could read. Before today, she has never seen a liquor bottle. She gathered them up in a burlap sack. Whiskey was sold at the mercantile, but it did not sit on the shelves. Emma did not even know it was illegal.

She thought it shameful for a person to allow their home to fall into such a state, but Mister Pearson was a widower, she did not want to judge. He has lived alone for years now with no one to help him.

She moved on from gathering up bottles to the next chore needing to be done. Emma has been in nearly constant motion since her mother died, so seeing the boys at work made her realize she should have been keeping them busy all along. She only cried when she was quiet and unoccupied.

The root cellar was just outside the kitchen door, and Emma found it to be in good order. There were barrels of potatoes under straw and carrots packed in moist sand. Dozens of Ball jars were arranged on shelves, and hams hung from the beams. She took down an empty basket and selected handfuls of potatoes and carrots. Then she carved a slice of ham using a huge knife she found stuck into a beam.

She carried her basket back up into the kitchen and put on a pot of water to boil. The twins were doing a mediocre job of dishwashing, so she sorted through what they had washed and only put away what was clean. She piled the rest next to the sink. The twins looked at each other, simultaneously poked each other, and began rewashing the dishes Emma rejected. It was the first time she saw them smile.

Tommy came into the kitchen carrying his broom. "I'm done, Emma."

Emma asked, "Did you do the bedrooms?"

He looked down at his feet and said, "I ain't going in there, it smells bad."

Emma agreed. She left Tommy standing in the kitchen and went to drag the sheets and blankets from the beds. She took them outside and piled them next to a big iron caldron hanging from a tripod by a chain. Tommy came outside to watch, so she put him to work carrying wood to make a fire and water to fill the cauldron. She went back inside and opened all the windows that were not stuck shut.

Emma was sweeping the bedrooms when Ike came into the kitchen carrying a pail of milk. Hearing him coughing, she went to check on him and found him sitting at the table holding a bloody handkerchief over his mouth. His grandsons stopped washing dishes and stood at the sink watching him.

He said through his handkerchief, "Girl, there ain't no use cleaning this house. I told you, it will not be long now."

The twins approached him and stood on either side. He pushed himself up from the table. Keeping his handkerchief over his mouth, he said, "Don't come no closer, boys. They ain't been sick, girl. Keep them back."

He groaned and walked outside to lean against the post that held up the clothesline.

Emma followed him outside. "Mister Pearson, those boys need you."

"I ain't long for this world. I'm begging you to take pity on them. Keep them safe."

Emma could not refuse him, she owed an unimaginable debt. He relieved her of the terrible burden of burying her mother. There was no grave marker, so she collected small white stones from the stream and arranged them to form a cross and spell out her mother's name on the grave. She reached into the front pocket of her dress and rubbed that awful letter to her father between her fingers. Tears blurred her vision.

She said, "I will wash the bedding so the sickness does not spread. You will ruin your Sunday clothes doing chores. Maybe you ought to change. Let me wash them."

Ike took his mind off his sickness and impending death to consider Emma. She looked up at him with tears on her face, a sweet, willowy girl. He was struck by her beautiful eyes—blue ringed with gold. Her mother's eyes were like that.

He said, "Your momma was holding Martha's hand when she died. Did you know? I have always been grateful for that."

Emma remembered. Her mother stayed at the

Pearson's farm for two days. There was a church service, and Missus Pearson was buried in the small plot on the Pearson farm. She could see it from where she stood now, a low hill surrounded by an iron fence.

The churches were closed now. Public funerals were banned for fear of spreading the flu. Doctors, nurses, and clergymen were among the first to be stricken. Families coped as best they could, left to bury their own and struggling to keep their faith. Healthy men and women in the prime of life volunteered to aid the sick and soon discovered they were the most vulnerable to this terrible disease.

Emma left Mister Pearson leaning against the post and went to check on her pot of vegetables and ham.

***

Emma did not own a watch, but it was well past noon. After she and the boys cleaned the house, she persuaded Mister Pearson to eat the meal she prepared. He refused to come in and sit at the table with her and the boys. Instead, he hunkered down on the back steps, still dressed in his Sunday best. She was relieved to see him eat. He seemed to gain strength.

When she came back to check on him, she found the empty bowl. He was out by the barn pitching hay to his milk cow.

The sun had dried the sheets, so she put them on the beds. The blankets were still damp. She would stop again on the way back from town and take them down.

She hitched Buck up to the wagon, and as she walked around it checking the straps, she saw that Mister Pearson had placed in the back a large ham wrapped in burlap, a bushel of apples, sacks of potatoes, and jars of what appeared to be blackberry jam. It was difficult to imagine him making jam. More likely, he bought them in town.

She climbed up into the seat and shook the reins. Buck pulled them out to the road, but she had to turn him toward town when he headed for home. He knew it was the wrong time of day to be heading into town.

Just beyond the Pearson's farm, they passed a small one-room schoolhouse. Emma attended school there along with more than a dozen other children. She had fond memories of that little schoolhouse. In good weather, she walked. On especially cold mornings, her father heated bricks on the woodstove and placed them on the footboard of their wagon to keep her feet warm while he drove her to school wrapped in a warm blanket.

Emma learned reading, writing, and arithmetic at home from her mother. She was more of a teacher's helper than a student, but she had learned things at that school. She learned to help those in need and to ignore the taunts of those more fortunate. She found her place in their community. She was Anna Taylor's daughter. Everybody who knew her said she looked and acted just like her mother. There was no higher praise.

The nearest town was Spencer, a small community of four thousand souls, situated on a flat spot on the side of a rise overlooking the White River. At the edge of town was the mercantile. It was more than a general store. The owner also purchased cash crops, sold gasoline, ran the post office, and the railway station. The road ran through a flood plain, and Emma could recall times when the river overflowed its banks and they were unable to reach the town. The town itself sat on high ground that the floodwaters never reached.

She could see the town up on the hillside. Buck leaned into the straps as the road took on a slight rise. The twins sat between her and Tommy on the wooden seat. She watched Tommy lean over, looking into the face of the boy nearest him.

"Is your name Clyde?" he asked.

The boy shook his head, so Tommy leaned farther out and caught the eye of the boy next to Emma. "Are you Clyde?"

That boy too shook his head. The twins looked at each other and giggled. Emma realized those two have probably traded names more than once in their short lives. She has studied them closely—looking for a freckle or a scar that would set them apart—but they were perfectly identical.

Tommy leaned back with a frown and said, "One of you is Clyde. If you don't speak up, I'll just pick."

Emma pulled up to the mercantile as the sun touched the treetops, worried about getting home before dark. She set the brake and climbed down from the wagon. The sign in the window said the place was open, but there were no cars and no other wagons. It looked deserted.

She left the boys sitting in the wagon and timidly went inside. Mister Anderson, the proprietor, looked up from behind a counter. "Where is your mask!"

Emma froze, clutching her letter. "I'm sorry. I don't know what you mean."

Mister Anderson came out from behind the counter and Emma saw that he wore a white mask over his mouth and nose—a miniature version of his white apron.

He pointed to a sheet of paper tacked to a bulletin board. "Everybody has to wear a mask, county ordinance on account of the influenza."

Emma began to tremble. "I don't have a mask."

Mister Anderson went back behind the counter and returned holding out a white gauze mask. Emma took it from his hand, and seeing how his was fastened, she pulled it over her face, tying it in back. It frightened her that Mister

Anderson shouted at her, and this thing over her face felt uncomfortable.

He held out his hand. "That'll be six cents."

The county provided the masks free of cost, but Emma didn't know that. She held out her letter in a shaking hand. "I just wanted to post a letter. I don't have any money."

Mister Anderson snatched the letter from her hand and examined it. He looked her up and down. "Are you Anna Taylor's daughter?"

Emma nodded her head.

Mister Anderson took her by the shoulder and led her to the postal counter. "No charge for the mask. Are you here to collect your daddy's pay? How's your momma?"

Emma began to cry. Lying was a sin, but Mister Pearson cautioned her not to let on that her mother was dead. She did not want to say it anyway, so she kept silent. Mister Anderson went behind the postal counter and counted out slightly more than thirty dollars. He placed it in an envelope and turned a ledger book around on the counter.

"I'm sorry I yelled at you. Your momma is the finest woman I ever met. You tell her I said to stay well." He pointed at the ledger book. "Make your mark, girl. You and your momma got letters."

Emma studied the ledger through tears. She carefully wrote her name and the date in the appropriate places. Mister Anderson placed two envelopes on top of the one containing the money. He pushed them across the counter, and she reached out slowly, half expecting him to snatch them back. Once she had them in her grasp, she whipped them away, stuffed them into the pocket of her dress, and ran for the door.

Emma shot out of the mercantile and ran to the wagon. She untied the reins and climbed up into the seat. The boys watched her in fear. She was crying and had something tied over her face. When she picked up the reins, one of them slipped from her hands. Buck stepped on the rein and his head dipped. He blew a complaint.

Emma jumped down to the ground and ran around to pick up the rein. She wrapped her arms around Buck's long nose. "I'm sorry, Buck. I'll be more careful."

Buck blew again and nuzzled into her. She pulled her mask down around her neck and sighed, glad to be able to take an unobstructed breath. She was no longer crying, but she thought this sickness had transformed the world. People she had known all her life were acting strangely—cruelly.

She ran to the back of the wagon and took a small apple from the bushel Mister Pearson left there. She ran back to the front and offered it to Buck, held out on a flat hand, and he took it in one bite, crunching this rare treat and rolling his eyes. Emma patted him on the neck and he lowered his head so she could scratch behind his ears. She knew he liked that. She gave him a moment to finish his apple and climbed back up into the seat. She did not have to shake the reins. Buck swung the wagon around and headed for home.

As soon as they reached the flat stretch of road, Emma untied her mask and stuffed it into her pocket. She would need it the next time she came into town. The sun was touching the tops of the trees, and the ride home would take more than an hour. She did not want to travel in the dark, so she urged Buck into a trot and whispered an apology. Once this ride was over, she would brush him and give him another apple. The boys had to hold on to the seat because the springs tended to launch them into the air on the bumpy road.

When they reached the Pearson place, the sun was behind the trees. Emma swung Buck into the yard, set the brake, and jumped down. They did not have much time. She was glad to see the blankets had been taken down from the clothesline. The twins started to rise, but she only had to give them a look and hold up one finger. They sat back down. She ran to the door and knocked. She wasn't sure, but she thought she heard a voice, so she went on in. A lamp burned in the kitchen.

She found Mister Pearson sitting at the table, eating the soup she left simmering on the stove right out of the pot. He looked up at her and gestured to the seat beside him with his spoon.

He said, "Thank you, Emma. This house does not feel so sad to me now that it is clean. I can meet my maker with a measure of comfort."

Emma sat down beside him and saw that he was still wearing his church clothes. She hoped he would not sleep in them again. The leaves on the trees were still green and the days were warm, but it was the end of September and the nights were cooling off. She stood up and placed another log in the woodstove. Ike watched her, knowing she was thinking of his comfort.

She said, "It's getting dark. I still have chores, and the boys need their supper. Thank you for the things you left in the wagon, but I have to be going."

Ike said, "Anna Taylor is surely an angel in heaven. I pray that I am privileged to meet her again before the sun rises."

Emma thought that some decent food had brought back a little of Ike's color, but his breathing was still labored. He wheezed and rattled. She looked up at him with concern.

"If you do not come to the house in the morning, then we will come and check on you."

She ran for the door. The last sliver of the sun was on the horizon when Emma drove the wagon into the barn. She set the brake and told Tommy, "Take the twins and feed the pigs and chickens. I'll take care of the horses and the cow."

She jumped down and started unhitching Buck. The boys still sat in the wagon, looking lost and exhausted. She clapped her hands and shouted, "Now, boys!"

They scampered down, and Tommy led them off to get the feed for the pigs.

Emma removed the harness from Buck and arranged it carefully over a wooden rail. She took another apple from the basket in the back of the wagon and fed it to Buck. He crunched away happily while Emma went to get the brush and her milk stool. Buck was the biggest horse she had ever seen. She had to stand on a stool to brush him down. He shivered when she ran the brush along his spine and she smiled. He loved to be brushed.

When she was done, Buck's coat was shining. She led him to his stall to find Jane already there waiting for him—or more likely for her dinner. Emma was late. She climbed into the hayloft and pitched hay through openings above the hayracks for the horses and their cow. Then she climbed back down and carried buckets of chopped corn and cob to dump into the troughs.

Emma and her mother had harvested all the corn. Buck pulled their wagon through the fields while they stripped the ears from the husks using corn pegs, sharp wooden pegs attached to leather straps that aided them in splitting the husks so the ears could be twisted free of the stalks. The ears were kept in a crib while they dried, and then loaded again into the wagon. They made a dozen trips to the mercantile. She did not know how much money they made, but her mother told her that because of the war, prices were exceptionally high.

They paid a crew of men to harvest their wheat. A

thresher crawled into their fields from a neighboring farm, belching thick black smoke. It was impossible to bring that huge machine up the wagon trail. Horse-drawn reapers cut the wheat and carried it to the thresher.

Emma spent that day carrying buckets of drinking water down to the thresher and pouring them into ceramic jars, wrapped in wet burlap to keep them cool. At noon, she and her mother laid out a spread of fresh bread, milk, ham, and boiled eggs on a table made from planks and sawhorses. The men were very polite and complimentary. They reaped and threshed twenty acres in a day and a half.

The harvest was in, and the animals were healthy. The farm was thriving, but Emma felt no joy. The center of her world was gone. Her heart was broken. A tear trickled down her cheek. *What would Momma do?*

Momma, she thought, *would do what needed to be done.* She wiped her eyes and dragged that big ham out of the wagon. She would hang it in the root cellar and come back for the rest. Where were those boys? She could use some help.

***

Emma ended her day with thoughts of her father. Where was he? Would he receive her letter? She knew that sometimes, letters to or from her father simply disappeared, lost in the chaos of the war. She sat down at her small writing desk and pulled the envelopes from the pocket of her dress. The evening was taken up by delayed chores, a late dinner, and then getting the boys ready for bed. She was exhausted and glad for the chance to read her father's letter in private.

Spreading the envelopes out in the lamplight, she selected the one with her name written in her father's spiky hand. She held it to her face and rubbed it against her cheek, hoping to feel some trace of his comforting strength. She opened it carefully using her ivory-handled letter opener, a gift from her grandmother. She unfolded the single piece of paper and took a deep breath.

Dear Emma,

This is a day I will always remember, June 25th. Happy birthday, daughter! I wish for you happiness and good luck on your birthday. I know that your mother baked you a chocolate cake as that is your favorite.

We are currently living in a cellar with excellent accommodations. It is a grand house, but the upstairs is ruined. I am in charge of the nightly guard. Few men have been injured in our group, but another was attacked with gas this past night having just arrived and foolishly lit a lantern.

I cannot say where I am or where I am going. I do not want the censors making black marks on my letters. Do not be alarmed if you do not receive a letter for some weeks. It may be difficult to post where we are headed. If it is not too much trouble, please include an envelope and a blank piece of paper in your letters as such things are often impossible to come by. Even now, I am using a borrowed pen. We pass it around and each man writes his letters.

Watch over your mother and Tommy. I know they will watch over you.

I love you, Emma,
Thomas Richard Taylor

She put her head down and wept, shaking with tears. His letter took three months to reach her! Hers might take just as long to reach him. Evil and suffering have taken over the world. She threw back her head and begged God, "Please! Please bring Daddy home!"

She sobbed uncontrollably. It all came crashing down around her and she was overwhelmed. She was only a girl. She could not do all that was being asked of her.

She felt a soft touch on her arm and looked up to find the twins standing beside her. The one touching her arm said, "Don't cry, Emma."

She gathered them into her arms and cried even harder.

Chapter Three

Emma opened her eyes and wished she could close them again, but she could hear the birds chirping and knew sunrise was near. Last night, she released her pent-up tears, and now she felt faded—a shadow of herself. She dragged herself out of bed and walked softly downstairs. It was time to begin her day.

She drew comfort from the warm feel of her home in the dim light of early dawn. The walls were solid oak, a foot and a half thick. There were four rooms upstairs and four downstairs. Her mother planned to have a large family, but it had not come to pass. Her mother's bedroom was downstairs. Emma was unable to go in there. She paused by the door, but once again she could not bring herself to open it.

Her father's desk was in the next room. He kept the farm's ledger books in his desk. There was a metal box containing every cent they had, hidden in a special place under the floor. They lived in a cash economy. Few farmers used banks for anything other than loans. Their farm was owned outright—free and clear. Her father inherited the land from his father. The original homestead was still there, but nearly disintegrated—a log cabin with a sod roof, empty now for many years. Emma used to play there. She barely remembered the girl in her that found the time to play.

She placed the envelope containing the money she was given at the mercantile on her father's desk. There were chores to do, and the boys would be up soon.

Their home contained a luxury that few outside of town could claim. Her mother called it a powder room, but really it was just a narrow room with a commode and a wash basin. Even so, indoor toilets were rare on a farm. The water came from a cistern her father dug into a hillside behind the house. Sometimes, the cistern ran dry or the pipes froze, and buckets had to be carried from the kitchen to fill the tank, but usually it worked perfectly well. Emma was no stranger to their outhouse. She used it when she was about her chores and had muddy feet, but on cold winter mornings, or when the urge came in the middle of the night, she was exceedingly glad to have a powder room.

She still remembered the day her father pulled the chain for the first time. The whole family stood over the bowl to watch the water swirl and disappear while they clapped their hands and cheered. Her mother kissed her father so long and hard that Emma blushed and turned away. It was the only running water in the house. There was a hand pump over their big kitchen sink that provided cold, clean water from the well for washing, cooking, and drinking. Hot water came from a reservoir in the side of their woodstove.

Emma took the empty pitcher from the washbowl and carried it into the kitchen to fill it with warm water from the stove. She carried it back into the powder room and closed the door. She usually washed in her room, but she was too tired to carry a pitcher upstairs.

Once she was clean, she poured the used water into the toilet bowl and stepped quietly back up the stairs to get dressed. She always wore a dress and cotton bloomers that fastened around her ankles. Her mother had done the same. Emma owned four everyday dresses and one for church. Cleaning Mister Pearson's house left her clothes too filthy to wear again today, so she selected a clean dress from her wardrobe. Slipping out of her damp nightdress, she shivered in the coolness of dawn. She quickly pulled her dress over her head and sat down on her bed to pull on her woolen socks. She laced up her shoes and stood up, feeling more like herself. She could do this. She was Anna Taylor's daughter.

She walked smartly down the hall allowing her heels to clack on the wood floor and knocked on each door as she went by. There were rules in the Taylor house. First among them was that you fed the animals before you fed yourself.

***

Emma placed plates of eggs and salted pork in front of the boys. She had roused them from their sleep, washed and dressed them, and taken them outside to acquaint them with their chores. Tommy was used to this morning routine, but the twins groaned until Emma clapped her hands. Then they snapped to attention, listened closely, and did their best to please her. They were wearing their only clean clothes, so today would be laundry day.

Tommy was drinking the milk he learned only this morning to take from Susie. Milking was one of Emma's chores, but she was burdened now with the things her mother had done, and her mother was burdened with the things her father had done. The twins proved to be inseparable, so she allowed them to work together, gathering acorns for the pigs, scattering feed for the chickens, and pitching hay for the horses and their milk cow. It took her longer to show them what to do than it would to have simply done those things, but she could feel herself growing weaker. They would have to learn quickly and do their share before she keeled over from exhaustion.

Clyde was speaking now. She tried to encourage him to talk. She would show them what to do and ask him, "Do you understand?"

Whether he understood or not, his reply was always, "Yes, Emma."

Being the head of the household had its own set of rules. Emma made her plate last and dropped into her chair.

When she picked up her fork, she heard the unmistakable rattle and chug of an automobile. It was a huge relief. She was worried that Mister Pearson would not show up this morning. She could not face death again.

She stood up and went to look out the window over the kitchen sink. Sure enough, Mister Pearson's truck was parked beside the house. He was unloading wood onto the woodpile, but she was alarmed to see that he still wore his suit. She put on a kettle to boil, picked up her plate, and carried it outside.

When Ike saw Emma come out of the house, he sank down to sit on the woodpile and coughed hard. Emma thought he sounded some better. He was coughing up the sickness, clearing his lungs, but he seemed dizzy, and he still had that strange sour smell about him.

She handed him her plate. "I'm happy to see you, Mister Pearson. We were concerned for you."

He tried to give her plate back. "Child, do not waste food on a sick old man. I am certain sure that this will be my last day on this Earth."

Emma clasped her hands behind her back and smiled. "You are welcome at our table, but if you prefer it, I will make your tea and bring it outside."

He did not answer, but he seemed to develop an interest in her eggs and crisp fried salt pork. She turned and went back inside to peek out the window. He was eating and seemed to be enjoying it. It warmed her heart to see him eat. She was starting to love that ornery old man.

Emma turned to make tea and found that the boys had taken down a clean plate and divided their breakfasts into four equal shares. She was hungry and grateful. She walked around the table and kissed each of them on the forehead— leaving smiles behind her. They had apples. If she could find the time today, she would bake them a pie.

When the kettle began to boil, she got up from her breakfast and made tea, snatching a piece of pork or a forkful of eggs each time she passed her plate. She added a dollop of honey to the tea and carried it outside.

Mister Pearson had cleaned his plate and was stacking wood. Emma was worried about the woodpile. She was too small to wield an axe and maul. Even if she had the strength, a crosscut saw required two people—preferably strong men. She planned to take a handsaw into the woods and cut branches she could carry. Stocking the woodpile was serious business, and the winters are cold in Indiana.

She handed Mister Pearson his tea and said, "Thank you kindly for the wood. I have been concerned about it."

Ike took the warm cup from her, and at the first sip, his eyes lit up. It had been a long time since he tasted honey.

"This here is seasoned white oak, burns long and hot. If I am still drawing breath near sunset, I'll bring another load. Certain sure, I will not live to see another sunrise."

Emma thought his fine suit of clothes was done for, but less sure Mister Pearson was on death's door. Even so, he was a pitiful sight.

She placed her hand on his arm. "Promise me you will come back before the sun sets. I can harvest corn, sew, cook, clean, and feed the livestock, but I cannot swing an axe. You promise me you will bring another load of wood and I promise you I will cook a fine dinner and bake an apple pie."

Emma did not wait to hear his promise. She picked up his empty plate and carried it back inside. There were things that needed to be done.

Ike had been listening hard for days, straining to hear the angels calling. He struggled to his feet and downed the rest of his warm tea. He coughed, spat, and felt a little better. An angel had finally called to him. Maybe tonight he would only drink a little—maybe. He had been alone for years now. Drinking himself into unconsciousness at night had become a habit, a way to cope with the loneliness of life without Martha.

Emma set Clyde and Claude to work washing the dishes. She figured they were experienced enough now to do the job well. She sent Tommy out to gather acorns and went up to her room. Her father's letter to her mother was resting on her writing desk, and it was weighing on her mind. She stood beside her desk, looking down at the envelope. On the outside was her mother's name written in her father's hand. Such a thing was incredibly valuable to her, but it was a personal thing that belonged to her mother. She dared not open it.

Placing the letter in her pocket, she went downstairs, out the kitchen door, and walked to the stream that ran beside the woods. It was only a few inches deep. Even when hard rains caused the river to flood, their stream flowed calm and gentle, fed only by a spring. The water was clean and clear. Their pastures were situated so the animals could drink from it.

The bottom was sand and gravel, but in places it exposed the hard, white limestone this part of the state was known for. A prized building material, it was quarried in Bedford some twenty miles away. She followed the stream into the woods until she found what she was looking for—a flat white slab an inch thick. She pried it from the bank, washed it clean, and carried it to her mother's grave. Pausing there for just a moment, she said hello with a prayer. Then she returned to the stream to find another.

She carried another stone, similar to the first, up the

hillside and positioned it carefully at the head of the grave. The earth was still soft, so it sank in. She took her father's letter and placed it on the stone, then covered it with the other. It was the best she could do. She clasped her hands in front of her, bowed her head, and prayed that somehow, her mother would know her husband had written to her and he loved them all.

Emma turned to walk away and paused. She did not know she was crying until she tasted tears. She could not understand why God would cut short her mother's life. It did not make her question her faith—without a doubt God existed. She was, however, beginning to question His divine plan. She turned back to the grave, and instead of bowing her head, she looked up into the sky and shouted defiantly, "I am Anna Taylor's daughter!"

Her words echoed back from the house, the barn, and the trees. It frightened her. She had never before shouted at the Almighty. A sob burst out of her and she looked all around fearfully. Then she ran back to the house—half expecting a bolt from the blue.

When Emma entered the kitchen, the twins were putting away the last of the dishes. She sent them out to help Tommy gather acorns before they saw her tears. She put on her mother's apron and used it to dry her eyes. Wearing it made her feel closer to her mother. It had large pockets and blue ruffles around the edges. Her mother wore it every day. It came down below Emma's knees.

She sat down at the table and started peeling apples, saving the cores and peels for the pigs. She considered how to hang on to their farm until her father's return. Almost certainly, it would be many months. Winter was coming, a time of short days and long nights when chores were made more difficult by cold, ice, and snow.

Tommy would start school this year—if the schools were open. The schools and churches have been closed for months now, by order of the state. Public gatherings of any sort were banned. Emma wondered if closing the churches contributed to the shameful way people were treating each other. Despite his recent kindness, Mister Pearson pointed a shotgun at her. Unthinkable in normal times! Mister Anderson shouted at her and forced her to wear a mask.

Her family attended a small country church just a few miles from their home. She longed for the far-off sound of church bells, calling the faithful to congregate and worship together.

After every Sunday service, Pastor Williams would gather with a few of the men and linger at the front near the pulpit. Even though Emma was never privy to those conversations, she understood that arrangements were being made to care for the needy. While those men did indeed make arrangements to care for the needy, what Emma did not understand was that they also kept the peace— Regulators. Her father stood among them.

She put her apple slices in a bowl, added a handful of dried cherries and a pinch of cinnamon. She tossed the fruit with sugar and flour and set it aside. Before making the dough for her crust, she wanted to get a nice, steady fire going in the woodstove. Kneeling down in front of it, she shook out the ashes. Then she tossed in two small logs of Mister Pearson's white oak and opened the dampers to let the wood burn quickly down to charcoal. Later, she would close them and bake her pie while the charcoal burned slowly into ash.

***

The sun was behind the trees when Emma heard Mister Pearson's truck struggling up the wagon trail. The boys were cleaning out the chicken coop, and hearing the noise, they came running toward the house.

Knowing her little brother, she stepped outside and shouted, "Tommy! Did you latch the door?"

He made a U-turn and headed back to the chicken coop.

Emma was waiting for him when Mister Pearson pulled his truck up next to the house and shut off the engine. When he climbed out, she was pleased to see he had finally changed clothes. He was wearing mostly clean bib overalls and a flannel shirt. He still looked horrible: gaunt and unshaven, but the back of the truck was filled with wood.

"I'm glad that you kept your promise, Mister Pearson. Would you join us at our table, so I can keep mine?"

Ike started piling up wood. "I am some recovered, but the Lord may take me yet."

He stacked the wood neatly but slowly. What he was unloading came from his own woodpile. He reasoned that if his health improved, he would hire the men who cut this wood to cut more. And if not—he would not need the wood. He didn't feel well, but he was no longer coughing up blood. Instead, his coughs produced thick jelly-like phlegm. His sides ached when he coughed. He was slowly clearing his lungs.

Emma watched him stack wood for a moment. The twins stood ten feet from their grandfather, casting glances at him, each other, and then Emma. She gave them a little frown and nodded toward Mister Pearson. Their faces lit up and they ran to throw their arms around his waist.

Ike stood up straight, holding a log over his head and shouted, "Boys! Get away from me. I ain't well!"

He tossed the log onto the ground and tried to pry the boys loose. When they looked up at him with identical smiles, he relented and put his arms around them, but only for a moment.

He pushed them away. "Boys! Keep your distance now. You do not want what I have."

They backed up and ran to cling to Emma. She said, "Let's get you boys washed up for supper. Mister Pearson, you must sit with us. It's Sunday and it would not be proper to allow a guest to eat on the steps."

She didn't wait for an answer. She turned and led the twins inside just as Tommy ran up from the chicken coop. He followed her inside.

Emma made the boys wash their hands and faces in a washbowl she placed in the kitchen sink. Then she lined them up and inspected them, just as her mother would have done. She had prepared a proper Sunday dinner of biscuits, string beans, fried chicken, and boiled potatoes, and had been defending her apple pie from three impatient boys all afternoon. She checked through the window to see Mister Pearson leaning against the woodpile. She put the kettle on to boil and went out to get him.

When Ike saw Emma come outside, he pushed himself onto his feet and stood up straight. Unloading his truck sapped his strength, leaving him dizzy. He placed a hand on the woodpile to steady himself, and Emma stopped in front of him. She looked him up and down and decided not to ask. She took his arm and led him into the house. If she asked, he would refuse, and she was in no mood to persuade him. She thought he must be some improved. He did not have that sour smell about him.

Emma worked hard on this dinner. The chicken on the table was a chicken in the coop earlier in the afternoon, and there had also been laundry to do. She was worn out. She wanted nothing more than a nice dinner and a quiet end to her day.

Mister Pearson hesitated at the door, so she pulled him inside and led him to the big sink. She dumped the washbowl and filled it again from the reservoir in the stove, then pumped a little cold water in to make it just warm. She handed him a bar of soap and busied herself with setting out plates while he washed. The twins watched him closely.

Their kitchen table was big enough to seat six. Emma placed Mister Pearson in her father's chair at the head of the table and sat down at the other end. She seated the twins beside her, and Tommy sat next to Mister Pearson. She did not think he was still contagious, but Tommy already had the flu, while the twins had not. Emma bowed her head. First the boys, and then Mister Pearson, clasped their hands in front of them and bowed their heads.

She closed her eyes and said, "Lord, we pray for those we love but cannot see. Please shine your warm light upon them. Tell them we are well and all together and we are thinking of them. Let our love for them bind us together. Amen."

Ike and the boys sat up but seeing Emma with her hands still clasped and her head still bowed, they bowed their heads again and waited.

Emma said, "Lord, I am sorry I yelled at you. I didn't mean it. Amen."

She sat up to find four sets of eyes upon her. It was the first time she saw Mister Pearson smile—ever. She pushed the platter of chicken across the table to him. On every farm, it was a tradition for the patriarch at the table to get the biggest piece of chicken.

Dinner was pleasant but quiet. The boys were digging in, too busy stuffing themselves to make polite conversation. Besides, since arriving here, Claude had yet to speak.

When Mister Pearson first tasted the gravy, his eyes lit up. "Emma, this is as fine a dinner as I have ever tasted. I do thank you for watching over the boys like you done."

"They're good boys." She continued to hold his gaze. She wanted answers, but her future was so uncertain she did not know what questions to ask.

Ike saw the unasked questions in her eyes. He put down his fork. "I have spoken to your momma and daddy many times, but I do not believe we ever spoke before you showed up in my yard and begged for help. I pointed a gun at you and sent you away. I have been ashamed of that ever since."

Emma could not look at him when she said, "I forgave you that day and prayed that God would ease your burden." She looked up. "You came in the morning and helped me do a hard thing. I will always be grateful."

Ike would never forgive himself for turning Emma away, but he was not surprised to hear she forgave him. She was just like her mother.

"I believe I was no more than a cup of tea and a bowl of soup away from death's door. I think that I did not want to live. It seems now, I will live awhile longer."

Emma had worked up an appetite. She sat chewing a mouthful of string beans, considering what Mister Pearson just said. Looking down into her plate, she pushed her food around with her fork.

"I'm only twelve. I can do chores, but I don't know how to run a farm. I can't even keep the woodpile." She looked up at him and her eyes filled with tears.

He said, "I ask that you keep the boys until your daddy comes home and then we will speak to him. Don't worry about the woodpile."

Emma had already assumed the boys would live here. Two boys on a farm were more help than hindrance. What frightened her was the world outside their eighty acres. Was it possible that someday men might come and take her and the boys away? Take their farm from them? She had to hang on until Daddy came home.

Fighting to hold back tears, she said, "Mister Anderson at the mercantile shouted at me. Has the whole world turned mean?"

Ike said, "If anybody ever shouts at you again, they will have to deal with me. Don't worry, Emma, you're a fine girl. Between us we can keep this farm going until your daddy gets back from the war."

Clyde listened to all this with keen attention. They were talking about life and death. He had faced too much death. His mother and father were his whole world, and now they were gone. He had not talked to Claude about it, but there was no need. They were identical.

He did not think it mattered what he wanted and he did not think anybody cared what he had to say, but they were deciding his fate. Just in case, he said, "We want to live with Emma."

Ike was slightly hurt to hear this. After a moment's consideration, he said to his grandson, "If I were you, I would too. You boys pay attention to Miss Emma and do what she tells you. You're fortunate she wants you here."

They nodded their heads, wearing identical scared expressions.

Chapter Four

It was the end of October of the year 1918, and the leaves had turned. It would be decades before anybody tallied up the numbers, but in that month, 195,000 people died of influenza on American soil.

***

Emma stood just outside the kitchen door and admired the trees in the early morning sun. Bright red maples and golden oaks surrounded their farm. The yellowwood tree that guarded her mother's grave was brilliant yellow. A cool breeze lifted a wisp of her soft blonde hair across her face, and she pushed it back behind her ear. She turned and went into the kitchen. There were things needing to be done.

She knew now that she lived on a prosperous farm. Ike Pearson helped her understand the ledgers; they found slightly more than five thousand dollars in their cash box—a fortune! Most people made around fifteen-hundred dollars a year. Ike Pearson showed her in the ledgers that the money had not come in a year or even two. It was the result of a decade of careful management.

The war was a boon to farmers all over the country. Their soaring profits attracted speculators, snapping up farms as quickly as they could, taking advantage of families left without their men due to the war or influenza. When they could not buy the land directly, they purchased the mortgages from the banks, and then foreclosed when payments fell even one month behind. Ike saw all this coming. He cautioned Emma that when the war ended, so would the profits. He told her the profiteers would only prosper until the end of the war. In normal times, it took hard work and careful management to make money on a farm—more than could be expected from sharecroppers and hired hands.

Emma wrote a letter to her father every week. Each one cost her dearly in heartache and terror. She repeated the heartbreaking news of her earlier letter, in case it had been lost, and begged his forgiveness again and again. Mister Pearson posted them for her at the mercantile, but there had not been a letter to bring back to her.

She had not left the farm since the day Earl Anderson shouted at her. Ike fell into the routine of coming for supper once or twice a week, and she came to depend on him for advice and the simple comfort of having an adult in her life. She would have to make a trip to the mercantile today. She would pick up her father's pay, and she and the boys needed coats and boots before winter came.

The schools and churches were still closed, so Emma started setting aside a few hours each day for schooling. Claude still had not spoken, and she was concerned for him, but he was able to write his letters just as well as his brother and could cipher numbers. It had only been a month since he lost his mother and father. She understood why he did not want to talk. If it were not for Tommy, she might well have retreated into silence herself.

The squash was ripe for picking. She sent the boys out to gather them before the first frost. They would spread them out on the back porch to cure for a week and then store them in the root cellar.

It was Saturday: bread making day. She tried to keep to the schedule her mother always followed, but some days there was too much to do and she fell behind. Her hands were rough and red from doing chores. She would rise from her bed every morning wanting nothing more than to climb back into that warm cocoon. She was keeping things together, but she felt like she was fading away.

Emma peeked into the oven to check on her bread and went back to making lunch for the boys: boiled eggs, cheese, fresh bread, and butter. She could hear Tommy and the twins coming up from the garden, dragging their burlap bags of squash behind them. Emma smiled when she heard them laughing. It was a rare sound on this farm.

They're only boys. They should be laughing.

The boys ran into the house and swirled around Emma. They tugged at her apron and hugged her around the waist. She was the center of their lives now. They orbited around her.

Tommy said, "Emma! What's for lunch? We're starving!"

Clyde asked, "Can we have strawberry jam? Grampa brought some last night."

Seeing their smiling faces, Emma said, "Okay, Clyde. You boys wash up and I'll open a jar. We can have it with the bread when it's ready."

Tommy laughed. "That ain't Clyde."

Emma looked down at the boy who spoke and asked, "Are you Claude?"

He said, "No, Emma, I'm Clyde."

Tommy was washing his hands at the sink. "No, he ain't. They take turns being Clyde."

Emma's mouth dropped open in surprise. She knew it was true! A dozen little details fell into place—a broken shoelace, a bruise, a scratch. It was perfect! She would give anything to have a double and take a day off from speaking and making decisions and all the other little burdens of her days. She started to laugh, giggling at first, which then turned into huge belly laughs. She fell into a chair and held onto her stomach while she laughed.

The twins looked at each other in concern and then

turned to give Tommy identical dirty looks.

He shrugged and said, "Well, you guys do take turns. Do you even know for sure which one of you is Clyde anymore?"

The twins have been using this little ruse all their lives, and in fact, they did not know which one of them was Clyde, they never had, but the joke was on Tommy. They were identical, so it did not matter.

***

Ike arrived early in the afternoon. He promised to take Emma to the mercantile in his truck. Having ridden in an automobile only a handful of times, she was looking forward to the experience. A trip that took more than an hour in the wagon could be accomplished in just twenty minutes, but she was dreading leaving the security of the farm.

Emma ran out to meet him. "Hello, Mister Pearson!" She hugged him briefly as she always did now, and he smiled, as he always did when she hugged him.

"Hello, Miss Emma. You are looking beautiful today."

Emma shyly looked away and touched her hair. She was wearing her Sunday dress, and her hair was tied back with a matching blue ribbon. It nearly felt sinful to dress like this on a Saturday, but there had not been a church service for months now. It felt good to dress up.

The twins ran out of the house with Tommy hot on their heels. They ran up to their grandfather and slammed into him. He laughed and put his arms around them. "Are you boys ready to go into town?"

Clyde said, "Can we get chocolate?"

"We'll see what they have. You boys get in back and hang on. I don't want nobody falling out."

Emma was tempted to tell him it was Claude who

had spoken, unaware that even the twins had lost track of which of them was Claude, but the twins had found a way to ease the burden of their short, tragic lives. She would allow them their little subterfuge. She climbed into the passenger seat.

Ike drove slowly down the wagon trail, riding the brake. When he reached the gravel road, he pushed the accelerator lever on the steering wheel forward and removed his foot from the gear pedal. Their speed approached thirty miles an hour, not that there was a speedometer. Emma's hair whipped over her shoulders and across her face. She was moving faster than she had in her entire life—incredibly fast! She gripped the seat with white knuckles and heard Tommy whoop with delight behind her.

She whispered, "So fast," and held on tightly while trees and tall grass flew past them in a blur.

Sooner than she thought possible, they were pulling up in front of the mercantile. Emma eased her grip on the seat. There was a horse drawn wagon and an automobile already parked in front. Ike pulled up next to the gasoline pump.

Emma brought her white mask with her, and Mister Pearson had one of his own. The boys jumped out of the bed and were waiting for her when she stepped out of the truck.

"Wait here, boys. You can't go in without a mask," she said.

She pulled the one Mister Anderson gave her from her pocket and tied it around her face. Then she counted out eighteen cents to buy masks for the boys. Ike held the door for her and they went inside.

Mister Anderson stood behind the counter making change for a lady Emma could not recognize. Half a dozen people milled about, examining merchandise, unrecognizable behind their white masks. Emma dreaded facing Mister Anderson again, certain the world had turned mean. She stood close to Ike Pearson and took his hand. He looked down at her in surprise. Her strangely beautiful blue and gold-ringed eyes were wide with fear above her white mask.

When the lady in front of them turned and left with her packages, Ike stepped up to the counter.

"Hey, Earl. I need some gas and Emma here needs a few things. Her momma ain't well enough to come." He leaned across the counter, and his eyes crinkled up above his white mask. "You be real nice to her. You hear?"

Earl Anderson intended to be nice to Emma. He was still feeling the sting on his conscience from a month before, and there was a letter waiting for her. Those yellow envelopes bordered with red and blue were all too familiar to him.

"Sure, Ike." He met Emma's eyes above her mask and said, "What can I do for you, little lady?"

Emma held a trembling hand over the counter and dropped eighteen cents. "Mister Anderson, sir, I need three masks for the boys so they can come inside."

Earl Anderson pushed the coins back to her and said, "No charge for the masks." He leaned down behind the counter and stood back up, holding out three masks.

Emma picked up her coins and dropped them back into the pocket of her dress. She slowly took the masks from him and looked up at Ike. He could tell from her eyes that she wanted him beside her, so he allowed her to take his hand and lead him back outside. Once they left the building, she released his hand, pulled down her mask, and took a deep breath. Then she went to fit the boys with masks.

Earl Anderson came outside holding a wad of keys.

He sorted through them and unlocked the gasoline pump. Ike lifted up the front seat, put the nozzle into the gas tank, and started cranking the pump handle. Before he could finish filling the tank, Earl took him by the arm and led him a few steps away. Emma frowned when she saw them speaking in low voices. Mister Pearson seemed to shrink down before her eyes. His shoulders were stooped and he glanced back at her. Then he looked away and walked back to the truck to finish pumping gasoline. When he was done, Earl locked the pump and went back inside.

Ike walked over to Emma just as she pulled her mask back up. Her eyes were filled with fear, and the boys picked up on it. He held out his hand and she gripped it tightly. He led her back inside, followed by the boys, so they could buy coats, boots, and a dozen little things that Emma wrote down in her best penmanship on a list in her dress pocket. He would collect the letter and give it to her later, when they were back at the farm—where she could grieve in private.

***

When they arrived back at the farm, it was after five o'clock. On the ride back, Mister Pearson drove slowly. To Emma, he seemed troubled, but she did not want to pry. The boys climbed out of the bed of the truck with chocolate-smeared faces.

They clustered around Emma. She pushed them away. "Don't you boys dare get chocolate on my good dress!" All three of them were licking their lips, and it amused her. "Go wait by the door. I don't want you touching anything before I get you washed up."

She went inside to get a washcloth, ran warm water from the reservoir in the stove to dampen it, and went back outside to clean the boys' faces and hands. Mister Pearson still sat in the cab of his truck. Once she had the boys all washed up, she allowed them to carry the packages inside.

***

Ike sat there trying to think of a way to give Emma the hard news. He considered waiting until after dinner. She would be in no shape to feed those boys once she knew, but he only waited until now for her sake. Convenience was a poor reason to delay any further. He got out of his truck just as she sent the last boy, laden with packages, into the house.

Emma walked up to him and smiled. It nearly broke his heart. Even though the top of her head came up to his shoulder, he had to remind himself that she was only a girl. Over the past two months, he watched this pretty little slip of a girl care for three boys and run a farm better than most people he knew. She worked hard and did not complain.

He took her hand and led her up next to the house to sit on the woodpile. She looked up at him in concern. He had collected her father's pay for her. She was all too willing to let him deal with Earl Anderson on her behalf. He noticed that she thought the masks cost money and knew they did not. One day soon, he would have a little talk with Earl Anderson.

He pulled a heavy white envelope from his pocket and handed it to Emma. "This is from your Pa."

Emma knew it was her father's pay, but the envelope felt heavy. She opened it to find a thick stack of ten-dollar bills and fanned through them.

"There's more than two-hundred dollars here!"

He removed the yellow envelope from his pocket and handed it to her. She examined it and saw her mother's name, written by the hand of a stranger. Her eyes filled with tears—she knew.

She ripped open the envelope. Inside was a single piece of yellow paper, a preprinted form filled out by some unknown and unfeeling person. She wiped at her eyes and struggled to read through tears.

At the top, it said. *Madam, it is my painful duty to inform you that on this day*, in a box someone had written, October 3, 1918, *a report has been received notifying the death of* and in another box, someone had written, *237843 Thomas Richard Taylor*. There was a checkmark next to 'Killed in Action.'

At the bottom, it said, *The United States government wishes to express to you our sympathy and regret at your loss. Any application you may wish to make regarding the late soldier's effects should be addressed to the War Department.*

Emma crushed the paper in her hands and screamed, "No!" She jumped to her feet. "It's a mistake! Daddy is coming home!"

Ike stood up and tried to embrace her, but she struck him in the chest and screamed again—wordlessly, a long wailing moan. She flung the crumpled death notice away and frantically rubbed her hand on her dress. Then she ran up the hill to her mother's grave and dropped to her knees in the mud.

Ike stayed where he was to give Emma a little time with her mother. There were many years when he had not shed a single tear, but this year had been hard. He heard the creak of the screen door, and the boys stepped outside, looking fearfully up the hill at Emma.

Tommy turned to him. "Pa ain't coming home, is he?"

Ike knew that he was not. The Army buried casualties near the place where they fell. His son was buried somewhere in France. He picked Tommy up, and the boy hung limp in his arms. He already knew the answer.

He sent the twins back inside saying, "Emma is not well today. You two find something to do that she would have done."

He carried Tommy up the hill to stand beside Emma. She was sobbing so hard she did not notice him. He watched as she straightened the small white stones that spelled out her mother's name. He put Tommy down beside her and he threw his arms around her.

Emma jumped when Tommy grabbed hold of her, then gathered him into her arms. She knew without question that her mother was once again secure in her father's arms. That certain knowledge was the only thing that kept her sane. She bowed her head and sent them a promise. She was Anna Taylor's daughter. She would always do as her mother would have done.

Chapter Five

The day Emma learned of her father's death, Ike spent the night at their farm and did not sleep. He made dinner for the twins, but Emma quietly went to her room. Tommy followed her. He checked on them after dark, holding up a candle, and saw the flame reflected in Emma's eyes while she lay in her bed holding Tommy—both of them still dressed.

When Emma rose before dawn, still wearing her good dress, she found Ike in the kitchen making her breakfast by the light of a kerosene lamp. No one had made anything for her to eat in months. She hugged him and cried quietly. He helped her into a chair and made tea for both of them while she ate her eggs with a slice of buttered bread.

He sat down across from her. "Emma, we have to figure what you are going to do."

She looked up into his eyes and sipped her tea, holding the cup with both hands to warm them, and tried not to cry. "I don't know what to do, Mister Pearson," she said quietly.

"Just call me Ike, girl. You been more of a grownup than me."

They spoke quietly as equals. He offered to bring her and the boys to live with him, but she refused, saying this was her home. Inwardly, he was relieved. It had been a hollow gesture.

He offered to take the twins, but she refused, saying they were more help than hindrance, and she had grown to love them. They were better off with her. A hard truth, but he knew she was right.

He explained to her that in Indiana, a minor could not own property. Their land was already in jeopardy. If the authorities learned of their situation, she and her brother would become wards of the county and be placed in an orphanage. The land would be auctioned, and if they were lucky, the money placed in trust. Even if they were so fortunate as to receive a fair price, he cautioned her that their guardians would hold the purse strings. It was likely that in the end, they would come of age with nothing.

Holding the warm cup in both hands, she met his gaze and said, "You can own the land."

Ike believed Emma saved his life, but his feelings on that account were somewhat ambivalent. More importantly, she took in his grandsons and treated them as her own kin. He knew for a fact that Indiana contained far more than its fair share of corrupt officials. If word got out that only children lived here, the most likely outcome was that this farm would be handed to some lackey for a pittance, and Emma and Tommy would be thrown into an orphanage already overflowing with the children of the war and the flu.

"If we had known before your momma passed away, maybe we could have put the farm in trust. It's too late now. Besides, I'm too old to keep this farm until you turn eighteen. You just have to be careful and not let on that your momma died."

Emma's eyes grew wide. She nodded.

Ike lost the spark of life when Martha died. He had good days and bad days, and he knew he was unfit to raise his grandsons. He felt that he was too old, too sad, and too often drank himself into oblivion. Those were poor excuses to leave these children alone, and he was ashamed of his weakness. A better man would give Emma and the boys a good home. Ike knew he should do more but felt that he could not. He stood up and left Emma sitting at her table looking scared to death. He nodded to her, went outside to get into his truck, and drove away.

***

The next few days passed quickly, taken up by chores. The loss of their father affected Emma more than Tommy. To his mind, his father had been gone for a good portion of his short life. To Emma, the source of her strength and security was taken from her. She carried a constant buzz of fear.

Emma was headed for the kitchen door with the boys on her heels, when she saw a trail of chicken feathers beside the barn. She ran to the chicken coop to find two hens torn to pieces. Throwing open the door, she ducked inside to count her birds. Another was missing! Some critter just robbed them of three Sunday dinners and hundreds of eggs!

The boys clung to the chicken wire, looking in at the carnage.

"What happened?" Clyde asked.

Tommy said, "I bet it was a fox. We got foxes around here. I seen 'em."

Every year was a constant battle against foxes, raccoons, hawks, and stoats. Emma followed the edges of the enclosure until she found where some animal dug down below the wire and slipped into the chicken coop. The animal that did this killed three hens, but only carried off one. Emma was angry. She and the boys would do without because of this intruder's attack on her birds.

When she looked up at the boys, the gold in her eyes glittered, and her face was red. They slowly backed away from the chicken wire and ran back to the house. Her father had hammered long spikes deep into the ground all around the enclosure. That worked well until today. Something managed to dig up two of them and slip under the wire. It made her even angrier that it happened in the middle of the

61

day.

The boys watched from the kitchen door while she replaced the spikes, filled in the hole, and tamped down the dirt. She scooped up the remains of her hens and buried them in a shallow hole. Then she put away her spade and marched toward the house, still steaming with anger.

When she entered the kitchen, the boys retreated to the parlor. When she entered the parlor, dragging a kitchen chair, they retreated up the stairs. When she dragged the chair up to the big stone fireplace and stood on it to take down her father's shotgun, they disappeared entirely.

The only gun in the Taylor house was a 1910 Marlin ten-gauge single-shot shotgun. Her father showed her how to use it, but she has never actually fired it. He told her that if the need arose and she had to fire this gun, she should be prepared to be knocked down. She should also check behind her to make sure she had a soft place to land before pulling the trigger. She laughed at his joke, until she looked into his eyes.

Emma stepped down onto the floor, holding that huge gun, and broke open the breech to ensure it was not loaded. It was longer than she was tall. She snapped the breech closed, carried it into the kitchen, and leaned it against the wall beside the door.

She shouted, "Boys!"

Three faces peeked around the edge of the doorway to the parlor.

She pointed at the shotgun. "Do not touch. Do you understand?"

Tommy said, "Yes, Emma."

Clyde said, "Yes, Emma."

Claude said nothing. Emma locked eyes with him and arched her eyebrows—her lips were compressed in a thin line.

Claude's eyes got big. "Yes, Emma."

Emma went into her father's study and took a single shell the size of a corncob from the top drawer. She put it in the front pocket of her dress, marched up the stairs to her room, closed her door, sat down on her bed, and cried.

She was worn out—emotionally drained and physically at her limit. It seemed that everything she loved was being taken from her. It was only three hens, farms lost hens all the time. To her, the evil that swept over the world crept onto their farm again today and took something else from her. She was drawing the line—right in front of her chicken coop.

***

November had taken hold, and the nights were cold. A hard frost killed the last green things. After dinner, the twins washed dishes while Tommy ran the scraps out to the pigs. It was fully dark under a clear sky filled with sparkling stars. The only light came from a lamp in the kitchen and a three-quarter moon.

Emma lit a candle and drew a pitcher of hot water from the stove to carry upstairs to her bedroom. Ike bought her a few bars of Ivory soap. Wonder of wonders, it floated! No more fishing around in murky water, searching for the soap.

She lit the kerosene lamp on her writing desk and blew out her candle. Her lamp was made from milk glass, a white globe at the bottom held the kerosene and another surrounded the chimney above. She adjusted the wick until it gave off a warm yellow light.

Emma sat on the bentwood chair beside the small woodstove in her bedroom. Her pitcher sat on a stand made from rosewood with a marble top and one drawer for her toothbrush, toothpowder, hairbrush, and comb. It was cream colored with daisies painted on it, matching her washbowl.

Every night, she washed from head to toe, ending up by soaking her feet in the warm water. Once she was clean and dry, she would put on a nightdress and adjust her mirror, so she could brush her hair. It was the only time her door was closed, and the boys understood that if they desperately needed her during those twenty minutes for a matter of life and death—then too bad, she was indisposed.

She knew they had already washed, more or less, and were waiting in the hall. She read to them in the parlor every night, but instead of waiting for her there, they would gather outside her door. Claude was speaking now. She could hear them whispering. They did not dare to knock.

"Is she coming?" one of the twins asked.

Tommy said, "She's coming. It ain't like we was out late or nothing."

Emma opened her door to find three smiling faces. She dearly loved her boys and did everything she could think of to keep them happy and healthy. She was a child herself, just twelve years old, but she was the only mother they had. They followed her everywhere she went, lined up like ducklings, until she gave them something to do.

She was reading *Twenty Thousand Leagues Under the Sea*, by Jules Verne. The book was older than she was. First published in French in 1869, it was translated into English four years later. Emma remembered being fascinated by this book when her mother read it to her, and now, she was reading it to Tommy and the twins. For half an hour every evening, they would gather in the parlor, and she would read a chapter.

The boys followed Emma as she carried a candle downstairs and sat in her mother's rocking chair next to the fireplace. Her feet did not reach the floor. The boys gathered on the rug in front of the dying fire. She opened the book and began to read. Soon, giant sea monsters, electric cannonballs, and underwater islands fascinated them. At the end of the chapter, she closed the book and looked up at the wide-eyed faces arrayed in front of her.

"Time for bed, boys. We will visit the underwater Island of Crespo tomorrow."

The boys struggled to their feet, yawning. The fire was only embers. The room was cooling off. She led them upstairs and tucked them into their beds—first the twins and then Tommy. She stoked the small stove in each room.

Finally, she knelt down beside her bed and sent to her mother and father a prayer and a promise, as was her habit. She was Anna Taylor's daughter. She would always do as her mother would have done.

***

Emma rose to the sound of birds chirping in the big oak tree outside her window. She wrapped herself in a blanket before going downstairs in the silvery light of early dawn. She started a fire in the kitchen stove, scooted her chair over next to it, sat down, and huddled in her blanket while she waited for it to heat up.

Now that cold weather arrived, she spent a good deal of her time shaking ash and carrying it outdoors to dump into the ash pit behind the house. She would start a fire in the kitchen stove in the morning and keep it going until supper. Then she built a fire in the parlor fireplace for the evening, and at the end of the day, fired up the small woodstoves in their bedrooms. In cold weather, all of the rooms in their big house were never warm at the same time. They only heated the rooms they were using.

Once the stove began to warm, she put on a kettle to

boil and ran upstairs to dress quickly in her cold room. On the way back down, she knocked on the boy's doors. Emma was making herself a cup of tea, when Tommy came into the kitchen rubbing his eyes.

He didn't even pause while he grabbed his coat from the peg beside the door and mumbled, "Morning, Emma," and went out to do the milking.

Clyde and Claude appeared soon after and headed off to feed the animals. Assured now that the boys were underway, Emma took down her egg basket and went to gather the eggs. She would have just enough time to gather the eggs and fix the boys their breakfast while they finished the early morning chores. It was a crisp, clear morning. The air was cold, but not freezing. The fallen leaves collected in drifts. She checked the chicken coop for mischief, and finding everything in order, went inside to collect her eggs.

Hot bowls of oatmeal were waiting on the table when Tommy brought in the milk. Emma poured a pitcher of raw milk for use during the day. Tommy would pour the rest into pans she would skim later to make butter and cheese. Most of the skimmed milk would be fed to the pigs.

The first killing frost was a week ago. Ike promised to come day before yesterday and help them harvest the carrots and potatoes, but he did not show up. Emma was not too concerned. When Ike said he would be there on a certain day, he often did not show up until the day after, or the day after that. The carrots were not a problem, she and the boys already harvested them by pulling them out of the ground.

She needed Ike to dig up the potatoes. It required more strength than she had. Once the mounds were dug up, she and the boys could gather them easily enough. They would have to be hardened off for a week before being packed in straw in the root cellar. They were running out of time, and if Ike did not show up this morning, then she and the boys would walk over there to check on him in the afternoon.

Clyde and Claude came in from feeding the animals, red-cheeked and chattering. Emma made them wash in the sink before sitting down.

Clyde asked, "Can we have honey in our oatmeal?"

Claude said, "Cherries too!"

Emma took down a ceramic jar and walked around the table sprinkling dried cherries. Then she went around again and dropped a dollop of honey into each bowl. Once she was able to sit down, she watched each boy take a bite and nod his head up and down enthusiastically. She tried it herself, and her eyes lit up.

It's really good!

They sat around the big oak table eating their oatmeal. Emma was happy to see the boys enjoying their breakfast, but she was also worried. Where was Ike?

At noon, she called the boys away from their chores and fed them a lunch of milk, boiled eggs, cheese, and buttered bread. Ike still had not shown up. It was annoying—she depended on him to do those things she could not. She was worried as well—he was a sad old man who lived alone.

After lunch, Emma bundled up the boys, and they started off down the wagon trail to the Pearson farm. She was accustomed to the walk. At this time of year, she walked this way every day on her way to school. It was a cold gray day, and a few scattered raindrops fell. Once they left the shelter of the trees and started down the gravel road, the Pearson place was in sight. The boys always lined up behind her everywhere she went. They trudged along in line, hunched down into their coats in the cold wind.

When they reached Ike's house, Emma had a feeling

of foreboding. There was no smoke coming from the chimney. His milk cow mooed loudly and the pigs crowded against the fence milling around in agitation. She could see Ike's truck through the open barn door, but he was nowhere in sight.

She turned to the boys, standing in the tall grass. "Stay here."

They huddled together in the wind while Emma stepped up on the rickety porch and knocked on the door. There was no answer, so she went inside.

The house was cold and dark. She called out, "Ike! It's Emma!" There was no answer.

Her heart began to race when she opened his bedroom door. The bed was empty, the blankets strewn on the floor. She closed the door and checked the other bedroom, but he was not there. She went into the kitchen, and the table was once again crowded with dishes and bottles, but there was no sign of Ike.

The kitchen door stood open. The wind blew back the screen door and the spring pulled it shut with a clap. Leaves were scattered on the floor. Stepping outside, she followed the well-worn path to the barn and found Ike propped up against a wall. A bottle lay beside him.

She ran to him, grabbed his hand, and held it to her face. It was ice cold! She grabbed the front of his shirt and pulled at him shouting, "Ike! Please, Ike!"

He stirred and groaned. Emma released him and choked back a sob. She had been certain he was dead.

Ike stood up, swaying from side to side. Seeing Emma, he patted her on the head, tripped over his own feet, and fell on his face. He laughed and rolled over in the straw to stare up at the rafters.

Emma had no experience with drunkenness. She had

read enough to know that these things happen, and depending upon the author, it was viewed with either humor or disdain. She would have thought he was sick, if not for the bottle and his laughter. She did not know what to do for him, but the cow needed milking, her teats were swollen. If a cow is not milked regularly, she will stop giving milk. It was obvious that the animals needed to be fed. Those were things she understood and could rectify.

She walked out of the barn. "Boys! Come here!"

They ran around the house and gathered in front of her.

"Ike is not feeling well, so we have to feed the animals. Clyde and Claude, you feed the pigs and chickens. Tommy, you come with me."

She led Tommy over to the barn and turned to see the twins still standing where she left them. She gave them a look and pointed at the pigpen. They scurried off in that direction.

She left Tommy by the barn door while she climbed into the hayloft and forked down hay for the cow and the horses. She found their feed, and once they were fed, she gave Tommy a clean milk pail and set him to work milking the cow. Then she went to see about Ike. He was passed out again. When she knelt down beside him, she learned to associate that sour smell with drunkenness.

Pulling on his arm, she called out, "Ike! Ike, get up!"

His eyes fluttered open and he sat up. "There's my angel! How you doin', angel darlin'?"

Emma pulled on his arm again. "Come on, Ike! Get up! Let's get you in the house. It's cold out here."

Ike picked up his bottle and held it up, still a quarter full. "I like it here. I ain't goin' nowhere."

Emma pulled harder. "You can't stay here. We need

to get you someplace warm."

Annoyed, he swung his bottle and hit her hard, just above the left eye. Emma fell over onto her side and moaned. The world dimmed. She struggled to remain conscious while she tried to sort out what just happened. She clung to her forehead. When she examined her hand, it was bloody.

She heard a distant, wordless scream. Tommy flashed past her and rammed a pitchfork bigger than he was into Ike Pearson's leg. Ike howled and scrabbled away, leaving the pitchfork with a bloody tine. His bottle was forgotten. Amber liquid trickled out into the straw—right in front of Emma's face.

She rolled onto her back and stared up at her bloody hand, unable to understand how she was injured. Tommy stood over her. She was concerned to see him crying, but oddly, even though his lips were moving, she could not hear what he said. He began to pull on her arm, glancing fearfully behind him. Emma sat up. The sound of his voice came through her fog like a distant echo.

"Emma! Get up, Emma! We have to run!"

When she tried to stand, her knees buckled. Tommy stuck his head under her arm and helped her up. She staggered out of the barn, leaning on her little brother, and everything suddenly snapped into focus. Her head was pounding. The cloudy daylight was incredibly bright. The rustling of the leaves beneath their feet was painfully loud. Unable to think through the assault upon her senses, she fell to her knees, dragging Tommy down with her, and vomited into the tall grass.

Tommy pleaded with her. "Emma, please. Get up!"

She struggled to her feet with Tommy supporting her, and they made their way to the road. Realizing that the twins were not with them, Emma stopped. She turned around to look for them, and her knees gave out again. On her hands and knees, she raised her head and tried to focus her eyes.

Ike Pearson stood in the doorway of his barn, gripping the door with one hand for support. The other hand gripped his bloody thigh.

He called out, "Emma! I'm sorry, Emma! Come back!" He began limping in her direction.

The twins stood beside the pigpen. Emma tried to call out to them, but her throat was burning. It didn't matter. Seeing she was hurt, they ran to her and supported her on either side. Ike sank down to sit on the ground and watched Emma stagger away, propped up between his grandsons.

Emma struggled to walk for more than a mile with her arms over the shoulders of the twins. By the time they reached the wagon trail, her feet were dragging in the gravel. She had to rest. Her head throbbed with every heartbeat. The boys helped her a little ways up the wagon trail into the shelter of the trees and eased her onto the wet ground.

She sat with her legs crossed and her head down. A drop of blood fell onto her new coat, and she sat up in concern. She reached up to touch her face. It was slick with congealed blood all the way down the side of her neck. She lifted up her collar and was heartsick to see that it was soaked with blood. Her new coat was ruined. She looked up to find all three of the boys standing in front of her. She was the only one not crying.

By the time they arrived back at the house, Emma was walking slowly without assistance. She made her way unsteadily into the kitchen and peeled off her coat. It saddened her to see it stained with blood. It was less than a month old.

She tried to stoke the fire, but Clyde, or maybe Claude, grabbed her hand and pulled her to a chair. Tommy stoked the woodstove while one of the twins filled a washbowl with warm water from the reservoir in the stove. All three of the boys soaped washcloths with a bar of Ivory and jostled for position around her, taking turns gently wiping away the blood. She closed her eyes and sighed. It felt so good to be taken care of for once, and she desperately needed to be cared for.

When one of the boys placed a towel in her hands, she opened her eyes and dabbed carefully at her face. The towel came away with a few tiny spots of blood. The bleeding had mostly stopped. The boys still had tears on their faces. They looked scared to death. The water in the washbasin was crimson.

She smiled. "I'm fine, boys. You can stop crying."

Truthfully, her head ached fiercely. Wanting to get a look at the cut, she stood up and walked slowly to the powder room, holding on to furniture along the way. She had to stand on tiptoe to see in the mirror, but she did not think it needed a stitch. The wound was not gaping. She doubted that she could stitch it up herself anyway. She once watched her mother put three stitches in her father's hand. While he smiled through the pain—to show how tough he was—tears rolled down his cheeks.

The boys clustered around her so tightly she could not take a step. She touched the tops of their heads, and each one she touched hugged her around the waist. None of them have spoken since they left Ike's.

"Go on now, get your chores done and I'll fix supper."

They were immensely relieved to slip back into their familiar routine and scurried off. She heard Tommy bang his milk pail on something and smiled. He did a fair job of milking for a six-year-old boy. She stretched to get another look at her head. The cut was half an inch long, just above her eyebrow, and the area around it was swollen—pink and sky blue. She dropped back down on her heels and swayed.

Able now to think about what happened, she closed the door, sat on the commode, and cried. Ike hit her with a bottle! There was no one they could trust. They were completely on their own.

Chapter Six

Emma lay in bed that night unable to sleep. She had made the boys a simple dinner of salt pork, bread, and carrots. They cleaned up the mess without being asked, carried up her pitcher of warm water for her, and respectfully closed her door so she could wash. They even skipped their nightly chapter from Jules Verne and sent her off to bed. Her head was less painful now, but it still throbbed every time she leaned over.

She desperately longed for the comfort of her parents, but everyone in this house was without mothers and fathers. She sat up in bed and made up her mind to do something she had been unable to do. It might help Tommy too—if she had the courage.

She lit a candle and stepped quietly into the hall. She always left her door ajar but closed the boys' doors to keep in the heat. She stood still for a moment—listening. There was only silence. She stepped softly down the stairs to stand in front of her mother's door. It had been two months since her death, and Emma still could not go in there, but there was something she desperately needed in that room.

Placing her hand on the doorknob, she took a deep breath and pushed the door open. The soft scent of roses wafted around her. She smiled. Her mother always wore a splash of rose water. When Ike carried out her body, she was wrapped in the sheets. Emma saw that he had straightened the covers. The bed was neat and tidy. Not a trace of pain and struggle remained—only the soft scent of roses.

Unafraid now, she walked into her mother's room and felt closer to her. There was a washstand beside the big four-poster bed. The pitcher and bowl were decorated with roses; her mother loved roses. She walked past it and gently ran her hand along the lip of the bowl. What drew her here sat on her mother's dresser. She held up her candle, and tears ran down her face, but she was smiling.

The light from her candle illuminated a picture of her mother and father on their wedding day. At the age of twenty, her mother did not look much different than she did on the day she died. Her long blonde hair was pinned up and she was wearing a white dress with bands of lace near the hem. It had a high collar and long sleeves, both banded with lace. It was a simple dress, light and airy, without trains or corsets. It hung in her wardrobe, wrapped in white paper, awaiting the day Emma would wear it.

Her mother was smiling, but her father looked stern. She knew that look. He could not keep it on his face for more than a second without smiling. He was dressed in his Sunday suit, or one just like it. That too was hanging in the wardrobe. She remembered his face now.

The photograph was mounted under glass in a silver frame. She picked it up carefully and carried it into the parlor. Placing it on the lamp table where she read to the boys, she hoped it would lift Tommy's spirits as it lifted hers.

As she crept back up the stairs by the light of her candle, it occurred to her the twins needed something similar. They had no mementos of their parents. They arrived here with nothing more than a sack of dirty clothes. She knew that someday she would have to face Ike Pearson again, but she would do so from a distance. She would never again let him come close enough to touch her.

Emma drifted off to sleep, unaware of the boys standing in the hall, peeking around her door. Tommy pulled it closed—to keep in the heat.

***

The next day dawned cold and clear. Emma sat at the

kitchen table, wrapped in a blanket, waiting for the stove to heat up. When she looked in the mirror on her washstand, her appearance alarmed her. There was a dark bruise above her left eye, and blood pooled beneath it in a crescent. It did not prevent her from doing what needed to be done, and it only hurt when she bent over.

Tommy was always the first of the boys to come down in the morning, and she noticed that his footsteps stopped in the parlor. It was several minutes before he walked into the kitchen. Emma sat at the table. He stopped in front of her, looking up into her face—frowning.

"Does it hurt bad?" he asked.

"It doesn't hurt. It looks worse than it really is. I'm fine, Tommy."

Still wearing a frown, he pulled his coat down from a peg beside the door and put it on. He stood in front of the door for a moment, doing up the buttons.

Without turning around, he said, "Ma is real pretty."

The door closed softly behind him as he went on out to milk the cow. They never spoke of their parents in past tense.

***

At breakfast and lunch, the boys were too quiet. Emma was bothered by it. The incident at Ike Pearson's farm was traumatic for all of them. There have only been a handful of days when the boys laughed and played. Those were good days, and she wanted more like them. She thought boys were naturally fun-loving and cheerful. All that was required to make them happy was to keep them safe and unharmed.

After lunch, Emma made up her mind; they had to get the potatoes out of the ground. She was used to using a spade to dig up a few new potatoes for lunch or supper, but it was a time-consuming task. She could dig them with a spade, but even if she did nothing else, at that rate it would take at least a week to dig them all up. They needed to harvest them and get them cured for storage before they lost them in the frozen ground.

She pulled on her coat, grimacing at the feel of the blood-encrusted collar, and went outside. She dragged the big potato fork out of the tool shed into the garden. It was taller than she was. She pushed the tines into the earth beside a potato mound and stepped up to bounce on them, driving them into the ground. Then she tried to pull it down to turn the earth, but she did not have the strength. She walked back a few yards and took a run at it, jumping up to grab the handle. It leaned slightly while she stood on the tines. She stepped down to consider the problem.

Seeing her in the garden, the boys gathered around her, staring up at that big potato fork. When they heard the unmistakable rattle and chug of Ike's truck, they all turned to face the road with looks of shock and fear. The boys converged on Emma and clung to her coat.

Ike pulled up and parked beside the house. The back of his truck was filled with wood. He stepped down out of the cab and limped in their direction. Tommy stepped around to stand in front of his big sister.

Ike limped toward them dressed in clean overalls, clean shaven, and with his hair combed. His long coat flapped behind him in the wind. Emma's heart jumped into her throat. This man caused her more pain than she had ever felt before. She grabbed Tommy by the shoulders and held him against her. She thought it quite likely he might rush Ike and take him on alone.

Ike stopped ten feet from her and the boys.

"Emma, please forgive me. It was the drink that

made me do it. I swear to you and those boys that I will never touch another drop."

Emma had no experience at all with liquor. It had simply never entered her world before. The concept of not being responsible for one's actions made no sense to her. She only knew for sure that the man standing before her carried the potential for violence.

"You hurt me, Ike." Her eyes filled with tears. She loved him and she feared him. Those things taken together made her cry.

Seeing Emma surrounded by the boys was intensely painful for Ike. Her face was cut and bruised, and her new blue coat was stained with dark blood all down the left side. He watched her count out her own money to pay for that coat. When she first tried it on, she quietly turned a circle in front of the big mirror at the mercantile—her unusual eyes wide above her white mask. All of them deserved better than he had done.

He was not surprised to see Tommy stick out his chin and ball up his little fists. That rascal put him in his place, darn near ran him through. He knew he deserved that and more.

He looked into Tommy's eyes. "You did good, boy. I'm proud of you."

Emma felt Tommy tense up in her hands and gripped him more tightly. The twins regarded their grandfather with the same tortured look that was on Emma's face. They too loved their grandfather—and feared him.

Their father had taken them to visit Ike only rarely, but they were familiar with the effects of his excessive drinking. More often than not, they sat on his porch while their father cleaned the house and sobered up their grandfather. Ike visited them in town a few times a year. On those rare occasions, they came to know and love him.

Clyde peeked around Emma and said, "Grampa, Emma can't dig up the potatoes. She's too little."

Ike could see that. He was here three days later than he promised. He was a constant disappointment to his grandsons and to Emma. The problem was that all these responsibilities fell upon him years after he gave up on life. His farm was prosperous only because he had farmed all his life. He ran his farm without thinking about it. Children, however, required constant thought and attention. He was struggling to cope.

He looked into Emma's eyes. "If you will let me, I'd like to help. I promise—no more liquor."

Emma did not know what to do. She needed Ike, but she no longer felt safe around him.

What would Momma do?

The answer came to her in The Lord's Prayer. She would forgive him. It was not what she wanted to do, and she felt a pang of guilt at that. What she really wanted to do was whack him on the head with a bottle and run for it, but she knew for a fact that was not what her mother would have done.

She untangled herself from the boys. Trembling with fear, she hesitantly walked up to Ike and hugged him gently. Then she quickly backed away. When she looked into his face, his eyes were full of tears. It was not until she saw his tears that she actually forgave him in her heart. At that moment, she came to fully appreciate the profound wisdom of her mother's gentle nature. She was Anna Taylor's daughter. She would do well to remember that.

Ike blinked away tears. "Thank you, Emma. That is more than I deserve."

He shivered and pulled his long coat around him.

"Cold today. How about you boys go stack that wood and I'll dig up these taters?"

The boys didn't move. They looked up at Emma. She said, "Go ahead, but make it quick. We have to get these potatoes spread out in the barn so they can harden off."

***

Emma was making supper, occasionally looking out the window over the sink at the boys as they gathered up the potatoes into burlap bags and dragged them into the barn. The bloody spot on Ike's leg concerned her. She would offer to clean and bandage it for him.

She added a string of beans from the root cellar to the new potatoes she gathered from the garden. Her grandmother always called strings of dried green beans leather britches. They had spent many hours together sitting on the front porch stringing beans. Green beans were preserved by using a needle and heavy thread to string them together and then hanging them up to dry. Emma never understood why they were called leather britches, and simply called them string beans. The thought of eating leather britches did not strike her as particularly appetizing.

A large pot bubbled on the woodstove, a rich broth made from two smoked hocks. The aroma had her stomach growling. She stirred the pot and dropped in the beans and potatoes. Supper would be ready in half an hour.

She was setting places at the table when she heard a commotion outside. Hens cackled. The boys shouted her name. She looked out the window and saw her hens flapping around in front of the henhouse. It was happening again! Some varmint was stealing her chickens!

Emma had been carrying that heavy shotgun shell around for weeks. She pulled it out of her pocket, snatched the shotgun from its resting place beside the door, and broke it open. Slamming the shell home, she snapped the breech closed and ran outside.

The boys ran toward the house calling her name, while Ike limped along behind them. Feathers were flying inside the chicken coop. In the same place that was penetrated before, a red fox squirmed out under the wire with a bloody hen in his mouth.

Emma lifted up the shotgun and struggled to aim. It was too heavy to hold steady, so she raised it high, and as it dropped, she gripped it tightly, as her father taught her. When she saw the fox looking back at her over the barrel, she squeezed the trigger.

There was a tremendous BOOM, and she flew back, flipping head over heels behind the woodpile. She jumped to her feet and looked over the logs to see a cloud of feathers in the air. Scrambling over the logs, she ran out to the chicken coop. Her hen appeared to have exploded. There was not a piece of meat bigger than a silver dollar, and no sign of the fox.

Tommy and the twins looked around at the carnage. Tommy ran back twenty feet and held up a headless tatter of red fur by the tail. "You got him, Emma! See, it was a fox! I knowed it!"

With her heart pounding in her chest and her ears ringing, Emma pointed a shaky finger at the scrap of fur and shouted, "Won't be killing any more of my…"

She frowned and lowered her arm slowly. Gripping her right shoulder with her left hand she said, "Ow!" The adrenaline was wearing off.

Ike limped past them to retrieve the smoking gun. He broke it open and pulled out the spent shell, examining it closely. He smiled.

Carrying the gun over to Emma, he showed her the

spent shell. "Girl, you just shot a varmint with a ten-gauge slug, must have been four-hundred grains."

Emma looked at the spent shell in his hand. "Bullets are bullets, aren't they?"

Ike laughed—something he thought just this morning that he would never do again. "First off, this here is a shotgun shell, ain't no bullet. Second, slugs are for deer— buffalo for that matter, big as this here gun is."

Emma cradled her arm and winced. Ike became concerned for her. "Are you hurt bad?"

The question itself tore at him, since her sweet face carried wounds he himself had made.

Emma worked her arm. "It isn't broken, but that hurt!"

Ike said, "Someday you may need to use that gun again. Before you do, let's take a look at your ammunition. Bird shot won't hurt you none."

Emma shivered in the cold wind and wrapped her arms around herself. She turned to go back inside, it was too cold to be standing out here in just a dress. She had yet to take a step when she heard a far-off gunshot, and then another and another. Off in the distance, they heard guns going off in every direction. The boys clustered around her, hanging on to her dress. She looked up at Ike, and he shrugged. Something strange was happening.

Gathering the boys in her arms, Emma ushered them inside. She turned to Ike. "Will you join us at our table? I'm grateful that you dug the potatoes."

Ike gave her back her shotgun. "Much appreciated, but I need a few things at the mercantile. Might be I can find out what these gunshots is for. If it is agreeable, I'll stop in later."

Jostling the heavy gun, Emma said, "You are

welcome any time, Ike."

She started to go inside, but there was something left unsaid, she could feel it. She turned back around and swung the barrel of her shotgun into Ike's face. "I love you, Ike, but don't you ever strike me again."

Ike's mouth dropped open, and he looked a little afraid. Feeling better now, Emma cradled her shotgun in her arms and went inside, closing the door behind her.

***

Supper that night was a sort of celebration. The boys were excited and proud of Emma. She shot a thieving fox right before their eyes! Emma too felt a measure of pride. She successfully defended their farm. Even though it was just a fox, she was determined to shoot at it, but actually shooting it was nothing but luck. For certain, she would have a close look at her father's bullets before she tried such a thing again.

Tommy said, for the third time, "Emma! When you shot that fox, you went flying. Your feet was straight up in the air!"

Clyde laughed and added, "Yeah, they was! You just flew over the woodpile. I thought you was hurt, but you come running!"

Claude just chuckled and smiled.

Emma looked around the table. All three boys were smiling, laughing, and enthusiastically spooning up their potatoes and string beans. It was the happiest she had ever seen them. She understood what they were feeling because she felt it herself. They were only children, all of them, and they have been battered by life. For the first time since they were thrown together, they no longer felt completely helpless. Emma, as it turned out, was a force to be reckoned with.

The boys cleared the table and carried her pitcher to her room for her. They felt more responsible now, a side-effect of having a measure of control over their fates. They even washed themselves more thoroughly than usual.

Emma sat on her bentwood chair beside the small stove in her room and damp-washed her hair using a little Ivory soap rubbed into a washcloth. She washed her face, gingerly dabbing at the cut above her eye with the soapy cloth. She washed from head to toe and then, as she always did, placed the bowl on the floor and soaked her feet. The warm water felt wonderful.

She heard the boys gathering outside her door, whispering. She dried her feet and slipped her nightdress over her head. Then she pulled on a clean pair of socks to ward off the chill. The nights have grown long and turned cold. She sat in front of her mirror, brushing her hair, and smiled when she heard the boys shushing each other so loudly it created a ruckus. Tonight, she would read to them, and together they would explore the underwater Island of Crespo.

Turning down her lamp, she carried a candle across the room to open her door. All three of the boys were tangled together, holding their hands over each other's mouths. When she laughed, they jumped to their feet and ran for the parlor. She followed them downstairs.

Tommy placed a log on the fire. Emma had just settled down to read when they heard Ike's truck coming up the wagon trail. She had literally lost track of time. When her mother first became sick, Emma neglected to wind their mantle clock, and ever since, it did not seem to matter. They lived by the position of the sun in the sky.

Ike said he would stop by, but it seemed late. She was used to him not showing up when he said he would. Emma closed her book and told the boys, "Wait here."

She lit the lamp on the kitchen wall and met Ike as he came to the door. The moon was near to full. It was lighter outside than in. She opened the door and he came inside carrying several packages. He seemed subdued.

"The war is over," he said. "That's what all the shooting was about."

Emma didn't know what to think. Her father was the only soldier she knew, and now that he was gone, the war no longer mattered to her.

"Who won?" she asked.

"We did, they say. Don't know what difference it all made."

"I'm glad for the soldiers. They can come home now."

Ike saw that this news was bittersweet for Emma. He felt the same way—peace came too late for them. Placing his packages on the table, he unwrapped the largest to reveal a long blue coat and held it open for Emma. "Try it on."

She slipped her arms into the sleeves and pulled it around her. "It's nice, warm."

Ike took her stained one down from the peg beside the door and folded it over his arm. "If you don't mind, I want to hang this one in my kitchen, to remind me."

Looking down at her new, new coat, a single tear ran down her cheek. "Thank you, Ike."

The muscles in Ike's jaw bunched up as he walked to the door. "Anyway, I, uh, picked up a few things for you and the boys."

He stepped into the moonlight and turned to leave. Emma walked out onto the back porch and called out, "Ike!" He turned back to her and she asked, "What time is it?"

He was surprised by the question. "I don't rightly

know. Don't pay much attention to time no more. I'm sorry, Emma."

Emma's breath formed puffs of vapor in the cold air. "That's alright, Ike. It doesn't matter."

She went back inside.

Chapter Seven

On the eleventh hour of the eleventh day on the eleventh month of 1918, a ceasefire was declared on the Western Front, and The Great War came to an end. Seventeen million people died in the war—a third of them from influenza.

In London, Big Ben chimed for the first time since the war began in 1914. In Paris, the gas streetlamps lit up after four years of darkness. Across the world, people rejoiced and gathered in the great open spaces such as Place de la Concorde, Trafalgar Square, and Times Square. Soldiers returned home to the kisses of their loved ones. In every city and town, the people turned out and celebrated in huge crowds.

As a result, another wave of influenza swept across the planet.

***

Emma and the boys had not left the farm since the day Ike hit her with a bottle, and they were perfectly happy to remain there. The flu was back, and the world outside their farm was rocked by death and despair. In the morgues and mortuaries, the bodies were stacked like cordwood.

They had not seen Ike in more than a week, but Emma had no intention of paying another visit to his farm. It was the twentieth-sixth of November, or thereabouts. A calendar hung in their kitchen, but some days were so traumatic she could not remember for sure if she crossed them off.

In the dim light of early dawn, she sat beside the woodstove wrapped in a blanket, waiting for the stove to warm. It was a cold gray day. She stretched to see through the window over the sink. The first snowflakes were falling.

Winter had arrived.

Everything they did throughout the rest of the year were done out of respect for winter. For those who were prepared, it was a time of holidays and fun. Little could be done on the farm aside from hauling wood and feeding the animals. For those who were unprepared or beset by misfortune, winter was a time of desperation when farms failed and were abandoned.

Ike butchered three of their hogs for them. Most of the meat hung in their smokehouse. The rest were submerged in salt brine in the root cellar. They had been tending a small fire in a pit beside the smokehouse for more than a week, adding hickory chips and bark several times a day. There was a long stovepipe buried in the ground that cooled the smoke and thereby kept the meat cool while it cured. It was nearly ready to be hung in the root cellar. Her father usually peppered the meat and wrapped it in parchment paper to discourage mold and insects. Since she had just a little pepper and no parchment at all, she would roll it in sifted ash instead. The meat did just as well, although the ash could be a nuisance.

She could have driven into town. She had money, but she would have to pass the Pearson place. In her mind, it was the place that harmed her. She did not want to go near there. The Ike Pearson who stood on his own ground was a different person than the Ike who stood upon hers. Eventually, he would come here—he always did. When he came, she would ask him to pick up what she needed from the mercantile. Mister Anderson was another bit of unpleasantness she hoped to avoid.

Before her father left for The Great War and the influenza came to Owen County, the people here were a community—centered on the church. When someone felled a tree for firewood, a dozen men would arrive with axes to trim the branches, crosscut saws to cut the proper lengths and mauls to split the logs so the wood could season.

On the days those men came to Yellowwood Farm, Emma and her mother prepared huge meals, served outside, and hard work became a celebration. The men would tell taller and taller tales about fishing, hunting, and farming—in an effort to outdo each other—until the lies became outrageous and the stories wonderful. Emma had listened with rapt attention, hanging on every word.

These days, people avoided each other, fearful and anonymous behind their white masks. The church remained empty. Emma fought off feelings of depression. If she allowed herself to feel sad, the boys would pick up on it and she would have her hands full. She did her best to be cheerful every day—as her mother would have.

She decided to make cookies for the boys, maybe oatmeal with cherries. Oatmeal cookies brightened the day of any small boy. And if the truth were known, they also cheered up any twelve-year-old girl who was raising three boys and struggling to find the strength. The kitchen was finally beginning to warm up, so she stood up and folded her blanket. It was time to gather the eggs.

Where are those boys?

Emma had taken to dressing Clyde in green suspenders, and Claude in brown ones, as a way of telling them apart. The whole idea depended upon one of them honestly giving her his name, so she was fairly certain she only succeeded in naming the suspenders. Even so, it was a convenience that saved her asking them their names again and again. It also helped the twins to remember who Clyde was...on that particular day.

After rousing the boys, again, and collecting the

eggs, Emma checked the meat in the smokehouse to see if it was ready for the root cellar. The bacon looked ready. She thought she would leave the hams another day or two, although she really did not know. She had watched her father do this every year, but this was the first time she did it herself. She wished Ike would show up. He would know for sure.

Snowflakes drifted down in the still air. Off in the distance, half a dozen turkeys gleaned seeds in the stubble of their wheat field. Emma and the boys had eaten nothing but pork for two months now. Their henhouse had been raided twice and they needed their remaining hens for eggs. Hens produced fewer eggs in the fall and winter anyway. She walked into the kitchen with a turkey dinner on her mind.

She laid her precious few eggs in a wire basket, placed them in the sink, and pumped water over them to rinse and cool them. Her eyes fell on the shotgun, still leaning against the wall beside the door. The boys did not complain outright, they were lucky to have meat at all, but they sighed when she put pork on the table, even ham. She felt the same way. She was sick of pork.

Her father always brought home rabbits, grouse, or a turkey at least once a week all throughout the winter. She never went hunting with him—her mother said it was unladylike—but the thought of a turkey dinner made her mouth water.

Standing on tiptoe, she peeked out the window over the sink. The turkeys were still there. Her mouth screwed up and she rubbed her cheek with her forefinger—considering. What would Momma do?

Momma would just eat the pork, thank God with a blessing, and not complain. But for sure Daddy would be out there collecting a turkey for dinner!

It wouldn't hurt to at least take a look at the bullets, or shells, or whatever they were. They didn't look like shells, they looked like bullets.

She went into her father's study and pulled out the top drawer of his big desk. She found a small box containing four shells, missing one, labeled 10 GAUGE SABOT SLUGS. She recognized them by the small dome of metal sticking out of the end. She carried around a bullet like that for weeks.

A bigger box was labeled 10 GAUGE BIRDSHOT. She recalled Ike saying that birdshot would not hurt her. There were also numbers across the box that meant nothing to her at all: 3 Dram, 1⅛ Shot. She had no idea what they meant, but it didn't matter. These two were the only kinds in the drawer. As far as she knew, she needed birdshot. It made perfect sense. She planned to shoot a bird, so she took two. They were crimped at the end and did not have a dome of metal sticking out.

Emma marched up to the kitchen door and stopped. Was she really going to do this? She looked into her heart for guidance, but her heart was in conversation with her stomach, and her stomach said she was going to do this.

Pulling on her coat, she dropped the shotgun shells in her pocket so they would be handy. She picked up her shotgun and went outside. A crescent of the sun peeked up behind the trees. Soon it would be fully light. The turkeys were still there.

Tommy came out of the barn carrying a pail of milk and nearly dropped it when he saw Emma with her shotgun. He ran up to her, slopping milk in every direction.

"Emma! Is there another fox?"

Feeling slightly embarrassed, she said, "No." She pointed out to the wheat field two hundred yards away. "I'm going to shoot one of those turkeys."

His eyes lit up. "Turkey! Shoot two, okay?"

Emma frowned. "Take that milk inside and quit spilling it. Go find Clyde and Claude. You boys stay right here. I don't want you getting hurt. I've only shot this thing once."

The ground had a light covering with snow that made the dark color of the turkeys stand out. Emma considered sneaking up on them, but they were too far away from the woods to use for cover. She decided to walk right up to them.

She walked into the cornfield standing between her and the wheat field. Each step between the dry stalks was silent, but when she reached the wheat stubble, it crunched beneath her feet. The turkeys were less than fifty yards away. The tom lifted his head and gobbled. Emma froze.

She brought her shotgun up to her shoulder and realized she had not loaded a shell. She quietly broke it open and slipped a shell into the breech. When she closed it, the metallic click sent the turkeys flying for the trees.

The birds flew low to the ground and disappeared into the trees. Emma ran after them. She stopped ten yards from the woods and listened closely. They were gone. She crept forward and stared into the trees—nothing, not a bird in sight. She heard a rustle and lifted the gun to her shoulder, watching intently—nothing. She lowered her shotgun, disappointed and empty-handed.

A loud scream came from the trees just in front of her! It sounded like Ike Pearson when Tommy stuck him with a pitchfork!

Emma jumped back and squealed, scared half to death, certain a giant grizzly bear was about to run out and snatch her up. With her heart pounding and a lump in her throat, she shakily raised her shotgun back up—wishing she had brought a slug. She backed away, afraid to turn her back on the trees. She jumped at the sound of a loud crash in the brush and stood perfectly still, gun at the ready. After half a minute—nothing.

She lifted her head from the sights, straining to see anything in the thick brush. A dozen turkeys nearly flew into her face. She screamed, closed her eyes, and pulled the trigger. BOOM! Her feet left the ground, and she landed flat on her back.

When she opened her eyes, she was looking up into a cloudy sky. A big crystalline flake of snow landed on her face. She jumped to her feet. The turkeys were already far across the field, nearly to the woods on the other side. She scowled, brushed herself off, and gripped her right shoulder with her left hand. "Ow!"

Rubbing her shoulder, hurting and disappointed, she turned to pick up her shotgun, and as she bent over, she heard a low growl. The bear was back! She slowly lifted her head with her heartbeat thundering in her ringing ears and saw a mound of dark feathers just a few feet away. Closer to the trees, a second mound of feathers was being dragged into the woods by a bobcat. Emma had seen this cat before, but only from a distance. He was scruffy looking and must be half-starved or deaf to hang around after that gunshot, but there he was, gamely dragging a big hen into the trees.

Frightened as she was, an odd thought crossed her mind—he had pretty eyes. Finally getting a good grip on his bird, he bounded off and disappeared. Emma snatched up her shotgun and quickly loaded the other shell with shaking hands—ready to defend herself. The only sound was a distant rustling of leaves. She stood there for a full minute with her shotgun at the ready before she slowly lowered it. Picking up her turkey by one foot, she ran like the dickens for the house.

The boys watched the whole thing from beside the barn and now, seeing Emma running their way, they took off to meet her. They met in the cornfield and swirled around her, pulling the turkey out of her hand and slapping her on the back.

Tommy said, "Emma! How come you only shot one? Did that big cat steal one of yours, or did he get his own?"

Clyde hung onto Emma's coat and asked, "Was that a mountain lion? I never seen a mountain lion before."

Emma rolled her eyes and said, "No. That was not a mountain lion. That was a poor old scruffy bobcat. If he had not helped, we wouldn't have this turkey, so do not begrudge him his share."

They walked back up to the barn with the boys taking turns carrying the turkey. Emma was quite accustomed to dressing turkeys. She would show the boys how it was done, relieving her of the tedious job of plucking the feathers. The boys would be thrilled to do it anyway.

They were standing beside the chicken coop celebrating their upcoming feast when one of the boys grabbed her arm. KABOOM—the shotgun flew out of her hands.

Emma screamed and grabbed the twins. "Are you boys okay?"

"I'm fine," Clyde said. Claude just shrugged. His eyes were huge.

She looked behind her to find Tommy lying on the ground. Emma threw herself on top of him. She took his face in her hands and he smiled.

"That gun kicks hard! Emma! Can you make stuffing with cornbread and cherries?"

She sobbed and smothered his face with kisses until

he said, "Hey! Enough already!"

Emma stood back up with tears on her face. She helped Tommy to his feet, and he rubbed his chest. "Ow!"

When she turned around, feathers floated down to the ground inside her chicken coop. One of her hens was splattered all over the side of the henhouse around a five-inch smoking hole.

Emma balled her fists. Her whole body shook. Another of her precious hens was gone! A chicken dinner and hundreds of eggs! They would have been better off without this blasted turkey! She couldn't take it anymore. She screamed into the sky in sharp, piercing tones, "DAMN STUPID CHICKENS!"

Having just alighted after the sound of that gunshot, the birds flew back out of the trees, and the pigs scurried back into the barn. Emma's eyes got big. She covered her mouth with her hand. The horses stopped grazing and lifted their heads to peer in her direction as the echoes died away.

Claude grinned, looked up at her, and said, "Damn stupid chickens."

Emma glared at him. "Shut up, Claude."

***

By the time the boys finished plucking and dressing the turkey, Emma came to realize that losing another hen was almost worth it—not worth it, but almost. They would be short on eggs until early summer, but the boys were laughing and thrilled to think that Emma could hunt.

She laid out a simple breakfast of oatmeal with honey and cherries. It was one of their favorites. She sat down to eat and listened while they told and retold the story. The bobcat became a mountain lion, and Emma's accuracy with a gun—never mind that it was a ten-gauge shotgun—came to rival Annie Oakley. They repeatedly whispered, "Damn stupid chickens," and burst into laughter.

Every time they repeated the phrase, Emma frowned and said, "Don't say damn." She could not bring herself to scold them. As a result, damn was said twice as often.

After breakfast, Emma dragged a big Dutch oven out from behind the curtain fastened around the kitchen sink. She could barely pick it up and wondered how much more it would weigh with a turkey in it. She wasn't sure, but she thought it might be Thanksgiving. If it was, then Ike should be here to spend the holiday with his grandsons.

Just because he hadn't shown up didn't mean it was not Thanksgiving. Ike was dangerously unpredictable. Better to wait until he came here than drop in on him.

Emma had never roasted a turkey by herself before. She had helped her mother often enough, so she felt confident she could do it. She even knew how to make cornbread stuffing. First, she needed cornbread. She poured two cups of buttermilk, left over in the churn after making butter, into a large bowl, and began mixing the ingredients. She wasn't really sure, but she would tell the boys it was Thanksgiving. This was the first time they have had a turkey in the oven, so she wanted to make the most of it.

Once she had the stove burning steadily, she closed the dampers a bit and put her cornbread in to bake. Then she went to the sink and started rubbing the turkey with salt and butter, looking out the window watching the boys pretending to shoot her chickens with a stick and laughing. It was a good day when she saw them laughing and playing. Was it a coincidence their best days were when she fired that blasted shotgun?

She picked up her turkey and placed it in the Dutch oven just as she heard Ike's truck chugging up the wagon trail. She was glad he finally came. The boys heard him too and surrounded the truck when he pulled up next to the house. The back was full of wood.

She watched the twins hug him around the waist, and he ruffled their hair. Tommy stood away from this touching scene with a little frown. He would never forgive Ike for hitting her with that bottle. A moment later, all three of the boys were stacking wood.

As usual, Ike knocked on the kitchen door and waited for Emma to open it and invite him in.

"Ike! Come in, please, it's good to see you," she said.

Ike stepped inside. Emma was pleased to see that his clothes were clean and he was clean-shaven. He removed his long coat and hung it on a peg beside the door. He was carrying a large cloth sack.

"Hello, Miss Emma. Do I smell cornbread?"

Emma said nonchalantly, "I'm making stuffing. I shot a turkey this morning and wanted to stuff it for the boys."

Ike's eyebrows went up. He peeked into the Dutch oven and said, "You did for a fact. Emma, you surprise me."

He placed his cloth sack on the table and said, "I brought a few things for you and the boys."

He took out a small white glass jar with a metal lid and held it out to her. She wiped her hands on her mother's apron and took it from him. The label said, *Velvet Hand Cream.* Sometimes, Ike surprised her. Her hands were red and rough to the point of cracking and bleeding between her fingers. She opened it and smiled at the scent of roses. She closed it tightly to preserve that wonderful smell.

She gave him a gentle hug. "Thank you, Ike."

Ike smiled. "Ain't nothing, considering all you done."

Emma looked up at him and asked, "What day is it?"

"I thought you knew, shootin' turkeys and all. It's November 28, Thanksgiving."

"I thought it might be, but I wasn't sure," she said.

Ike could never get over the sight of this pretty little girl, bustling about this big kitchen, doing better than he could ever hope to do for those boys. He took her bloodstained coat back to his house weeks ago, hung it up in his kitchen, and swore off alcohol for good. He could not touch a drop within sight of that painful reminder—so he only drank in the barn and never before coming here. As a result, he did not come here nearly often enough, but he knew that on the days he stayed away, they were better off without him.

Seeing the pink scar above Emma's eye, Ike swallowed hard. He was often haunted by the memory of that day. He asked her, "Want to know what time it is?"

Emma looked up at him in surprise. She did in fact want to know the time. Not that it mattered. Time had nothing to do with life on this farm, but not knowing made her feel disconnected from the rest of the world.

Ike reached into his shirt pocket and pulled out a locket on a gold chain. Untangling the chain, he dropped it over her head so the locket hung on her chest. Emma flipped up her hair in the back so the chain rested against her neck, picked up the locket, and opened it. It was a watch! She had never owned one, nor had her mother. They kept time on the mantle clock. It looked expensive. She lifted it to her ear and heard it ticking. It was just after ten o'clock in the morning.

Her lip trembled when she said, "Thank you, Ike."

"It belonged to Martha. I won't be having no granddaughters, but you been like a daughter to me. Martha would be proud for you to have it."

Emma hugged him again, harder and longer this

time. Ike clumsily patted her on the back. He did not feel that he deserved her affection.

"Anyways," he said, and Emma stepped back to look up at him. "I brought some pepper and parchment so's we can finish off the meat in the smokehouse."

Ike took his coat down from beside the door. "I'll have the boys help with the meat. You fix your supper."

"Tell the boys we're skipping lunch today. We'll have an early supper. Will you join us at our table?"

"I would be pleased to have a taste of turkey." He went outside, pulling on his long coat.

Opening her locket, Emma checked the time again. Only one minute had passed. It lifted her spirits to know the time. It was the sort of thing people used to come together— meeting at a certain time. She closed it back up and tucked it inside her dress to keep it safe. Then she crossed off two days on her calendar and dragged a kitchen chair into the parlor to wind and set the mantle clock.

***

Emma prepared a proper Thanksgiving dinner. There were bowls of potatoes, carrots, and squash. Her turkey sat on a platter, tender and moist, owing to her Dutch oven. The bread was still warm, and a plate of oatmeal cookies with cherries sat beside it. She used her mother's wedding china, scared to death one of the boys might drop something. She would serve them herself to minimize the risk.

Once she had everyone seated at the table, she admired her supper for a moment. Ike and the boys admired it as well, with hungry eyes. As was their habit, Emma bowed her head and clasped her hands to say the blessing. Everyone else did likewise.

"Lord, we pray for those we love, but no longer see. Tell them we are well and thinking of them. Let our love for them bind us together. Thank you for the turkey, I know it was your gift to us. Amen."

Ike and the boys sat up but, as sometimes happened, Emma still had her head bowed. They glanced around nervously, bowed their heads again, and waited.

Emma said, "Lord, I'm sorry I cursed the chickens. I didn't mean it. Amen." She looked up to find smiles at her table.

Claude said quietly, "Damn stupid chickens." The boys laughed themselves silly while she frowned and sipped her milk.

Ike was given the honor of carving the turkey. He took for himself only a polite portion and loaded the plates of everyone else. Emma jumped up to serve the vegetables before one of the boys picked up one of her mother's dishes. Then she climbed back into her chair to partake of the best meal she'd had in months. When she took her first bite of the turkey, her eyes closed and she smiled. Wild turkeys actually fly, so they are entirely dark meat. Even the breasts are moist and flavorful. Several minutes of silence passed while Emma, Ike, and the boys dug in.

Emma's eyes met Ike's, and he nodded to her politely. This was the Ike she loved. It was her mother's gentle spirit that led her to forgive him, despite her fear and anger. She knew he battled demons she did not understand and prayed for him often. Today was one of his good days.

She briefly closed her eyes and sent a prayer to her mother, thanking her again for her guidance. Without her, she would have forsaken Ike, and their tenuous hold on this farm might have been lost. The people she loved, sitting at this table, might have been torn apart and left in the hands of strangers. She was Anna Taylor's daughter. It was the only thing that saved them.

***

Thanksgiving at Yellowwood Farm in the year 1918 was a celebration of belonging. Their odd little family came together and formed strong bonds. The boys continued to retell the story of Emma and the mountain lion all through supper.

Ike repaired the henhouse and did not comment on Emma's accidental discharge. It frightened her badly and she vowed to be more careful around that big shotgun. It was a little funny. She could not help but laugh when Tommy relived the moment by shaking from side to side and damned all chickens, Bantams, Leghorns, or otherwise. It turned into a contest of who could name another breed of chickens, and they damned them one at a time while Emma sank down in her chair and silently begged for their forgiveness.

Supper began early and lasted long. By the time everyone had eaten their fill and laughed themselves out, it was fully dark. Emma checked her watch, surprised to find it was only a quarter of six. Once darkness fell, she and the boys were usually winding down for a chapter in the parlor and then off to bed.

Emma sent the boys out to feed the animals. She would wash the dishes herself. They were too precious to trust to the twins. Meanwhile, she and Ike sat alone at the table.

She said, "Thank you again for the watch. It's a comfort to know what time it is."

Ike stood up and stretched. "Least I could do. That was as fine a Thanksgiving meal as I have ever had. Your momma would be proud."

Emma was wondering about something. She did not want to pry, but the twins needed a reminder of their parents. Her own parents' wedding picture had brought comfort to her and Tommy. Even without it, they were far better off than Clyde and Claude. Everything they touched on this farm held memories of their mother and father.

"Ike, Clyde and Claude don't have anything from their mother and father. They need something to remember them by. Is there a picture of them?"

Ike considered this for a moment. He sat back down at the table with a troubled look on his face. "Their momma was a fine woman and my son was a good man, but they was barely making ends meet. Donny worked at the lumberyard. The house was rented. When I went there that day, Helen was already dead, in bed beside Donny. He begged me to bury them next to his momma, and he died later that day. I'm ashamed to say that I did not claim their things. Don't know what became of them."

Here was a glimpse of the Ike that frightened Emma. In most families, sons took over the management of their father's farms when they grew old. She did not ask why Ike's son had not done so—she already knew.

"Do you think you could maybe ask? Just a picture or a keepsake, they only need a little thing. Nobody else would value it."

Ike met Emma's eyes and felt shame. She was doing more for his grandsons than he even thought to consider—a girl, only twelve years old. He stood up again and looked out the kitchen window. There was no moon. The night was black.

"I'll try. When Donny and Helen died, I just buried 'em and tried to forget."

He took down his long coat, pulled it on, and without looking back he said, "You're a fine girl, Emma. You done real good by my boys."

The screen door clapped shut behind him.

Emma got up from the table and went to stand in front of the sink, looking out into the night. She heard Ike's truck start up and watched the yellow glow of his headlamps appear and then fade away into the darkness.

Chapter Eight

The first heavy snow fell on Yellowwood Farm four days before Christmas. Emma lay in her bed, snug and warm beneath her blankets, dreading the moment when she crawled out from under them. She could see her breath in the cold air, lit by starlight and a sliver of the moon shining through her window. It was the shortest day of the year.

Fully awake and unable to delay any longer, she swung her stocking feet onto the floor and wrapped herself in her warmest blanket. Lighting a candle to light her way, she walked quickly down the hall and down the stairs to the kitchen—the heart of her home. She used the candle to light the kerosene lamp hanging on the kitchen wall and adjusted the wick until the room filled with soft yellow light. Crystalline frost covered the windows.

She shook the ashes from her woodstove, took a handful of kindling sticks from a basket, dropped them into the firebox, and struck a match. When they began to burn, she added larger pieces of wood and finally, some small logs. Then she scooted a chair up next to the stove, climbed up into it, and huddled in her blanket to wait for the stove to heat up.

She felt very small. The world was made for giants, she thought. Sitting in her chair, her feet did not quite reach the floor. Every tool, every cup, every door, gate and ladder was made too big for her—especially that blasted shotgun.

She tried to shake off her sad thoughts but failed. Each day was a test of her strength. She worried constantly that she would somehow lose their farm. Holding back tears, she closed her eyes, bowed her head, and clasped her hands together. She sent a prayer to her mother and father, asking what to do. Then she opened her heart and waited for an answer. It came in an instant. A memory of a day she had forgotten.

She saw in her mind, clear as a bell, her mother and father, standing together beneath the cascading blossoms of the yellowwood tree. Her mother was smiling, touching her father's face. Her father was laughing, holding up Tommy so he could reach out to touch the blooms. For a moment, she was there. They found joy in each other's company.

Their answer was clear. Love is its own reward. She opened her eyes and pushed her hair back behind her ears. Three little bundles of love were just up those stairs. She would turn her mind away from sad thoughts and set to thinking instead of ways to make this a good day for them. It was a simple thing to find happiness; just love those boys. Their happiness was the key to finding her own.

The stove was heating up. She folded her blanket and warmed herself in front of it, turning slowly to get all sides. Then she draped her folded blanket around her shoulders and dashed upstairs to dress quickly in her cold room. She knocked on the boys' doors on the way back down—time to start the day.

The eastern sky glowed a pale orange, hinting at the impending sunrise. The door to the root cellar was tilted back at a sharp angle, buried beneath nearly a foot of snow. Emma used a spade to remove enough of the snow so she could lift the door and pull it open. She stepped down into the gloom and lit the lantern hanging from the rafters. Taking down a basket and carrying it over her arm, she unstrapped the top of a small barrel containing sweet potatoes packed in straw and oak leaves. She would make a sweet potato pie for the boys.

She selected a few nice sweet potatoes and strapped the lid back onto the barrel before carving off a thick slice of ham. Breakfast would be ham and bread. She would save their two eggs to make a pie. Climbing back up into the orange light of early dawn, she heard a far-off growling wail and giggled. That scruffy old bobcat must be claiming his own breakfast. She struggled to lift the heavy root cellar door out of the snow and dropped it closed.

Emma felt connected to that old bobcat. The two of them came together and collected two turkeys— something neither of them could have done alone. She stood in the cold air with her basket over her arm and gazed out across the fields, wishing him good luck. Then she picked up her spade and waded through the deep snow back to the house. The boys would be done with their morning chores soon. She would have their breakfast ready for them.

A loaf of bread warmed in the oven, and sliced ham sizzled in a frying pan when Tommy came in. He stomped his feet to shake the snow from his boots and hung his coat on a peg beside the kitchen door. His cheeks were red from the cold. He went straight to the woodstove and held out his hands to warm them.

He looked up at his big sister, turning ham in the frying pan with a fork and asked, "Emma! Can we make snow cream?"

Pulling him up against her with one arm, she said, "I was going to make a sweet potato pie. We can have pie and snow cream."

She put down her fork and knelt down to rub his hands between hers to warm them. She had taken to using lard to keep their hands from chapping. Once the weather turned bitter cold, they used up her little jar of hand cream in only a week. What they really needed were mittens. The coldest months were yet to come. She knew how to knit, but just barely. Without a pattern to follow she could not knit more than a scarf.

Last week, she rummaged through the storage benches in the parlor and found her mother's knitting basket, but no patterns. Her mother gave her a pattern for stocking caps, and she put it to good use knitting hats for her and the boys. She could not understand how her mother knitted mittens every year without a pattern to follow. Thinking back, she could not recall ever having seen her with any kind of pattern at all. She never paid much attention to it at the time. Now, it seemed impossible. Emma learned how to knit for fun, but this year it was serious business. The next time she saw a lady knitting, she was going to ask a hundred questions.

They hadn't seen Ike in nearly two weeks, and the heavy snowfall made it unlikely they would see him at all before Christmas. On his last visit, Emma asked him to pick up a few things for the boys to have on Christmas morning. She had offered him the money to pay for them, but he would not accept it. He told her not to worry, that he would take care of it. She was worried about it now. Somehow, he always came through at the last minute, but it caused her to worry when he failed to show up on the days he promised.

Clyde and Claude came in from feeding the pigs, and after hanging up their coats, they made a beeline for the stove. The three of them crowded around Emma, warming their hands at her woodstove.

Tommy said, "Hey guys, we're gonna make snow cream!"

"What's snow cream?" Clyde asked.

"You never had snow cream! It's real good. Me and Emma make it. Emma! Can we put cherries in it?"

Emma smiled. "Sure, Tommy."

Once they were warm, Emma sat them down for

breakfast and served hot ham with warm bread and butter. They ate as if they were starved, laughing and wolfing down their breakfast. It made her happy to see them this way. She closed her eyes and sent thanks to her mother and father for their wisdom and guidance.

On snowy days, farm life slows down, but the cold does create a few extra chores. Emma sent the boys to check the creek and make sure it was not frozen over. They found it mostly free of ice. When it froze, the ice had to be broken up so the animals could drink. The water, however, was fast flowing so it seldom froze over completely. Clyde and Claude came back in after only a few minutes, but without Tommy.

"Where's Tommy?" Emma asked.

Clyde said, "He went up the hill."

Emma peeked through the curtains of the kitchen door and saw Tommy, wading through the snow toward the yellowwood tree. She put on her coat and went after him.

The yellowwood tree was stripped bare of leaves. Emma kept her eyes on Tommy as she made her way through the snow and stopped beside him. He seemed to be visiting the tree and not the grave beside it. When she caught up to him, he stood looking up into the branches.

She stood beside him for a moment, looking up, but there was nothing out of the ordinary, just branches. Emma laid her hand on Tommy's shoulder.

He turned to her. "Pa used to hold me up so I could touch the flowers."

"I remember," she said.

The yellowwood had not bloomed in two years. He would have been only four, but he remembered. He was standing in snow up to his knees recalling a May memory that Emma knew was placed in their minds by their mother and father. She was not surprised. She always felt their presence.

When she looked up again, she saw what he saw; long white clusters of blooms with tiny yellow centers. His father could no longer lift him up, and his mother could no longer knit his mittens, but they had the powers of the angels—to comfort and inspire.

Emma was smiling, looking up at the tree, when a snowball hit her in the back of the head. A dusting of snow found its way down her collar, making her squeal. Tommy knew better than to hang around. He was plowing through the snow toward the house, laughing. They pelted each other with snowballs all the way back to the house.

When they came back inside, Emma was alarmed at how cold and red his hands were. She resolved to do something about it immediately. She might not know much about knitting, but she knew how to sew quite well. She sacrificed an old woolen blanket to make mittens by cutting two sides and then stitching them together.

Her first attempt produced a three-quarter size mitten, and her second would have fit a chimpanzee perfectly. It took her several hours, but in the end, the resulting product turned out better than she expected.

On an inspiration, she made them come halfway up the boys' arms and cuffed them. She and the boys now had warm mittens, actually better than if she knitted them. In fact, she thought they were the nicest mittens she ever owned.

The boys did their lessons at the kitchen table, played checkers, and passed the short day quietly—all together, all day, while Emma made bread around them.

Supper that night was potatoes, carrots, and string beans cooked in a rich broth, one of the boys favorites. It was a good thing they liked it, because that was what they had the most of in the root cellar.

A pan of cream simmered on the stove. Emma checked it frequently so as not to scorch it. It was nearly ready, cooked down to a thick golden consistency. She added sugar and cherries and stirred it with an appraising eye. Then back to the table to take another spoonful of her supper. She scooted her stepstool over in front of the pantry, took down a small dark bottle of vanilla extract, and added just two drops to her condensed cream. Then back up her stepstool to replace the bottle and back to her bowl for another bite.

Many of her meals were taken one bite at a time while she bustled about her big kitchen, scooting her stepstool here and there, so she could reach. She scooped up some of the condensed cream in a big wooden spoon and watched it drip back into the pan, judging the consistency—perfect. Using a dishtowel, she picked up the pan by the handle and carried it outside to place it in the snow. She dashed back inside rubbing away the goosebumps on her arms and jumped back up into her chair to finish her supper. Her sweet potato pie was already on the table.

After supper, Emma gave the boys a measuring cup and a large bowl with instructions to collect exactly eight cups of tightly packed snow. Three did not divide into eight evenly, so it took them half an hour while they fought over the cup, threw snowballs at each other, and started over many times, having lost count. When they finally managed to place eight cups into the bowl, they called for her.

She pulled on her coat and went outside to find them covered in snow, smiling and rosy-cheeked. Pouring her little pan of cold condensed cream over their bowl of snow, she mixed it up thoroughly—snow cream. She left it beside the door and ushered them inside. In the time it took them to collect eight cups of snow, she washed the dishes and laid out slices of sweet potato pie. Topped with a big scoop of snow cream, her pie was a huge hit with the boys.

After supper, Emma sat in her bentwood chair, pulled close to the little woodstove in her room, and washed. Her bar of Ivory soap was just a sliver. She would use it down to nothing before opening another. The soap was precious to her, a little indulgence. She knew there was an unfathomable amount of money in their hidden cash box, but Ike cautioned her that it would be barely enough to get by on. The war was over now, so farms would struggle over the coming years. Her mother was always frugal, and now Emma was too.

The feel of the warm water and the scent of the soap soothed her. It was a good day for her and the boys, but she was worn out. She would read to them in the parlor. She enjoyed that as much as the boys did, but she longed to crawl into her bed and sleep. She dreamed of a morning when she would sleep until she could sleep no longer, getting out of bed long after sunrise. And if a bird wanted to chirp at her window—there was always that big shotgun.

She dried herself thoroughly, hung her towel and washcloth on her washstand, and slipped her nightdress over her head. Pulling on a pair of warm socks, she lit a candle. When she opened her door, she found the boys sitting in a line, quietly waiting for her in the dark. They followed her downstairs, placed a log on the fire, and took their places on the rug in front of the fireplace. Emma climbed up into her mother's rocking chair and opened her book. This was how they ended their good days.

***

The next day was Sunday. Long before sunrise, Emma sat beside the woodstove in her kitchen wrapped in a blanket—her usual morning routine. The white snow reflected the dim light of the stars and a crescent moon, giving the appearance of twilight.

Even though it was Sunday, there would be no church service. She had no experience outside their little country church, but there the pastor served because he heard the call and was elected by the congregation. He was not paid in any way, and farmed, just like everyone else. On this Christmas, her church was without a pastor, and the law prohibited the congregation from coming together.

Her mother had taught her the everyday lessons of life by quoting scripture, and she in turn learned those lessons from her mother and so forth. A long line of Annas, Emmas, Ruths, Marys, and Elizabeths stretched back into the mists of time—all joined together by their faith.

Emma was concerned for the boys because there was no spiritual component to their upbringing. She did not in any way consider herself capable of preaching and besides, listening to sermons was the least thing she learned at church. Her greatest lessons came from watching people gather for common cause: to sew, harvest, cut wood, or any of the other thousand things that needed doing and were more easily or more enjoyably done together. On those occasions, an air of celebration was lent to hard work.

She was learning now, as were the boys, that in times of most desperate need, people often turn away. Emma would never live her life that way. She was Anna Taylor's daughter—a child of God. She would always do as her mother would have done.

The stove was warming up, so she folded her blanket and dashed upstairs to dress. The day was cold and the snow deep, so she did not hold out much hope of seeing Ike today. She was worried about Ike—for a lot of reasons.

She dressed quickly in her cold room and knocked on the boys' doors on her way back down. It was time to gather the eggs. She slipped on her coat and pulled on her new mittens, glad to have warm hands on a cold morning. Her hens were accustomed to her gentle touch. She lifted them up to retrieve the eggs and settled them back down without ruffling a feather. They barely opened their eyes. It was a normal part of every morning.

She was down to just five hens, and each one only produced an egg every other day or so—fewer still in fall and winter. She found three precious eggs. Yesterday, there were only two. She would hard boil these three and give them to the boys for lunch.

It was still fully dark, the morning star bright on the horizon. Tommy came out from the kitchen and headed off to the barn with his milk pail.

Emma shouted, "Tommy! Where are your mittens?"

He held up his pail, and without turning, he shouted back, "I can't milk with mittens, Emma!" He continued on his way.

She would speak to him later about wearing them before milking. One of these days, Susie might kick him for having cold hands. She carried her three eggs back inside and started making oatmeal for breakfast.

After the morning chores were done, and the breakfast dishes washed and put away, the boys gathered at the table. Emma was familiar with teaching young boys from her experiences at her little schoolhouse. She always made the lessons fun.

She asked them, "If you have ten chickens and a fox steals three, how many chickens do you have?"

The boys laughed while they held up ten fingers, folded down three, and counted.

"Seven!" Clyde said.

Claude said, "Yeah! Seven damn stupid chickens."

Emma glared at Claude until he stopped smiling. "Sorry, Emma."

Tommy said, "If the fox steals three and Emma blows one to bits with a shotgun, you only have six!" They nearly fell out of their chairs laughing. Most of their arithmetic was learned by counting the demise of chickens.

They took turns writing their letters on Emma's slate, the one she used when she was six years old. Then she wrote words and held them up for the boys to identify. They passed the morning this way until she allowed them to go outside and play in the snow after lunch.

While she was mixing a little honey with butter to put on bread for her lunch, Emma saw Ike drive a sledge up next to the house. Nearly every farm had a sledge, but it never occurred to her that Ike might drive one up the wagon trail. Mostly, they were used for hauling heavy loads in the snow and seldom went off the farm. Ike's sledge, like those on most farms, was homemade with wooden runners faced with metal barrel stays. It was just a platform on runners. Ike stood in front, and the back was loaded with wood. She watched as he unhitched a team of big draft horses and jogged alongside, leading them into the barn.

She put on a kettle to boil so she could make tea. She was glad to see Ike, although he was here four days later than he promised. It caused her to worry. He appeared at her kitchen door and knocked softly. She could hear rattles and clunks as the boys stacked the wood.

Emma opened the door. "Come in, Ike. I was worried for you."

Ike was dressed in his long coat and knee-high boots with a broad brimmed hat. He stomped his feet to shake off the snow, tipped his hat, and stepped into the warm kitchen. "Miss Emma," he said.

Emma waited for him to hang up his coat and gave him a gentle hug. He hung his hat over his coat. He never answered her concerns over his tardiness. He never knew what to say.

Ike carried his big cloth sack. He laid it on the floor and started removing packages, placing them on the table.

"I picked up the things on your list and a few others. It should be a fine Christmas for you and the boys."

Emma sorted through the packages, many of them wrapped in gift paper. She suspected they were wrapped at the mercantile or wherever Ike purchased them. Emma did not write anything on that list for herself, but there were two packages with her name on them. There was also honey, tea, sugar, and a case of Ivory soap—twenty-four bars! She leaned over the case, inhaled the scent, and smiled. Twenty-four bars of Ivory soap were a treasure!

She cleared a space on the table and seated Ike in front of his tea. "You should let me pay for some of this."

He warmed his hands on his mug and blew on it. "I'm an old man, Emma. When I was young, I valued money more than the things it could buy. Now, I ain't even sure I recall where I hid it all."

Emma kissed him on the cheek while he sat drinking his tea, surprising him. "Thank you, Ike. At least stay for dinner," she said and ran off into the parlor.

She returned a moment later, carrying a hatbox. She looked everywhere but did not have any paper she could use for wrapping, so she borrowed a hatbox from her mother's things. She hoped Ike did not walk off with it. She wanted to put her mother's hat back in it.

"Merry Christmas, Ike." She placed it on the table in

front of him.

He started to lift the lid and stopped to look at Emma standing beside him with a big smile. She nodded at the box and said, "Go ahead."

He removed the lid and began pulling out a long yellow scarf. It was six feet long with tassels at each end. He stood up and draped it over his neck, holding up one end.

"It's as fine a neck-wrap as I have ever seen."

Emma smiled and replaced the lid on her mother's hatbox before carrying it back into the parlor. She knitted Ike's scarf more than a week ago, using up every bit of her mother's golden yarn. It looked good on him. He was always dressed in such drab clothes that a spot of color did wonders for his appearance.

In Ike's long life, he had seen everything there was to see. He was jaded and hard-bitten, and he could not understand how there came to exist in such a cruel and unforgiving world a girl like Emma Taylor. Every time he was in her presence, she surprised him.

"I…uh…I promised the boys we would cut a white pine for your parlor. If you don't mind none."

Emma said, "The boys would love that."

She stood there in a blue dress, heavy boots up to her knees and a frilly apron that came down below them. Her appearance was an odd mix of little girl, farmer, and homemaker. He reached into his cloth sack, pulled out a five by seven frame, and handed it to Emma.

"I asked Donny's landlord about their things. Said he burned the clothes and such. They wasn't much, no pictures. He saved this, said he knowed I'd come back for it someday. It's them, I can tell."

It was a silhouette of a man and a woman, shown in profile, facing each other and holding hands. Inside an oval of black matting, was an image cut from black paper and pasted onto a cream-colored background. Such things were an inexpensive alternative to photographs.

"Thank you, Ike. This will mean a lot to the boys. We'll hang it in the parlor."

Ike was always uncomfortable around Emma. He looked everywhere but directly at her, to avoid seeing the scar on her face.

"Well, I uh, I reckon we'll go cut down that tree then." He stuck his hat on his head, pulled on his coat, and went outside.

Emma carried the silhouette into the parlor and laid it on the lamp table beside the photograph of her mother and father. It was beautifully done, very detailed. She would hang it low, where the twins could see it. It was exactly what they needed. It captured the certain knowledge that this man loved this woman.

Chapter Nine

Christmas day dawned cold and gray on Yellowwood Farm. Emma had been up for hours before the weak gray light revealed a clean, new, blanket of white under fast-moving clouds, still spitting snow. Fresh footsteps ran from the house to the barn, the root cellar and the woodshed.

Emma made griddlecakes and hot syrup by boiling molasses and water flavored with cherries and honey. The special breakfast was the only thing that drew the boys away from the gifts under their Christmas tree. They gathered at her table.

Emma did not often say a blessing at breakfast, but this being Christmas, she held on to the syrup until the boys got the idea. They bowed their heads when she did and waited.

She looked into her heart, as her mother always did, and found the words to say.

"Lord, it's us again. It's Christmas and we celebrate the birth of your son. We thank you for his gift of rebirth and eternal life. Please shine your warm light on our mothers and fathers. Tell them we are well and we are thinking of them. Let our love for them bind us together. Amen."

Emma sat up and Tommy reached for the syrup, but Claude still had his head down. Emma held on to the syrup and bowed her head. Tommy looked around the table and seeing Claude, he did likewise, but he had a frown—Emma said the blessings around here.

Claude said softly, "Lord. Please watch out for Grampa. If it ain't too much trouble, tell him it's Christmas. Amen."

Claude looked up to find all eyes upon him. He shrugged. "I ain't never talked to God before. Do you think he heard?"

Emma said, "He always listens, you don't even have to say it out loud. That was a fine blessing, Claude."

There was a look of astonishment on Clyde's face. It never occurred to him that he could talk to God. Or that He would listen! Did God actually care what he had to say?

Breakfast began pleasantly enough, but as everyone's appetites were curbed, thoughts of unopened gifts awaiting them under the tree pulled them into the parlor. Emma was no less attracted than the boys. Every twelve-year-old girl loves Christmas morning just as much as any boy half her age. She was the last to leave the table, wolfing down a final mouthful of griddlecake and running after the boys. She found them holding presents, waiting for her.

She wanted to immediately tear open the two mysterious packages under the tree with her name on them. She has shaken and prodded them for two days, but there was a proper way to do these things. A sharp pain passed through her at the sight of her mother's empty rocking chair. In all the excitement, she forgot—for just a moment. She fought back tears and climbed up into the chair, to do what her mother would have done. They opened one gift at a time.

The boys were thrilled to find toy trucks, marbles and new socks. They were mostly thrilled by the trucks, but some article of clothing was an obligatory Christmas gift and they understood that. Each truck was different. They took turns pushing them around on the floor, hauling marbles across the parlor.

Emma opened her gifts last—as her mother had always done. Inside a thin light box, she found a pair of gloves. She never owned gloves before. Children wore mittens. They were soft, supple and lined with fur. She felt as though she was holding something that belonged to someone else. She put them back in the box and thought that someday, she would wear them to church.

The last gift was Emma's. It was a small yet heavy little cube she has puzzled over for days. She tore away the wrapping to reveal a finely made wooden box. She turned it over in her hands, not sure what it was. When she lifted the lid, she saw that it had a small felt compartment for jewelry or a keepsake. The only such thing she owned was her watch. Then it began to play music.

Emma and the boys had not heard music in many months. The soft tinkling tune was unfamiliar to her, but it was beautiful. All of them sat in stunned silence as the wonder of music soothed them. When the music ended, Emma wound the key and they listened again without saying a word. The boys crowded around her, enthralled by the miracle of music from a little wooden box.

***

The holiday tradition at Yellowwood Farm is to skip lunch and have an early supper. Emma was struggling to lift the door to her root cellar out of the snow when she heard the twins shouting, "Grampa's here!"

She let the door drop closed and waded through the snow around the corner of the house. Ike drove his sledge up the wagon trail. Once again, it was loaded with wood. Emma never stopped worrying about their woodpile. She considered moving Tommy's bed into the twins' room to save on wood, but now they might have enough to comfortably heat all three bedrooms through the rest of winter and the cold of early spring.

Ike struck sort of a dashing figure. He was tall and thin, and he was wearing his wide-brimmed hat, his long gray coat, and the long yellow scarf she gave him. He drove his sledge up next to the woodpile and jumped down to unhitch his big draft horses. The boys went straight to the sledge and started stacking the wood.

Emma headed for the kitchen to make tea, glad that Claude's prayer was answered.

By the time Ike knocked at her kitchen door, Emma had a kettle boiling. She opened the door and said, "Merry Christmas, Ike. Your tea is almost ready."

Ike stomped his boots on the steps and came inside carrying his cloth sack. He closed the door behind him and said, "Merry Christmas, Miss Emma." He hung his coat beside the door.

Emma thought he looked better than he had since they became acquainted. He was clean-shaven, his cheeks were pink, and his eyes were sparkling. It took her a moment to realize there was something else. "You cut your hair! It looks good. I should cut the boys', they're getting shaggy."

"Drove into town couple days ago and the barber was open. Still have to wear a mask, but I got me a proper haircut."

He picked up his sack and placed it on the table, rooting around in it. He took out a paper bag, and holding it out to Emma, he said, "Smell."

She closed her eyes and inhaled. "Oranges! I haven't tasted an orange in a year!"

Digging through his sack, he placed on the table a box of chocolates, a jar of hand cream, and a large bundle wrapped in butcher paper. Then he tossed the empty sack beside the door and sat down at what had become his place at the table.

Emma placed his mug of tea in front of him. "Thank you for the gifts. The boys love their trucks. And thank you for the gloves and the music box. I've never worn gloves before, it almost does not seem proper."

Ike sipped his tea and tasted honey. Emma stood beside him, and he noticed she kept glancing at the bundle of butcher paper.

He said, "I thought y'all might like a beef roast for Christmas supper."

Emma threw her arms around his neck and kissed him on the cheek. "Thank you, Ike! Oh thank the Lord we will have something besides pork for supper tonight!"

Ike felt a twinge of guilt. He never thought to provide them with any meat other than pork. He himself sometimes grew tired of it, but when he did, it was no trouble to hunt up a rabbit or a woods pheasant. He knew Emma shot a turkey, but according to the story the boys told, that was something of a fluke. Common sense should have told him that a twelve-year-old girl and a ten-gauge shotgun did not work well together.

Beef was a rare treat in this part of the country. Cattle required more than an acre of forage each. Crops were a more profitable use of such fertile land. Most beef came in by train and had to be refrigerated. Electricity for refrigeration was only available in town.

Emma ran to the door and pulled her coat down from its peg. Putting it on she said, "Excuse me for a minute. I have to get some potatoes and…Oh wait! I have cherries soaking for a pie…"

With one arm in her coat, she stopped while she worked out the logistics of heat and space in her oven. She pulled her coat the rest of the way on and dragged her Dutch oven out from under the sink. Then she grabbed a basket and opened the door.

She turned back to say, "Thank you, Ike." Then she shouted out the open door, "Boys! We're having beef roast for supper!" She ran out into the snow, slamming the door behind her.

Ike could hear the boys cheering for beef roast. He made up his mind to hunt for them now and then, so as to break up the monotony of their meals. He had been sober for four days, more days in a row than in the past four years. He was trying very hard.

***

Christmas on Yellowwood Farm was a happy celebration of the birth of Jesus, new toy trucks, and the coming of music into their isolated little world. The remainder of the year passed quietly, taken up by chores, studies, quiet meals, and the warm comfort of a big woodpile. Emma's music box sat on the lamp table in their parlor, and it became part of their nightly ritual when she read to the boys.

Emma and the boys never left the farm. They did not want to and they did not need to.

Chapter Ten

It was the first week of April, and the first green things were rising out of the ground—lilies and daffodils. It was a fortunate early warm spell. Some years, snow fell on this date.

The flu was ebbing. A few people were still getting sick, but the disease seemed to have lost its virulence—none died. The Public Health Service identified the most recent cases as the common cold. The ordinance requiring people to wear masks was lifted and businesses reopened.

Emma sat at her mother's sewing machine, putting the final touches on a shirt for Tommy. He was growing like a weed, as were Clyde and Claude.

She called out, "Tommy!" He ran in from the kitchen, already holding out his arms.

Emma held the shirt across his shoulders, judging the fit. With a mouthful of pins, she pinned a seam. Rocking the pedal on the sewing machine, she laid down the last row of stitches while Tommy watched over her shoulder.

Cutting the thread with a tiny pair of scissors, she held up Tommy's new shirt, turned it right side out, and snapped it in the air. She wasn't sure why she did that, but she always had an irresistible urge to do it when she finished sewing a garment. "Okay, try this on."

Tommy unbuttoned the few buttons he could still fasten on the shirt he was wearing and put on his new one, buttoning it all the way up. Emma lifted up his arms, spun him around, and tugged at the sleeves and tails. It was a little too big—perfect, room to grow.

Tommy pin-wheeled his arms and twisted from side to side. "It fits! Thanks Emma." He ran back to the kitchen.

Emma had declared today bath day and hung sheets

around the tub when they dragged it into the kitchen. No doubt, the boys were still bailing out the water into the sink so they could drag the tub back onto the porch. All four of them were as clean as she could make them, hair washed and scrubbed until they were all pink and glowing.

Gathering up the loose thread on the bobbin, Emma unthreaded the sewing machine and carefully replaced everything in her mother's sewing box. In the minds of the boys, this was Emma's sewing machine, and every night, she sat in her rocking chair, but in her mind, those things belonged to her mother. She was very careful when she used her mother's things.

Now that Tommy had something decent to wear, Emma dashed up the stairs to change. The weather finally broke and the snow melted. The temperature was barely sixty, but after months of ice and snow, it felt like a heat wave.

She took out her church dress and held it in front of her while she peeked at different angles in the mirror on her washstand. Her good shoes were a tight fit, but if they did not have to walk too far she thought she could wear them one more time before she gave up and bought a new pair. She took a few steps in them.

Maybe not.

There were butterflies in her stomach when she slipped into her good dress and sat down to brush her hair. Ike promised to take them to a moving picture show! And then to the ice cream parlor! She could hardly wait to see an actual moving picture, but they had been isolated for so long she was frightened as well. The town had not been kind to her, but she longed to be with people again—nice people, who did not shout at her.

Ike had been fairly dependable lately. There were

two weeks in March when they did not see him, but he blamed it on a bad cold and icy weather. Emma did not want to disappoint the boys. They have been preparing for this trip for two days and were brimming with excitement. So was she.

She checked the watch in her locket—it was almost noon. The motion picture did not start until three o'clock, but Tommy and the twins needed new shoes. All they had were their boots. They were going to visit a shoe store, and if Emma saw something reasonably priced, she thought she might go ahead and get new shoes for herself. She took ten dollars from the cash box and was so nervous about carrying it around she pinned it inside the pocket of her dress.

She checked her appearance in her mirror one last time, practiced a smile, and ran downstairs. Limping into the kitchen, she sat down in a chair to pull off her good shoes. She could not possibly wear them. She would have to wear her boots to the shoe store and buy new ones. It seemed a shame. She hardly had a chance to wear her church shoes before she outgrew them. Brushing the mud off her boots, she pulled them on.

As soon as she had the boys ready, Emma made them sit at the kitchen table where she could keep an eye on them. They were dressed as well as she could dress them and they were as clean as they had ever been in their lives. There were two blankets folded neatly on the table that she intended for them to sit on during the trip into town. She was watching the second hand move slowly around the dial of her watch when she heard Ike's truck coming up the wagon trail.

She jumped out of her chair, and so did the boys. She blocked the door, holding out her arms. "Sit!" They sat.

They were accustomed to walking through puddles and thought nothing of throwing mud balls at each other. She planned to escort them one at a time into the bed of Ike's truck and park them on clean blankets.

When Ike appeared at the door, Emma opened it. "We're ready," she said. "Don't let those boys out of their chairs. I want to walk them to the truck and get them settled before they jump in the mud."

Ike wore gray pants and suspenders with a nice white shirt. He even went to the trouble of putting on a string tie and shining his black boots. Emma thought he looked like a country gentleman in his wide-brimmed hat and long jacket.

He tipped his hat. "Yes, Miss Emma. You look beautiful today."

Emma blushed—it had been a long time since anyone said she was beautiful. She had brushed her hair until it shined and worried at her nails until they were perfectly clean. If only she had a decent pair of shoes.

"I've outgrown my church shoes. I need to buy a new pair, if we have time. I don't want to wear these boots to the theater."

"Don't you worry none. We got plenty of time to get shoes for all y'all."

Once Emma had the boys safely sitting in the back of the truck, she climbed into the passenger seat. It was the first warm spring day. The sky was azure blue and the trees carried a hint of green as the leaf buds began to open. She glanced up at Ike nervously. The world changed quickly in spring. Today it was on the verge of blooming into life. She could feel the highly charged energy of possibilities.

They drove slowly down the wagon trail. The farther they went from her farm, the faster Emma's heartbeat was. When they reached the gravel road and left her property, she huddled down in her seat, half expecting some sort of unpleasantness to fall into her lap.

When they drove past Ike's farm, Emma felt a pang of fear. She hated that place. She resisted the urge to reach up and touch the thin ridge of scar tissue over her eye. Today was the first time they left the farm since that awful day.

Soon the sight of her schoolhouse brought fond memories. She wondered—would she ever set foot in her school again? Attendance through elementary school was compulsory, mandated by the state, but she would have graduated this year. She had learned as much as her little school had to offer. She had responsibilities now. They were sitting behind her in the bed of the truck. Her mother hoped for her to attend the high school in town, but Emma could not imagine a future where such a thing was possible. Too many other things needed to be done.

When they passed the mercantile on the edge of town, half a dozen cars and a few wagons were parked out front. People came and went without masks, nodding and speaking to each other. It looked—normal. Ike drove past, and Emma turned in her seat to watch the people. She thought she heard laughter.

When they drove down Main Street, it was lined with cars. The sidewalks were crowded with people enjoying the warm day. Men and women walked arm in arm with children trailing after them. Emma was amazed to see it all, astounded! It all seemed so—normal. Something burst inside her and tears poured down her cheeks. She hung her head and was wracked with sobs.

Ike pulled to the curb and placed a hand on her shoulder. "What's wrong, Emma?"

"I don't know," she said. "It's just that…I don't know!"

Tommy's face appeared in the back window. Seeing Emma in tears, he jumped out of the truck and ran around to stand beside his sister, gripping her arm. "Don't cry, Emma."

She pulled a pink handkerchief from her pocket and wiped at her eyes. "I'm okay, Tommy. I don't mean to cry." She lifted her head to watch the people passing by and said, "I thought this was gone!"

She looked down at Tommy, standing beside the truck and laughed through her tears. She trimmed and combed his hair so carefully, and now, after riding in the wind, it was sticking up every which way. She tried to smooth it down, but it was hopeless. Thankfully, she knew, he did not care in the least.

Once Emma recovered from her shock at finding the world where she left it, they drove a few more blocks and parked in front of the shoe store. When they got out of the truck, she and the boys were wide-eyed with wonder. So many people! They could hear music!

When they approached the shoe store, a stranger held the door for them and tipped his hat to Emma. She blushed and mumbled, "Thank you." Then she scooted quickly past him into the shop.

A pretty, dark-haired young lady met them at the door, and Ike pulled her aside. She returned smiling and gracious and led Emma to a chair. "Mister Pearson over there said to fit you with whatever you want. I am not allowed to discuss the cost."

Emma leaned to the side to peek around the young lady. "Ike!" He turned to her and she said, "I can't allow you to do that."

He waved his hand in dismissal and went back to looking at boots.

Emma sat back in her chair, and the smiling young lady asked, "What sort of shoes do you need?"

Emma considered it for a moment. "Well, I need

something for church and a motion picture show."

The young lady pulled Emma's heavy leather boots off her feet and holding them at arm's length, she said, "I think we have just the thing. I'll box these up so you can wear your new ones."

The boys lined up in front of Emma, wide-eyed and staring. She was relieved when Ike gathered them up and handed them off to a young man who sat them down and measured their feet. Buying new shoes felt like too intimate a thing to have them watch.

The young lady returned carrying a large box tied with string and a shoe box. She pulled a low stool up in front of Emma and slipped a shoe onto her foot that had a one-inch heel. It was so shiny it appeared to be wet. Emma frowned and stood up. She alternated between standing on the tall heel and dropping down onto her other foot.

"Do you have something with a lower heel, maybe something not so shiny?"

She resisted an urge to apologize for having complained, slipped the shoe off her foot, and sat back down. In a moment, the young lady returned with a pair of shoes Emma suddenly had to have. They were brown brushed leather with a low heel and little brass adornments. They fit her perfectly. She stood up, walked back and forth and jumped up and down. "These are perfect. Thank you so much!"

Once everybody was wearing new shoes, Ike sent them outside to put the boxes containing their boots in the truck and settled up with the clerk. When he stepped outside, he was gratified to see Emma lifting one heel and then the other, swishing her dress back and forth to admire her new shoes.

When she saw Ike, she ran over to him and hugged

him. "Thank you, Ike. It feels so good to be properly dressed again."

They walked to the theater down a crowded sidewalk. As usual, the boys lined up behind Emma. She said hello to everyone she passed, fascinated by each person she encountered and unable to just walk past without acknowledging them. Everyone she met was courteous and polite.

The theater had a marquee out front that announced *Daddy-Long-Legs* was playing, starring Mary Pickford. Emma had only seen one other motion picture: *20,000 Leagues Under the Sea*. Both Emma and her mother begged her father to take them. They were awed by the moving pictures yet confused by the way it mixed several Verne novels into a single story. Still, it was an amazing experience. Ike purchased their tickets and they found seats inside.

Emma sat between Tommy and the twins. The lights went out and the screen lit up with moving pictures. To Emma and the boys, photographs themselves were miraculous, let alone moving ones. A lady played a piano up front. The music too was a wonder.

In the opening scene, a policeman found a baby wrapped in a newspaper in a garbage can. Emma was appalled. She covered her mouth with her hand. The word orphan brought goosebumps to her arms when she read it on the screen. She and the boys were orphans too! The orphaned baby girl was delivered into the hands of Missus Lippett, the cruel headmistress of the John Grier Orphanage. Emma cried.

At age twelve, the orphaned girl was known as Judy. Emma gasped. She was the same age! Judy rebelled against the long hours of work and their diet of bread and prunes.

She stuck up for the younger children and led a hunger strike. Emma scowled with righteous anger.

Tommy said, "Emma, how come…" Emma covered his mouth with her hand without taking her eyes off the screen.

When Judy stole a doll from a spoiled rich girl and gave it to a dying orphan girl, Emma cried. When Missus Lippett punished Judy by giving her a taste of the hell to which she was destined by holding her hand against a hot stove, Emma was outraged!

At age eighteen, Judy was sponsored by a rich trustee to attend college. The conditions of her sponsorship were that she write to her unknown benefactor once a month, to communicate her progress, and that she never attempt to contact him in person. Judy missed meeting him by seconds and glimpsed his shadow with long legs. She called him Daddy-Long-Legs in her letters. Emma was intrigued. She longed to go to college.

Tommy said, "Emma, how come…" She covered his mouth with her hand without taking her eyes off the screen.

Judy did well in college, but she was a homespun girl. She did not fit in with her affluent classmates. Emma felt that way when she walked into the shoe store wearing her clunky farm boots.

Judy repaid her benefactor when she became a successful author. Emma was proud of her. She dreamed of someday writing a book.

When Judy became caught up in a love triangle involving a brash young man and an older sophisticated gentleman, she eventually chose the older gentleman and discovered that he was her Daddy-Long-Legs. Emma was glad she chose Jervis over that smart-alecky Jimmie Wyckoff.

When the film ended, Emma jumped to her feet and applauded along with every other female and most of the males in the theater.

The boys looked around, looked at Emma, and jumped to their feet to clap. Unable to read the captions well enough to follow the story, once the novelty of moving pictures began to wear off, they were frustrated by having to sit still for nearly an hour and a half. Everybody else was yelling, clapping and making noise, so they joined in—mostly as a way of releasing pent up boyish mischief.

Ike rose slowly from his seat and clapped softly, watching Emma. Tears rolled down her cheeks. Emma clapped enthusiastically, bouncing up and down and clasping her hands in front of her. Ike assumed this picture would be about dancing, given its title. Instead, it struck close to home. He saw Emma as the heroine in her own story of orphaned hardship.

Ike threw his grandchildren into Emma's life out of desperation. He sincerely believed he was about to die, but he recovered from the flu. He saw the look Emma gave his house when they drove past it. To her, it was a house of horrors.

On the day her mother died, he chased her off with a shotgun—and she forgave him. He split her head open with a bottle in a drunken fit—and she forgave him. He paid three men fifteen dollars to fell an oak tree and cut it into firewood, far more than he could possibly use. Then he drove it to Yellowwood Farm one load at a time to heartfelt thanks. He could have shown her how to hire the work out for herself and what to pay—but then she would not have been dependent upon him.

He knew that in Emma's mind, he was keeping them warm and providing for them. Each time she hugged him in gratitude it changed him a little. He was slowly becoming a better man, drinking less and doing more for Emma and the boys, but he did not deserve a single one of those warm little hugs.

He constantly rationalized it. He was too old to raise his grandchildren. He drank too much. Clyde and Claude were better off without him. Ike came up with all sorts of things that made him feel better about it, all of them true. The unavoidable truth was—he was using her.

He knew that Emma wanted to go to the high school in town. That was her mother's wish and Emma's dream. Instead of helping her achieve her dreams, he completely consumed her for the price of firewood and some odds and ends. She was raising his grandchildren for him.

Ike watched Emma dry her eyes and smile at people in the aisle. When she reached him, she hugged him and said, "Thank you, Ike. That was wonderful."

He patted her on the back. As Ike slowly became a better man, he was getting to the point where he could not stomach his own company.

Chapter Eleven

Emma stood in the barn rubbing her cheek with her forefinger—thinking. She pulled away the canvas tarp covering her father's plow and knelt down to examine the blade. It had a thick covering of grease and was mostly free of rust. She had occasionally been given the chore of removing any rust with a piece of limestone. Emma understood that it had to slip easily through the soil. A good plow had a mirror-like shine. She stood back up and tried to imagine the twenty-foot long train of horses and plow that turned their soil.

They had not seen Ike since he took them into town. Planting time was drawing near and their fields were untouched. Yellowwood Farm had sixty tillable acres. By definition, an acre took a day to till, but that number was based upon a team of oxen. Buck and Jane averaged one and a half to two acres a day.

Last spring, her mother hired out the plowing. Then she and Emma drove their team of draft horses back and forth, pulling the harrow to smooth the fields. Planting was actually a lot of fun, taking turns walking behind their planter while the other person moved the wire for the next row. Buck and Jane knew more about it than Emma and her mother, so they simply allowed them to do their jobs.

They rotated their crops in three twenty-acre fields: the near field and two far fields. The near field grew corn last year, so this year it would grow soybeans. The far fields were rotated wheat-wheat-sorghum-fallow. One should be seeded with sorghum and the other left fallow.

Emma had no illusions about plowing those fields herself. Ike should be plowing his own fields, if he did not hire it done. She needed help. She was considering loading the boys into the wagon and driving to the mercantile, when she heard Ike's truck coming up the wagon trail. She was relieved he finally showed up, but annoyed that he appeared at the last minute.

Ike parked next to the house and stepped down out of his truck. Emma walked out to meet him but did not hug him. She stopped in front of him with a frown. He looked fine: clean-shaven and wearing clean clothes. Whenever he did not show up when he promised, she always worried that he was either drunk or sick. She did not make a distinction between the two. She did not know the difference.

"I'm glad you finally came. I'm worried about the fields. They should be half plowed by now."

Ike regarded Emma, looking up at him as if he were some sort of truant adolescent. He felt like one. He should have been here days ago. After taking Emma and the boys to that motion picture show, he returned home and indulged in a four-day bout of alcohol-fueled self-loathing. His farm suffered as a result—something that rarely happened.

"Good afternoon, Miss Emma." He seated himself on the remains of the woodpile. He patted a log beside him, but Emma did not sit down. She walked around to stand in front of him.

"I need to hire some help, but I don't know how," she said.

Ike might not be much of a human being, but he was an excellent farmer. With more than sixty years of experience, he seldom made mistakes.

"I'm sorry I'm late. I had some things that needed tending. I brought y'all a crate of chicks. They're in the back of the truck."

Her annoyance momentarily forgotten, Emma ran up and hugged Ike while he sat on the woodpile, nearly dislodging him. "Thank you, Ike! We'll have eggs again!"

She ran around the side of the house to find a ventilated cardboard box under a canvas tarp in the bed of the truck. Ike followed her and removed the lid. A dozen chirping little yellow chicks danced around inside.

She picked one up and held it to her cheek. "Oh they're so cute! I just love them when they're little."

She placed the little chick back in the box and replaced the lid. She would keep them in the kitchen by her woodstove until they got a little bigger and then turn them out in the coop. She picked up the box and headed for her kitchen.

"I'll make some tea," she said.

Ike followed her around the side of the house and opened the screen door for her.

Emma left the box of chicks beside the door and put on a kettle to boil. She tossed a small log into her stove and scooted her stepstool over to take down two cups. Ike sat down at his usual spot, at the head of the table, and watched Emma scoot her stepstool over to the pantry and take down a canister of tea.

He said, "Your Momma hired the plowing out last year to the Coonce boys. I asked their pa and they ain't available. Reckon I waited too long to ask. I got a boy I hire now and again. He ain't real experienced, but he does what he's told."

Emma said, "The field by the house should be planted in soybeans and the far field with sorghum. The other one is supposed to lie fallow this year."

Ike considered this and said, "Your daddy was a real smart man. This is going to be a hard year. The war is over. All of them farms in Europe are going to be producing again. Prices are going to drop."

Emma sat down across from Ike with a concerned expression. "What does that mean? Will we be okay?"

He said, "Your land is owned free and clear, so y'all can still make a profit. It won't be as much as these past years, but y'all will make some money. Seed is priced high right now on account of the scarcity from the war. This year will be a hard turn. Seed will cost dear and crops will sell cheap."

The kitchen door flew open and the twins ran inside shouting, "Grampa!" They threw their arms around Ike and he smiled. "Are we going into town?"

"Not today, boys, me and Miss Emma got business to talk over."

Clyde, or at least the one in green suspenders, picked up the box of chirping chicks by the door and gave it a shake, causing the chirping to intensify. Emma wrestled it away from him.

"Clyde! Do not shake the baby chickens, please." She placed them back on the floor.

Clyde leaned over to stick a finger into one of the holes in the box. "Hi, little chickens. Watch out Emma doesn't shoot you." He glanced sideways at her just in time to dance out of the way of a snapping dishtowel. He laughed and ran outside, followed by his brother. The screen door clapped shut behind them.

Ike watched them go and thought how happy and healthy they were. The smile left his face when he realized they would not have fared so well under his care. Now that the weather had broken, he spent most of his time in the barn, as far away as he could get from the little blue coat hanging in his kitchen. He relieved himself of feeling guilt by focusing on the problem at hand.

He said, "I asked a fella I know to send his boy over

today. He ain't a growed man, but he does a tolerable job with a plow. He knows how to treat a team proper."

"Thank you, Ike. How much should I pay him?"

"Don't you worry none about pay. I'll take care of it."

While she poured their tea, Emma said, "No Ike. I need to learn if I'm to run this farm. We can't be waiting for you to take care of things. What if something happened to you? God forbid."

They couldn't be waiting for him to take care of things. That phrase did not go unnoticed by Ike. "I don't rightly know if he would take orders from a girl."

"If he doesn't like my money, I'm sure there is someone else who will. How much should I pay him?"

Ike was surprised to find a piece of iron in Emma. He was willing to accept the cost of hiring a farm hand. He hadn't thought it through, but now that it was slipping away, he realized that he wanted control over the lives of Emma and the boys. He should have been more careful about showing up when he said he would. When he told Emma he would take care of something, it didn't mean a thing to her.

He reluctantly said, "I usually pay three dollars for a ten-hour day. Him being a boy, I'd say two-fifty."

To Emma, it seemed like an extraordinary amount of money, but she had no choice. "I'll talk to him. If he doesn't mind taking money from a girl, I'll pay him two dollars and fifty cents a day and feed him a nice lunch."

Ike said, "I reckon that would be agreeable. Emma, I know this is a hard thing, but I told his pa that your momma was sick. Maybe you ought to take them rocks off her grave so's nobody knows she's buried there."

Emma was about to take a sip from her cup and stopped short. She put the cup down and went to stand at the kitchen door, looking up the hill at the yellowwood tree. It was shrouded in a mist of green as the leaf buds issued tiny immature leaves.

She hung her head. "Alright, Ike." She walked out the door and started up the hill, leaving him alone in the kitchen.

Ike got up and stood at the door. He watched her climb up the hill in her blue dress and heavy boots. She dropped down on her knees beside her mother's grave and clasped her hands in prayer. It was a hard thing to watch as she gathered up those small white stones.

***

Joe Hansen was fourteen years old, but he could pass for older, tall with dark hair and brown eyes. He was the youngest of three boys and he understood that he would inherit none of the family farm. He worked as hard as any of them, maybe harder, being the youngest, but the Hansen tradition was to hand the farm down to the eldest brother, so he was expected to make his own way. At least he was allowed to find work.

His father told him to ride over to Yellowwood Farm today and talk to Ike Pearson about a job. He said that Tom Taylor was killed in the war and Old Man Pearson was helping them out. It was a good five-mile ride, but it was a warm spring day and he was glad to get out and about. With the schools being closed, he had been cooped up all winter.

Anna Taylor was a legend in these parts. When he was younger, he went to school with her daughter, Emma, and they had been good friends. He had never spoken to Anna, the most beautiful woman he had ever seen. He wasn't sure if he could stand in front of her and speak. He was just hoping for a chance to admire her from a few feet away.

He was riding a tan quarter horse that he raised

himself named Verne, after his favorite author. He owned his horse, this saddle, and the clothes on his back. He was looking forward to making a little money.

He had been to the Taylor farm, but never in the house. It was said they had an indoor commode. He wanted to see that. The Hansen farm only had an outhouse. Over the winter, he found that extreme cold induced constipation—a result of his reluctance to visit that freezing little shed out back.

When he reached the wagon trail that led up a hill from the main road, he urged Verne into a trot. It could not hurt to ride in like somebody who wanted to get there. He topped the rise, and the road leveled out. Yellowwood Farm was laid out before him.

The house was two stories tall, made from square cut oak with big windows. There was a red barn with YELLOWWOOD FARM painted on the side in white letters. The fields were situated between areas of hilly forest just starting to turn green. He headed for the house. Ike Pearson's truck was parked beside it.

When Joe rode up next to the house, he found Ike sitting on the woodpile. He jumped down from his horse, and holding the reins behind his back, he held out his hand. "Afternoon, Mister Pearson."

Ike stood up stiffly and shook his hand. "Afternoon, Joe."

Joe saw a young girl walking down the hill behind the house. Ike nodded in her direction. "That there is Emma. You'll be workin' for her. Her momma ain't well enough to leave her room."

"That's fine, Mister Pearson. Me and Emma went to school together. What's the wages?"

"Two dollars and a half, but y'all should talk to

Emma."

Joe nodded to Ike and led his horse in Emma's direction. Her head was down. She had not yet noticed him. He remembered Emma from grade school as a bubbly little girl with a sweet disposition. He went on to attend the high school in town, and since then he only saw her at church. Over the past two years, from one Sunday to the next, he watched her turn pretty. She looked just like her mother. They had rarely spoken, just shy hellos and how ya doin's.

Emma came to within ten feet of Joe before she looked up and saw him standing there, holding the reins to his horse. She stopped and turned around, embarrassed to be seen crying. Wiping away her tears, she took a deep breath and turned back around. The man standing there was nearly as tall as Ike, but he was young and handsome. He looked like he could handle a team and a plow.

Joe said, "Hi, Emma."

Emma looked closer and thought she recognized him, but it hardly seemed possible. "Joe?"

When he smiled, Emma was sure. She ran into him and threw her arms around him. "I'm so glad it's you, Joe!"

Joe shyly patted Emma on the back while she clung to him. Was she crying? He didn't know what to do, but he was certain he had never been hugged by a prettier girl.

Emma backed away from him and turned around again, wiping her eyes.

Joe asked, "Are you okay?"

She turned back to face him with a teary-eyed smile. "I'm fine, Joe. I was just worried about who Ike might get to help out. You got so tall!"

Emma's eyes always fascinated Joe. He looked into the depths of her blue eyes, ringed with gold. He'd never seen anything like it. It was said her mother had eyes like that, but he was never close enough to see them.

Ike watched all this from beside the woodpile. While he could not hear what they were saying, when Emma hugged that boy, his hands balled into fists. He watched while Emma pointed to the fields, apparently describing what needed to be done. He turned to go and then turned back to squint up the hill. Emma's laughter was like a far-off tinkling bell. He spat on the ground, got into his truck, and drove slowly down the wagon trail.

***

That night, Emma sat on her bentwood chair and damp washed her hair with a washcloth. The nights were still cool, so she had a fire in her stove. On really cold nights, when she built a fire in the evening, she felt cold on one side and hot on the other. Warm weather was coming. She could hardly wait to open every window in the house.

Joe Hansen's presence today was comforting. He was a friend. She desperately needed a friend. When she attended elementary school with Joe, he kept the bullies in check. He had two older brothers, so he knew what it was like to be picked on and how to knock down a boy bigger than himself. Even when he turned thirteen and moved on to the high school, he left behind a sense of fairness in the other children that did not tolerate cruelty. Emma and every other girl in the school fell madly in love with him.

She washed her face with a soapy cloth and rinsed with warm water held in her cupped hands. There was a bump at her door. She smiled, picturing the boys gathering there. They bonded to Joe immediately, seeing in him an older brother or maybe even a father figure. They begged for rides on his horse, and when he told them his name was Verne, they surprised him by recognizing that name. They told him all about the Nautilus and Captain Nemo.

Placing her washbowl on the floor, Emma soaked her feet and sighed. She could hear the boys whispering to each other. They worked in the garden all day, turning the soil, and they were bone tired. She dried herself quickly and dressed in clean socks and a nightdress. The boys had earned their nightly chapter, but if she didn't hurry she would likely find them asleep in the hall. She lit a candle, turned down her lamp, and went to read to them.

When she opened her door, she found them all slumped together, trading yawns. They climbed to their feet and followed her quietly downstairs into the parlor. She was reading *Journey to the Center of the Earth*, another Verne novel. Tommy tossed a log onto the fire and they gathered on the rug while she sat in her mother's rocking chair. This nightly ritual made their lives happier.

***

The next morning dawned cold and gray. A light rain fell. Emma made a fine breakfast for the boys of crisp fried salt pork, fried potatoes, and biscuits. She made extra and kept peeking out the window, watching for Joe.

When he arrived, he was hunkered down on his horse, wearing a rain slicker and a wide-brimmed hat. He rode straight into the barn. Emma pulled on her coat and ran to the barn to find him brushing down his horse.

"Good morning," she said.

Joe smiled. "Good morning."

He laid his saddle over a rail and turned his horse out into the pasture. Emma watched him closely. Tiny drops of rain gathered on her blue wool coat and sparkled in her hair.

"Will you join us for breakfast? I made salt pork and potatoes."

"I ate at home," he said. "I thought the deal only included lunch."

"I already made extra. You are welcome at our table. The boys would like for you to join us."

Joe's breakfast was a soft, wrinkled apple, barely hanging on from last year. "Well, I wouldn't want to disappoint the boys. Are you sure your mother won't mind?"

Emma turned away and said softly, "Momma will not be at the table. I'm sure she would want you to join us."

Joe saw that his innocent question hurt Emma. He wondered how serious her mother's illness must be.

He said, "Breakfast would be great. Truth be told, I'm starving."

Emma smiled, and Joe followed her out into the soft rain. When he came inside, all three of the boys converged on him.

"Joe! Hey, Joe, can we ride Verne today?"

"Joe! Joe! Can we help plow?"

Joe laughed as they pulled his rain slicker off his shoulders and hung it beside the door. He hung his hat over it. He had never been the center of so much attention. He looked around and was impressed by the size of the big kitchen. Varnished, square cut oak gave it a warm yellow glow. Light tan paint covered the finished interior walls. It was a beautiful house, far nicer than the one he grew up in.

Emma dashed around the table, setting out plates and filling glasses with milk. She seated Joe in her father's chair, at the head of the table. Joe knew her father was killed in the war. He was reluctant to sit there. He had never sat at the head of any table—ever. He was especially uncomfortable sitting there with Emma and three boys staring at him.

Emma finally sat down and pushed a platter of fried salt pork across the table to Joe. This was another farm tradition reserved for the head of the household. He could not recall a time when he was served first or got the biggest piece of anything. His mouth was watering, but he pushed the platter back to Emma. "You first."

Emma never served herself first. She pushed it back across the table. "It wouldn't be proper, you first."

Tommy looked from Emma to Joe and frowned. "If you two don't decide, it's going to be me first."

Joe saw himself in Tommy, as a feisty little mop-headed boy. He knew exactly what it was like to be the littlest one at the table.

"I think we should take turns." He pushed the platter over to Tommy. "Today is your turn."

Tommy looked over at Emma and she nodded. He stabbed the biggest piece with his fork and dragged it onto his plate. Joe made sure he was served last, and their breakfast erupted into happy chatter, planning their day.

Emma was thrilled to have Joe at her table. She loved that he insisted upon Tommy being served first. It was just like the Joe she remembered from school to do something like that. The hard times had not changed him, but he was so tall! Only his smooth complexion and soft voice revealed him to be a boy. They were five now, their odds had improved. It took some of the tension out of her shoulders.

Every day, Joe arrived at sunrise and worked hard until sunset. In a mere twelve days, he plowed the near field and smoothed it with the harrow for planting. Emma persuaded him to take his suppers with them, so he extended his hours to repay her generosity. Every night, he rode off just after sunset and arrived home in darkness. He was puzzled that he never saw a sign of Anna Taylor. Her illness must be serious to keep her in bed for so long.

***

Easter Sunday of 1919 was on the twentieth of April. Emma sat in front of her washstand brushing her hair in the mirror. She rubbed at the pink scar above her eye, which seemed to be fading. They had not seen Ike in nearly two weeks, but that was not unusual. He did, however, tend to show up on holidays. She hoped to see him. She needed to buy seed and wanted his advice.

Joe told her there would be a church service today. She could hardly wait to return to her little church and see her neighbors for the first time in almost a year. Today they would meet to elect a new pastor. They would also sing hymns and pray together. It was something she needed, long overdue. She checked her reflection one last time. Her blonde hair was shining—held back by a blue ribbon. The blue ribbon in her golden hair matched her blue eyes ringed with gold.

She stood up and smoothed down her dress. It had gotten shorter over the past year, it came up to her knees. The light stain near the hem was a painful reminder of the day she learned of her father's death. She decided to make a new one. When she went to buy seed, she would purchase a few yards of cloth.

Chores did not recognize holidays. The animals still needed feeding and the cow still had to be milked, but Joe had the day off. He had worked twelve days in a row. When Emma asked him to attend church with them, he readily agreed. She expected him any time now.

She ran downstairs to find the boys still sitting at the table, clean and dressed as well as she could dress them. She had forbidden them from getting out of their chairs. Even so, she was surprised to find they were still there. They were good boys and usually did what they were told, but boys their age had natural limitations. They could only sit still for so long.

Impressed that they lasted this long, she said, "Okay

boys, you can go play with your trucks in the parlor. Stay indoors! Okay?"

They jumped out of their chairs and ran for the parlor.

Emma had saved a little dab of her hand cream for a special occasion. She scooted her stepstool over to the pantry and took down the small jar from the top shelf where she kept it hidden from the boys. She scooped out the last bit with her finger and rubbed it into her hands, inhaling the soft scent of roses. She turned around just in time to see Joe ride into the barn.

Resisting the urge to run, she walked outside to greet Joe. She found him in the barn, brushing down Verne. He looked like a boy today. His church pants came up to his ankles and his good shirt rode up over his wrists. He had his back to her. She watched as he pulled at his sleeves, brushed at his trousers, picked off some invisible piece of something, and turned around. He stood up straight when he saw her.

"Morning Emma," he said. He was holding a bouquet of lilies.

Emma's heart soared. Joe brought her flowers!

He held them out to her. "Ma sent these for your mother. She said to wish her well."

Joe watched as Emma's expression faded from joy to sorrow. She hung her head, her lip trembled, and a tear ran down her cheek. He had no idea what to say. He just made Emma cry, the last thing in the world he wanted to do.

Emma was unable to lie to Joe any longer. She never told him an explicit lie, but that was a poor excuse. She allowed him to believe that her mother was in her room and took her meals in there. She could not continue to deceive him, especially on a Holy day.

When she looked up into his eyes, it broke Joe's heart

to see her that way. Tears rolled down her cheeks. She was far beyond sad, desperate misery written on her face.

She took the flowers from him. "Thank you."

She turned and walked away, disappearing around the corner of the barn door. Joe went outside to see her walking slowly up the hill with the flowers cradled in her arms. He felt himself to be a poor choice in this situation, but there was no one else around. He would have to do, so he followed her.

Emma stopped beside a tree with smooth gray bark that stood away from the forest. Joe watched from a little ways off as she dropped to her knees beside a rectangular patch of raised ground and placed the flowers there. He suddenly realized it was a grave. Emma arranged small white stones on the low mound of earth. When he walked up behind her, he saw her head turn ever so slightly at the sound of his footsteps. She knew he was there. He watched as she arranged the stones to spell out Anna Taylor. Then she bowed her head and clasped her hands in prayer.

Joe's eyes gradually opened wide and he inhaled sharply. This was a grave. Emma's mother had died. He stood there for a moment, fidgeting in his too small church clothes, not knowing what to say. He finally knelt down beside her. It was all he could think to do, so he prayed for Emma and the boys.

Emma's prayer was simple, "Help me, Momma."

No images entered her mind, but she could smell her rosewater perfume. A soft breeze brought her mother's touch, brushing her hair, their nightly ritual. She felt her mother's love.

After a few moments, Emma raised her head. Without turning, she said quietly, "Momma died last September from the flu. Ike Pearson was sick too. He asked me to watch over his grandsons. He thought he was gonna die, but he didn't. The boys just stayed here. Ike can't raise children."

Joe said, "I'm sorry, Emma. I was real sorry to hear about your pa too. How did you make out, all alone up here?"

"Ike helped me. Please don't tell, I'm not supposed to say this."

"I won't tell anything you say not to."

Emma threw her arms around him and clung to him tightly, "Please don't tell, Joe! I couldn't lie to you anymore. We need this farm."

"I won't tell nobody." Inside he was alarmed to think that only children lived here. Emma was capable of things he could not imagine himself doing.

Emma lifted her head. "Did you hear that?"

Joe listened. "Church bells, they ain't rung in nearly a year."

Emma jumped to her feet and frantically wiped the mud from her knees. "Church bells, Joe! We're going to church!"

Joe stood up and watched Emma run down the hill toward the house, calling out for the boys. He could not understand anybody being so excited about church, but he knew Emma well enough to think that if anybody could get worked up over going to church, it would be her. He looked back down at the grave with Anna's name spelled out in small white stones. He closed his eyes and wished her well. She left behind a legacy of beauty and kindness—a smaller version of herself.

Joe had Buck harnessed and hitched to the wagon by the time Emma was able to gather up the boys. She scrubbed away the smudges of fireplace ash they were hauling in their trucks. She should have known they would find a way to get dirty. Next Sunday, she would dress them at the last minute, but today she was too excited to wait. She herded them outside to find that Joe had already pulled the wagon up next to the house.

Emma spread out a blanket in the back and boosted the boys up. Then she climbed up into the seat, right past Joe's outstretched hand, too excited to notice. She could hear the bells, calling the faithful to worship. Buck headed off to the church before Joe shook the reins. He knew the sound of church bells.

Emma noticed that Joe was no stranger to driving a wagon. He rode the brake on the way down the hill. He seemed to know everything there was to know about farming. The near field was perfect—dark, smooth, and ready for planting. His presence lifted her spirits and made her feel more secure. She trusted him more than she ever trusted Ike, but she was still worried about Ike. It had been too long since they saw him.

When they reached the gravel road, the bells were clearer, still distant but unmistakable. She bounced up and down on the seat. Joe laughed at her.

The closer they came to the church, the louder the bells. Once the church was in sight, she grabbed Joe's arm. "I've missed this so much. When all the sickness was here, people turned mean. We didn't leave the farm for months. I was afraid it would stay that way."

The church was a one-room building with a high peaked roof and a small bell tower. There were thousands just like it, all across the country, but this one was special— it was Emma's. It had a small pasture where people turned out their horses during the service. Joe pulled the wagon up next to the fence beside half a dozen similar wagons and unhitched Buck.

Buck was another of the things people admired about the Taylor farm. He was big, strong, and beautiful. Joe had to run alongside as he pranced toward the field gate to meet with his own long-lost community of horses and mules.

Now that they had arrived, Emma turned shy. She stood beside the wagon waiting for Joe with the boys hanging on to her. People gathered in front of the church, talking, embracing, and shaking hands. She knew most of them, but not all. The new faces were mostly children, taken in by relatives when their parents died from illness or war.

Joe came around the wagon, surprised to find Emma still there. He expected her to be in the middle of things. She looked up at him. "We're here."

Joe smiled. "Yes, we are."

Emma surveyed the crowd of people standing in front of the church. "I'm scared, Joe. People change when times are hard."

He said, "You're still the same. Hard times don't change good people."

Joe's mother saw them and came their way. Emma knew Mary Hansen. She was an older lady, her dark hair streaked with gray. She walked right up to Emma, took her face in her hands, and kissed her squarely between the eyes. The boys ran around to hide behind the wagon before they got kissed, but Emma smiled.

"Emma Taylor! As I live and breathe, you have grown into the image of your momma. How is she, dear? Joe says she's real sick."

Joe took his mother by the arm and led her two steps away. "Ma, Emma cries when she tries to talk about it."

Missus Hansen covered her mouth with her hand. "Oh, Joe, I'm so sorry. I'll tell the ladies not to pry. I hope she gets well soon."

She walked back over to Emma and put her arm around her. "Come, dear. It's been too long since we spoke." She turned back to Joe and shouted, "Joey! Get those boys out from behind that wagon and sit them down up front."

Emma smiled. Joe hated being called Joey. It was starting to feel like church. Missus Hansen led Emma inside and seated her between herself and Joe's father. Jack Hansen was a handsome man in middle age, tall and muscular. His dark hair had gone gray at the temples. He smiled at Emma and patted her hand. She wanted to jump up and hug him for that small gesture of kindness.

Once the congregation was seated, four men stood near the pulpit and the people quieted. They were older men, all grandfathers. All four of them helped to build this church. The oldest, Mister Turnquist, stepped up behind the pulpit. He was gray and grizzled with a scraggly white beard and piercing blue eyes.

"I see many familiar faces. I also see the faces of children I do not know. All are welcome here. The doors to this church have stood open for forty years. They ain't even got locks. We welcome all to come here and worship."

A baby cried loudly. Old Mister Turnquist smiled when the young mother frantically shushed her baby.

"Let that child cry!" he shouted. "God speaks through children. I suspect he is sayin' stop blathering and get on with it. Well here it is! I'm an old man and I apologize for that. In my old age, I have heard the calling. If y'all will have me, I would be pleased to preach."

The other three men standing in front of the congregation raised their hands. Other hands went into the air, and after a few moments, everyone had their hands up. Even Tommy, Clyde, and Claude raised their hands, but only after Emma did.

Mister Turnquist nodded his head. "I thank you. I am too old to serve well, but I will do my best until a better man can be found."

He took a folded piece of paper from his pocket and smoothed it out in front of him.

"We have endured a hard year, what with the war and the sickness. I ask that we bow our heads. This being Easter, I think it would be fitting if our first prayer together be the names of those that have departed Earth and been reborn in Heaven."

The people there bowed their heads, and he began to read. Each name brought a gasp or a sob as their loved ones were touched. He paused for half a minute before he read another. When Emma heard Thomas Richard Taylor, she sobbed. Missus Hansen pulled her to her bosom and held her while she cried.

There were twenty-two names on that list. Fewer than thirty people were sitting in the church—it was half-empty. When a mother or father is lost, whole families disappear.

Pastor Turnquist finished by saying, "Our dear ones are with the Lord. May He shine His warm light upon them and may our love for them bind us together. Through Christ our Lord, Amen."

It was a familiar prayer to Emma. She had learned it from her mother. When she lifted her head, every person sitting in the pews was wiping away tears. Emma and her boys had suffered more than most, but they remained together despite impossible odds. She knew that Ike made that possible. If he did not show up soon, she would have to check on him. She owed it to him. More importantly—it was what her mother would have done.

Chapter Twelve

Cecil Hammond led a comfortable life. At thirty-three years of age, he was married to the most beautiful woman he had ever seen. He stood beside his county-issued Ford Coupe, filling the gasoline tank under the front seat, while his wife perused the goods inside the mercantile.

In sharp contrast to his lovely wife, Cecil was pear-shaped, with long skinny arms and short heavy legs. Combined with his weak chin and bulging eyes, he bore an uncanny resemblance to a bullfrog. Everyone who knew him has asked at least once, "How did a man like Cecil end up married to a woman like Florence?"

It was Easter morning, so he was dressed in his best finery—his deputy sheriff's uniform. Some of the ladies at their church frowned at the sight of a gun in God's house, but he had permission. Cecil and the pastor shared membership in a certain secret organization.

Cecil received a salary of one hundred and five dollars a month, but he earned more than twice that amount. Business boomed when the flu and the war increased the demand for repossessions. He earned a dollar for every summons served and three dollars for attending the proceedings when property or possessions were auctioned off. Not exactly according to law, but it was customary.

It was not unheard of for the neighbors of a repossessed farm to show up at the auction with shotguns and purchase the property for a pittance, only to give it back to the dispossessed. The presence of an armed deputy discouraged this practice, ensuring those who were intended to buy the property were not chased off and could in fact purchase it—for a reasonable price.

An even more lucrative source of income fell into his

lap last year, when Indiana went bone dry. Prosecutors received a twenty-five-dollar bonus, collected in fines, for every case they successfully tried in violation of the new liquor law. The prosecutors knew where their bread was buttered, so they shared their good fortune. Deputies could make five dollars for every alcohol-related arrest they made, as long as they provided an illegal beverage as evidence. Even hair tonic was admissible.

Cecil's tank was full, so he replaced the seat and went inside to settle up. Florence stood in front of the counter. He walked up behind her and put his hands around her waist.

Florence jumped and slapped him away. "Cecil, not in public!"

Florence had a slim waist and long brown hair, pinned up today under her Easter bonnet. She treated her husband and everyone she met with kindness. She did not wish anyone ill, quite the opposite. Florence was a crusader for goodness—sober, Protestant goodness. She firmly believed she could convert every Papist and alcoholic she met through intelligent conversation.

They were paying for their purchases when Ike Pearson came through the door and bumped into a racked display of oil cans, sending them rolling across the floor.

Earl came out from behind the counter and danced around trying to corral the rolling cans with his feet. "Ike! Watch where you're going."

It was not a good day for Ike. His eyes were bloodshot, his clothes were filthy, and he smelled of vomit. He carefully stepped over the rolling cans and made his way up to the counter—holding onto it for support. He wasn't drunk, just very hung over. He wanted to be drunk, but he had run out of drink.

Florence Hammond wrinkled her nose, gathered up her purchases, and hurried out the door. That was all it took. Ike Pearson was a marked man. Cecil nodded to Earl and left.

Earl replaced the cans in his display and went back behind the counter. Ike didn't look too good today, but he had seen him looking worse.

"What can I do for you, Ike?"

Ike swung around to scan the store—they were alone. He turned back to Earl. "I'm out."

Earl shrugged. "Out of what?"

"You know damn well what! Don't play stupid, Earl."

Earl waved his hands in a placating gesture. "Keep your voice down. Didn't you see that copper? Where you parked?"

"Out front," Ike said.

"Pull around back to the dock. How much you want?"

Ike reached into his pocket and pulled out a thick wad of cash. "Gimme a case of Kentucky."

Earl looked up at the ceiling while he calculated. "Forty-two dollars."

Ike scowled, but he counted out the cash. Whiskey cost five times what it did only a year ago. Earl was taking on considerable risk, but he was making a lot of money with little effort. The black market opened the day the new law took effect. In eight months, when liquor could no longer simply be purchased in another state and driven to Indiana, Earl Anderson would get rich. Even at exorbitant prices, alcohol consumption would increase by five-fold before Prohibition was over.

Ike drove back to his farm with his illicit cargo

concealed beneath a tarp in the back. The pleasant day revived him. He was only vaguely aware it was morning when he climbed into his truck and drove into town. Now, in the cool air and sunshine, his head was beginning to clear. His fields looked good: plowed, harrowed, and nearly all planted in sorghum.

Ike knew he would make a modest profit, even though he hired out most of the work. It was all he could do to feed his pigs, gather the eggs, and milk the cow. More often than not, the pigs got the eggs and milk. He had enough money to live comfortably in town for the rest of his life, buried in Ball jars around the farm. He just kept farming because he was a farmer. He didn't know how to be anything else.

He turned off the gravel road and drove his truck into the barn. After he shut off the engine, he sat behind the wheel trying to collect his thoughts.

It might be Easter, should have asked at the mercantile. Maybe I should clean up and go visit my grandsons.

That thought went through his mind every day, but holidays always put the extra edge on his guilt that helped him pull it off. It was easier when he had a full case of whiskey on hand. The less liquor he had the more he wanted it. When he ran out, he desperately needed it. He wasn't entirely sure of the date, but he made up his mind to go and see his grandsons. Besides, their root cellar must be running low. He would take them some potatoes. His own stores have hardly been touched.

He stepped down out of his truck and his knees buckled. Staggering back to lean against the truck, he fought off a bout of nausea.

For sure, it's time to sober up, maybe this time for

good.

He thought that every day too. Once he felt strong enough, Ike headed for the house. He would eat a little something and then work on cleaning himself up.

Once he had a fire going in the woodstove, he filled the reservoir with water from the pump over the sink. While he waited for the stove to heat up, he gathered up the mess. After years of living in filth, he found that he liked the feeling of a clean house—once Emma and the boys cleaned it for him. He touched her bloody coat, deepening his despair, but he also found the resolve to sober up. He continued to clean up his kitchen and tried not to look at it.

The stove was ready, so he put on a pot of water, tossed in three potatoes and the end piece from a ham. It would take a little while for it to boil. He would use this time to run out to the barn and hide his liquor under the floor. He walked slowly out to his truck and threw off the tarp covering a small wooden case. Picking it up made him feel weak. He despised what it contained and what it had done to him. Even so, he carefully concealed it under the floor.

When he walked back into the kitchen, his soup was hot. He carried the pan over to the table, wiped a spoon off on his shirt, and after the first spoonful, he ate ravenously. He ate all of it and then he picked up the pan and drank the broth. Pushing the pan across the table, he was suddenly overcome with exhaustion. He laid his head on the table and went to sleep.

***

When Ike awoke, it was fully dark. He sat up groggy and disoriented. His head was pounding and his mouth was dry as cotton. Holding onto the table, he made his way over to the sink and pumped cold water over his head. It helped. He drank from a cupped hand and that helped too.

He was feeling better, but he was alarmed that he somehow missed another day, another chance to see the boys. Now, he would have to face a long sober night so as not to spoil his chances of visiting them tomorrow. He dried his face on a dirty towel and stared out into the moonlight. He needed to feed his animals. They did not complain when he fed them at odd hours, grateful to be fed at all. He stretched and twisted, trying to crack his back, but to no avail. Sleeping at the table left him stove up and aching. He limped out into the night.

Ike carried buckets of feed through the barn doors to dump into the pig troughs. He saw a white flash. Suddenly, he was on his back staring up at the stars. His head felt ready to burst. Four hooded figures gathered over him, silhouetted against the night sky. *White Caps!*

Most people thought they died out after the ruckus over the lynching in Corydon, but somebody always hated somebody in these parts. Two of the hooded figures grabbed his ankles and dragged him into his barn.

Someone yanked his shirt up over his head while he lay on the floor. Ike tried to roll over onto his back, and was kicked in the side of the head. He groaned and struggled to stay conscious. His wrists were tied together.

"Haul him up!"

The rope went taut. Slowly, Ike was hauled up until his feet just touched the floor. He twisted and turned, struggling to free himself.

The four hooded men gathered in front of him in the flickering light of a lantern. One of them uncoiled a long whip.

The first lash left a searing line of pain across Ike's chest and back. He gritted his teeth and kept silent. He didn't want to give these bastards the satisfaction.

The second lash wrapped around him and opened a cut on his belly. He groaned.

The third lash coiled around his shoulder and left a line of blood blisters on his neck. He cried out in pain.

When the fourth one wrapped a fiery tendril around him—he howled like a newborn child.

***

Emma awoke before dawn to a dim gray light and the chirping of birds. She stretched and yawned. Yesterday was a good day for her and the boys. The church service was sad, but it did what it was intended to do. The people there came together.

When Pastor Turnquist read her father's name, she was grateful to Missus Hansen for holding her while she cried. Later, she guiltily wondered who held Tommy at that moment. He probably just stuck out his chin and held it in. He was like his father. Singing hymns was awkward at first, until they found their voices and a ringing harmony made people smile.

Her room was cool, but not cold. Spring was here. She wrapped a blanket around herself and walked quickly downstairs to begin her day. Shaking the ashes out in her woodstove, she dropped in some kindling, and once she had a good fire going, she scooted her chair over to sit and wait for her stove to heat up. The days were getting longer, so she waited in the dim light of dawn without lighting a lamp.

Last night, Joe stayed for supper and helped prepare the meal. She was surprised to find he was not without skills in the kitchen. He made excellent biscuits and even made the dough for her cherry pie. It was a quiet and pleasant afternoon, and when the sun touched the horizon, she was sorry to see him go.

He'll be back soon. The sun is nearly up.

Today she had to buy seed and check on Ike. It has been two weeks since they saw him. It wasn't something she wanted to do by any stretch of the imagination. She has found nothing but pain and misery at Ike's farm. Joe said he would go with her. She wasn't sure she could have found the courage otherwise.

The stove was heating up, so she put on a kettle to boil and ran upstairs to dress. Joe always arrived when the first crescent of the sun appeared behind the trees. She did not intend to answer the door wearing her nightdress. Ten minutes later, she had the boys up and out doing their early morning chores.

When she checked her roosting boxes, Emma was thrilled to find four eggs. If she scrambled them, she could make them stretch a little farther with some milk and cheese. When she emerged from the henhouse, the sun peeked over the horizon, and Joe topped the rise on the wagon trail. It made her smile to have something so dependable in her life again.

She ran out to meet him beside the barn, carrying her basket of four eggs. "Good morning, Joe!"

Joe looked more like a man today. His work clothes fit him. He always wore dungarees and a denim shirt with red suspenders to work. He jumped down off his horse and said, "Morning, Emma."

Knowing that Emma lived alone up here with three young boys gave Joe a hollow feeling in the pit of his stomach. He didn't think he could maintain the pace she kept up all day. Yesterday, he helped her with the cooking and tried to get her to sit down and eat. It was in her nature to adopt and care for everybody, and once he came in sight, she immediately started treating him like one of the boys. He admired her sweet nature, but he worried it was too much for her. He wanted to help.

He said, "I told Pa you needed to buy seed today. He said he'd go with us to make sure Earl doesn't take advantage."

Emma brightened. "Thank you! That is much appreciated."

She was worried about having to negotiate with Earl Anderson. Jack Hansen, on the other hand, sat beside her in church yesterday. He was kind to her, something she no longer took for granted.

She said, "Come inside and I'll make breakfast."

"I'll be right there," he said.

Joe watched Emma smile, turn, and walk away—a beautiful girl wearing a frilly blue dress, work boots, and an apron too big for her. She was trying to be several people at once. He himself was not yet a man, but he was the closest thing they had on this farm.

Joe brushed down his horse. It was a firm rule at the Hansen farm that you brushed your horse down as soon as you took off the saddle. He had watched Verne being born, and gentled him to a saddle when he was a yearling. Joe was twelve then—Emma's age.

Tommy came out from the back of the barn carrying a pail of milk and stopped to watch Joe. After a moment, he said, "Morning, Joe."

Joe said, "Morning, Tommy."

"I saw you yesterday up on the hill with Emma. She was crying."

Feeling like he was in trouble with this boy, Joe turned to face him and said defensively, "I didn't make her cry. I hate it when Emma cries."

Tommy put down his pail and rubbed his hand on his trousers. He carried that pail around so much the wire handle was wearing a callous across his palm.

After eying Joe up and down, he said, "I went up there this morning. Ma's name is spelled out again. I was real happy to see that. It ain't right not to have her name there. Ike made her move them rocks."

Joe said, "Don't worry boy. I won't tell nobody. I promised Emma."

Tommy said, "Good, we ain't supposed to tell. Emma's scared all the time somebody's gonna find out."

He gave Joe one more hard look and picked up his pail. He turned his back to Joe, and as he walked off he said, "If you make Emma cry again, I'll make you cry."

Tommy only came up to his chest, but Joe believed him. Tommy walked through the barn door with his pail of milk, while Joe was still trying to think of what to say.

Is that boy only seven?

After breakfast, Joe hitched Buck to the wagon and Emma rounded up the boys for the trip into town. Jack Hansen said he would meet them at eight o'clock. She was checking the time on her watch, and at precisely eight, Jack and Joe's oldest brother, John, topped the hill from the wagon trail riding horses. Quarter horses like these and Joe's horse, Verne, were uncommon in these parts. Most people kept draft horses, but the Hansen's preferred horses to wagons and automobiles. They rode them everywhere they went.

Joe's oldest brother was barely twenty, but he already had the permanent tan and crinkled eyes of a man ten years older. He was a handsome young man. He looked like his father. All the Hansen amen wore the same broad brimmed felt hats, practical in sun and rain. Those hats made them look sort of dashing, like cowboys but more Midwestern.

Emma could hardly bring herself to speak to John. Her thoughts sometimes drifted away and she would end up just staring at him with a goofy grin, while she admired how pretty he was.

She had on her good shoes, and her good shawl was wrapped around her shoulders. She considered wearing her church dress, but they were just going to buy seed. She walked out to stand looking up at Jack and his son as they sat hunched over on their horses.

"Thank you for going with us, Mister Hansen. I was concerned about it."

Jack said, "Your momma done earned any help we can offer."

Emma had never been involved in these sorts of transactions. She was shy about it, but she had to ask. "Mister Hansen, we're planting twenty acres in beans and twenty in sorghum. How much money should I bring?"

Jack sat up straight on his horse and said, "Seed is costly this year, maybe two dollars an acre for the beans, less for milo."

Emma knew from studying the ledgers that her father paid a dollar thirty for beans only two years ago. Ike told her to expect seed to cost more, but this seemed excessive. "My goodness," she said.

Jack said, "I know how you feel. Could be we ride down to Bloomington and get it cheaper, but I don't hold out much hope. May as well bite the bullet and buy your seed, Miss."

Emma nodded and reached into the front pocket of her dress to touch the envelope containing sixty dollars. Between her father's pay and his life insurance, she has put more money into the cash box than she has taken out of it. It still felt like stealing every time she took money out, so she only did it when she could not think of another way. She would buy seed and enough cloth to make a new church dress. Buying a dress did not occur to her. She and her mother had made every dress they owned.

She ran back inside to take another twenty from the cash box. Gathering up the boys, she ushered them outside and boosted them up into the bed of the wagon.

Emma was headed for the front of the wagon when Clyde peeked over the side. "Emma, can we stop and see Grampa?"

Emma knew Clyde was just as afraid of his grandfather's farm as she was. She understood what he was feeling, because she felt it too. The longer they went without seeing Ike, the more they worried about him. She already told the boys they would stop at the Pearson farm, Clyde was just making sure. She was more grateful to Jack Hansen than he knew.

"We'll stop and check on him," she said.

Emma stood beside the wagon, working up her nerve when she heard Joe say softly, "Emma."

She looked up to see him leaning over the side of the wagon with his hand out. She took his hand with both of hers, and he lifted her up into the seat. She looked back over her shoulder at Jack and John Hansen, tall and capable men mounted on handsome horses. She turned to look at Joe, sitting beside her. He had been by her side every day for two weeks. She felt safe in their presence. She was so accustomed to carrying a constant buzz of fear that she had to ask herself what she was feeling when it left her. It was the feeling of family.

Joe shook the reins and Buck headed for the mercantile. Jack lead the way down the wagon trail and John fell in behind the wagon.

When they reached the gravel road and headed north, Ike's plowed, harrowed, and seeded fields were in sight. Emma could not imagine Ike doing all that. As they approached his farm, the house and barn became visible. Jack Hansen urged his horse into a trot and rode ahead. When he reached the dirt road onto Ike's property, he turned off the gravel and disappeared behind the trees.

When the wagon reached Ike's farm, John rode up next to them and leaned over in the saddle to say to Joe, "Pull over and wait for Pa."

Joe turned the wagon onto the dirt road that led to the house and reined in Buck. It was a warm spring day. The trees were budding. Redbuds and the dogwoods bloomed pink and white, widely scattered among the taller trees. Emma, Joe, and the boys sat in the wagon listening to birdsong in the warm sunshine. Jack's horse was beside the barn, but there was no sign of him.

Emma had a feeling of foreboding. She hated this place. The pigs squealed and clustered against the fence. The cow mooed a complaint. The horses pressed up against the corral fence, watching them. She looked behind her and found the twins wearing identical little frowns. The last time they were here was a cold rainy day last fall. Even in the sunshine with the smell of spring blossoms in the air, it felt the same as on that awful day.

***

When Jack Hansen rode ahead, Ike did not answer the door. When he went inside, he found the woodstove in the kitchen still warm, but there was no sign of Ike. Every cabinet door and drawer was thrown open. Dishes and other belongings were strewn across the room. Canisters of sugar, flour, and salt were smashed on the floor in big starbursts. He checked the bedrooms and found them in the same condition.

He stood in the kitchen door, looking out at the barn. A child's coat hung beside the door, stained with blood. Jack ran his fingers along the blood-encrusted collar and frowned. Something unholy had happened in this place. He walked quickly out into the barn and found Ike.

Ike's wrists were tied together with a rope, thrown over a beam and lashed to a rail. His feet barely touched the ground. He was shirtless and his pants were down around his ankles. Weeping, red welts striped his stomach, back, and legs.

Jack ran to him and lifted him up. Ike groaned—he was alive! Jack pulled a knife from the sheath on his belt and sawed through the rope. Ike dropped into his arms, and he gently laid him in the straw.

"Ike! You alive, old buddy?"

Ike's eyes fluttered open. "That you, Jack?"

Jack had never seen a man whipped so hard. Whoever did this must have used a yard whip. The way the welts ended in cuts where the tip of the tail laid into Ike spoke of hatred—or sadistic pleasure.

While he unraveled the knots holding Ike's wrists together, Jack asked, "What happened here? Who did this?"

Once his hands were free, Ike tried to pull his pants up to cover himself, but only one arm was working. He groaned and rolled from side to side in the straw. Jack helped him get his pants up and fastened them for him. Ike sat up and put his head between his knees.

"Water," he croaked.

Jack ran out of the barn to the kitchen and pumped cold water into a pitcher he found on the floor. He ran back to the barn and helped Ike to drink. Ike could only raise one hand.

***

When she saw Jack run out of the barn, a knot tightened in Emma's chest. When he ran back into the barn, carrying a pitcher, she jumped down from the wagon and ran after him.

She found Jack kneeling beside a shirtless Ike, sitting in the straw. Red, weeping welts and cuts covered his chest and back. She ran to him and knelt down, afraid to touch him.

"Oh, Ike! I'm so sorry!"

Ike looked up and reached out to touch her hair. She gripped his hand and kissed his fingers with tears streaming down her face.

"I ain't hurt bad, Emma. Don't cry." He looked over at Jack. "Git her out of here. She don't need to see this."

Joe and the boys appeared in the doorway, lit from behind by bright sunlight. Jack tried to pull Emma away, but she screamed, "No! He's hurt! I have to help him."

Jack took Emma's arm and tried to lead her away, but she struggled. He held on to her arm until she settled down and led her over to Joe.

"Take her back home. Tell John to go fetch your Ma."

Joe led Emma out of the barn, leaving Tommy and the twins still standing in the barn door. Clyde and Claude were crying, but Tommy was unaffected. He walked up to Ike, sitting in the straw.

"Remember when you hit Emma?"

Ike looked up at Tommy in despair. He remembered. He thought about it every day.

Tommy met his watery gaze with a hard look. "She fell down right where you are now."

Then he turned and ran after Joe to see to his big

sister. The twins chased after Tommy.

Joe lifted Emma up and placed her into the seat of the wagon. When the boys climbed up the wheel and over the side, they went to the front and reached out to her. She climbed over the back of the seat, and the four of them hung on to each other in a little ball of misery. Joe picked up the reins, but Buck was already headed for home.

Jack Hansen heard what Tommy said and he connected it with the bloody coat hanging in Ike's kitchen. He had an urge to tie him back up to the rafters and whip him himself. Everybody knew Ike was a drunk, but he'd never hurt anyone except himself before. He found Ike's shirt near the wall. The buttons had been ripped loose when someone tore it off him. He picked it up and tossed it over Ike's head.

He looked forward to helping Old Man Pearson re-articulate his shoulder. It would hurt like hell. "Stand up and we'll see if we can pop that arm back in place."

Chapter Thirteen

Emma sat at her table, desperately worried about Ike. The boys found distraction in going about their chores, but they were quiet all day. Once again, Ike's farm revealed itself as a place of misery. Joe sat across from Emma, uncomfortable and mystified. He made lunch for the boys, but Emma would not eat. She got up from the table and stood in front of her kitchen window, watching the wagon trail. Joe went to stand beside her. Her head only came up to his shoulder.

She looked up at him and asked again, "Why would somebody do that to Ike?"

"I don't know," he said.

Not having an answer bothered him. He wanted to give her a reason, but he suspected that even if he knew, Emma would be unable to comprehend something so cruel.

The sky was overcast and gray. A few drops of rain splattered on the windows. Joe felt awkward. He had no idea what to do for Emma, or what happened to Ike. He wished his mother was here. She had a way of soothing worry.

Emma pulled her shawl around her shoulders. "I'm going to talk to Momma."

Joe followed her outside. She stood looking up the hill at the yellowwood tree. Shyly taking Joe's hand, she drew strength from him. Together, they walked up the hill in a light rain to stand beside Anna's grave. When Emma knelt down, Joe knelt beside her.

Emma carefully straightened the small white stones that spelled out her mother's name before she bowed her head. When she closed her eyes, a tear fell from her cheek and dropped onto the soft earth, lost among the raindrops.

She clasped her hands together and prayed,

"Momma, I am lost."

A vivid memory crystallized in her mind, of a crisp fall day three years ago. A dozen men came to their farm that day to cut firewood. She was sitting on a log in front of a fire and Joe sat beside her. She always found comfort in Joe's quiet presence. The smell of the wood smoke and the heat from the flames seemed real.

Jack Hansen was telling some improbable tale, while the men gathered around the fire laughed. Her father sat across from her, holding an axe across his knees. Her mother stood behind him with her hands on his shoulders, but her eyes were on Emma. She nodded her head.

Emma opened her eyes and looked over at Joe to find him looking back at her. She wiped her eyes and smiled. Joe's eyebrows arched.

"Momma told me to listen to your father and stay close to you."

Joe looked alarmed. "Really?"

Emma nodded and smiled. "She really did."

She stood up and hugged him while he knelt beside her mother's grave. She felt better now. She would raise Ike's grandsons to the best of her ability and do what she could for that sad old man, but she could no longer depend on him for help or guidance. She would turn to Jack Hansen.

The rain began to come down harder. "Come on, Joe. We're getting wet."

Joe got to his feet, and Emma pulled him down the hill toward the house. A brilliant blue flash lit up the dark clouds, followed by a boom of thunder. The rain poured down. Emma squealed and ran for the house, dragging Joe along behind her.

When they came through the kitchen door, Emma and Joe were drenched. She took two towels from a drawer, tossed one to Joe, and began to dry her hair while she stood in front of the window watching the rain. The boys stood just inside the barn doors, looking out at the storm. Rather than be cooped up in the house, they took refuge there.

Joe stood on the rug just inside the door, shaking off the rain. He dried his face on the towel and regarded Emma, standing in front of the window. She was a beautiful girl, but she was just a girl. They were vulnerable here. He draped his damp towel over the back of a chair and went to stand beside her. He never knew what to say to her, but he felt he had to say something.

"Emma," he said, and she turned to look up at him. "Are you going to tell Pa that your mother died?"

The smile left Emma's face. She looked back out at the rain. "Momma told me to listen to your father. Will he help us?"

"Pa always does what he thinks is right. He might not think it's the right thing to leave you and the boys here alone."

Emma considered this. "In five years and two months, I'll be eighteen. We have to hang on until then. People can't know Momma is gone. I'll do whatever it takes to keep this farm."

She looked up at Joe, and he saw grim determination written on her delicate features, but there was fear in her strangely beautiful eyes. He had known Emma for most of her life. She was the kindest person he knew. These past few weeks, he came to know a different side of her. She changed the world with relentless gentle nudges—punctuated by the rare shotgun blast.

Emma tried hard to hold back her tears. They were talking about her future and that of the boys. Serious, hard decisions had to be made. She needed someone she could trust, and Jack Hansen had her mother's blessing. She looked back up at Joe.

"I'm going to tell your father the truth. Momma said I could trust him."

Joe didn't know what to say. He was a quiet boy anyway, and being around Emma robbed him of the rare words that did come to his mind. He didn't have a way with words, but he knew how to help.

He took down his hat from the peg beside the door. "The wood box is empty. I'll get some wood and we can start supper."

Emma watched Joe step out into the rain and smiled. Her mother's vision was filled with meaning. She understood the feelings, if not the reasons. All true things, she knew, were felt, not figured out. She felt that she would spend her life with Joe. She wondered if he knew.

***

Emma had just gotten the boys settled at the table and was ladling out their string beans and ham, when she saw Jack Hansen top the hill on the wagon trail riding his dark horse. He rode straight into the barn.

She glanced over at Joe and saw that he too saw his father ride up. She didn't say anything in front of the boys. She wanted to find out what happened to Ike and have a chance to think before she talked to them.

"Joe, will you look after the boys? I have to run out to the barn."

Joe nodded. Tommy sat up straight in his chair and peeked out the window. He opened his mouth to speak, but the look on Emma's face silenced him. He shrugged and turned his attention back to his supper.

Emma slipped outside and sprinted for the barn. She had been waiting all day to hear about Ike. When she ran into the barn, Jack already had the saddle off his horse and was brushing him down. He saw her coming and turned to her.

"Slow down Emma, Ike's gonna be just fine."

Emma stopped in front of him, breathing hard. "What happened?"

Jack went back to brushing his horse, a dark stallion with a white star on his forehead. He was turning over in his mind what to say to Emma. Hard things needed to be said and he was not comfortable discussing them with her.

He turned back to Emma, and her breath caught in her throat. Jack looked angry. The muscles in his jaw were clenched. She shrank from his intense gaze.

Seeing this, Jack sighed and knelt down on one knee in front of her. He had raised three boys, but he was struggling with what to say to this delicate young girl. He took her hands in his and was alarmed to find that she was trembling.

"How did you get that scar on your face?"

Emma pulled her hands out of his and backed away. She touched the thin, pink ridge of scar tissue above her eye.

"It was an accident."

Jack stood up and approached her slowly. She looked scared and ready to bolt. He gently laid a big, hard hand on Emma's shoulder and tried to smile. The sight of that bloody little coat hanging in Ike's kitchen would haunt him for the rest of his life. After he helped Ike pop his shoulder back into place, he took him inside to sit at the table.

Jack took down that bloody coat, wadded it into a ball, and stuffed it into the woodstove. Then he grabbed Ike by the hair, pulled his head back so he could look into his eyes and said, "If you ever touch her again, I swear to God— that will be your last day on this Earth."

The old man had cried, but Jack felt no pity for him.

When Mary arrived, he did not tell her what he had found. She was too good a person to be burdened by it. He left her with John, to dress Ike's wounds, and rode off to Yellowwood Farm.

"It's alright, Emma. I shouldn't have asked. I know your momma isn't well, but I need to speak to her."

She fell to her knees and sobbed. All the grief of the past seven months turned to tears and poured out of her. Jack thought his business here would be the sort of thing that needed a man. He was wrong. He fervently wished Mary was here, because he had no idea what to do. He reacted instinctively to the sight of a crying child and picked her up.

Emma wrapped her arms tightly around his neck. The feeling of being lifted high into the air by strong arms reminded her of her father. She thought she would never feel this again. She buried her face against Jack's chest and cried. He smelled of soap, sweat, and horses—just like her father.

Jack was completely at a loss. He could only guess that Emma needed her mother. He took two steps toward the barn door and felt her stiffen in his arms.

She raised her head and said through her tears, "No! Please don't let the boys see me crying."

Jack stopped and just held her for a minute. Then he walked back into the barn, sat down on a wooden crate, and let her cry.

He arrived at dusk, and now, it was nearly dark. Emma had been still for a while. Her grip on his neck relaxed, but he could not see her face. It was still pressed against his chest.

Joe appeared in the barn door, looking worried. Seeing his father holding Emma, he approached quietly and sat down beside him. Jack looked over at him and shrugged as best he could with Emma in his arms.

She did not want to break her tenuous grasp on the illusion that her father was holding her, but she knew she was not in her father's arms.

She raised her head. "I'm fine now, Mister Hansen. You can put me down."

Jack stood up and carefully placed her next to Joe. She rubbed at her eyes and sniffled.

Joe leaned over to her. "Did you tell him?"

Emma shook her head and said quietly, "You tell him, Joe."

Joe was alarmed. Jack, however, was relieved. Emma had him flustered, but he knew quite well how to deal with his sons.

"Tell me what?"

Joe stood up. He looked down at Emma and then back at his father. He walked over beside the barn door, and Jack walked over to stand beside him. Joe looked back at Emma, slowly disappearing into darkness as the last glimmers of the day faded away.

Standing close to his father, he said softly, "Emma's ma died of the flu last September. She's buried up on the hill."

Jack felt a sudden and terrible loss. Everyone who knew Anna Taylor loved her. Her beauty was legendary, but the people that knew her loved her for who she was, not what she looked like.

Joe could see that his father was shaken. He said, "Ike Pearson was sick too. He thought he was gonna die, but he got better. He asked Emma to take care of his grandsons and helped them get through the winter."

Jack understood now what set Emma off. He called into the darkness, "Emma!"

A few seconds later, she emerged from the shadows

and stepped out into the dim moonlight peeking through the scudding clouds.

"Let's go inside," he said.

Joe took the boys upstairs to settle them into bed. The news that their grandfather would be okay brought smiles to the faces of the twins. They were used to him being remote and unavailable, but they had never seen him injured by anyone other than himself before.

Emma sat at her table drinking the tea Joe placed in front of her. A bowl of string beans and ham remained untouched by her elbow. Jack Hansen sat across from her. He didn't have a clue what to say.

Emma could see that Jack was struggling to find words, so she said, "I prayed to Momma today. She told me you would help us."

Jack was a God-fearing man, but he did not believe that the dead spoke to the living. "Your momma spoke to you?"

Emma frowned and said, "Prayers don't work that way. She showed me a memory of a day when you came here to cut wood. Her answers come in memories and feelings, not words."

Jack was taken aback. This young girl just opened his eyes to the honest core of spirituality. Having prayed all his life, only now did he realize that he has often been answered. It was something her mother might have said, the sort of thing that made people love her.

"You're just like your ma."

Emma looked up from her teacup and smiled. "Thank you, Mister Hansen."

She looked back down into her tea, unable to meet Jack's penetrating gaze. "Ike told me if anybody finds out Momma died, then people will come and take the farm away.

I need help. Momma said I could trust you."

Jack's mind was reeling. Even so, it only took him a few seconds to realize that what Ike said was true. Yellowwood Farm was the envy of Owen County. If word got out Anna died, then it would be a matter of days before some corrupt official blatantly robbed Emma and Tommy of their land. He was more than willing to take them in, but that would not save this farm.

Joe walked into the room and took a seat next to Emma. "The boys are in bed. They griped about not reading a chapter, but they're worn out, probably asleep by now."

Jack fixed his gaze on Joe and asked, "How long have you known about all this?"

Emma saw Joe shrink under his father's withering gaze and sprang to his defense. "I only told Joe yesterday! He works hard and he even helps cook."

Jack knew that Joe was a good kid. He didn't talk much, but there was nothing wrong with being quiet. Somebody has to listen. The only one at the table who was making any sense was Emma.

Jack asked her, "What else did your ma tell you?"

Emma sat up straight in her chair and glanced shyly over at Joe. She didn't want to say.

Jack could see that he had touched upon something important. He raised one eyebrow, making him look even more intimidating and said, "Well?"

Emma felt trapped, but considering what was at stake, she had to be honest. She said, "You know I don't hear words, right? It's just memories and feelings."

Jack said, "I understand. You can trust me, Emma, so your ma was right about that. What else did she say?"

She glanced back over at Joe and he smiled. A warm feeling came over her, giving her the courage to say out loud,

"She told me Joe would always be beside me."

It was a full three seconds before the smile drained away from Joe's face. "She said what?"

Jack rocked back in his chair and laughed.

Chapter Fourteen

Ike lay in his bed, staring up at the cracked ceiling. The kerosene lamp on the dresser was turned down to a flickering blue flame. Mary Hansen had stripped him of his clothes and applied salve to his wounds in a no-nonsense manner that did not make allowances for modesty. Then she had fashioned a sling for his arm, cooked him a meal, and left.

More embarrassing than being laid bare in front of Mary, was the way Jack burned Emma's bloody coat. The sight of it always caused Ike pain. He knew it was an unhealthy and macabre thing to keep in his kitchen, but he never anticipated anyone other than himself would be in this house. He realized now that it was a stupid thing to do. It hadn't even served its purpose—curbing his urge to drink.

The White Caps had whipped him until he passed out. Then they had ransacked the house and took his wife's jewelry. Martha never had much, her few necklaces and brooches were more keepsakes than heirlooms. The only thing she owned of any real value was the watch he gave to Emma. Being robbed of the handful of things Martha cherished infuriated him more than the whipping. He felt like he deserved the lashing. Martha, on the other hand, did not deserve to have her things stolen.

Ike rolled out of bed and groaned. He savored the pain of his wounds as penance for the way he had treated Emma and the boys. He staggered into the kitchen and eased himself into a chair. Moonlight streaming through the window lit the kitchen.

He carefully poured a glass of water from the pitcher Mary left on the table and drank all of it. His stomach churned. She and her son, John, cleaned up the mess the

White Caps had made. The Hansen's were good people, hardworking and honest. Mary treated him with kindness and compassion, so Ike knew her husband hadn't told her about Emma's coat. Jack was that kind of man. He would deal with Ike himself, if need be, but he would not gossip about it.

Ike was ashamed that Jack Hansen knew he struck Emma. That single second of drunken anger defined him as a worthless human being. Emma forgave him, but he would never forgive himself. He sat in the moonlight and battled his demons. They chattered incessantly about the case of whiskey hidden under the floor of the barn.

***

Emma sat in her bentwood chair, washing away the dirt and grime of yet another terrifying and painful day, but it ended well. Jack Hansen agreed to help her.

Jack sat at her table and spoke plainly about the corruption of government officials and the dangers of the world. He told her about the White Caps and explained that they probably whipped Ike for his drunkenness. Her life, up to last September, was so sheltered she did not even know drinking liquor was against the law. Lastly, he told her she was too young to know these things, but she had no choice.

Joe would continue to work as a hired hand. In front of Emma, Jack told his son that in five years, she would be of age. And then, if she was still so inclined, Joe would be the luckiest man in the world if Emma still wanted him by her side. She was the spitting image of her mother, the kindest, most beautiful woman Jack had ever met.

Joe listened, wide-eyed and subdued. Considering the beauty of Emma's mother, her reputation as a good woman and the desirability of Yellowwood Farm, he could not imagine a more promising future. Even so, it was unsettling. A twelve-year-old girl staked her claim on him.

***

Emma placed her washbowl on the floor and soaked her feet. It was after eleven o'clock. On any other day, she would have been asleep hours ago. She was exhausted, yet excited to think they might actually make it through the next five years. She had been struggling to hang on to their farm one day at a time. Jack Hansen gave her hope. She could think now about what she might do next year and stop focusing on getting through tomorrow.

She dried her feet and pulled on a warm pair of woolen socks. The nights were still cool. She adjusted the mirror over her washstand and brushed her hair by the yellow light of her kerosene lamp. She thought she looked different tonight. It took her a moment to realize the frown lines were gone from her brow. She rubbed at the thin, pink scar above her eye, wishing it would fade. She did not want to carry that painful reminder for the rest of her life. What was Ike doing right now? When would they see him again? The frown lines came back.

Emma sighed, put away her hairbrush, and blew out her lamp. Kneeling down in a pool of moonlight beside her bed, she pressed her hands together, closed her eyes, and prayed, "Thank you, Momma."

The scent of roses filled the air. Feelings of love and contentment washed over her. Her mother always answered her prayers.

***

The next day was warm and sunny. Emma sat on the wagon seat beside Joe as Buck turned off the wagon trail onto the gravel road. The boys sat in the bed behind her. Jack rode out in front and John rode behind. When they passed Ike Pearson's farm, the boys became quiet and clung to the side rail, looking for Ike. He was nowhere in sight.

Jack told them Ike was fine and they would see him soon, but not today. Today, they had to buy seed and get started planting. Emma leaned over to look past Joe into the dark windows of Ike's house. She wanted to know if he was okay, but she did not want to set foot on his land. His pigs were out in their enclosure and his horses grazed in the pasture. They did not look distressed.

Maybe things are as they should be.

Joe saw the look on her face. "He's fine, Emma. Pa checked on him before he came to your place."

Emma already knew that. She sat up straight. "Ike's been alone for too long." She turned around to face the twins. "Your Grampa is fine, boys. Mister Hansen checked on him this morning."

Clyde looked up at her and smiled. Like Emma, he had no desire to set foot on that farm. He did, however, love his grandfather. That sad old man was the only family he and his brother had left.

Once they were past Ike's farm, Emma allowed herself to enjoy the trip into town. It was a beautiful day. Tender new leaves sprouted from the trees and the dogwoods were in bloom. Soft flowers and tender new shoots filled the woods. The thorns and stickers of summer were months away.

Joe kept glancing over at Emma. While he was flattered that she found him to be a worthy future husband, those choices were years away. He was certain that once she matured, she would realize he wasn't good enough for her and turn to a more worthy suitor.

Emma caught Joe looking and smiled. He turned his attention back to the road, not that Buck needed his help. She scooted across the seat and placed her hand on his arm.

"I'm sorry if I scared you last night, but Momma is always right about these things. You're beside me right now."

Joe managed to smile. "Five years is a long time."

"I hope it goes by quickly. We'll be out of danger then."

Joe kept his eyes forward. "We're just kids."

Emma gripped his arm more tightly. "I wish that was true."

When they pulled up to the mercantile, Jack rode up next to the wagon. "Pull around back, Joey. Emma, you come inside with me."

Jack tied his horse to the rail while Emma climbed down from the wagon. She ran a few steps to catch up to him. He held the door for her and they went inside.

The place was bustling with people browsing the merchandise and talking in small groups. Earl Anderson was talking to a lady wearing a long dress and a ridiculous hat. When he saw Emma, he excused himself and came around the counter.

"Emma Taylor! How's your momma?"

Emma looked up at Jack for help. She hated lying, especially about something as monumental as her mother's death. She would tell the lie if she had to. She felt cowardly for expecting Jack to do it for her, but she was afraid that she could not do it without crying.

Jack said, "Howdy, Earl. Anna's not well. Do the girl a kindness and don't make her talk about it. Me and the boys will be helping them out this year. Emma here needs enough soybeans to plant twenty acres. What's your best price?"

Earl frowned and shuffled his feet. "Soybeans are costly this year. Y'all have got a corn planter—so figure two forty-pound bags an acre. A dollar ten a bag is the going price."

Looking down at Emma, Jack said, "Bloomington is twenty-five miles. I reckon we can make it there and back by sunset."

Earl was unruffled, but when Jack turned to leave, he said, "A dollar is the best I can do."

Jack turned back around. "How's them boys of yours? As I recall, Anna taught them when they was in school."

Earl snorted and laughed. "Alright! Ninety-five cents, but only for Anna Taylor. Don't tell nobody, or I'll go broke!"

Jack looked back down at Emma. She was pressed against his side, looking up at him. Her eyes were huge—sparkling blue in rings of gold—just like her mother's. Anna's eyes always fascinated Jack and every other person who got a good look at them.

"Shake the man's hand, Emma. I think we have a deal."

Emma shyly held out her hand.

Earl grasped it and shook it firmly. "You drive a hard bargain, young lady."

"Thank you kindly, Mister Anderson."

Earl laughed again and said to Jack, "She's just like her momma. She even has those pretty eyes."

"The wagon's out back. She needs to buy milo too and a few other things before she settles up."

Earl said, "I'll have my boy load the wagon."

***

On the ride home, Emma felt light as a feather—thrilled to have accomplished something she had been dreading for weeks. The boys sat behind her, high up on the bags of seed. She turned to check on them and frowned at their chocolate-smeared faces. She could not understand how they managed to eat everything else without getting it all over themselves.

They were all set to start planting. She lifted her locket out of the front of her dress to check the time. It wasn't quite eleven o'clock. The smile left her face when she realized she was holding something Ike gave her. They were nearing his farm. She turned around to find Clyde and Claude staring over the side of the wagon at their grandfather's house in the distance.

"Can we stop and see Grampa?" Clyde asked. Claude sat beside his brother looking hopeful.

Emma did not want to set foot on Ike's land, but she felt the twins needed to see their grandfather. If she was going to do this, she would only do it with Jack Hansen standing beside her. She turned back around and called out, "Mister Hansen!"

Jack stopped his horse and waited for the wagon to catch up. He rode alongside and tipped his hat to Emma.

"Can we stop and check on Ike?"

Jack considered it for only a moment and said, "I'll go and see about Ike. If he's feeling well enough, he can come to your place."

Emma said, "Thank you, Mister Hansen."

Jack touched the brim of his hat again and trotted his horse down the dirt road to Ike's house. He was standing on the porch, knocking on the door, when the wagon passed a grove of trees and Emma lost sight of him.

***

When Ike didn't answer the door, Jack went around back to look for him in the barn. When he came to the house this morning, he found Ike asleep at his kitchen table, and fed his animals without waking him.

Jack walked into the barn and saw Ike sitting in his truck. He walked around to the front, so as not to surprise him, and leaned against the frame.

"How you doin', Ike?"

Ike saw Emma and the boys drive past in the wagon. He watched Jack ride down the road to his house and was waiting for him. This man knew his darkest secret—something known only to an innocent young girl and three small boys. On reflection, Ike was relieved that Jack was aware of what he did. It was comforting to know that if he ever harmed Emma again, Jack would kill him.

"How's Emma and the boys?"

"They're fine. We bought Emma's seed."

Ike felt a pang of guilt. The men he hired had already planted his fields. He intended to help Emma with planting hers, but too many days escaped him. He always had good intentions.

"Thanks, Jack, I kept meaning to," he said.

Jack said bluntly, "I know that Anna died."

Ike sat up straight and turned to look him in the eye. "What are you going to do?"

"Emma's secret is safe with me. She's got it in her head that someday she's going to marry Joey."

Ike chuckled. "If that's what she thinks, then I reckon that's what's gonna happen."

Jack looked at Ike closely. "You feel like driving over there? Emma and your grandsons want to see you."

Ike said, "I was considering it."

Jack leaned in to examine the inside of the truck. "Can you drive that contraption one-handed?"

Ike lifted his arm out of the sling and winced. He moved it back and forth. "Feels a might better. I can manage."

"You need help with the livestock?" Jack asked.

Ike said, "I'll be fine."

Jack stood up straight and said, "Wait a few hours and come for supper. Maybe shave and clean yourself up a bit."

Ike rubbed the stubble on his chin. "Tell Emma I'll come for supper. I'm glad you're gonna help her out. She's scared witless the law will find out her momma is dead and she'll lose their farm."

"She's raising those boys for you. Might be you could do more for her."

Ike leaned over to rest his head on the steering wheel of his truck. "I've lived too long."

Jack stood beside the truck for a few moments longer. Ike had nothing more to say, so he walked out of the barn. He whistled and his horse trotted around the house. He never liked Ike Pearson. Now, he despised him. Jack was a Christian—he helped anyone who needed his help, but he was also a Regulator—he took vengeance when it was due. He swung up into the saddle and rode off toward Yellowwood Farm.

***

Joe wasted no time loading up the corn planter with soybeans and hitching up Buck and Jane. By the time his father arrived, he was already in the field closest to the house. Emma was in her garden, planting potatoes, when she saw Jack ride up. She dropped what she was doing and ran to him.

"Mister Hansen! Is Ike okay? Did you talk to him?"

Jack stepped down off his horse. When she looked up at him, her unusual eyes sparkled in the sunlight. He forgot what he was about to say.

"Mister Hansen?"

"Your eyes are just like your ma's."

Emma blushed and looked away. "Is Ike okay?"

Jack blinked. "Ike's fine. He said he'd be over in a little while for supper, if you don't mind."

Emma sighed in relief. "Ike is always welcome at our table. Thank you, Mister Hansen."

Jack climbed back up onto his horse and said, "If you need anything, tell Joey."

He rode into the field and followed alongside Joe while he drove the team pulling the planter. Joe reined in the team and looked up at his father.

"Ike is coming for supper. You stay here until he leaves. Do you understand?"

Joe nodded, even though he did not understand at all. Jack wheeled his horse around and rode off.

***

Tonight, Emma's table would be full for the first time since her mother died. She bustled around her kitchen, making cornbread to have with the ham, potatoes, and string beans that made up the majority of their diet for the past six months. They used the last of the carrots a month ago, and their supplies were running low. She had searched through the barrels and bins to find the best of their remaining vegetables.

Tommy came in carrying his milk pail. He watched Emma scoot her stepstool over to the pantry and climb up to take down a sack of cornmeal. She placed it on the table and scooped out four cups into a large bowl.

"Emma, do you think you could shoot us a deer? I saw some out in the fields this morning."

Venison sounded good to Emma too. Her father always shot a deer or two after every spring planting, when they came to graze on the tender shoots of their crops. It served the dual purpose of keeping the crops safe and feeding the family.

She said, "I don't know how to dress a deer, but Joe probably does. Maybe he can collect one for us."

She poured a little buttermilk into her mixing bowl and began working it around with a wooden spoon. Tommy poured off a pitcher of raw milk for supper. The days were getting warm, so he would pour the rest into the milk can that sat in the cool water of their spring-fed stream.

"Joe thinks you're pretty," he said.

Emma stopped mixing her cornbread and looked up at Tommy in surprise. "How do you know?"

"He watches you when he thinks you're not looking. And his cheeks turn pink when you talk to him."

Emma laughed. She thought Joe had pink cheeks all the time.

Tommy grinned, picked up his pail, and went back outside. He had done what he set out to do—make Emma laugh. She rarely laughed.

Emma looked out the big kitchen window. Their cherry trees were in bloom. Soft pink petals rained down in the warm breeze. Joe was in the near field behind the planter. She watched him make the turn at the end of the field and start a new row. From this distance, he looked like his father. She went back to making her cornbread and smiled.

***

When Ike's truck topped the rise on the wagon trail, Clyde and Claude ran to meet him. He parked beside the house and slowly climbed out.

Clyde wrapped his arms around Ike's waist and said, "Grampa! Are you alright?"

Ike's grandsons clung to him. He squirmed in pain, but did not push them away. "I'm fine, boys."

Emma stood just outside the kitchen door, to give the twins a little time with their grandfather. She noticed that Ike's left arm hung at his side, but other than that he looked good. He was wearing clean clothes and had shaved.

Claude said, "Grampa! Emma made dinner, cornbread and ham."

"Emma's a fine cook. You boys are lucky she wants you here."

It seemed to Emma like an unkind thing to say, but the twins did not notice. Ike walked up to her with them hanging onto him.

"You are looking beautiful as always, Miss Emma."

She said, "Supper is nearly ready. I'm glad you came. Come inside and I'll make tea."

Tommy stood beside Emma, hanging on to her apron. He gave Ike a dirty look.

Unable to look into the boy's eyes, Ike turned away. "I brought some things in the back of the truck. How 'bout you boys go fetch 'em."

The twins ran for the truck. Tommy, however, stayed where he was and looked up at Emma.

She said softly, "Go help Clyde and Claude."

Tommy walked toward the truck, looking back over his shoulder at Ike. He was in a hurry to grow up. Someday, when he was tall and strong, he would take his revenge on Ike. He thought about it every time he saw the scar on his sister's face.

Emma looked Ike over carefully. He was favoring his left arm. A red welt rose up from his collar and wrapped around his neck. Liquor and whippings—it was all beyond her understanding. What else was there that might rise up unexpectedly? She knew now that her mother and father had sheltered her from the hard things in life. It was her turn to stand in the forefront. She would have to learn how to shelter her boys in a gentle world of her own creation.

Ike saw that Emma was lost in thought. He placed a hand on her shoulder and she jumped. Then she smiled and took his hand.

"Come inside and sit down." She led him into the house.

Ike sat down at the table, and Emma put on a kettle to boil. She checked her cornbread and used a dishtowel to take it out of the oven. She gave her stepstool a push with her foot and it slid across the floor to stop in front of the pantry. Placing her cornbread on top of the stove, she turned and climbed up to take down their last jar of honey. She stepped down to place the honey on the table and, without turning around, she gave her stepstool a little kick that slid it over in front of the cupboards. She turned back around and ran up it to take down two teacups.

All this was highly amusing to Ike. "Girl, why don't you move them things down where you can reach?"

"Honey and Momma's teacups have to stay up high, where the boys can't get at them."

Ike smiled. Somehow, at the lowest points in his life, Emma always amused him.

Clyde and Claude came through the door dragging burlap bags. "Emma! Grampa brought carrots and potatoes!"

Emma ran to peek into the bags. "These are nice, Ike! Thank you! Boys, take these to the root cellar. Pack the carrots in sand and put the potatoes in an empty barrel. We'll use what's left of ours for planting."

The boys dragged their bags off to the root cellar while Emma made tea. She placed a cup in front of Ike and sat down across from him.

"I told Jack Hansen about Momma. He's going to

help us," she said.

Ike stared into his cup. "He told me. Be careful who you trust. Jack's a good man. He'll do what's right, but don't tell nobody else."

"I don't like lying."

Ike knew that. He also knew he didn't have to convince her it was necessary.

She got up from the table and walked to the door. "Supper is ready. I'll go tell Joe and the boys."

The sun was behind the trees when she walked outside. Cherry blossoms drifted down in the warm, springtime air. Tiny buds grew on her mother's roses. She found Tommy and the twins in the root cellar, packing away the things Ike brought.

She shouted down into the dim light. "Boys! Supper is ready. Come wash up."

They ran up the stairs and shot past her, racing toward the house. She hauled up the heavy door and dropped it into place. When it was covered with snow, it took all three of the boys to lift it. Joe was not in the field, so she walked out to the barn to find him brushing down Buck.

"Supper is ready."

He turned to her and smiled. "I'll be there soon as I brush down the team. They did good today. I was just following them around."

Emma knew that Joe was meticulous about caring for horses. She retrieved her milk stool—Tommy's now—from Susie's stall in back and placed it beside Jane. She stepped up on it to brush down their big mare.

"I'm glad you're here," she said.

Joe looked over Buck's back, and she nearly laughed at his pink cheeks.

"Me too." He shyly looked away.

After they brushed down the horses, Joe climbed up into the loft to fork down the hay, while Emma dumped buckets of grain into their troughs. Once the horses were squared away, they walked together back to the house.

****

That night, after she tucked the boys into bed, Emma lit a candle and went downstairs to stand in front of her father's desk. She opened the drawer and felt around in the dark. When she touched a smooth dome of metal, she pulled out a heavy sabot slug. She didn't know what terrible new thing might confront them, but she would carry this with her from now on. It was up to her to keep them safe.

Chapter Fifteen

The First World War taught Hoosiers how to manage large-scale organizations. Each township established a war council, and from a population of less than three million people, ninety-three thousand of Indiana's sons went to war. Governor Goodrich formed the Liberty Guards, whose purpose was to "stamp out treason and discover disloyalty."

Scotch-Irish, English, and Germans settled Owen County. During the war, the Liberty Guards kept a close eye on people with German surnames, denying them public office and expelling them from the teaching profession. The idea that you could not trust your neighbors and that patriotism had to be proven, was an important part of the success of the Klan in Indiana.

***

On a warm May evening, Florence Hammond approached the pulpit at the First Baptist Church with pride and purpose. She was a longstanding member of the Women's Christian Temperance Union. They met at the church every Wednesday night. She and the roughly thirty other members of the Owen County chapter, were flush with their victory of Prohibition. Having subdued the evil John Barleycorn, the ladies of the WCTU were eager to announce the new initiatives handed down from the national office in Evanston, Illinois. They were seeking the Prohibition of golf, movies, and baseball on the Sabbath—to increase attendance at church—as well as outlawing the use of tobacco on any day.

Florence was a beautiful woman. Her long dark hair was pinned up today, revealing her slender neck. She took the podium to polite applause from the other ladies and nodded.

"Thank you, ladies, you are too kind. Our agenda is to discuss how best to publicize our new initiatives, but first, we have some very special guests. I am pleased to present our esteemed guests, the twelve Terrors of the Invisible Order of the Klan!"

A murmur passed through the members of the WCTU. Twelve men dressed in white robes with red and yellow trim, entered through the doors of the church and marched together to the pulpit. White hoods hid their faces. Florence blushed and backed away from the lectern, proud of her husband's commanding and ghostly presence.

Cecil Hammond stood at the lectern and waited for the whispers to subside. Few people in Indiana were old enough to remember the days of the Underground Railroad and the Klan of the Reconstruction Era. In the new Klan of the Progressive Era, whipping and hanging on the basis of race alone was outlawed, unless ordered by the Exalted Cyclops of the local klanton. Besides, there was not a single person of color living in Owen County. Their new mandate was the enforcement of Prohibition and the persecution of Catholics.

Catholics drank sacramental wine, which was sinful and illegal. They pledged their allegiance to a foreign pope. Most people viewed the new wave of Catholic immigrants with suspicion and indignation. Outright hostility, however, did not arise until Catholic churches and schools began to appear in the Bible belt.

Most of the ladies in the pews knew the names of one or more of their hooded visitors. The WCTU did not accept Catholics, Jews, or women of color. Neither did they accept any woman not born in North America. The members of the

WCTU were mostly middle-class evangelical Protestants. The largely anti-foreign, anti-Catholic, and anti-Semitic nature of the temperance movement meant that the women who held office in the WCTU, often held office in the WKKK.

When the ladies fell silent, Cecil said, "Let us bow our heads and pray." He stood tall at the lectern, on tiptoe in fact, aroused by the sight of dozens of women bowed in submission before him. He puffed himself up and began to speak in his deepest voice.

"We proud members of the Klan pledge our lives to God, the Constitution of the United States, and the preservation of pure womanhood. We pledge our allegiance to God, America and none other, in Rome, or otherwise. We pray for the strength to pursue those who partake of demon rum. We pray for your blessings upon these pure and gentle women gathered here tonight. They have done more than their share. We pray that they find their just rewards in Heaven, your angels on Earth, Amen."

Cecil was gratified to hear the quiet echoes of amen from the ladies in the pews. His lovely wife had gotten down on her knees beside the lectern. He reached down and helped her to stand.

"Missus Hammond, please accept our prayers for continued success in all your endeavors and this modest gift."

He dramatically waved his arm, and one of his companions stepped forward, got down on one knee in front of Florence, and held up in his cupped hands—five crisp, new twenty-dollar bills.

Florence gasped in genuine surprise. It was five times more than she expected! She gathered up the bills, waved them in the air, and giggled. The ladies applauded.

She spoke the words she rehearsed for her husband a few hours earlier. "We ladies of the WCTU thank you for your generous gift, oh kind and noble strangers."

Cecil and his silent companions bowed as one to the ladies and marched in lock-step down the aisle and out the doors of the church. The last man out slammed the door behind him, and the ladies in the pews jumped in unison. Similar scenes played out in churches all across Indiana. It was official now. The Klan had inducted the White Caps into their ranks.

***

Emma sat in her bentwood chair and washed her face. Her washcloth left little soap bubbles on her brow, and she giggled when they popped and tickled. It had been a good day, long and tiring, but filled with rewards. She and the boys trekked through the woods to a sandy hillside covered with strawberries. They filled their baskets, picking every ripe berry, and she spent the remainder of the day making strawberry preserves. At supper, she surprised the boys and Joe, with strawberry shortcake and fresh whipped cream. It more than made up for the pork she placed on the table.

From now, until the first frost, work on the farm would consume them as they prepared for another winter. She felt great satisfaction in placing her jars of preserves on the shelves in their root cellar. Arranging them carefully in perfectly straight rows, she stood in the dim light and admired them. She finally managed to place something onto those shelves, instead of taking something down.

She washed her neck and arms and squeezed her washcloth to let warm water run down her back. Work on the farm went from sunup to sundown, and the longer days meant more hours of work. She didn't mind. She loved spring. Laughter and the sweet taste of strawberries filled this day. On every day in her memory, she has danced to the cadence of the seasons—sometimes in joy and sometimes in sorrow, but always in tune with nature.

Placing her washbowl on the floor, she soaked her feet, wiggling her toes in the slippery soapy water. She picked up her watch from her washstand and checked the time. It was nearly eight thirty, yet it was still light enough to see. On a winter's night, she would have been asleep more than an hour ago. She wondered if she would be aware of the longer days, if she did not know the time.

She dried herself thoroughly and slipped into a nightdress. The boys whispered outside her door, waiting for their nightly chapter. They were healthy, happy, and growing like weeds. With her mother and father gone, she had found somebody to love—a purpose. She took very good care of the people she loved. When she opened her door, she found them waiting for her to read to them.

***

The next morning, Emma awoke to the familiar chirps of sparrows. She rolled out of bed, wrapped herself in a blanket, and stood at her open window in the cool breeze. Only the brightest stars were still visible in the sky. Sunrise was minutes away. Joe would be here soon, so she dressed quickly and went downstairs to make breakfast, knocking on doors along the way.

By the time Tommy came down, she had already checked her roosting boxes and found enough eggs to make griddlecakes. The chicks Ike gave her were growing quickly, but it would be at least another two months before any of them laid eggs.

Last night, two of their sows gave birth in the farrowing pen. Today Joe would clip their needle teeth to prevent them from hurting each other or the sow's udders. When the sun appeared behind the trees, Joe topped the rise from the wagon trail.

Emma watched him ride into the barn. She would wait a few minutes before frying her griddlecakes, to give him a chance to brush down his horse. Having guessed that breakfast today would be a rare treat from the jar of molasses warming on the back of the woodstove, Tommy, Clyde, and Claude were already at the table. While they waited, they took turns stealing strawberries from a bowl whenever Emma turned her back.

When Joe came into the kitchen, she dropped hot griddlecakes onto his plate. The boys were already happily chewing away. Unable to speak, they all raised their forks in a silent salute and then pointed at their plates. Joe took off his hat and hung it beside the door.

Emma said, "Sit down, we have griddle cakes."

Joe sat. "I need to go into town today. There's a strand of wire rusted out in the pasture fence."

Emma served herself and sat down across from him. "We'll go too, if that's okay. I need a few things."

She pushed the warm jar of molasses across the table. Joe pushed it back. It made her smile, he always did that. She spooned some molasses onto her griddlecakes and pushed the jar back to him.

"I need thread and tea. We can just go to the mercantile," she said.

Joe took a bite of his griddlecakes and sat up straight. "These are good!"

While he chewed, he glanced across the table at Emma and went still. The sun was near the horizon, shining through the window and lighting up her blue eyes ringed with gold. He was fascinated by her eyes, yet embarrassed to be caught staring at them. It was impossible to look at her eyes without being seen. Emma smiled and he looked away. His cheeks turned bright pink.

Tommy mumbled through a mouthful of griddlecake, "Told ya."

After breakfast, Joe hitched Buck to the wagon and drove it up next to the house. Emma boosted the boys into the back and climbed up into the seat beside Joe. Whenever she found herself beside him, she was reminded of her mother's message to her. She was only twelve, but she had been in love with Joe since she was seven. She had never heard him raise his voice or say an unkind thing. He came and went with the rising and setting sun. He brought light and warmth, and when he left, the world turned cold and dark.

She watched him drive the wagon down the trail and turn onto the gravel road. Five years seemed like an eternity, but someday, she knew, she would unwrap that beautiful white dress hanging in her mother's wardrobe and stand beside Joe. Until that day, she would do her best to get them through.

When they came within sight of Ike's fields, Emma looked behind her to find the twins clinging to the sideboard, staring off into the distance at their grandfather's house. It had been two weeks since they last saw him. Emma turned back around to look up at Joe. He met her gaze and shook his head very slightly. His father had told him not to let Emma go there.

Ike's fields looked good—green and growing. When they passed the house, the animals were out in their enclosures. They did not appear to be distressed. Emma could see into the open barn. His truck was gone. Maybe they would run into him at the mercantile.

When they passed the schoolhouse, Emma turned to Joe. "Remember when we would trade lunch?"

He smiled. "I always had apples and you always had cherries."

Emma turned around. "You boys will go there this fall."

Tommy sat up straight and peered over the sideboard. "How come you can't just school us Emma?"

"You boys need proper schooling. There's more to learn there than what you're taught."

Tommy frowned up at his big sister. Sometimes the things she said made no sense at all.

When they rode up the hill into town, cars and wagons surrounded the mercantile, more than Emma had ever seen before.

"What's going on, Joe?"

"I don't know. It ain't a holiday or nothing."

They parked the wagon in a grassy clearing across the road, and Joe attached a long rope so Buck could graze. A train was stopped alongside the mercantile building. That wasn't unusual, but a large crowd had gathered on the platform.

Emma stood beside Joe and watched the crowd. She looked up at him. He shrugged. It looked as though half the town was there. She felt uneasy. Taking Joe's hand, she checked behind her to find the boys lined up the way they always were.

When they reached the top of the steps in the front of the building, Joe stopped by a large poster taped inside the window. He pointed to it, and Emma paused to read. In big block letters it said:

> **WANTED**
> **Homes For Orphan Children**
>
> A company of orphans, under the auspices of The Children's Aid Society of New York, will be in Spencer, Indiana on Thursday, May, 22. These children are available for placing out to caring parents able to provide good homes.

Orphans, that word drained the life from her. She and the boys were orphans, and keeping that secret ruled their lives. She looked up at Joe with tears in her eyes.

He swallowed hard. "It's an orphan train."

Emma never heard of such a thing.

Charles Loring Brace, a missionary dedicated to improving the lives of the thousands of orphaned children living on the streets of New York, organized the Orphan Trains in the middle of the nineteenth century. He reached the conclusion that orphanages were a cruel and ineffective way of dealing with the problem. Instead, he proposed to send them into the farmlands in the Midwest and place them with families who would welcome another child to assist with the never-ending work of running a farm.

At each stop, the children departed the train, and their escort arranged them in a line. Local residents and farmers inspected the children. Some of the prospective parents looked into their mouths and felt their arms and legs to make sure the child was sound and healthy. Train depots were often the place where brothers and sisters saw each other for the last time. Families seldom took more than one child. There was no means of legal adoption, these children were simply taken to new homes and given new names. Often, they went to good homes, but not always.

The war and the flu filled the streets of New York with tens of thousands of orphaned and abandoned children. More than eighty children climbed down from the train beside the mercantile and lined up on the platform. Many of the older boys and girls held infants or toddlers. They were all dressed in new clothes, wrinkled now from the long trip, and each of them carried identical little cardboard suitcases.

The crowd buzzed with excited chatter while they examined their prospective children. Emma made her way through the gathering, pulling Joe along with her, while Tommy, Clyde, and Claude stayed in line behind her. When they reached the front, she felt as if she was going to be sick. It was their eyes! She had seen that look in her own eyes and those of Tommy and the twins. Orphans, she thought, could recognize one another by their haunted eyes.

A well-dressed, matronly lady stepped out in front of the children and raised her hands in the air. The noise from the crowd subsided.

"Thank you all for coming. As you already know, these children are available for placing out to good, Christian homes. Feel free to speak to them, but please refrain from taking a child without first entering your name into the register."

An older man, dressed in a gray suit, stepped forward and pointed to a lithesome, dark-haired girl, around sixteen years old. "I'll take that pretty little thing. I need a girl to keep the house."

Their escort turned to him. "Absolutely not! These are children, not house servants. Begone with you, sir! Girls will not be given into the care of men unaccompanied by their wives."

The man scowled and stormed off. A handful of other men followed him.

***

Florence Hammond stood among that crowd of people, horrified to learn that such men existed in their community. Children were meant to be cherished. She has been married to Cecil for nearly six years and God has not yet blessed her with a child. She considered the children, lined up before her, and her gaze fell upon a red-haired little girl holding the hand of a small boy. She was desperate for a daughter, someone she could truly love. She whispered into her husband's ear.

***

Emma trembled in fear. If anyone ever discovered their secret, then she and her boys might end up standing in that line of frightened children. Seeing them examined like livestock made her aware of how tenuous her grasp was on their farm and their lives together. She wanted to run away, but she felt connected to the children on the platform. If she took three steps, she would be one of them. Joe squeezed her hand. Emma looked up at him.

He said, "Let's go. We don't need to be here."

Men and women moved along the line, briefly speaking to a child and then moving on to the next one.

What would Momma do?

She had no idea. The circumstances were more horrible than anything she could imagine. Joe pulled at her hand, and she turned to walk away.

A tiny voice called out, "Anna!"

Emma whipped around to see who called out her mother's name. The escort held onto a small boy around four years old, while a girl of perhaps ten was dragged away by a man in a policeman's uniform.

The girl looked up at the man who had her by the arm and said through tears, "He's my brother! You have to take both of us!"

The man continued to drag her forward. "The boy is sick. Besides, Florence wants a girl."

A beautiful woman Emma had never seen before leaned over the young girl. "Come with us, dear. I'm sure your brother will find a good Christian home."

The girl struggled to escape from the policeman's grip. Her long auburn hair fell into her face and she screamed, "No! He needs me!"

That did it for Emma. She pulled her hand out of Joe's and ran forward. The boys converged on Joe and hung onto his shirt.

She ran up to the matronly escort, still holding the squirming little boy. "Brothers and sisters have to stay together!"

The escort gave her a pitying look. "It's just not possible, daughter. This train will not return to New York empty. The boy has had pneumonia. He will likely ride it the whole way."

Emma balled up her fists and screamed, "I am Anna Taylor's daughter! God would never grant a daughter to a mother as cruel as you!"

The crowd fell silent. A few men chuckled at the horrified look on the escort's face.

Emma heard a whimper of pain and spun around to see that the policeman had the girl by the back of the neck. He forced her down to her knees. A crucifix on a silver chain fell out of the front of her dress. She grasped it with her left hand, and with her right, she made the sign of the cross.

The policeman's wife stood up straight and backed away with a horrified expression. "She's a Papist." Then she shook her head, as if waking from a trance. "Let her go, Cecil! You're hurting her!"

"She's not going anywhere until I say so. Calm down, girl! I ain't hurting you!"

Joe struggled to take two steps toward Emma, while three terrified boys tried to hold him back. He knew what was about to happen, but he was too late. Emma took four long strides and kicked the policeman in the shin with an audible thunk. He howled and let go of the girl.

The young girl jumped to her feet and dashed toward her brother. She did not stop to plead her case, she tackled him. Together, they rolled off the platform and disappeared.

***

Florence realized that what she just witnessed was a heroic act of love. Was she really so thoughtless as to try and separate them? Her certainty that she stood upon moral high ground evaporated. She felt as if she was falling.

She watched her husband pull his revolver and grab Emma by the hair. An instant later, a small boy slammed into him and pummeled him in the ribs. He pushed the boy away with the barrel of his gun and looked up into Joe's face, only inches away.

Joe stood ramrod straight, his fists clenched and his eyes glittering with rage. "Let her go."

Earl Anderson appeared behind Joe. "Let her go, Cecil. That's Anna Taylor's daughter."

Murmurs of, "Anna Taylor's daughter" echoed through the crowd. A dozen angry men surrounded Cecil, while he clutched Emma's hair in his fist.

Florence watched it all happen in slow motion. That small boy was trying to free his sister from the painful grip of a fully-grown man armed with a gun—her husband. It was another selfless act of love. Once again, children were defending other children from the cruel acts of her and her husband. When did they become so evil?

She ran forward and grabbed her husband's arm, trying to pull him off the girl. "Cecil! You let her go this instant!"

Realizing he had gone too far, Cecil released Emma's hair and holstered his pistol. "I'm sorry, Flo. It's a reflex. I can't control it."

Emma was on her knees, crying. A crowd of angry men surrounded Cecil, while his lovely wife got down on her knees in front of Emma.

"I'm so sorry. Please forgive us," she said.

Emma looked up at her, and Florence placed her hand over her heart. Golden halos encircling deep blue, glistening with tears, transfixed her. She reached out to take Emma's hands in her own. It all made sense to her now. They had stumbled upon a band of angels—and molested them.

Tommy stood beside Emma with tears streaming down his face. He smoothed down her hair. "Are you okay?"

She sniffed and nodded.

He turned and made his way through the men surrounding Cecil Hammond. Unnoticed, he took careful aim and punched Cecil in the testicles as hard as he could. Cecil grabbed his crotch and doubled over. He was now face to face with Tommy.

Tommy poked him in the forehead with a little finger. "You made Emma cry, so I made you cry."

The men surrounding Cecil burst into laughter. They led Tommy away before he got into further trouble, slapping him on the back and making him stumble.

Earl Anderson grasped him by the shoulder. "Your

pa would be real proud of you, boy."

Tommy wiped away his tears and smiled. Then he ran back to Emma, unaware that he just saved Cecil Hammond from a well-deserved beating.

Joe stood over Cecil, watching him cradle his balls and moan. He shook his head. "I shoulda seen that coming."

He nudged his way through the line of children at the edge of the platform and looked down between the platform and the train. The girl and her brother were gone. They must have crawled under the train.

When he turned to look for Emma, she was still on her knees. The policeman's wife was still holding her hands and gazing into her eyes. He walked up behind Emma and helped her to her feet. He had to pull her away from the woman holding her hands.

When Joe pulled Emma away, Florence reached out to her with an expression of terrible loss. There were tears on her face. She pressed her hands together and begged God to forgive her.

Joe led Emma away from the crowd, while a dozen men searched under and around the train for Anna and her brother. He walked her quickly back to the wagon and lifted her up into the seat. The boys climbed up the wheel and over the side while Joe attached Buck's harness.

He jumped up into the seat beside Emma. "I'm taking you home. I'll come back for the wire tomorrow."

She nodded her head and wiped her tears on the back of her arm. Looking back over her shoulder at the train beside the platform, she hated it. She never imagined so much misery could be gathered together in one place. The men searching under the train fanned out, calling, "Anna!"

Every time she heard someone call out her mother's name, Emma felt a chill. She stood up and looked in every direction. She knew what Momma would do now.

She took a deep breath and shouted out, "I am Anna Taylor's daughter!"

She looked all around, and after a few seconds, she called out again, "I am Anna Taylor's daughter!"

There was a wagon shed a little farther down the road, where people could rest their horses during prolonged visits to the mercantile. A small face peeked around the door. Emma jumped down and ran for the wagon shed.

***

When Anna Kennedy saw Emma running her way, her heart jumped into her throat. Her little brother was half-buried in the straw behind her, gasping for breath. He ran as far as he could and then she carried him. They could not run any further. Hiding under the straw was their only protection.

Emma ran into the wagon shed and pulled the girl away from the door. They stood facing each other in the dim light. Anna had long, reddish brown hair, delicate features and large hazel eyes, crinkled in fear.

"Thank you." Tears ran down Anna's cheeks. "I don't know what to do."

The young boy wheezed and gasped for breath. Emma dropped down beside him and lifted up the hem of her dress to wipe the sweat from his face. He had dark circles under big brown eyes. He reminded her of Tommy, when he was that age.

Joe appeared in the doorway. Tommy, Clyde, and Claude stood behind him.

Emma looked up at them with an expression of grim determination. "Go get the wagon. We're taking them with us."

Joe stepped out of the sunlight, into the shadowed

interior. "Emma, we can't."

She stood up, walked past him and shouted, "Buck!"

A few seconds later, Buck's massive shadow appeared outside the door. Emma stepped out into the sunlight, took him by the halter, and led him into the shed.

Anna was on her knees beside her brother. Emma touched her shoulder. "You can come with us. Brothers and sisters stay together."

Anna looked up at her. "Who are you?"

"My name is Emma and I will take care of you."

Chapter Sixteen

Overruling Joe's objections, Emma concealed Anna and her brother under a tarp in the back of the wagon. They rode out of town without any trouble, right past some of the men who were searching for them. Once they were on the gravel road near the schoolhouse, Emma climbed over the seat into the back of the wagon.

She lifted the tarp. "You can come out now."

Anna threw off the tarp and sat up. He brother was breathing easy now. He sat up beside her and held on to her dress with one hand. Emma smiled; the boys did too.

"What's your name?" she asked him.

He looked up at his sister and she nodded. He turned back to Emma. "Christopher."

"That's a fine name. My name's Emma."

He nodded. "I heard."

The boys sat with their backs against the sideboard. They had never shared the back of the wagon with strangers.

Emma pointed to each of the boys. "That's Tommy, Clyde, and Claude. And that grumpy guy driving is Joe."

Anna's eyes locked onto Clyde and Claude. "You're twins!"

Clyde said, "We are—?" He glanced over at his brother. "Hey! That's me!"

Claude just smiled, but Tommy laughed out loud. "Clyde is supposed to wear green suspenders, but they take turns being Clyde."

Anna looked out over the side of the wagon. The fields were green with newborn crops. Pale green, fresh, new leaves filled the trees on the hills surrounding the flat farmland. Pink redbuds and white dogwoods stood out among them.

"Where are we?" she asked.

Emma said, "Owen County, our farm is just a mile or so ahead."

Anna turned to her. "What state?"

The depth of their disorientation finally registered with Emma. "Indiana."

Gazing off into the distance, Anna said, "Indiana, I've heard of it. It's so green. There are no buildings."

When they passed Ike's farm, Emma saw that his truck was still gone. Where was he?

Joe turned around. "There's a car coming."

Anna did not have to be told to hide. She ducked down and pulled Christopher down beside her. Once the car passed, she raised her head to peek cautiously over the sideboard.

Emma said, "Don't worry, we're almost home."

That word registered with Anna—home. She gathered her little brother into her arms and looked about fearfully.

Emma fought to hold back tears. Anna and Christopher were the very image of herself and Tommy, less than a year ago. Their anxiety reminded her of that terrible day, when they sat in the swing in their front yard, clinging to each other in pain and fear.

When Buck turned off the gravel road and started up the wagon trail, Emma patted Anna's arm. "You're safe now. We're home."

When they topped the hill, Yellowwood Farm was laid out below them. Anna gazed down into the valley in awe. "It's beautiful. I've never been to a farm."

Joe drove the wagon down the hill and parked it next to the house. They all climbed down and gathered beside the wagon, shyly exchanging glances.

Joe said, "Emma, we have to tell Pa."

"I know. I plan to," she said.

In fact, she has planned nothing. From one second to the next, she was operating solely on the basis of what she thought her mother would do. She never saw her mother kick a policeman in the shin, but she was certain that under the same circumstances, she would have done it.

Before they went any further, there was one important fact Anna and her brother had to know. It was hard for Emma to say, but it was only fair she tell them. She turned to Anna. "We're all orphans here, except for Joe."

Anna went stock-still. "Is this an orphanage?"

Joe said, "No, of course not!" After a moment's consideration, he was not so sure.

Emma said, "Tommy is my brother. Our father died in the war and Momma died from influenza last September. We can't let anybody find out, or they might take this farm away from us. Everybody thinks Momma is just sick. I'm not old enough to own land in Indiana."

"How old are you?"

"I'll be thirteen next month. When I'm eighteen, we'll be safe."

"What about the twins?"

Claude said, "Let me tell her."

Emma was surprised. She suspected that those green suspenders were still traded on a regular basis. Even so, it was unusual for the boy not wearing them to speak at all.

He said, "Ma and Pa died of the flu. Grampa came and took us to his house. He buried Ma and Pa. I always pray for them when we go by there. Emma taught us how to pray."

Emma was certain now that this was in fact Claude. Between the two of them, Claude was the spiritual one. She never heard him say so many words at once.

"Their grandfather knows about Momma and so does Joe's father. They promised to help us. We can't let anybody else know."

Claude looked down at his feet, shuffled them in the dirt and said, "It's nice here, better than at Grampa's. He says we're lucky Emma wants us."

"We're not entirely safe. Someday, people might come and take this farm away from us. If you want, Joe can take you back to town."

Anna looked up at the big house, nicer than any she had ever set foot in. She looked around at the green fields and the trees. The air was crystal clear and filled with birdsong. Lastly, she looked closely at each of the children standing around her. They were healthy and happy. This place was so clean and pure, it seemed like heaven.

Dropping to her knees in front of Emma, Anna grabbed her hands. "Please let us stay. I beg you!"

Rocked to her core, Emma pulled Anna to her feet and held her hands. She tried not to cry, but her face contorted and she bawled. "Don't cry! You can live here if you want! We can be sisters!"

Anna sobbed and emphatically nodded her head. "Thank you."

Hearing a quick inhalation of breath, Emma glanced up at Joe. There were tears in his eyes! In all the time she had known him, she never saw him shed a tear. He turned away from her and mumbled something about the wagon. Taking Buck by the halter, he led him towards the barn.

Feeling that this occasion needed to be solemnly sealed, Emma sniffled and said, "Everybody follow me." She headed up the hill.

The yellowwood tree was in bloom. Foot-long clusters of white flowers with tiny yellow centers cascaded from the branches. As they approached it, the scent was soothing. When Emma got down on her knees beside the grave, the other children did too. Together, they straightened the stones that spelled out, Anna Taylor, and pulled up the grass and weeds encroaching upon the bare earth.

Emma pressed her hands together and bowed her head. "Lord, it's us again. We thank you for bringing us Anna and Christopher, our new brother and sister. Please shine your warm light upon our mothers and fathers. Tell them we are all together and we are well and we are thinking of them. Let our love for them bind us together. Amen."

There was a quiet chorus of amen spoken all together, and Anna made the sign of the cross. When they stood up, they traded shy smiles and glances.

Anna said, "That was a fine blessing."

Tommy asked Anna, "How old are you?"

"Ten. Chris is five," she said.

Emma thought he was small for five years old. She wondered how long he'd been sick.

Tommy said, "I'm seven, my birthday was in February. Clyde and Claude are eight."

Looking up at his sister, Tommy asked, "Is Chris my brother now?"

Emma smiled and ruffled his hair. "We're all brothers and sisters now."

Tommy walked over next to Chris, who was hanging on to his sister's dress and stood up straight. He was a good five inches taller than Chris.

"I been the littlest for a long time. Now it's your turn. Don't worry none though, everybody is the littlest at first."

Anna touched one of the long white strings of blossoms and asked Emma, "What kind of tree is this?"

"It's a yellowwood tree. Momma loved this tree. She

named our farm for it."

She pointed to the barn. The words, Yellowwood Farm, were painted on the side. "Can you read?"

Anna said proudly, "I went to Holy Cross for four years. I can read."

Tommy tugged at Emma's dress. "We're hungry. Can we have strawberries? Can we? Please?"

Emma had no idea what time it was. Their traumatic trip into town completely disrupted the rhythm of her day. She opened her watch to find it was past noon.

"You and the boys go see Joe. Ask him what needs to be done. Anna and I will make lunch."

Tommy ran back to the other boys, and they all ran down the hill with Chris trailing after them.

Emma walked down the hill with Anna at her side. "I hope you like ham. We have it almost every day."

Anna stopped in her tracks. Emma went back to her. "Are you okay?"

"Truly now, do you eat ham every day?"

Emma laughed and said, "Soon enough, you'll be wishing for something else."

Anna had a look of wonder on her face. "I've wished often enough for a crust of bread. I cannot imagine having ham every day."

Emma felt shamed for complaining. Her mother would have just eaten the pork and thanked God with a blessing. She vowed to be more humble, but if a turkey or a deer wandered into their fields, then all bets were off!

When they entered the kitchen, Anna looked around in amazement. "*Begorrah!*"

Emma gave her a puzzled look. "What's *begorrah* mean?"

Anna blushed. "It means by, ah, well, it's something

we say rather than take the Lord's name in vain."

"Oh! We say by golly, means the same thing though."

Anna stood in front of the woodstove. "This stove is so big! Everything here is big—this house, even your horse. That's the biggest horse I've ever seen!"

Anna's arms were thin and her complexion pale. Her dress hung loosely upon her. She was a pretty girl, but timid. She would reach out to touch something, and just before she made contact, pull her hand back.

Emma said, "We have to figure out where you'll sleep. Can you cook?"

Anna clasped her hands behind her back and rocked on the balls of her feet. "Oh yes! Ma taught me."

Peeking through the doorway into the parlor, Anna saw an enormous stone fireplace at one end of a large room, comfortably furnished with padded chairs and a conversation table. A rocking chair sat in front of the fireplace. She leaned in for a better look and saw two big windows, swung open, that flooded the room with light and the scent of cherry blossoms.

Tears filled her eyes. "It cannot be true that we are to live here."

She buried her face in her hands and began to sob. Emma understood why she was crying and embraced her until she quieted. She held her in silence for a few moments longer, stroking her hair.

Two barely audible words rose up from that tangle of tears and auburn hair. "Thank you."

***

Cecil Hammond sat in the driver's seat of his Ford Coupe with his beautiful bride beside him. She wasn't speaking to him. According to her, he molested an angel.

"For God's sake, Flo, that girl attacked me!"

Florence made a face that indicated she'd swallowed a bug and turned away. He had never seen her so angry. In the space of ten seconds, he was kicked in the shin and punched in the nethers. Those kids were lucky he hadn't shot one of them—purely by reflex of course.

His injuries were not severe, or even detectable, but serious damage had been inflicted upon Cecil Hammond. In front of half the town, he manhandled two young girls and stuck the barrel of his gun into the chest of a small boy. He had whipped men for far less. In fact, he thought he might be whipped himself for what he did today. Dues-paying Klan members were seldom expelled, but it was likely he would lose his title of Terror, one of the twelve avenging archangels in the local klanton.

Cecil dearly loved being a Terror. It meant his hand held the whip. After long deliberation, he was selected because he owned a pistol. Not many men did in this part of the country. Most men owned rifles or shotguns and used them often—for hunting. Pistols, on the other hand, were useless for hunting. Their only practical application was killing people.

When he pulled up in front of Sally Ingram's house, Florence jumped out of the car. She ran daintily along the stone footpath and threw her arms around Sally's neck just as she opened the door.

He watched from the car, while Florence gestured and spoke to her friend. She poked herself in the chest with her finger and reached up to grab her own hair. Both women turned to glare at him. They hitched up their dresses, stuck their noses in the air, and marched into the house.

Cecil sighed and slid down in his seat, trying to get comfortable. It looked as though he was going to be here awhile. His nice comfortable life had been turned upside-down.

***

Emma made a big lunch of sliced ham, boiled potatoes, and carrots, to celebrate Anna and Christopher's arrival. Anna followed her closely the whole time and happily took over when she saw Emma doing something she could do. She peeled potatoes, turned the ham in the skillet, and nearly cried again at the sight of fresh strawberries.

The screen door squeaked open and the boys swirled into the room like leaves in a strong wind. Emma chased them away from her bowl of strawberries and herded them over to the sink to wash up.

Christopher ran to his sister and grabbed her dress with wet hands. "Anna! I rode a pig!"

She knelt down to dry his hands with her dress. "You did!"

He wheezed and caught his breath. "It was fun! You have to try it."

Joe came through the door and hung his hat on a peg. "Them boys are gonna run all the fat off the livestock."

Emma was laying out plates, when she saw that they were out of chairs. They were seven now and their table only had chairs for six. Her father's desk chair was similar to those around her table, except it had arms. She ran off to return moments later, scooting it through the parlor.

Once everyone was seated at the table, Emma shushed the boys and said, "I think we should say a blessing for lunch today. We have more to be thankful for than we know."

Christopher sat up straight and looked at the food on the table. "Is all this for us?"

Emma said, "We don't usually have such a big lunch,

but today is special. This is your home now. Anna, would you say the blessing?"

Anna was still unable to imagine that this was her home. She struggled to believe. "I know a prayer from school. It would be right for us."

Emma pressed her hands together and bowed her head. The boys did the same.

Anna looked around the table at her new family. She took a deep breath, bowed her head, and hoped she could remember her prayer.

"Hail, Holy Mary, mother of Jesus, our life, our sweetness and our hope. To thee do we cry, orphan children of Eve. To thee do we send up our sighs. Turn then, Holy Mother, cast your eyes of mercy upon us. And after our long exile, lead us home. O clement, O loving, O sweet Virgin Mary. Amen."

They raised their heads slowly and stared at Anna in awe. She had struck a solemn chord in every one of them.

Except for Christopher, he was in awe of the ham. "Can I have some ham now?"

Joe was more affected by Anna's prayer than any of the children. He tried to wipe away a tear, under the guise of rubbing his nose, and pushed the platter of ham in front of Christopher. "We take turns here. Today is your turn to go first."

He felt changed. He never cried. He was, in fact, somewhat famous for it among the members of his family. And now, twice in one day, he had fought off tears. That phrase, 'orphan children of Eve,' was still ringing in his mind.

***

The boys spent the afternoon weeding the garden and helping Joe apply iodine to the umbilical scars of the newborn piglets. Joe was always kind to the boys, but now he felt different. He felt responsible for them. Emma, Anna, and these boys, chasing squealing piglets in every direction, did something to him today he could not put into words. Without him realizing it, they connected his heart to his mind.

***

Anna was still gasping at the wonders she found in the Taylor house. It was so big! Emma took her upstairs and showed her the spare bedroom. There was a double bed, wardrobe, dresser, and washstand, untouched for years.

Emma swung open the window to air it out and said, "This can be your room. Christopher can sleep with you if you want, but there are twin beds in Tommy's room."

Anna looked around. "It's so big."

Emma smiled. Anna had said that at least a dozen times. She opened a cedar chest at the foot of the bed and pulled out sheets and blankets. Seeing what she was doing, Anna hurried over to help her.

While they stretched the sheet tight and tucked in the corners, Anna said, "Truly, is this to be my room?"

"If you want," Emma said.

"Our whole family lived in three rooms. Altogether, they would fit in this one!"

Holding a pillow under her chin, Emma saw that Anna was struggling again—fighting back tears. She yanked the pillowcase over the pillow and tossed it at the head of the bed. Taking Anna by the shoulders, she sat her down on the bed and sat down beside her. She put her arm around her, and Anna leaned into her, quietly weeping and wiping her eyes.

Emma said, "I promise, this is your home now. This is your room and we are your family."

Anna looked into her lap, clasped her hands together, and shook with pent up tears. "Are you an angel?"

Emma was shocked that anyone could think such a thing. "No! Of course not."

Without looking up, Anna said, "Your eyes, you have an angel's eyes."

Emma smiled and said, "I have my mother's eyes, so I guess you're right on that account. How did you come to be on that train?"

Anna wrung her hands and tried not to cry. "Da died in the war. Ma and me sewed to pay the rent, but then she got sick and—" She broke down and sobbed. *"Ní raibh mé in ann a shábháil di."*

Emma held her while she quaked in her arms and whispered to her, "I don't understand."

Anna rubbed her eyes. "I'm sorry. Sometimes I don't know what I'm saying. When I was little, Da and Ma mostly spoke Irish at home. When Chris was born, we mostly spoke English."

Emma asked, "Are you from Ireland?"

Anna nodded her head. "We came here when I was a baby, I don't remember. Chris was born here. When Ma died, I did na know what to do. Me and Chrissy stayed in the front room, but there were rats, they—"

Emma held Anna while she moaned, and tears came to her own eyes. She knew that moment of terrible loss and uncertainty. What she could not imagine was the horror of seeing her mother's body mutilated by rats.

Anna took a moment and then tried to finish her story. "Early in the morning, when the flu was bad, men would come down the street and shout to bring out the dead. We could na carry her down the stairs, me and Chris. Our neighbors did na answer the door. I ran down to the street and begged the men to come and take her, but they would not.

A tear rolled down Emma's cheek. "The twins' grandfather helped me bury Momma. I will always be grateful for that."

After a few moments, Anna said, "The next day, when they came, I took down Da's violin and traded the men to come and take Ma."

She cried out, *"Ní raibh siad milis léi!"*

Then she gasped and took a deep breath. "I mean—they were not gentle with her. They threw her on a pile of others and took her away."

Emma and Anna clung to each other in tears, sharing a tragic bond.

***

Supper that night was a celebration. Christopher bonded to Tommy, who was thrilled to have a little brother. The seven of them sat around a table laid with all the same foods they had for lunch, with the addition of fresh bread and string beans.

When Emma glanced around the table, they quieted down. Joe sat at the head of the table, alarmed to see so many children arrayed before him.

Emma said, "Anna, can you say another blessing?"

Anna was still awestruck by the events of the day, still nervous and uncertain, but now she understood why this place existed. Anna Taylor had raised her children well.

She said, "There is a blessing, but I cannot remember it all."

Pressing her hands together, Emma said, "Just say what's in your heart. That's what Momma always did."

Anna nodded and bowed her head. She struggled to recall her prayer, but could not, so she looked into her heart.

"Father in Heaven, please keep us, your children, faithful to your calling. Let us become one family in your service. May we live as your children, as Jesus once lived. And please Lord, keep our secret, so we can be brothers and sisters. Amen."

Anna raised her head and smiled. It wasn't the prayer she learned years ago, and she was unaccustomed to making up a blessing, but it felt right.

Tommy raised his head and gazed at her, wide-eyed. "Golly! You pray as good as Emma."

All of them burst into laughter, except Joe. His dark brows knitted together. He watched Anna laugh, the first time he saw her do so. That skinny little red-haired girl, he thought, contained a powerful spirit.

Chapter Seventeen

Emma awoke to the chirping of sparrows. The sun was still below the horizon, gray light filled her room. She sat up, stretched, and saw Anna asleep beside her. Her auburn hair covered her face.

Christopher eagerly agreed to sleep in Tommy's room. He viewed it as an adventure. For the first time in his life, he had his very own bed! Tommy was puffed up with the important duties of an older brother, imparting his wisdom and such.

Anna, on the other hand, was too terrified to sleep in that huge room alone. Last night, she knocked softly on Emma's open door and asked if they could sleep together.

They talked quietly well into the night, unburdening themselves of the hardships of the past year. Anna told her that after their mother's death, she managed to pay the rent by sewing, taking on the work her mother had done. She barely earned enough to get them through the winter. They struggled to buy food and coal for their stove.

In February, both Anna and Chris grew sick. For two weeks, she was unable to sew. To pay their rent, she was forced to give the landlord her mother's sewing machine—the last thing they owned of any value. Two weeks after that, the police came to evict them.

In the spring of 1918, ten million people lived in the city of New York. By the spring of 1919, half a million of them were killed by the flu. Gatherings of more than ten people were outlawed. Schools, churches, and theaters were closed.

Tens of thousands of children were abandoned on the streets, Anna and Christopher among them. Children just as desperate as they, but bigger and stronger, robbed them of the few possessions they carried in their arms. They ran away from everyone they saw, hiding in alleys and abandoned buildings—eventually on rooftops, huddled next to warm chimneys.

Anna earned a little money by singing. Singing girls were a common sight on the streets of New York. She learned to stand on corners in good neighborhoods, Irish neighborhoods, and sing the songs her mother taught her in Gaelic.

She and Christopher would stand holding hands while she sang. Passersby, wearing white masks, dropped change into a tin can she placed on the sidewalk, a little distance away, because the people did not want to come near them. On good days, a policeman sent them on their way. On bad days, the gangs of other desperate children took her handfuls of coins.

They lived that way for weeks. When Anna said she did not know how long, Emma recognized that feeling of living outside of time. Again, she counted her blessings. She and the boys suffered sadness and loss, but Anna and her brother endured far more. Exposed to the depravity and cruelty of life, they had grown fearful and cautious.

It was little more than a week ago, that a woman approached them while Anna stood singing on a corner. Anna tried to run, but when she pulled on Christopher's hand, he sank down onto the sidewalk and told her he could not run anymore. The Children's Aid Society took them in.

Emma reached out to brush Anna's hair away from her face. The moment she touched her, Anna instantly came awake and sat up moaning. She felt all around her with a terrified expression, saying, "Chris? Chris?"

Seeing Emma sitting beside her, she calmed down. She reached out to touch Emma's arm. *"Shíl mé go raibh sé ina aisling.*"

Emma said, "Good morning, sister."

Anna yawned, smiled, and pushed her hair out of her face. "Good morning, thank you, sister."

Climbing out of bed, Emma said, "You can sleep if you want. You must be tired after, well, after everything."

Anna climbed out behind her. Emma's nightdress was so big on her it touched the floor.

"I want to learn how to be a farmer today."

Emma smiled. "Okay, but mostly it's just cooking and cleaning up after the boys. Joe does the hard work around here."

She dug around in her wardrobe and then turned to go through the cedar chest at the foot of her bed. She pulled out a blue dress, only a little tattered, and a pair of white cotton bloomers.

"We have to find a way to buy you some clothes. I've outgrown these, so you should be able to wear them."

"Are we so rich that we buy clothes?"

Emma realized Anna and her namesake were very much alike. "You're right. Joe has to buy some wire today. I'll ask him to get us some cloth and thread."

When Emma sat down to change into her clothes, Anna sat down beside her and pulled her nightdress over her head.

Emma gasped. There was a bruise half the size of a dinner plate on Anna's back. "How did this happen?" she asked.

Anna reached around to touch the bruise gingerly and said, "When we fell by the train."

"Why didn't you tell me?"

"It's nothing. I can work. I want to learn farming today."

Emma helped her get a camisole over her head. Now that she was aware of the injury, she could see the telltale signs when Anna pulled on her clothes and leaned over to tie her shoes, but she did not complain, and she was bursting with joy and enthusiasm.

"Will you teach me to make strawberry jam? Tommy says you make the best."

Emma thought they should make another trip to the strawberry patch to collect the ripened berries. They were nearing the time when the raspberries would ripen, then blackberries. With two more mouths to feed, they should take advantage of every opportunity to stock their root cellar.

She said, "We can go and pick strawberries. We should pick them while we can."

The sky was turning blue. The sun would be up soon. Emma sat down at her washstand in her bentwood chair and took out her hairbrush.

Anna ran around behind her. "Can I brush your hair? I used to brush Ma's."

Anna took the brush and stood behind her, gently brushing her hair. Emma closed her eyes and sighed. It was a feeling she almost forgot. Her mother used to brush her hair. Then she would press her cheek against Emma's and they would look at each other in her mirror—mother and daughter, nearly identical, their blue eyes ringed with gold.

On their way down the hall, Emma knocked on the boys' doors. Anna stayed close on her heels, still awestruck by her new home. Knowing now the things she had been through, Emma was amazed at her cheerful demeanor.

Emma only looked at the woodstove, and Anna ran to fill the basket with wood to start the fire. When she went out to gather the eggs, Anna watched her check under one hen and checked the other four hens herself, lifting them gently without ruffling a feather. She insisted upon carrying the basket with their three precious eggs.

Tommy came down with Chris, and Emma saw that he managed to find some old clothes for him. The pants were rolled up, but the shirt fit decently. Anna and Chris were still wearing the dress shoes they were given by the Children's Aid Society. Not ideal for working on a farm, but at the moment, they are all they have.

Tommy picked up his milk pail. "Morning, Emma. Morning, Anna."

Chris ran to Anna and grabbed her dress. "We're gonna go and see a cow. I never seen a cow before."

Anna said, "That sounds like fun."

He turned and ran after Tommy, slipping through the screen door before it closed.

When a crescent of the sun appeared over the horizon, Emma left Anna tending a pot of bubbling oatmeal and stood in front of the window over the sink. Joe appeared on the wagon trail, and his father rode beside him.

Emma was dreading this. She respected Jack Hansen. He was a good man, but he was practical and disciplined. She did not think he would approve of what she had done.

"Joe's here. I'm going out to the barn," she said.

Anna turned to her with a smile. "I like Joe. He's quiet."

Emma walked out to the barn to find Joe and his father brushing down their horses. Joe's father must plan to be here awhile to unsaddle his horse.

"Good morning, Joe, Mister Hansen."

They turned to her. Beneath his black, broad-brimmed hat, Jack Hansen looked furious. Joe looked subdued.

Emma stuck out her lower lip and prepared to do

battle. She had made up her mind. Nothing could convince her to allow Anna and Chris to be taken off this farm.

Jack tossed his brush over his shoulder, and Joe fumbled to catch it. He approached Emma and stood with his hands on his hips. Jack Hansen was an impressive looking man, tall and lean with gray hair at his temples.

"I hear you kicked a deputy sheriff."

Emma resisted the urge to take a step back. "Momma would have kicked him too!"

Jack took off his hat and slapped it on his thigh to get the dust off. Joe kept brushing down the horses, nervously glancing at Emma. He looked worried.

Jack said, "I hear Tommy punched that deputy in his sensitive area."

Emma looked puzzled. "I don't know what you mean."

Jack's eyebrows arched. "You know, in his private parts."

Emma was shocked. "He did! I didn't know!"

Joe shooed the horses through the gate to the pasture and walked past his father to stand beside Emma. That he was standing beside her was not lost on Emma. She looked up at him and smiled.

He said, "It should have been me, Pa. I should have broken that bastard's neck. You would have done it."

Jack gave his son a withering stare, but instead of slumping down and looking at the ground, as he usually did, Joe stood up straight and looked him in the eye. Jack didn't know if he liked that or not.

Chris ran out from the back of the barn and went straight to Joe. He grabbed his hand and said, "Joe! Joe! Guess where milk comes from."

Joe placed a hand on his shoulder. "I don't know.

Where does milk come from?"

Wheezing and puffing, he said, "You would na believe me if I told you."

Then he ran through the barn doors toward the house, calling out, "Anna! Anna!"

Jack tried not to smile, but he did. Then he stuck a frown back on. "Emma, you can't take in every orphaned child."

She said, "It's been decided. Anna and Chris live here now. They've been through horrible things. I'm going to take care of them."

"What if that deputy comes looking for them?"

"Nobody sets foot on my land if I don't want them to."

He gave her a hard look and said, "You don't own this land."

Emma's resolve melted away. Her lower lip trembled and she burst into tears. She put her face in her hands and ran for the house.

Jack was still scowling, frustrated by the whole situation.

Joe turned to face his father. "If Tommy finds out you made Emma cry, he's gonna punch you in the nuts."

Then he turned and walked out into the early morning light, leaving his father astonished.

Jack Hansen looked up into the rafters. "Lord, why do you get me mixed up in these things?"

Looking into his heart to find the answer, he heard the Almighty chuckle. He hung his head and headed for the house.

When Jack walked into the kitchen, he found Emma sitting in a chair—still crying. A little red-haired girl, dressed just like Emma, had her arm around her, and the boy he saw earlier was hanging on to the red-haired girl. Joe was leaning against the sink.

When the little girl saw him, she grabbed her brother by the arm and pulled him around to put the table between him and themselves. Her eyes were huge and she was shaking. He was frightening small children. Jack felt like an ass.

Joe stood up straight and walked over to pat Emma on the shoulder. She threw her arms around his waist and sobbed.

"It's okay Emma. Pa's going to help us." Staring directly into his father's eyes, he squinted. "Ain't you Pa?"

Jack had never seen his son behave this way. Joe was his youngest—the quiet one. He always did what he was told, and he usually had his eyes on the ground. How many times had he grabbed that boy by the shoulders and told him to stand up straight? He was standing up straight now.

Realizing that his mind had been made up for him, Jack said, a little too loudly, "Alright!"

The little girl across the table from him jumped. Her brother hid behind her.

He said more softly, "Alright. These two can stay here, but no more, Emma. It's too risky."

Emma looked up at him through tears, and Jack's heart melted. He knelt down beside her. "I'm sorry. I shouldn't have said that."

Emma switched her grip from Joe to his father and hugged him around the neck. He smiled in spite of being choked and patted her back. She sniffled and wiped her eyes.

Tommy came through the door carrying his milk pail. He put it down on the table and frowned. "Who made Emma cry?"

Joe chuckled and pointed at his father.

***

The sun was just up when Cecil Hammond sat up slowly and groaned. He slept in his clothes on the parlor settee. Florence finally emerged from Sally's house last night, but she was still giving him the cold shoulder. His dinner consisted of a peanut butter sandwich. Flo went straight to their room and locked the door.

He stood up slowly and cracked his back. He smelled coffee. Hitching up his trousers, he staggered into the kitchen. Flo was seated at the table, wearing a long robe. Her dark hair hung halfway down her back.

Cecil took down a cup and poured himself some coffee. He sat down across from her. "Morning, Flo."

She picked up her cup, stood, and walked away. The kitchen door swung closed behind her. She stepped so lightly her footsteps could seldom be heard, but he heard a stair creak and the quiet click of a door.

It was agony for Cecil. He dearly loved his wife. He married out of his league, way out of his league, and he knew it. He would do anything for her, but he could not think what to do. What he had done could not be undone.

Unbeknownst to Cecil, Florence was in love with his uniform. She was a perfect wife, and she longed to be a perfect mother. She wanted nothing more than to be what people wanted her to be, and she saw in Cecil's uniform a symbol of conformity. She was not a rigid woman. In fact, she conformed too easily. Having grown up in a small town filled with evangelical Protestants, she was molded into their image of the perfect Christian woman. Her opinions were those of the people around her. Everything in Florence's life had been perfectly clear to her—until yesterday morning.

Cecil drained his cup and headed upstairs. He hoped Flo had not locked the door again. He needed a clean uniform. And he needed to know—who in hell is Anna Taylor!

***

Joe sat in the wagon, holding the reins. He respected Buck. That big horse knew how to work Yellowwood Farm better than he did, so he usually followed his lead. When they reached the gravel road, Buck turned left. He only turned right when he heard church bells.

Emma gave him a list of things she needed, and he needed a roll of wire. It still felt strange to have Emma hand him money, but if things worked out the way she thought they would, he had better get used to it.

He promised Emma he would check on Ike. He was riding along lost in thought, when a pig ran across the road right in front of Buck. He sat up straight and watched it high tail it into the field. Now that he was looking, he saw half a dozen others rooting among the newborn crops. Apparently, he wasn't the only one needing to mend fences today. He wondered if those were Ike's pigs rooting up his milo.

When he reached the Pearson place, he turned Buck down the dirt road and saw Ike's truck, titled at an angle halfway into the pigpen. That explained the pigs. He parked the wagon next to the house and jumped down to run to the truck.

He looked in, under and all around the truck, but there was no sign of Ike. He checked the barn and the horse pasture. Still no Ike. He was on his way to the house when he saw him in the chicken coop, sitting with his back against the henhouse.

Joe ran up to the chicken coop and stood looking through the wire. He saw that Ike was breathing, and released a long sigh. Ducking through the door and latching it behind him, he knelt down beside Ike. A bucket of chicken feed was spilled in his lap. A dozen hens pecked at the feed.

He shook his shoulder and said, "Mister Pearson! You okay?"

Ike's eyes fluttered open and focused on Joe. "Joe Hansen, little bastard."

His eyes fluttered and he went limp. Joe tried shaking his shoulder again, and he slumped over onto his side—snoring.

Joe's only experience with drunkenness was four years ago, when his oldest brother arrived home well past dark, covered with lipstick and reeking of alcohol. His father had picked him up by the scruff of the neck and the seat of his pants and threw him through the front door. It was not open at the time.

That was as close as Joe ever came to alcohol. He was not curious about the liquor, but the lipstick piqued his interest. Sadly, John refused to discuss it.

Joe considered leaving Ike where he was, but it didn't seem right. He pulled him away from the wall and managed to get his arms under his shoulders. He dragged him out of the chicken coop toward the house. He was struggling to open the kitchen door without dropping him, when Ike started to squirm. He lowered him onto the ground, and Ike rolled over onto his hand and knees. He groaned and vomited onto the steps.

The smell sent Joe reeling. He staggered away, trying not to throw up himself. He gagged and his eyes watered. He bent over with his hands on his knees, drooling and spitting. The screen door clapped shut. When he looked up, Ike was gone. He must be in the house.

Good enough.

Joe had better things to do than chase Ike Pearson and his pigs over half the county.

Using the hand pump over the horse trough, Joe pump water over his head and drank from a cupped hand. He had a strong stomach, but that was the most vile-smelling stuff he ever encountered. When he raised his head, the horses were looking over the fence at him. Ike had some nice stock. He reached out to rub the head of a big gray mare. He couldn't let them go unfed, so he went into the barn to find their feed.

He ended up feeding the horses, milking the cow, and collecting the eggs. Most of Ike's pigs were in the field. He figured he would feed them anyway. It might entice some of them to come back. When he carried out the buckets of feed, he saw egg shells scattered all around the troughs—hundreds of them.

Joe seldom got angry, but he considered kicking Ike Pearson in the ass. He had watched Emma collect her few eggs every day and carefully ration them out, sometimes giving them to the boys while she did without. She made shortcake, shortbread biscuits and all sorts of things like that because she was short on eggs. Ike Pearson lived less than two miles away with more than a dozen hens laying— feeding the eggs to his pigs!

Emma had told him, with an air of excitement and gratitude, that Ike had brought her a crate of chicks. Those chicks were still months away from laying eggs. Besides, Joe knew that around the time Ike brought them, the mercantile had those crates stacked by the counter. All Ike did was shell out four bits and pick one up.

Joe dumped the milk into the pig trough, but the eggs were for Emma. To keep her from asking questions, he would say they were from Ike. He left them in the egg basket, padded them with straw, and tucked them away under the tarp in the back of the wagon to keep the sun off them.

He was considering taking off, but it didn't feel right to leave that truck up on the fence like that. It took Buck less than two minutes to pull it off the fence.

He was on his way again, but he couldn't leave with that fence down. He spent an hour scavenging up the materials to fix it.

Finally, he told himself that he really had to get going. As it was, he could not in good conscience allow Emma to pay for a full day, when Ike Pearson's carelessness had occupied his morning. Then again, he didn't want to tell her Ike was drunk. He would just have to find some way to make it up to her.

It didn't feel right to leave those pigs out in the fields. The Hansen boys were well known for rounding up escaped livestock, but without Verne it would take him all day to run them down. He climbed up into the wagon and headed for town.

When he reached the mercantile, he went inside to find Earl Anderson stocking his shelves. "Morning, Mister Anderson."

Earl turned to him and said, "Morning, Joe. How's Emma? I coulda punched Cecil for pulling her hair like that."

"She's fine, sir. Sorry we caused such a ruckus."

Earl said, "Tell you what. After you folks left, nobody broke up brothers and sisters. Half a dozen of them kids was taken home. They was a couple of people wanted to take that little red-headed girl and her brother, but nobody could find 'em."

Joe nodded and handed Earl the list. "Emma needs a few things and I need some wire."

Earl examined the list. People did not just gather up what they needed. Many of the smaller items were on shelves behind the counter. You gave your list to the shopkeeper and he pulled it all together.

Earl asked, "Roll of double twist?"

Joe nodded again, distracted by his thoughts. If Emma had listened to him, would Anna and Chris have been placed together in a good home?

Doesn't matter now, what's done is done.

Besides, at the time, he had not been the least bit concerned for Anna and Chris. His only concerns were for Emma. Emma, on the other hand, fought hard for two strangers.

Earl brought out a sixty-pound roll of barbed wire on a hand truck. Joe pulled his leather gloves out of his back pocket and pulled them on. "Thank you, sir. I'll load it."

He was maneuvering the hand truck through the front door, trying to back through it, when he heard a feminine voice say, "Allow me." The door was held open for him.

He pulled the hand truck through the door. "Thank you, ma'am."

When he looked up, he came face to face with the woman from yesterday, the policeman's wife. She was a beautiful woman, but her beauty was of the frail and delicate variety. She had an aura of helplessness that attracted good Samaritans—and predators. She recognized Joe immediately. Her mouth fell open and she stood there blinking.

Joe tried not to panic. He nodded to her and started dropping the hand truck down the front steps. He heaved the roll of wire up into the back of the wagon, and when he turned around, she was only two feet away. He tried to back up and bumped into the wagon. She took a step closer, and he was nearly knocked down by a whiff of subtle perfume.

"I want to apologize for yesterday. What my husband and I did was unforgiveable. I don't know what came over me, trying to separate a brother and sister."

Joe was scared half to death, partly because of this lovely woman, but mostly because of her husband. He looked not into her eyes, but over her shoulder. Was that asshole somewhere nearby?

She noticed. "My husband isn't here. Please forgive me. I came to apologize to Mister Anderson, but I'm glad I ran into you."

Unable to escape, Joe faced her and hurriedly removed his hat. "No problem, ma'am."

Florence said, "I'd especially like to apologize to those poor girls. Cecil should never have laid a hand on them."

She embraced Joe. His cheeks turned bright pink.

"I'm so sorry," she said.

Joe stood at rigid attention with his arms pinned to his sides. "Nobody got hurt."

She leaned back to look into his face. "Cecil hurt both of those girls! Please tell your sister how sorry I am."

Pulling out a dainty kerchief, she dabbed at her eyes. Then she nodded and turned to go into the mercantile. Joe stayed where he was. She thought he was Emma's brother, but he didn't feel up to clarifying the misunderstanding. He could barely talk to that woman.

Ten minutes later, she came out of the mercantile, and Joe pretended to be busy moving things around the back of the wagon. She nodded to him and walked off toward town on the side of the road, stumbling a little on the rocky roadside. Joe watched her go and thought she seemed to be a nice enough lady. Her husband was another matter.

Now that the coast was clear, Joe went back into the mercantile to finish his business. Earl had Emma's things all wrapped up.

Joe was paying for his purchases, when Earl said, "I don't know what Florence sees in Cecil Hammond."

"You mean that lady who was just in here?"

"Pretty little thing, just as nice as can be. Don't know how she ended up married to Cecil."

Joe just shrugged. He had never seen Florence or her husband before and hoped he never would again. The mercantile sold mostly to farmers. The few clothes they had were coats and heavy-duty work clothes, and the dry goods were sold in bulk. If not for that train, Florence Hammond would not normally have been here.

Earl said, "She wanted to apologize to Anna on account of Cecil pulling Emma's hair. I thought that was right nice of her. Wanted to know where she lived."

Joe's struggled to appear calm. "Did you tell her?"

Earl said, "Yeah, any reason not to?"

"I don't think Emma wants that deputy showing up on her doorstep."

Earl's eyebrows rose up. "Come to think of it, I wouldn't want him at my house either."

Joe carried his purchases out to the wagon. He led Buck across the road to the wagon shed and let him drink from the trough. Then he climbed up into the seat, and Buck headed for home. Along the way, Joe considered how to handle Florence and her husband.

Chapter Eighteen

When Joe topped the rise on the wagon trail, he saw Emma and Anna down behind the house in the garden, dressed identically in blue dresses. He realized that from here, he could not recognize either one of them. If Cecil Hammond were to come here, then at best, he would see two girls.

He drove the wagon down into the valley, parked next to the barn, and unhitched Buck. He was in the barn brushing him down, when Emma walked in, followed by Anna.

Emma said, "Hi, Joe. Did you check on Ike?"

"Ike's fine. He sent you some eggs."

Joe retrieved the eggs from the bed of the wagon and handed her the basket. Her eyes lit up at the sight of seven eggs.

"We can have griddlecakes again!"

Anna asked, "Did you get the cloth?"

Joe took a big bundle from the wagon and placed it in her arms. She could barely see over the top of it.

"Cloth, thread, buttons and whatnot," he said.

"Thank you!" She headed for the house, turning sideways every few steps to get her bearings.

Emma started to follow her, but Joe took her arm. "That woman from yesterday, the deputy's wife," he said.

Emma's expression became solemn. She nodded.

"I ran into her at the mercantile. She wants to apologize to your mother for her husband grabbing your hair. She asked Earl where you live. He told her."

Emma frowned. "They're not welcome here."

"Yeah, well, from what I hear, they're not welcome in a lot of places."

Emma's indignation turned to worry. She glanced up the rise to where the wagon trail emerged from the woods.

Joe said, "You can't recognize anybody from the top of the ridge. Tell Anna if she hears a car coming, she should hide."

Emma considered it for only a moment. Her cheeks flushed with color and her eyes crinkled in outrage.

"No! They should just leave us alone! She already said she was sorry. We'll go into town and find that lady and tell her never to set foot on our farm. Anna and Chris should feel safe here."

***

Ike Pearson came awake slowly and groaned. He was sitting at his kitchen table, feeling like death warmed over. He raised his head and closed his eyes to block out the painful glare of sunlight. He had vague recollections of running out of whiskey and getting into his truck. After that, his memory was blank. That was not unusual. Passing time without recollection was the whole point of getting drunk.

The sun sat low in the sky, sending painfully bright beams through the window. He climbed to his feet, stumbled to the big window over the sink, and yanked the curtains closed. He pumped the well handle over the sink. It took all his strength to lift a column of water and drink from a cupped hand. He spent several minutes holding on to the pump, waiting for the room to stop spinning.

He had no idea what day it was. The sun was low in the eastern sky, so it must be morning. He was sober, an intolerable cruelty. Thoughts of all the things he should have done and should be doing would soon begin to eat away at him. He had no way of drowning them.

He could hear his cow mooing, needing to be milked. He was an uninterested observer of his life—a passenger.

Running purely on reflex, he headed for the door to do the things he did every day.

***

Emma watched Anna sitting at her mother's sewing machine, furiously pumping the pedal. At only ten years old, she could sew like a demon. Yesterday afternoon, she made a new dress for herself in only an hour. It would have taken Emma days.

The sewing machine sat beside a window in their parlor to take advantage of the light. Anna looked up from her work and smiled.

"I like this sewing machine. It runs easy," she said.

"You're so fast. It takes me days to make a dress."

"Ma could sew faster than me. I used to cut patterns while she laid stitches."

Shaking her head, Emma said, "Joe is going to take me into town today. I want to buy some things at the market. Can you keep an eye on the boys?"

Anna stopped her sewing and snipped a thread. She jumped up and clasped her hands behind her. "Oh yes! They're good boys, they won't be any trouble."

Whenever Anna answered a question in the affirmative, she clasped her hands behind her like that and rocked back and forth on the balls of her feet. In only two days, Emma had grown to love her. She made her realize how lucky they were to be living here. Anna was grateful for every stitch of clothing, every mouthful of food, and the extraordinary comfort of having a home. She was constantly on the lookout for anything she could do to earn their welcome.

Anna pulled a small pair of pants out of the sewing machine and held them up against her. She lifted one pants leg, cut it to length, and sat back down to sew the hem.

Whether she was sewing for herself, or for Christopher, Emma noticed that she measured everything by holding it up to herself.

Joe called through the kitchen door, "Emma! The wagon's ready."

She turned back to Anna and said, "There are boiled eggs and cheese for lunch. We'll be back in time to make supper."

Anna jumped up and followed her to the door. "Can I make your new dress?"

Emma said, "I can make it. You should try to have a little fun today."

"I don't mind. Besides, if, um…I can have it ready when you get home."

Emma laughed. Anna watched her sew last night, trembling with anxiety at her imperfect stitches and leisurely pace.

"Thank you, but I really should do it myself."

Anna said, "Me and Ma used to look into the shop windows. Then we would go home and make dresses just as good as those. I can make you one."

Anna wore the dress she made last night. It fit her perfectly. Emma had no way of knowing her own dresses were old fashioned with ruffles and bows. Anna's new dress seemed stylish in its simplicity, so she gave in.

"Okay then. That would be very nice. I like the one you're wearing."

Anna clapped her hands and ran back into the parlor. "You'll see. I'll make a fine dress for you."

Joe climbed up into the wagon and reached down to help her up. Emma took his hand and he lifted her up to sit beside him. It would be the first time she was separated from the boys since her mother died. She could hear them shouting and laughing. They were off in the horse pasture playing some sort of game, completely unaffected by a moment that had Emma close to tears.

When Joe picked up the reins, Buck headed for town. Emma turned around in the seat for one last look at the boys. The little scamps were throwing horse dung at each other.

She would stop at the market today, another first since her mother died. She wanted to buy a beef roast, a few jars of honey, and some other things only the market had, to celebrate Anna and Christopher's arrival. They also needed shoes. She traced the soles of the ones they were wearing to help her select the right size, but there was one errand she dreaded, the reason she and Joe went alone.

It was Saturday morning, so she reasoned they should be at home. She would be polite and courteous, but she would do her best to persuade Florence and Cecil Hammond that they need not visit their farm to make amends. If need be, she would tell them they were not welcome.

The dappled shade of the oak trees on the wagon trail were cool and comforting. Emma glanced over at Joe and caught him looking at her. He turned to watch the trail, and his cheeks turned pink. She smiled.

When they turned onto the gravel road into full sun, Emma pulled her sun hat up onto her head. She wore it nearly every day when she was working outside. It was made of straw and threaded with a long strip of blue cloth that she used to tie it on in the wind, or to keep it handy, hanging down her back.

Ike Pearson's place was in sight. "Can we stop by Ike's, so I can thank him for the eggs?"

Joe stared straight ahead. "No."

Emma was surprised. It was not actually a question.

Nobody has said no to Emma in quite some time, and she was unaccustomed to it. Even Joe's father was unable to make it stick. She let it stand because she knew Joe was looking out for her. Besides, she didn't really want to do it.

When they rode past the Pearson farm, things looked fine. Ike's truck was parked beside the barn, and the horses were grazing. She peered into the dark windows of his house, but there was no sign of Ike.

Soon, they were past the schoolhouse. Buck leaned into the straps to climb the slight rise on the switchback into town. Emma scooted over next to Joe. She was afraid of facing that policeman again. Hooking her arm through his, she snuggled up against him. Joe made her feel safe, but when Joe was around Emma, Joe did not feel safe at all.

They rode into town, past the mercantile, until the gravel road became Main Street and the gravel turned to brick. There was a wagon shed at the end of town. They stopped there and unhitched Buck so he could graze in the small pasture while they did their shopping.

Emma took a large basket out of the back of the wagon. They would ask at the market where the Hammonds lived. It was a small town, and this was the only market, so it seemed likely the shopkeeper would know. She grabbed Joe's hand and looked up at him. In full sunlight, he was always surprised by her beautiful eyes.

The shoe store was on their way to the market, so they stopped to buy shoes for Anna and Chris. The pretty girl who had fitted her with shoes a month ago met them at the door.

"How may I help you," she asked.

Emma said, "I need to buy shoes for a boy and a girl. I traced shoes that fit them."

She reached into the pocket of her dress and pulled

out a sheet of paper. The tracing of Anna's shoe was on one side and Chris' was on the other.

"They need comfortable work shoes. We live on a farm."

The clerk examined the tracings "I have just the thing. Please sit down. May I offer you some tea?"

Emma looked up at Joe and saw his mouth hanging open. She frowned, stepped on his foot, and bore down on his toes until she had his attention.

He jumped and said, "Uh, no thanks, Miss, just the shoes."

She smiled at Joe, showing perfect white teeth and brushed back a wisp of dark hair, stylishly left free. "I'll be right back."

Emma watched Joe watching that girl walk away. It occurred to her that she simply claimed Joe as her own. She wasn't even grown up yet and she had not consulted Joe. She decided it didn't matter and bore down on his foot again anyway.

Joe yanked his foot out from under hers, laughed, and held up his hands. "I didn't do nothin'."

That was true, so she begrudgingly gave him a smile. She had shared Joe with half a dozen girls all through grade school. One day she would claim him as hers and hers alone. Until then, she would just have to keep an eye on him.

Joe carried the shoe boxes, wrapped in brown paper and tied together with string, while they walked to the market. They came alongside a small ice cream shop with fancy, white, cast-iron tables and chairs arranged on the sidewalk.

Joe stopped. "Let me buy you an ice cream."

Emma turned around in surprise. "I can't let you do that."

"Why not? Just sit down and let me get you some ice cream. You're always doing for everybody else, let me for once."

It was a lot for Joe to say in one go. He pulled out a chair and she sat down.

He went inside and came back out a moment later with scoops of chocolate ice cream in little cut-glass dishes. When he placed them on the table, they threw rainbows of color onto the white tabletop.

Emma placed a small spoonful in her mouth and sighed. "This is so good. I feel guilty doing this without Anna and the boys."

Joe put a spoonful in his mouth and nodded in vigorous agreement. He was happy to see Emma do something, even such a little thing, for herself. She spent all her time taking care of everybody else.

Keeping his head down, he said to his ice cream, "I'll wait for you."

She looked up at him in confusion and asked, "Wait for me to do what?"

"Grow up," he said.

She knew Joe cared for her, but he had never said anything like this before. She jumped out of her chair and left a perfect chocolate kiss on his strawberry-colored cheek. She sat back down and smiled so big it hurt.

He looked down into his ice cream again and said, "It ain't proper to be courtin' at twelve years old, but if you promise to stop stepping on my foot, I promise to wait for you."

They were at an awkward age. He was only two years older than Emma, but those were formative years. In less than a month, she would turn thirteen, and just one year would separate them. He meant what he said. He would wait for her.

They finished their ice cream, sharing shy glances. When they stood up, Emma felt freer, more at ease. Joe just gave her something she had wished for nearly every day since she was seven years old. In his own way, he told her he loved her.

They walked down to the market, and Emma gave her list to the shopkeeper, an older man gone completely gray. He examined her list and began taking down the items and placing them on the counter.

"How big a roast you want?"

Emma had never bought a beef roast before. She looked to Joe for help. He shrugged.

She turned to the shopkeeper. "I'll know it when I see it. I don't often weigh things."

He waved her over to the meat case and she picked one out.

They were paying for their purchases, when Joe said, "We're looking for Florence Hammond. Would you happen to know where she lives?"

The shopkeeper smiled and said, "Florence is such a sweet girl. The Hammond's live just two blocks over on Jackson, number six eighty-two."

Emma said, "Thank you kindly, sir. It is much appreciated."

The old man looked down at her and took on an expression of wonder. He stepped around the counter and leaned over to look into Emma's eyes from only a foot away.

"Young lady, you have the prettiest eyes. Are you Anna Taylor's daughter?"

Hearing her mother's name was so unexpected she fought back tears, nodded, and turned away.

***

Cecil sat in his parlor reading *The Fiery Cross*, the Klan's daily newspaper. He was in a foul mood. Last night, the Exalted Cyclops had given him a good tongue-lashing, far better than the literal lashing he expected. When he thought it was over, he was fined fifty dollars. Half a month's pay! His paycheck made up less than half his income, but he was living beyond his means, and he counted on every cent.

Women like Florence did not come cheap. She wore the finest clothes. She lived in a nice house. In spite of all he had done for her, she would not speak to him. He could hear her even now. She was washing the few dishes he had left on the table after making his own breakfast.

He was still a Terror, but just barely. He saved his position by claiming the red-haired girl was a Papist. He was attempting to rescue her from the deviltry of the Pope. One of his Klan brothers had backed him up. He had seen the girl make the sign of the cross.

Fuming with anger, he slapped his newspaper down onto the floor, jumped to his feet, and kicked over the conversation table. A carved crystal candy dish shattered against the bricks of the fireplace, scattering shards of glass and candied mints into every corner of the room.

When he looked up, Florence stood in the kitchen doorway. Her expression was one of supreme sadness. She glanced at him and quietly climbed the stairs. He heard a soft click when she locked the bedroom door. He was desperate for her love. If he had to, he would demand that she give it to him. She owed him!

A knock at the door brought him to his senses. It wouldn't do for a Klan brother to find him kicking around the furniture, especially after last night. He righted the table and danced around, kicking broken glass and mints under the furniture. There was another knock at the door.

Before approaching the door, he smoothed down his hair, tucked in his shirt, and buffed a shine onto his badge with his sleeve. Taking a deep breath, he opened the door.

Standing on his front porch was the little blonde girl that had humiliated him, and behind her stood the boy who had threatened him. Cecil could not believe his good fortune. He smiled.

***

Emma was frightened half to death. The last time she saw this man, he caused her pain. His smile looked evil. She reached back to touch Joe's arm and backed up to press against him.

She wanted to turn and run, but if she did, then this man might come to her home. He was still smiling. She didn't like that.

She said, "M-Mister Hammond, s-sir, is Missus Hammond at home?"

Cecil stepped outside, making them back up, and closed the door behind him. He pushed Emma aside and stepped up to poke his finger into Joe's chest. "You in a heap of trouble boy. You assaulted a police officer."

Joe leaned into Cecil's finger. "I believe you're mistaken. The boy that put you on your knees was only seven years old. I'm fourteen."

Cecil pulled his pistol and whipped it hard across the side of Joe's head. His eyes rolled back and he crashed through the porch railing to land flat on his back in the yard.

Cecil holstered his pistol and smiled.

Emma screamed. She ran down the steps and got down on her hands and knees over Joe. "Joe! Oh please, God, no!"

Joe was bleeding, flat on his back, perfectly still,

surrounded by groceries. His eyes were blank and staring. Emma shook him and screamed, "Joe! Joe, please wake up!"

Unbearable pain radiated up her spine, and she somersaulted over Joe. Cecil had kicked her in the tailbone. She screamed wordlessly and wailed, unable to get up.

Joe moaned, and Emma clawed her way toward him.

Cecil put his foot in her back and pressed her into the ground. "Hurts don't it! Little girls shouldn't go around kicking people, 'specially when they kick back!"

The front door flew open and Florence ran down the steps screaming, "No! No! No!"

She slammed into Cecil and clawed at his face. He outweighed her by a hundred pounds. Her best efforts were little more than a distraction. Joe was on his hands and knees now, trying to get up. Cecil pushed Florence away and kicked him in the ribs, throwing him onto his back again.

Florence was desperate to stop this. She picked up a jar of honey and swung it as hard as she could. It glanced off Cecil's chin, flew from her hand, and smashed on a flagstone. Grabbing the front of her dress, he backed her up until she fell on the steps. Hauling her to her feet, he pushed her through the door.

When he turned to go back outside, she screamed, "You're a worm, Cecil, a worthless little worm!"

He stopped cold, closed the door, and turned to her. It was what she wanted. She would give herself up to distract him from hurting those children. She raised her arms, closed her eyes, and surrendered.

***

Wracked with pain, Emma moaned and clawed her way to Joe. She could not bear the agony when she tried to move her legs, but the pain was ebbing. She could bend her knees a little now. She dragged herself over to Joe and laid her head on his chest—sobbing. When he reached up to touch her hair, she clutched his hand.

Joe was regaining his senses. His head throbbed and his side ached, but he was coming back to full consciousness. Emma was hurt!

"Emma!"

She pushed herself up to look into his face. "I can't walk Joe! It hurts so bad!"

He scooted out from under her and jumped to his feet. Shouting and sounds of things breaking came from inside the house. He gently picked Emma up and she moaned. His ribs burned with every breath. He looked around to get his bearings and started the long walk back to the wagon shed. He walked toward an elderly couple, standing in the yard next door.

The elderly lady called out, "Is that girl okay?"

Joe passed close by them. "No! She's not."

Emma clung tightly to Joe, crying and moaning. Blood ran down the side of his head, dripped from his chin, and collected in her golden hair. He carried her down Jackson Street for six blocks to the edge of town. He began to stumble. The few people they passed gave them curious glances, but no offers of help. He avoided looking at them and focused on taking each careful step. What could he say to them? That they were running from the police?

Emma raised her head. "Put me down. Let me try to walk."

He held her more tightly. "I can make it."

She touched the side of his head and held her bloody fingers in front of his face. "Put me down. Please."

He staggered across the last street in town and carefully got down on his knees to lay her in the tall grass. The wagon shed was only two blocks away, but he needed to rest. Black spots obscured his vision.

Emma rolled over and carefully got to her feet. Standing in a crouch, she said, "It's getting better. I can walk."

Joe was on his hands and knees, breathing heavily. Blood dripped onto the grass.

Emma stood in front of him and said, "I'm so sorry. It was stupid to go there."

"No it wasn't. You did the right thing. That man ain't right in the head. Somebody ought to put him down."

She said, "Wait till your father finds out what he did. I wouldn't want to be Mister Hammond tomorrow."

Joe raised his head to look at her. He couldn't stand to see her hair matted with blood, even if it was his. She had suffered enough over the past year.

He said, "Pa will kill him. He'll ride straight into town, kick in the front door, and knock him down with a twelve-gauge slug."

Emma's eyes grew wide. She let her head drop down and stared into the grass. She took two painful steps. "I can walk now."

Joe stood up and stumbled backward before he managed to stand in one spot. Emma limped over to hold him steady.

He said, "Ain't we a pair."

She propped him up. "Ain't we though."

They held on to each other and walked along the edge of town toward the wagon shed. When they were less than a block away, Buck raised his head up high and inhaled deeply. He rolled his eyes and pushed his way through the split rail fence, snapping logs as if they were twigs.

He trotted up to Emma and stuck his head in her chest. She wrapped her arms around his long nose and cried, safe at last. Nobody would dare to touch them with Buck by their side.

***

Emma and Joe arrived back at the farm in a terrible state. She was barely able to walk, and Joe was still bleeding.

Before they even stepped down from the wagon, Anna climbed up beside Emma and started going through her hair, looking for an injury. "What happened?"

Emma said, "That policeman from the train, his wife wanted to come here to apologize to Momma. Me and Joe went to her house to tell them not to come."

Anna climbed all around Emma, parting her hair and examining her neck. "I don't see any cuts."

"It's Joe's blood," she said.

Anna stepped over in front of Joe and bent his head down. "Here it is! It's not too bad."

Once they were in the house, surrounded by Anna and the boys, they told them what happened.

Anna stopped fussing over Joe. "It's my fault. If you had na kicked that man, none of this would have happened."

Emma said, "You didn't kick him, I did. Momma would have kicked him too. And Tommy punched him in the nethers!"

Anna turned to Tommy in surprise. "Is that true?"

Tommy frowned when everybody turned their attention to him. He stuck out his chin. "He made Emma cry."

Anna chuckled and returned to cleaning Joe's face, examining the wound critically. She ran to the parlor and returned with a needle and thread.

Joe looked at her wide-eyed. "What's that for?"

"It needs stitching. Don't worry. Me and Ma are famous for stitching cuts. I'll be quick."

Joe gave Emma a worried look and she said, "It's true. She's really good with a needle and thread."

"She's only ten!"

Emma shrugged.

Joe sat in stoic silence. In half a minute, Anna put five stitches in his wound while the boys danced around making exclamations of horror and disgust. Anna applied a bandage and wrapped a strip of white cloth around his head to hold it in place.

She kissed him on the cheek. "You were very brave."

Joe turned pink.

Anna said, "Ma always does that when she puts in stitches. She says it makes them feel better."

Rubbing his cheek, Joe said, "It kinda does."

She took Emma's arm. "Will you please sit down? I cannot bear to watch you limp about that way."

Emma smiled. "Actually, I'd rather stand than sit."

Anna dashed out of the room. Moments later, she returned with a pillow and placed it in Emma's chair. "Now will you sit down?"

Emma hobbled over to her chair and carefully sat down.

Anna sat beside her and asked, "This man who hurt you, do you think he has hurt others?"

Emma was between them, so Joe leaned over the table to get a good look at Anna's face. She kept surprising him. What was she up to now?

Emma said, "I don't know."

Anna shivered. "I felt evil in him when he touched me."

Chapter Nineteen

Florence Hammond opened her eyes long before sunrise. She was lying in bed beside her husband. Blood crusted the sheets. Yesterday, he beat her badly. Hours later, when she regained consciousness, she found herself in bed. When Cecil's face appeared above her, he helped her to sit up and take a drink of water through split and bloody lips. Then he begged for her forgiveness. Foolishly, she whispered only one word, the last thing she remembered—no.

Cecil snored loudly beside her. She rolled out of bed very slowly, quietly dropped to the floor on her hands and knees and crawled away from him into the hallway. Gripping the banister, she pulled herself up and limped down the stairs in the dark. She was naked from the waist down, covered only by her bloody camisole. She struggled to focus her eyes on the clock hanging in the parlor. Four-thirty, it must be early morning. She had to escape before he killed her.

Where can I go?

If she went to her mother's house, then Cecil would come for her. Right after he struck her for the very first time, he told her she was an animal, to do with as he pleased. At that moment, she realized he could do that. As an officer of the law, he could do things that would get any other man hanged. She had to leave Owen County, get beyond his jurisdiction. She was acquainted with a pastor and his wife who lived in Bloomington, thirty miles away. She would go there and beg for sanctuary.

Cecil never awoke until well after sunrise. She had an hour, perhaps two, to make her escape. She dampened a towel with warm water from her stove and sat down in the dark to tend her wounds. The cuts and bruises would heal, but there was a knot on her forehead that worried her. She could not bear to touch it.

She pressed the damp towel to her face and noticed that in the darkness, her blood appeared to be black. Her whole body ached, but she could walk with only a little more pain than she felt sitting down.

Opening the back door produced an audible click that made her gasp. She froze and listened closely. Only crickets broke the stillness of the night. She crept out the back door into the yard and took down a few clothes from the line. Sitting on the back steps, she dressed as best she could in the moonlight. She had no shoes and stockings, but she dared not go back upstairs.

It was time. She stood up and took one last look at her home for the past six years. She loved her house and her garden, but she realized on her wedding night that she did not and could not love her husband. Until two days ago, she admired him. He was a dashing figure in his uniform, and even more so in his white robes, but when she saw him naked for the first time, it turned her stomach. He was soft and paunchy with stick-like arms and flabby legs. Without his uniform, he looked like a toad. Even so, she had done her duty and tried to be a good wife. She found fulfillment elsewhere by seeking the approval of her peers—the women of the WCTU.

Everything had changed for her when she had seen Cecil force that little red-haired girl to her knees. That sweet little girl, begging to remain with her brother, had clasped her cross at the moment of her greatest despair and prayed to God. It was beautiful in a way. Children have no allegiance to Popes or priests. She begged God to help her and God sent a child to her rescue—a blonde-haired girl with the eyes of an angel. That single moment revealed to her the foolishness and cruelty of prejudice against the faithful. God answered that poor girl's prayer—a Papist. It was an epiphany.

She crept back into the house, taking care to avoid the creaky floorboards. Her rainy-day fund contained nearly eighty dollars. She kept it in a soapbox, something Cecil would never touch. She quietly retrieved her hidden treasure and tiptoed into the parlor.

Cecil kept his keys on a hook beside the front door. She carefully took them down and crept back into the kitchen. The front door creaked, so she left through the back door, leaving it wide open, and walked around to the front of the house.

The packages carried by the children who came to her door were still scattered across the lawn. She knew now where Anna Taylor lived. She had passed that isolated road dozens of times and wondered where it led. She picked up the basket and stared hard at the upstairs window. No lights appeared, but the sky was turning gray. Sunrise was less than an hour away. She had a little time. It was only right to leave these things on the road to Anna Taylor's farm. It would not take her out of her way.

She picked up a tin of cinnamon, a small bottle of vanilla, and a can of baking powder. Her head ached every time she leaned over. Keeping an eye on the upstairs window, she scanned the yard, and a glint of gold in the moonlight caught her attention. She found a gold pendant on a chain. Holding it out of her shadow, she saw that it was a watch. No doubt this was the most valuable thing that little girl owned, given the way she dressed. She dropped it into the pocket of her dress, picked up a large parcel wrapped in brown paper and string, and placed it in the back seat of Cecil's car.

Florence had driven Cecil's patrol car a handful of

times, when he was stricken with gout and unable to work the gear pedal. She felt confident she could manage, and hoped it contained enough gasoline to get her to Bloomington. She stepped out into the street, wincing at the feel of coarse gravel under her bare feet. The car door opened with only a quiet click.

She had made up her mind the moment she opened her eyes. She was going to do this. Holding up the keys in the moonlight, she located the ignition key. A white arrowhead dangled from the keychain. It appeared there only recently. She inserted the key in the ignition switch and leaned over to see what position it was in. She switched it over to battery and pressed the starter button.

The car whined, coughed, and began to chug. It was incredibly loud. Florence glanced fearfully up at her bedroom window. It remained dark. She switched the key over to the magneto position, pressed the accelerator lever on the steering wheel forward, and stepped on the gear pedal. The car lurched, and she was off.

Aching from head to toe, with the noise from the engine setting off sharp bursts of pain in her head, she smiled. "I'm free."

***

Ike Pearson sat at his kitchen table in the cool gray dawn and shaved by the light of a lantern using a small mirror propped up on the table. He had not slept. He awakened last night, sitting where he was now, and spent the night recovering. Washed and wearing clean clothes, he was attempting to shave without cutting his own throat.

Dawn was breaking pale orange in the east. He had eaten a little salt pork and a boiled potato, hoping for a chance to see his grandsons before his urges forced him to drive to the mercantile. Only nicked a little, he wiped away the soap from his face and stood up to look out the window.

He heard a car approaching. Leaning over to get a look, he saw the yellow glow of headlamps. It was time for his morning chores, so he headed off to do the milking and feed the livestock.

Ike had just stepped outside when he heard a loud crash. He walked around the house and peered out at the road. He saw nothing out of the ordinary. He walked out to the gravel road, and just beyond a grove of trees, a Ford Coupe lay on its side in the ditch.

Checking both directions, the road was deserted. It was damned inconvenient. With nobody else around, he thought maybe he should see if anybody was hurt. If they were, he would have to find somebody to help them— damned inconvenient.

He started down the road. A half-grown pig lay on the shoulder. He knew right away it was one of his. Half his hogs were missing, and he reasoned he must have left a gate open. Even in his most inebriated state, he has never left a gate open before, but it seemed the most likely explanation.

***

Emma walked carefully around her kitchen, still wearing her nightdress, while Anna orbited around her. She led her to a chair, still with a pillow on it, and helped her to sit down.

"You stay there while I fetch the eggs."

Anna had only been here for three days, yet in that short time she learned how to do nearly everything Emma did on a daily basis. Last night, she fussed over Emma, washing the blood from her hair and fixing supper.

Tommy came in carrying his milk pail with Christopher on his heels. He poured off a pitcher for breakfast and walked over to lay his head on Emma's shoulder.

She gave him a gentle hug. "I'm fine. Don't worry."

When the sun peeked over the horizon, Emma stood up and limped over to the window. She stood there for a minute and frowned. No Joe. It was Sunday, but given the events of the previous day, they agreed to skip church today. Emma could not imagine leaving Anna and Chris alone after their run in with Cecil Hammond. Joe said he would be here. She wondered if his mother had changed his mind for him.

Last night, for the first time she could remember, Emma locked their doors. Joe had insisted upon it.

Anna came back inside carrying three eggs in her basket. "You could not sit?"

Emma just smiled. "My backside hurts."

Frowning, Anna placed her eggs in the wire basket and pumped cold water over them. Then she skipped over to the stove and peeked into the oven. "I made biscuits. I'll be right back. I still cannot believe we eat ham every day."

She grabbed a basket and ran out the kitchen door. Emma could hear her calling for the boys. She couldn't lift the root cellar door on her own.

A few minutes later, Anna came back through the door. "Ham, biscuits, and fried potatoes, we should give thanks."

Emma said, "From now on, we will say a blessing at every meal to thank God for our good fortune." She looked down at her nightdress. "I can't go around like this all day. I should get dressed."

Anna looked up at her with sparkling eyes. "I made you a dress. Come, I'll help you."

Emma walked slowly through the parlor and up the stairs to her room. Anna still slept with her, and last night she was grateful to have her there.

Anna took down a dress from Emma's wardrobe and snapped it in the air. Emma recognized that gesture. It must be common to all women who sew.

Anna ran over to hold it up to her, and Emma could hardly believe it was hers. It was simple, yet elegant. She had seen women wearing dresses like this in town, but she had never considered wearing one herself.

Anna took her arm and sat her down on the bed. It was carefully made with the corners tucked in. Emma never tucked in the corners, but it looked nice this way—tidy.

Tugging at her nightdress, Anna helped her to get it over her head. Emma stood up and stepped out of her undergarments.

Anna gently turned her around and exclaimed, "Oh! Your poor bottom! You have an awful bruise."

Emma blushed and said, "Would you get me some bloomers please?

Anna ran to her dresser, but instead of bloomers, she returned with a cotton undergarment and held it up. "I made you a camiknicker," she said.

Emma took it and held it in front of her. "Is this what they wear in New York?"

Anna shyly looked around the room. "Well, um, bloomers are sort of old fashioned. Most girls wear a chemise. This one is a step-in."

Struggling to stand on one foot, Emma tried to step into it. Anna ran around and knelt down to help her. She pulled it up and guided Emma's arms through the straps.

"See! It's all one piece, so you don't have to wear a camisole."

Adjusting the mirror on her nightstand, Emma looked at herself. It was a simple and comfortable undergarment, but she worried that it might be sinful. It only came down to just above her knees. It did, however, make her look pretty—less like a potato. She smiled at her reflection. She felt a little naked without the familiar pinch of a pair of bloomers, cinched around her waist.

While she admired her reflection in the mirror, Anna pulled her new dress down over her head. She struggled to get her arms through the sleeves while Anna did up the buttons in the front. Anna tugged at the hem and sleeves and then stood back.

When Emma looked into the mirror, she could hardly believe what she saw. A young lady looked back at her. "I can't wear this. It's too nice for every day."

Anna gave her a puzzled look. "It's made for wearing every day. It's got big pockets and it won't bind you no matter what. I left the seams open a little in the sleeves and skirt, so you can bend and work in the garden."

Emma turned to her in amazement. "You're a wonder." She hugged Anna so hard she squeaked. "Thank you."

Anna shyly looked away. Then she stood bolt upright and shouted, "My biscuits!" She ran through the door.

Left alone in her room, Emma looked again at her reflection in the mirror. She could hardly believe that was her. Her new dress had slim sleeves that came halfway to her elbows; her old dresses had big puffy sleeves. Her new dress made her look slim; her old dresses puffed out from her waist.

She sat down on her bed and pulled on a pair of white stockings that came up to her knees. She felt comfortable—and pretty. She was about to make her way back down the stairs when she heard a commotion coming from outside. The boys were shouting her name. She stepped over to her window and looked outside.

Joe walked toward the house, carrying a woman in his arms. Ike Pearson followed behind him, leading Joe's horse. As best she could, she hurried downstairs. When she reached the kitchen, Joe came through the door carrying a young woman.

"She's hurt bad. She crashed on the road down by Ike's place."

Emma gasped at the sight of the woman's swollen and bruised face. "Put her in Momma's bed." She hurried to open the door. Joe carried her into the room and gently laid her on the bed.

Emma said, "Anna! Get some hot water and clean towels!"

The boys stood just outside the door, looking in. Nobody went into this room. When Anna asked what was inside, Emma told her it was her mother's room. Anna never went near it again. Only Emma came in here, and only then to keep it clean.

The woman struggled to rise. Emma held her down. "Don't move. You're hurt."

Anna came in with a washbowl and towels. She laid them on the bed and soaked a towel. Examining the woman carefully, she said, "These cuts are not bleeding. I think she was hurt before. We need a cold towel to keep down the swelling."

Joe hurried out of the room and returned a moment later. He handed Emma a towel soaked with cold water, and she draped it across the woman's forehead.

She reached up to touch it and said in a hoarse whisper, "Thank you. That feels good."

Anna shooed Joe and the boys out of the room and closed the door. "We should check her from head to toe. She might be hurt somehow that we canna see."

Anna had a sort of practical sophistication that Emma admired. When she became excited or upset, she spoke differently. Anna was undoing the buttons on Florence's dress and checking her over carefully. There were bruises on both her chest and back.

Isn't a person thrown forward in a car wreck?

Her injuries did not seem consistent with wrecking a car. The cuts on her face appeared to have been cleaned, there was no blood.

Lying on the bed beside her was a gold locket on a chain. Emma picked it up and immediately recognized the watch Ike gave her. She thought it was gone forever—lost in the scuffle yesterday. It slowly dawned on her who this woman was and what had happened to her.

She leaned over her. "What's your name?

She could barely hear the answer. "Florence."

Emma's turned to Anna. "That man from the train, the one who held you down. This is his wife! She tried to stop him when he attacked us yesterday and he did this to her."

Florence moaned. Emma leaned over her and brushed her hair out of her face. This beautiful young woman was unrecognizable.

Florence's eyes opened slowly. When she saw Emma, she smiled weakly and asked in a raspy voice, "What is your name, child?"

Emma took her hand. "My name is Emma and I will take care of you."

***

Ike Pearson sat at Emma's table, turning a small white arrowhead over and over in his hands. He found it hanging from the keychain in the wrecked car. He knew every vein and chip in that knapped piece of stone. Martha had found it on his farm just after they were married. He took it into town and had it fashioned into a pendant for her on their first anniversary.

He was more than a little surprised to learn Anna and Christopher lived here now. When Joe explained how that came to be, Ike took notice of the name Cecil Hammond.

Joe leaned against the sink, and the boys were out in the yard. Emma came into the room looking frightened, with Anna close on her heels. "I think she'll be okay. There's a bump on her head that's worrisome." She looked up at Joe. "That's Florence Hammond. Her husband must have done this to her, when she…"

Emma put her face in her hands and sobbed. Anna ran around to stand in front of her, reaching out—but not quite touching her—uncertain what to do.

Ike knew right off the woman in that car was not injured in the crash. He started adding up the casualties. Far too many of the people in this house were nursing injuries inflicted by a man named Cecil Hammond.

He stood up. "Joe, put a harness on that big draft horse out there. Let's get that car out of the ditch."

Joe nodded and went outside.

Although outwardly quiet and subdued, Ike was enraged that someone had laid a hand on Emma. It brought to him a calm he had never felt before. He didn't want a drink, he had things to do. He briefly wondered why Jack Hansen hadn't killed him when he had found Emma's bloody coat. He went outside and headed for the wagon trail. At his age, he needed a head start on Joe and that big horse.

Buck was able to pull the car back up onto the road in a matter of minutes. Joe dragged the pig carcass up onto the wagon trail.

Ike said, "We don't want nobody finding this car. I'll

steer while you pull it up into my barn."

Joe said, "What are you gonna do with it? We can't be stealing cars."

"It's already been stole. I'll figure a way to get rid of it."

Ike climbed behind the wheel and Joe took Buck's halter. They pulled the car down the gravel road and up into Ike's barn without being seen. Joe retrieved the package containing shoes for Anna and Chris, and Ike pulled a big tarp over the car.

He asked Joe, "You know how to roast a pig, boy?"

"Yes, sir."

"Ain't no sense letting that meat go to waste. Take that weener up to Yellowwood and roast it for them kids. Shouldn't take long, it ain't that big. Tell Emma I'll be along maybe tomorrow. I got a few things to do."

Joe watched Ike walk off in the direction of his house. Taking off his hat, he ducked into the chicken coop. Gathering up the eggs in his hat, he came back out to find Ike standing next to his truck giving him a strange look.

He held up his hat. "I'll take these to Emma. She's been short on eggs for six months. Ain't no sense feeding them to the pigs when she's got all those kids up there."

Ike's expression did not change, but he seemed to lose two inches in height. Why hadn't he thought to give Emma a few hens? Why hadn't he hunted them up some game? Why hadn't he done a lot of things? Ironically, he could not figure out why the obvious often eluded him.

He picked up the packages from the back of Cecil's car and handed them to Joe. Then he gave that big draft horse a swat on the rump and Joe followed Buck as he headed for home.

Ike had things to do. He climbed into his truck and

headed for town.

271

Chapter Twenty

Florence Hammond awoke to a dream. She was lying in a soft four-poster bed in a room flooded with sunlight from two big windows. A delicious smell carried on the breeze. She was thirsty and ravenously hungry. In the past two days, she had eaten only a handful of crackers.

She struggled up onto her elbows and heard the squeals and laughter of children playing. Through the open window, she saw a cherry tree. Pink petals rained down. A glass of water sat on the bedside table. She only wished for it, and a small hand picked it up and held it to her lips. She drank gratefully.

When the glass was taken away, she licked her cracked lips and looked beside her. The little red-haired orphan girl from the train depot placed the glass back on the table.

The girl turned to her and smiled, her hazel eyes sparkling. "I'm glad you're awake. We were worried for you."

Florence had a vague memory of the girl with an angel's eyes standing over her. Was she dead? Surely those in heaven did not feel pain. She must still be on Earth. "Where am I?"

"Yellowwood Farm. Joe carried you up from the road."

She remembered a road. An animal ran out in front of her and she was unable to avoid it. Her memory flooded back to her in an instant. She struggled to get out of bed, looking around in fear.

The girl placed a hand on her arm. "You're safe. Nobody knows you're here."

How did she know? Florence struggled to swing her

legs over the side of the bed. The girl knelt down and placed soft slippers on her bare feet.

"Emma said you could wear her mother's clothes. I think everything will fit you."

Emma, that name seemed familiar. Florence tried to stand and dropped back onto the bed. The little red-haired girl stuck her head under her arm. "Let me help you," she said.

Florence managed to stand up with the girl supporting her. "What's your name?"

"I'm Anna. Your name's Florence. Or do you want us to call you Missus Hammond?"

Florence's face twisted in disgust. "Please call me Florence."

Looking around, she thought this was a lovely room, but it was so big, as big as the whole upstairs of her house. Rather, what used to be her house; she had no intention of ever setting foot in that house again.

Her head was clearing. She asked, "Is this Anna Taylor's farm?"

Anna slipped out from under her arm and stood looking up at her. "That man hurt you and you're running away. Aren't you?"

Florence looked closely at Anna. She was frail but pretty. She had a sparkle about her. "Could I please speak to Missus Taylor?"

Anna said, "We helped you. You can't tell our secret."

"What secret?"

Anna had been sitting at Florence's bedside all afternoon. She thought about this for hours and she didn't want Emma to have to say it. "Anna Taylor died last year. Only kids live here. If the police find out, they'll take the farm and send us away. Emma says brothers and sisters have to stay together. She's Anna Taylor's daughter."

Florence was ashamed of what she did at the train depot that day. Now that she was attempting to think her own thoughts, she was ashamed of much of what she had done for the past six years. She took Anna's hands in hers and began to cry. "Please forgive me."

Anna had never seen an adult do anything like this. She worried that when Florence woke up, she would simply run to the authorities and their new life here would be over. She had nearly collected Christopher and ran away with him, before they found themselves back on a train.

Florence was so bruised and battered, Anna was afraid to touch her. Instead, she gently squeezed her hands. "You have to promise not to tell. This is the nicest place me and Chris have ever been. Emma is our sister now. Brothers and sisters have to stay together."

Florence was lost, broken, and afraid. Almost everything she believed in was revealed to her as cruel. She no longer trusted her own judgment, so what better guide than the innocent pleas of a child? She had no idea what was going on outside this room, but whatever it was, love was holding it together.

She felt like a child herself, when she clasped Anna's hands and said, "I promise not to tell."

***

Joe had the small pig roasting on a spit. Emma sat down next to him on one of the logs he placed around the fire. She was slowly losing her limp, and if she sat carefully on the back of her thighs, there was only a little discomfort.

"It smells really good," she said.

Joe said quietly, "You look nice."

Emma glanced up at him, but he had already turned

away. He often spoke without facing her. She could tell he was looking from his pink cheeks. "Anna made this dress for me. She's a wonder with a sewing machine. What did your pa say when he saw your head?"

"Pa ain't seen it yet, but Ma made a fuss. I told her I did it stringing wire. She un-bandaged it and looked it over. Said next time somebody needs stitched up she's sending them to you."

Emma chuckled. "I've never stuck a needle in a person in my life! I wonder how Anna got to be so good at it."

She stood up and kissed him on the cheek. "You were very brave."

They both burst out laughing, and Joe turned beet red. When the kitchen door opened and Florence stepped out into the sunshine of late afternoon, Emma and Joe jumped up and went to her. The boys ran up from the pasture. Within moments, the children surrounded Florence. Half a dozen frowning little faces looked up at her in silence.

Joe fetched a padded chair from the parlor and carried it out to place it beside her. She smiled at him and sat down. The swelling was down, but bruises still marred her face.

Anna took Emma by the arm and pulled her aside. "She promised not to tell."

Emma gave her a puzzled look, so Anna said, "About your ma, or me and Chris, about this place. I think she has secrets of her own to worry about."

Emma released her breath in a long sigh. She had been trusting to God that this woman would not turn them in.

Tommy stepped forward and stood close to Florence with Chris hanging onto his shirt. "Does it hurt?"

Florence said, "Only a little. What's your name?"

"Tommy. This here is Christopher, but we all call him Chris. That there is Clyde and Claude. Clyde is supposed to be the one wearing green suspenders, but they take turns being Clyde."

"It's very nice to meet all of you," she said.

Tommy looked at her closely. "I got a black eye once. It hurt fierce, but I didn't cry. Did you cry?"

Emma grabbed him by the suspenders and pulled him aside. "Tommy! You mind your manners."

Florence was surprised to see so many children. Then she looked past them at the green fields surrounded by virgin forest. A big red barn had the words, Yellowwood Farm, painted on it in white letters. Horses grazed in the pasture and the house fit into the landscape perfectly: rustic and solid. The place was so idyllic, she asked herself once again if she had died. She didn't think so, but she wasn't entirely sure.

Emma stepped around in front of Florence and her eyes sparkled in the full light of the sun—deep blue ringed with gold. Florence reached out to her. Emma looked up at Joe and he shrugged. She stepped into Florence's arms and frowned while Florence embraced her. Gradually, her embrace began to feel familiar.

Florence held on to Emma and said softly, "You have the eyes of an angel."

Anna stood up straight. "See! Did I na tell you!"

Emma pulled herself away from Florence's grasp. "We're roasting a pig. Are you hungry?"

All eyes were on Florence. She looked around and counted seven children. "I'm starving. I hope you didn't go to so much trouble on my account."

Joe chuckled. "You bagged the pig."

They moved her padded chair into the shade of the big oak tree in the front yard. Children swarmed around her, catering to her every need. She could not get over the fact that only children lived here. When Joe, the closest person here to being an adult, told her he was just a hired hand and has been working here for only two months, she was amazed.

When the meat was ready, they loaded their plates and gathered around Florence. Joe too, sat in the grass with Emma, Anna, and the boys.

Emma said, "You're welcome to stay as long as you want. Since you're new here, would you like to say the blessing?"

Florence was taken aback. These children viewed her as another orphan, seeking shelter at Yellowwood Farm. She was running for her life. She never made it out of Owen County, but she felt safe here—and welcome.

***

Ike spent the afternoon in town, preparing for—he wasn't sure what—the end maybe. Was it possible he could redeem himself and avoid an eternity in Hell? Would what he had in mind damn him to Hell? He didn't know. His own sense of righteousness told him any man who laid a hand on Emma deserved to die. He could name two—himself and Cecil Hammond.

He paid Sunday wages to have the papers drawn up placing his farm in Jack Hansen's name. Now, all he needed was for Jack to sign in the presence of a notary and register the title transfer with the county clerk. He knew Jack despised him, but Jack was an honest man. He trusted him to do right by his grandsons. He didn't want them to fall into the same situation Emma was struggling to overcome.

In the last two hours of daylight, Ike dug up Ball jars buried next to fence posts all over his farm. He had a habit of burying his money when he accumulated more than a thousand dollars. Very rarely had he dug any of them up. Each location was marked by a cross carved on a fencepost. As each jar came to light, he dropped it into his big cloth sack. He had twenty-two jars in that sack, hidden where he normally concealed his booze. He knew he had not found them all.

Late that night he managed to get Cecil's Ford Coupe running. The body was smashed up, but the engine was fine. He pulled out on the gravel road and drove toward town. Just past the one-room schoolhouse, he turned right, headed for the bluff beside the river. He knew Cecil and his buddies would keep looking for this car, so he would make it easy to find. The water below the bluff was not deep. Somebody was sure to spot it from town tomorrow.

The headlamps were smashed, so he drove slowly by the light of a half moon. When he reached his destination, he pulled well off the road and shut off the engine. Walking up to the steep drop-off, he peered down into the darkness. He could just make out the river, rendered in black and white. The lights of Spencer twinkled on the hillside above.

Taking his double-barrel shotgun out of the back, he laid it in the grass. Then pushing for all he was worth, he got the car rolling down the gradual incline. It bounced and rattled to the precipice and disappeared into the darkness. He heard the rustle of grass and then a series of crushing impacts as it went end over end and landed upside down in the White River.

Ike picked up his shotgun, laid it over his shoulder, and looked up at the sky. It was a nice night, cool and clear. He had a long walk home, but he felt up to it. He had never seen a woman beaten as badly as Florence Hammond. He was glad he could help her escape. Not to mention the satisfaction he derived from trashing Cecil's patrol car. He strongly suspected that he and Cecil had already met—at either end of a yard whip.

He took the first step of the long walk home. He felt good, maybe even noble.

***

By the time the sun dropped behind the trees, Florence was exhausted. She ate her fill and then some. Roasted pork, boiled potatoes, and carrots washed down with fresh milk gave her body the fuel it craved for healing. Now, she desired nothing more than sleep.

The boys instinctively adopted her as their new mother. Nothing was said, and they didn't even realize what they were doing. They competed for her attention, showing off with cartwheels and somersaults and spelling out the longest words they knew.

Florence was surprised to receive so much attention. She loved children, and she had begged God for children of her own. She suspected that these particular children knew perfectly well how to take care of themselves. Even so, she felt a powerful urge to care for them.

When the littlest of them, Christopher, crawled up into Florence's lap, the other boys envied him. She wrapped him in her arms and held him. He fell asleep and now she was nodding off. Holding that small boy helped to heal her deepest wounds.

The pig carcass was picked nearly clean. Joe kicked dirt over the embers and looked for Emma. She was sitting in the tree swing, gently swaying back and forth. He walked up to her. "I have to go. I have to tell Pa. I have to tell him everything."

Emma stopped swinging and looked up at him with concern. "I'm sorry."

"It ain't your fault. You couldn't send her away."

"Will your pa shoot that deputy?"

"He probably will, especially when he gets a look at Florence."

She jumped out of the swing and hugged him as hard as she could. "You were very brave."

He chuckled and said, "I have to take your word on it. I don't remember getting hit."

Anna was collecting the scattered plates and glasses left by the boys and carrying them off to the kitchen.

Emma said, "I should help her."

She released Joe and started picking up. The sun was on the horizon, so Joe went to saddle up Verne.

When she walked into the kitchen carrying plates and glasses, Anna already had the sink filled with soapy water. She had even refilled the reservoir in the stove and had a small fire going to warm water for washing.

Emma was grateful for the help and Anna's unshakeable cheerful attitude. She was slowly recovering from her bruised tailbone. More damaging was the trauma of a grown man attacking her. Seeing what he did to Florence magnified the fear brought on by that attack a thousand-fold. She tried not to hope Jack Hansen would kill him. She knew those thoughts were the most evil sort of sin.

The ten-gauge slug she carried in the pocket of her dress weighed her down. If she had to use it, she would. She would protect her brothers and sisters at the cost of her immortal soul.

Anna stood on Emma's stepstool so she could reach down into the sink. She turned to Emma and smiled. "I've never had such a fine meal."

Anna's very presence pulled Emma away from dark thoughts. Anna spent her time searching for ways to be helpful. She was a fountain of cheerfulness and good deeds.

Emma walked up to stand beside Anna and soaped a washcloth. "I'm glad you're here," she said.

Anna turned to her and whispered confidentially, "I still think you're an angel."

She looked so serious it made Emma laugh. It was good to find a little childish wonder in her.

Tommy burst through the kitchen door and held it open. Florence came through it holding Christopher's hand, followed by Clyde and Claude.

"I'm sorry, I fell asleep."

She looked horrible. Blood pooled below her eyes, creating swollen pouches. She walked up to the sink and pulled up her sleeves.

Anna climbed down from the stepstool. "You need to rest."

Emma took her hand. "You can wear one of Momma's nightdresses. You look like her size."

Anna ran off into the parlor and returned a moment later carrying a pitcher, decorated with roses. She knelt down beside the woodstove and filled it with warm water.

Seeing that pitcher being put to use was hard for Emma. She kept her mother's room in perfect order, even going so far as to place a bar of Ivory soap on her washstand. A few strands of her mother's hair were caught in her hairbrush. Emma cherished them.

Letting Florence stay in her mother's room was forcing her to let go. Florence gave herself up to distract Cecil Hammond from beating her and Joe. Without that sacrifice, Emma knew she could be wearing those bruises, or worse.

She swallowed hard and pulled Florence toward her mother's room. It would always be her mother's room, but she would allow Florence to stay there. It was what her mother would have done.

Anna pulled Chris away from Florence and led him off to get ready for bed, yawning and rubbing his eyes.

Emma sat Florence down in a bentwood chair beside her mother's washstand and pulled a clean nightdress from the dresser. Florence could see what she was feeling.

"This must be hard for you."

Emma looked up at her, clinging tightly to her mother's nightdress.

Florence said, "Losing your mother and father, you're too young to do all you have done. Thank you, for letting me stay here."

Florence held out her arms. Emma hesitated for a moment and laid her mother's nightdress on the bed. She walked into Florence's arms and embraced her. Again, it felt familiar: comforting and warm. When she closed her eyes, the air filled with the scent of roses. She felt her mother's presence and sent a silent prayer.

I miss you, Momma.

Florence held her while she cried.

***

When Ike reached his own property, it was well after midnight. He never kept track of time. He lived by the position of the sun in the sky, and on some days, he didn't even pay attention to the sun. Tonight, he felt highly in tune with the moon and stars.

He walked past his farm and continued down the road to the wagon trail leading to Yellowwood Farm. A little ways into the darkness under the big oak trees, he found a comfortable spot. Easing himself down onto a bed of moss, he sat with his back against the old oak and laid his shotgun across his knees. The prairie grass on the other side of the road rippled in the moonlight. It had been a long time since he had seen the beauty of this place.

Chapter Twenty-One

Early Monday morning, Cecil Hammond stood in water up to his knees, searching through the remains of his patrol car. The county sheriff, Bill Robertson, walked the bank.

"I'm sorry, Cecil. I don't see any footprints."

Cecil climbed back up onto the bank. "She ain't dead, Bill. We got to find her!"

Bill didn't think she was killed in the crash. Cecil's neighbor, Hannah Zeller, knocked on his door yesterday afternoon and told him she saw Cecil beat two kids in his front yard. She said she saw him drag Florence into the house and heard screams. Was this some sort of cover up? He never liked Cecil, and he could not understand why Florence had married him.

The bank was soft and muddy. If anyone walked away from that crash, there would be footprints. The current was certainly strong enough to carry off a body, but he didn't think anyone was in that car when it went down the embankment. It didn't make sense. There was nothing on this road but a few widely spaced farms. Florence had no reason to be here. It was, however, the perfect place to stage an accident.

Bill said, "Let's go. She ain't here. We'll ask around to see if anybody saw anything."

Watching Cecil dejectedly climb the hill back up to the car, Bill saw genuine despair. He started to think Cecil really didn't know what had happened to Florence, but that didn't mean he didn't beat her. Maybe she ran off.

***

When the sun crept up behind the trees, Joe and his father started up the wagon trail on horseback. Jack Hansen was angry—again. Last night, he shouted at Joe while they stood outside in the dark until his mother came out and asked what was going on.

Jack made up a lame excuse about brushing down a horse. Mary shrugged and went back inside. She had no idea what was going on at Yellowwood Farm, and Jack dreaded the day she found out.

Joe followed along behind his father. He figured he would have whipped him, if he didn't already have five stitches in his head. It wasn't so easy to tell Emma no. He only went with her to make sure she didn't get hurt. As it turned out, he hadn't done so well on that account, but he had tried.

They had just started up the wagon trail when Ike Pearson stepped out of the trees carrying a shotgun. They reined in their horses.

Ike said, "Morning, Jack, Joe. Gonna be a fine day."

Jack gave him a hard look and decided he was sober. "What's up, Ike? Hunting up some game for those children?"

Ike knew what Jack meant by that comment, but he was redeeming himself. He hadn't slept a wink, yet he felt better than he had in years. He spent the night keeping watch over Yellowwood Farm.

"You might say that. I reckon Joe told you about Florence Hammond."

Jack scowled. "He did. I can't say I approve of Emma taking her in."

Ike looked him in the eye and said, "Maybe we shoulda left her in the road. Maybe we shoulda given her back to her husband, the fella that beat her half to death, pistol whipped your son, and kicked Emma black and blue."

Jack sat up straight on his horse and glared at Ike. "I'll deal with that man soon enough."

Ike chuckled. "You're a good man Jack, but you got a wife and kids to look after. You can't mess with the law in these parts until you have lived too long."

The leather creaked when Jack leaned over in his saddle and stared hard at Ike. That shotgun took on new meaning. "You been here all night?"

"Mostly. I pushed that car down the hill over by the Carrington's before I walked over here. Somebody probably found it by now. Probably think that poor woman was carried off in the river."

Jack considered this. "Might have picked a better spot, but at least they ain't looking for the car."

Ike saw a glimmer of respect in Jack's face. It was a bad situation all around, but if they were careful, maybe Emma and the boys could come through this. Ike, however, was resigned to taking a life—and losing his own. He figured he had everything to gain and little to lose.

"You go on up and talk to this woman, but you be real nice to Emma. Your boy here done all he could, he carried Emma all the way across town. You should be proud of him. When you're done, stop by my place, if you would. We got business."

Being lectured on how to behave by Ike Pearson, and rightfully so, drained the anger from Jack. Ike laid his shotgun over his shoulder and walked away. Jack looked over at Joe and regretted shouting at him.

He looked like he had a mouthful of bitters when he said, "I'm sorry I yelled at ya, boy."

Joe's mouth fell open in complete surprise. It was the first time in his life he heard his father apologize for anything.

Jack scowled and said, "Shut your mouth before you catch a fly in there. Let's go."

***

Emma stood at the window when Joe and his father topped the rise from the wagon trail. She hated it when Jack Hansen yelled at her. She figured it was best to get it over with out in the barn, where Florence couldn't hear.

Anna was setting out breakfast for the boys. Florence had not yet stirred. When Emma checked on her, she found her fast asleep. Her mother always said people healed better when they were sleeping.

She turned to Anna. "Joe's here and his father is with him. I'm going out to talk to them."

Anna put down a bowl of oatmeal and wiped her hands on a little apron she threw together in just fifteen minutes.

"Mister Hansen is loud, but he isn't mean. Just let him yell awhile and hug him."

Emma smiled. That was good advice. She would do just that.

She walked out to the barn and, as expected, she found Joe and his father brushing down their horses. Taking in Florence was what her mother would have done. She would defend that decision if she had to, but hopefully she could get by with a hug.

Jack turned to her and smiled. "Morning, Miss Emma. Joe tells me you've been adopting strays again."

Emma wasn't sure what to say. Mister Hansen didn't seem to be upset with her. He knelt down in front of her and took her hands. "Are you okay, Honey?"

She frowned, waiting for the yelling. It took her a few seconds to realize Jack wasn't going to shout at her. She threw her arms around his neck and hugged him for all she was worth.

Jack smiled and patted her on the back. "Your ma

would have done the same thing."

Emma wiped her eyes. "Thank you." She took Jack by the hand. "We have tea. Would you like some?"

"That would be fine. I'd like to speak to Missus Hammond, if she's up to it."

Emma said, "She doesn't like to be called that. Call her Florence. She's still sleeping."

Joe was as surprised by his father's behavior as Emma, but he thought he understood what was changing this tough old man. Emma had that effect on people. He smiled while he followed her toward the house—still holding his father's hand.

***

Florence came awake slowly. When she opened her eyes, a pair of brown eyes under a mop of dark hair looked back at her. The boy was only visible from the nose up, but she could tell when he smiled.

"Good morning, Florence."

She sat up slowly. Her back ached and her ribs burned on one side. She stretched the arm on her good side and looked around. Another small face appeared beside the first, a little higher up.

"Good morning, Florence."

She said, "Good morning, Tommy. Good morning, Christopher. What time is it?"

Tommy looked confused. "Why?"

Two identical little faces with blonde hair peeked through the door, and one of them whispered, "Is she awake?"

Tommy turned and whispered back, "She's sitting up ain't she."

They looked over their shoulders and came quietly into the room to stand beside the bed. Four little faces, filled with hope, stared up at Florence. She patted the bed beside her, and all four faces lit up. They circled around and crawled carefully up onto the bed in a row. She whimpered when one of them bumped her the wrong way.

Tommy said, "Be careful! She's hurt, you guys!"

Anna appeared in the doorway. "Did I na tell ya to let her sleep!"

They squealed and scampered off the bed in every direction, dodging swipes from Anna as they ran past her and escaped through the door.

Anna approached Florence and looked her over with an appraising eye. For such a small girl, she had the demeanor of a middle-aged woman.

"You look some better, but the second day after it always hurts more."

To find that this young girl knew such things saddened Florence. She was right though, she hurt all over.

Anna said, "Joe's father has been waiting to speak to you."

Florence felt a moment of panic. It must have shown on her face, because Anna took her hand. "Don't worry. Mister Hansen promised to keep our secret. He helps us. He shouts sometimes, but he's a nice man."

Florence drew aside the covers and moaned when she swung her legs over the side of the bed.

Anna said, "Let me help you to the powder room. Just as soon as you're done you are going back to bed."

Florence winced. "I'd rather meet Mister Hansen on my feet."

Anna put her hands on her hips. "Today, you will do as I say. Now let's get you to the powder room and then straight back to bed. Mister Hansen can wait until you've had a cup of tea. If you're feeling better this afternoon, maybe you can come to the table for dinner—or supper, or whatever people call it here."

Smiling weakly, Florence said, "Some tea would be wonderful."

Anna stuck her head under Florence's arm and helped her walk slowly to the powder room just outside the door.

Jack Hansen had been waiting for over an hour when he was finally allowed to speak to Florence. During that time he became acquainted with Anna Kennedy. In his estimation, she was a lot smarter than he was.

When Jack stepped into the room, Emma stood guard beside Florence. Anna stood beside the open window, wearing a little frown. Both of them had already cautioned him to be on his best behavior.

The woman sitting up in the bed was beaten so badly his stomach turned. She had long dark hair and delicate features, marred by cuts and bruises. In spite of her injuries, she was beautiful.

She held out her hand. "It is a pleasure to meet you, Mister Hansen."

Jack was seldom speechless, but he completely forgot what he intended to say. He reached out to take her hand and only brushed her fingers—afraid to grasp something so fragile.

Florence said, "I understand you have been helping Emma. That's very noble of you."

"Emma don't need much help on this farm. I only help her out when she has to dicker for seed and such."

Florence was embarrassed by her helplessness and by the stupidity of having married a man like Cecil. "I'm sorry to be such a bother. I'll leave as soon as I'm able."

Emma spun around to face her. "No! We want you to

stay."

Jack could see what Florence meant to them. A grown woman on a farm full of orphans filled an obvious need. "There's no hurry. Ike dumped your car in the river, so your husband likely thinks you drowned."

Florence gave him a look of fright. "If that's so, then my mother must think I'm dead! Please, Mister Hansen! You've got to tell her I'm okay."

Jack thought she was far from okay. Still, it was only right that he let her mother know she was alive. "Alright, I'll let her know."

Emma focused on Florence, still upset by the thought of her leaving. "Please don't leave," she said.

Florence didn't want to leave. Emma, Anna, and the boys gave her something she had sought her whole life, but they didn't understand the sort of danger she was in. Just being here put them in jeopardy. Her foolish behavior was the reason Joe and Emma were injured.

"It's beautiful here. I would dearly love to stay, but if my husband finds out I'm here…"

Her own thoughts huddled together deep inside of her, too timid to step out and be heard, but she could not so easily bottle up her feelings. She felt joy when those four boys sneaked into her room, seeking *her* acceptance. Nothing awaited her in Bloomington.

Emma said, "We're safe here. If you want, just stay."

Jack said, "She can't hide here forever."

Anna gave him a dirty look and stepped around the bed to take Florence's hand. "Me and Chris are hiding here. We can't leave, but we don't want to. I don't ever want to leave this place. Would you be happy if you never left here?"

Would she be happy here? Could she give up every bit of the world outside this farm? Did she have anything to offer these children?

She broke down in tears. "I have nowhere else to go."

Anna put her arms around Florence and glared over her shoulder at Jack. Emma stuck her finger in his chest and backed him up all the way through the door.

Jack found himself standing just outside the door, surrounded by the boys. They were all peeking in at Florence, when Emma closed the door in their faces.

***

That night, Joe gave up his seat at the head of the table to Florence. She wore only a nightdress and a robe. Having slept all day, Anna had to wake her for supper. They were completely out of chairs now, so Joe sat on Emma's stepstool.

Emma bowed her head. "Lord, it's us again. We thank you for sending us Florence, our new sister. Please Lord, watch over us. Please keep us safe. Amen."

Florence had never heard anyone genuinely pray for protection before. These children have survived far more than a beating from a spurned husband. She stopped feeling sorry for herself and tried to imagine what they have been through.

The table erupted into happy chatter as the boys told Florence about their exploits of the day. She found them to be highly entertaining, and they made a contest out of trying to make her laugh.

***

Emma watched all this while she ate her bowl of ham, carrots, and string beans. It was a relief to have the boys focused on someone else for a change, but it also bothered her. Upon closer inspection, she found that it wasn't jealousy she was feeling. It was fear, fear that they would come to love Florence—and lose her.

She waited for a break in the boyish storytelling. "Florence, would you be happy living here? What if you could never leave?"

Florence already knew the answer. She had never seen such a lovely place and never felt so needed. All she had to offer was love, but these children craved her attention.

"When I woke up here, I thought I'd died and gone to heaven."

Anna sat bolt upright. "I know! It's Emma's eyes. Sometimes they scare the dickens outta me!"

Florence laughed. "They do, don't they. She has an angel's eyes."

Emma frowned. "You didn't answer my question." She looked around the table, and everyone stopped eating, waiting to hear Florence's reply.

Florence became solemn and took Emma's hand. "I would be perfectly happy if I never left this place."

Emma relaxed. "You only have to keep our secret for five years. I'll be old enough then to own the land. I don't know about your husband though."

Joe said, "Pa will take care of him."

Emma didn't want to know how. She was struggling with her conscience over that.

After supper, Florence was tiring. The sun touched the horizon. Joe excused himself and went to saddle his horse. Emma felt that bringing Florence into their growing family deserved a solemn ceremony, so she took her hand and led her outside. They walked slowly up the hill to the yellowwood tree, surrounded by Anna and the boys.

Florence touched one of the long strings of blossoms. "This is beautiful. What kind of tree is this?"

Tommy said, "It's a yellowwood. It was Ma's favorite."

Looking down, Florence suddenly realized what was at her feet. Hundreds of handprints covered the grave. Small white stones spelled out, Anna Taylor.

The children gathered here often. Whenever a major decision had to be made, or just to renew their bond, they came together here. Emma came here every day. They knelt down all around the grave and started pulling up grass and weeds. Florence got down on her knees beside them and added her own slender handprints to theirs.

The sky turned a deep orange when the sun dropped below the horizon. Emma pressed her hands together and bowed her head. The other children did the same.

"Momma, we have a new sister today. This is Florence. She's not an orphan, but she needs our help."

A warm breeze carried the scent of roses. The sky took on a pinkish hue. She felt her mother's touch gently brush her hair, and feelings of love washed over her. With her mother's blessing, she accepted Florence into their family.

Chapter Twenty-Two

Jack Hansen knocked softly on the door of a small house on the edge of town. The house was quaint but falling into disrepair. The yellow paint was peeling and there was a broken step out front.

A thin, birdlike woman in her late sixties answered the door.

He removed his hat. "Missus Cavanaugh?"

"Yes. Can I help you?"

"Your daughter asked me to tell you that she is fine and not to worry if you don't hear from her for some time."

The old lady's eyebrows arched, and her lips compressed into a firm line. "What is this about?"

Jack realized this woman didn't even know her daughter was missing. "Florence is staying with some friends. Her husband beat her up pretty bad."

Bea Cavanaugh stepped out onto her front porch and grabbed Jack by the arm. Her claw-like grip was surprisingly strong. "The devil you say! Cecil would never lay a hand on Flo. I'm proud to call him my son-in-law! Who are you?"

Jack regretted coming here. He pulled his arm loose and stuck his hat back on his head. "Jack Hansen, Ma'am."

She looked him up and down with disdain. "Where is my daughter?"

Jack had not expected this kind of reaction. Offended, he leaned over Bea and gave her a hard look. She cringed and backed away.

"Your son-in-law whipped my boy with a pistol and kicked a little girl so hard she couldn't walk! Then he beat your daughter half to death. Are you proud of that ma'am?"

She looked around. "Come inside. I don't want the neighbors to hear."

She went back into the house, and Jack made up his mind. This woman did not deserve one more second of his time.

Bea came back to the door and held it open. "Well?"

Jack shook his head. "I reckon not."

He went back down the steps and swung up into the saddle. Tipping his hat to her, he whirled his horse around and rode off.

Jack travelled slowly on the gravel road out of town, moving to the shoulder when he could. He didn't like riding on gravel. It was hard on a horse's hooves and made for poor footing. When he turned off the gravel onto the dirt road that led to his farm, he urged his horse to a trot. It would be dark soon. He didn't like riding a horse past dark, they weren't naturally inclined to work at night.

All the little oddities of Yellowwood Farm had consumed yet another day. He didn't hold it against Emma, but farmers did not have time to spare. He worried that Bea Cavanaugh couldn't keep her mouth shut, he worried that Emma was trying to do too much, he worried about that big sack of money Ike Pearson entrusted to him, and he worried less about that little red-headed girl than the rest. He figured that whatever happened, she would be just fine.

***

The moment Jack Hansen rode off, Bea Cavanaugh started walking to her daughter's house only five blocks away. She stepped quickly with indignant anger. That man was lying to her, but she couldn't figure out why. There had to be some sort of swindle involved. What was it? Cecil would know. He was clever about things like that.

It took her only fifteen minutes to reach Florence's house. It was close to sunset, so she figured they would be home, but Cecil's car was not out front. She stepped up the flagstones and stopped. A jar of what appeared to be honey, was smashed on the flagstones. It had attracted bees, so she scooted around it. It wasn't safe to leave shards of glass lying about like that. She would say something to Cecil.

When she saw that the porch railing was broken, alarm bells went off in the back of her mind. Instead of knocking on the door, she stepped to the side and looked through the window. The conversation table was up against the fireplace and one of the chairs was on its back.

She was peering into the deepening gloom of the house, when a hand touched her shoulder. Bea jumped and squealed before she recognized Hannah Zeller, Florence's neighbor.

Bea covered her heart with her hand. "Hannah! Oh my goodness, you frightened me half to death!"

Hannah gave her a pitying look. "How is Flo? We haven't seen her since that ruckus on Saturday. She's such a sweet girl. I hope she ain't hurt bad."

Bea said, "I don't know what you're talking about."

Hannah looked around before speaking. "Cecil hurt a couple of kids that came to the door Saturday. He kicked a little girl so hard she couldn't get up. The boy with her was bleeding. He carried her off."

Bea looked shocked. "Cecil wouldn't do anything like that. He's an officer of the law!"

Hannah was ashamed to say, "When Cecil dragged Flo into the house, and we heard her screaming, me and Levi was too scared to do anything. We thought about calling the law, but Cecil is the law."

There was a bump from inside the house. Hannah took two quick steps away. "I'm sorry, Bea. I hope Flo is okay." She ran back to disappear through her own front door.

Bea turned back to the house. For the first time, she

felt a touch of concern for her daughter's welfare. Florence was a flighty child, requiring constant guidance, lest she associate with the wrong sort of people. Hannah Zeller, for example, was destined for Hell. Yet Florence often had tea with that woman—a Jewess!

She could understand Cecil having to apply a little discipline. She was forced to do so often enough herself. Her father was gone now, God rest his soul. When he was alive, he had kept his daughter squarely on the path to righteousness.

The door opened and Cecil stepped outside. He looked terrible. His uniform was wrinkled and he had two days of stubble on his face.

"She's gone, Bea. Took my car and run off. I don't know where she went."

Bea took his arm. "You poor boy! Let me make you some supper. Have you eaten today?"

***

Ike sat in the dark, chewing a piece of hardtack. He had slept part of the day, and now he felt refreshed. Washing down the dry cracker with water from his canteen, he wiped his mouth on his sleeve. Keeping watch over Emma and the other children made him feel useful.

His farm would be put in Jack Hansen's name in the morning. Jack refused to sign the title transfer until Ike pointed out that his grandsons were perilously close to being in the same situation as Emma. He also placed into Jack's hands, twenty-eight thousand dollars—his life savings. Upon his death, half was to be given to Emma and half put away for his grandsons until they came of age.

Jack had tried to argue with him, and had insisted that Ike put the money into a bank. Ike cautioned him never to trust banks. Banks, he told him, were going to fail. Not just one here and there, but all of them and all at once. Borrowing to buy land is hard, but workable. Borrowing to buy things that get used up is a losing proposition. Borrowing to buy stocks on margin? That's a disaster waiting to happen. Eventually, one of the little guys would miss a margin call, causing a not so little guy to miss his, and bigger and bigger dominos would fall. To Ike's mind, it was inevitable.

Jack did not appear to believe him, but he gave his word to hide the cash. Ike expected him to come by in the morning, and they would go into town to make everything nice and legal.

The creatures Ike was waiting for did not come out during the day. Sitting here at night connected him with the creatures of the night. Raccoons waddled up the trail, undoubtedly on their way to the stream on the other side of the hill. Every now and then, an owl silently swooped down to snatch up a mouse. He even saw an old bobcat, padding silently down the wagon trail toward the fields below.

He leaned back against the tree, laid his shotgun across his knees, and settled in to watch the show.

***

At nine o'clock on Tuesday morning, Cecil Hammond stood beside Sheriff Bill Robertson while he knocked on Jack Hansen's front door. Mary opened the door, surprised to find the sheriff standing there with one of his deputies.

"What's going on, Bill?"

He said, "This here is Cecil Hammond. Cecil's wife is missing, and her mother said that Jack might know where she is."

Mary didn't know what he was talking about. Bill could see that, so he asked, "Is Jack home?"

Mary knew Bill and trusted him, so she said, "Jack's

not here. Anna Taylor has been sick and Joe's working over there as a hired hand. Jack said he was going to check in on them and then he had to go into town."

Bill nodded. "Appreciate it, sorry to bother you."

Mary stepped out onto her front porch and watched Bill and his deputy get into his car and drive off. This didn't feel right.

***

Emma was out in her garden, planting tomato seedlings. She loved the new dresses Anna had made for her. They were so comfortable she dreaded wearing her old ones. Anna watched her closely, eager to learn how to grow a tomato.

Anna was now the proud owner of her own garden trowel. She dug a small hole and placed a seeding into it, careful to bury exactly two thirds of the stem. She ran four steps to pick up the watering can, ran four steps back, and watered the seedling. She smiled, nudged Emma, and pointed to it.

"That's good. They'll grow roots along the stem," Emma said.

Anna twirled around in excitement. "That is my very first tomato plant. Actually, that is my very first time planting anything!"

Emma laughed. Anna's enthusiasm made everything they did together fun.

Anna examined the box containing the seedlings. "How many kinds are there?"

"Four. They get ripe at different times, and sometimes they get wilt or blight, but usually only one kind gets sick."

"When did you plant the seeds in the box?"

"The second week of March. The hot box is on the

south side of the barn, so it gets lots of sun. I put horse manure in there too, that keeps them warm and fertilizes them."

Anna had a look of astonishment. "Begorrah! I did na know horse manure kept things warm!"

When Emma glanced up at her, Anna was sparkling with excitement, selecting her next seedling. Florence came out of the kitchen door fully dressed. Emma recognized that dress immediately. When Florence arose early and tried to help with breakfast, Anna would not allow it. She seated her at the table and put a cup of tea in front of her. After breakfast, Emma and Anna escorted her back to bed. Yet there she was, all dressed and walking around.

The boys ran up from the pasture and the barn. They surrounded her and she laughed. Emma could almost see her mother standing there. Florence looked nothing like her mother, but that was her dress, and children were drawn to her—just like her mother.

Anna looked up from her planting. "I knew she would not stay in bed. A little sun might be good for her."

Emma stood up and wiped her hands on her garden apron. "Maybe we should give her something to do. It isn't healthy for a person to have nothing to do."

Anna shrugged. "Is she good at anything?"

"I don't know. Let's ask her."

Florence was already headed their way, while the boys ran circles around her. Emma walked out to meet her.

"How are you feeling?" she asked.

Florence rubbed the top of Tommy's head and he smiled, looking up fondly at the first grown woman to touch him in nearly a year.

"I'm feeling much better. I'd like to help with the planting."

In Emma's opinion, it hurt just to look at her. The knot on her forehead was greenish gray, and the blood pooled beneath her eye on that side in a dark purple pouch. Her lips were cracked, but she was smiling.

Emma recalled that when a person had a knot on their head, it hurt to bend over. "Can you make bread?"

Florence brightened and stood up straighter. "Of course. Do we need bread?"

"We do, if you don't mind. These boys eat more bread than I can keep on the table.

She turned to the boys. "Clyde, Claude, go fetch some wood for the stove. Tommy, bring in a bag of flour from the root cellar."

They took off in a flash and she shouted, "After that, you boys get back in the barn and finish cleaning those stalls! And put it in the spreader, so Joe doesn't have to shovel it again!"

Chris was left standing next to Florence. He looked up at Emma. "What can I do?"

Florence tried to pick him up and failed. Clutching her side, she said with a smile, "You can be my special helper."

She took him by the hand and they walked back toward the house.

Anna and Emma were nearly finished planting the tomatoes when they heard an engine coming up the wagon trail. Emma stood up. "Ike's here."

A sheriff's car topped the rise. As it came down the hill, Emma stared hard at the two occupants. She grabbed Anna by the arm and hauled her to her feet.

"Run! Get in the house!"

Anna did not hesitate—she took off. Emma turned to look for Joe. He was out in the far fields, but he was already sprinting in her direction. She ran after Anna.

The car reached the house at the same time Emma did. Anna held the door open. She ran inside, and Anna slammed it closed while two men jumped out of the patrol car.

Florence looked up from kneading her dough, and a familiar voice called out, "Florence!"

Her face took on a look of terror. Cecil was looking through the glass in the door at her.

Anna pushed Chris into the parlor. Then she grabbed Florence's arm and pulled her in that direction.

Emma locked the door just as Cecil grabbed the knob. The door rattled. His face was two feet away from her! Sobbing, she took the shotgun shell from the pocket of her dress. She reached for her father's shotgun beside the door and it fell to the floor.

Frantically hauling it up, she broke it open while Cecil watched though the window in the door. She was shaking so hard she dropped the shell. Glancing up at the window, she screamed when she saw Cecil point his gun at her. The other policeman wrenched the gun from Cecil's hand and knocked him to the ground.

She scooped the shell from the floor, slammed it into the breech, and snapped the shotgun closed. Raising it up to her shoulder, she approached the door. The policeman who knocked down Cecil briefly appeared in the window and jumped aside when he found himself looking down the barrel of a ten-gauge shotgun.

She heard the boys call her name and saw them standing outside the barn. She dropped the shotgun to the floor and pressed her hands against the glass. "Run!"

They must not have heard her, or maybe they did. They took a step toward the house. Joe flashed into view and scooped up Tommy and Clyde, one under each arm. He carried them into the barn. Claude spun around and ran after him.

Emma sobbed and stooped down to pick up the shotgun. The policeman she didn't recognize kept his hands in the air. Emma raised her shotgun to aim at him through the glass. His eyes got big, but he stayed where he was.

Cecil was on the ground behind him. When Emma saw him roll onto his stomach and get on his hands and knees, she shifted her aim. Bill glanced back just in time to see Joe run out of the barn, and without slowing down, he kicked Cecil in the ass so hard his face went into the dirt and his knees came off the ground. Cecil screamed in pain and rolled onto his back, clutching his backside.

Joe stood over him, panting and red-faced. "You shouldn't go around kicking people, especially when they kick back!" He kicked Cecil in the ribs.

Bill looked over his shoulder. "That's enough!"

The exertion caused Joe's head to bleed and ache. Breathing hard, he reached up to touch the bloody bandage and examined his fingertips. Cecil was rolling around on the ground, howling in pain.

Bill carefully used one finger of his raised hand to point at Joe's head. "Did Cecil do that?"

Joe nodded.

"You can kick him one more time."

Joe smiled and laid one upside Cecil's head. His eyes rolled back and he quit screaming.

Bill turned his attention back to the door. Through the glass, only three feet away, a trembling little girl with tears running down her face was pointing a ten-gauge shotgun at his chest. He figured he was closer to being dead right now than he had ever been.

An odd thought went through his mind—she had pretty eyes.

Florence struggled through the doorway while Anna tried to hold her back. "Emma! Put the gun down!"

Emma looked back over her shoulder at Florence. "No! I'll go to Hell before I let those men hurt us!"

Florence gasped and started to cry. "This is my fault. Please put down the gun."

Emma kept the shotgun at her shoulder, until Florence gently took it from her hands and laid it on the floor. Emma released a long wailing moan. Everything she feared, all her worst nightmares, were coming true.

"I nearly went to Hell, Momma!" Realizing what she just said, she choked back a sob. "I mean…"

Florence wrapped Emma in her arms. "Hush now. It's okay." She reached out and unlocked the door.

Bill Robertson walked into the kitchen to find Florence and Emma clinging to each other in tears. A little red-haired girl reached for the shotgun. He placed his foot on it and she looked up at him. Her hazel eyes sparkled. When she blinked, tears ran down her cheeks.

When he saw Florence's face, Bill's heart hammered in his chest. She was barely recognizable, but the cuts and bruises only served to magnify the protective urges she naturally engendered. "Did Cecil do this?"

She nodded and buried her face in Emma's hair.

He looked around the room. "Where's Anna Taylor?"

Emma held on tightly to Florence and said, "Momma is…she…"

Florence said, "I'm Anna Taylor."

Bill gave her a puzzled look. Little Anna smiled.

"Please, Bill. Do this for me. I am Anna Taylor."

He tried to understand. "Where's Anna?"

"She died of the flu. These children have been working incredibly hard to hang onto this farm for a year! I'm begging you Bill. Let me be Anna Taylor."

The Spanish flu was a horrific experience for the entire world. At least once a month for almost two years, Bill took children from homes where their parents lay dead beside them. Corrupt state and county officials closed in rapidly, and those children did not fare well. Their homes were auctioned off to a select group of buyers at pennies on the dollar and then quickly resold for fair value.

"Look, Flo, I'm on your side. I know what happens to kids left without their parents. It ain't right. It ain't even lawful, but it happens all the time."

"If you say I'm Anna Taylor, then who's to say I'm not?"

Bill chuckled. Assuming a new identity was not unheard of, or even uncommon. All a person had to do was cross a state line and they could make a fresh start. This was different. "What about Cecil? What about your mother?" he asked.

Florence looked up from the floor, wounded and desperate. "What if I never leave this place?"

Emma began to understand what was happening. She stood up. "Please, sir, this farm is all we have."

When Bill turned around, he saw that the little red-haired girl had gotten hold of the shotgun again! She was smiling like a little angel, but she was a well-armed little angel. Thankfully, she was not pointing that big gun at him.

He grabbed the barrel. "Give me that, you little minx!"

When he pulled on the barrel, the gun went off with a tremendous BOOM! Anna flew back to land flat on her bottom. The shock wave went up Bill's arm and rattled his teeth. There was a big smoking hole in the door.

Emma screamed and threw open the door. She ran into Joe, who was running in. She untangled herself from him and screamed, "Tommy! Clyde! Claude!"

The boys stood in front of the barn, apparently unharmed.

Cecil Hammond sat up and put a hand to his head. Climbing slowly to his feet, he searched for his gun. It was nowhere to be found. He staggered toward the house. He was bruised and battered, but Florence was in there and he had to have her.

When Emma saw Cecil get to his feet and walk toward the house, she slammed the door and locked it. She stepped in front of Florence. "He's coming!"

When he reached the door, Cecil pressed his hands against the glass and stared into the kitchen at Florence. Tears streamed down his face when he saw what he had done to her, but she had brought it on herself. Until two days ago, she was a dutiful wife.

"Florence!" he screamed. "Florence!"

Bill Robertson unlocked the door, stepped outside, and pushed Cecil back. "You're an idiot!"

Cecil wept and blubbered, "She's mine, Bill."

"Not any more she ain't."

Bill grabbed Cecil's badge and ripped it off him, leaving a three-cornered flap of fabric. "You're done."

Cecil's face went red with rage. "You can't do that! On what grounds?"

"On the grounds that I can't have an idiot running around my county with a gun."

Pointing to the Colt revolver stuck into Bill's belt, Cecil said, "That gun belongs to me! County don't provide side arms if you recall."

Bill pulled out the pistol and stuck the barrel against Cecil's forehead. "Try to take it. You're lucky there are women and children here."

Cecil backed up, but Bill followed, keeping the gun pressed to his head. "Must be eight or ten miles back to town. How about I give you a ride?"

Cecil turned and headed up the wagon trail in a plodding jog, as close as he ever came to running. Once he disappeared over the ridge, the boys shot out of the barn and surrounded Bill—cheering. He smiled. He had kids of his own.

Florence came outside, followed by Emma, Joe, and Anna. Christopher's face peeked through the hole in the door before he ran out to hang on to Florence.

Florence leaned in to kiss Bill softly on the cheek. "Thank you."

He said, "He'll be back."

"I know. I can't stay here."

Emma looked up at her in alarm. "If you don't stay, he'll be back anyway."

"Not if he knows where I am."

When Florence reached out to grasp Emma's shoulder, she turned away.

Emma pouted. "Brothers and sisters have to stay together." She whirled around and shouted, "No matter what!"

Anna grasped Florence's hand and pleaded with her, "Please stay! We're more afraid of you leaving than we are of that fat little man."

Florence smiled at that description of her husband. Not until the past few days had she seen him as a pathetic, fat little man—even in his uniform.

Realizing what was happening, Tommy said, "We'll watch out for you, Florence. Please don't leave!"

All four of the boys were crying now. Everyone started talking at once.

Joe shrugged and walked away. He knew that Ike Pearson guarded the trail at night, but he figured the minute anybody counted on him to do that, he'd let them down, so he kept silent. He could see the team patiently standing where he'd left them. Buck and Jane were the only ones paying attention to the farm. If the farm was not successful, then all this other stuff wouldn't matter.

Emma watched Joe walk off toward the far fields, and she knew right away he was doing what needed to be done. He was just like his father: practical and focused. What was most important here? What should she do?

Frightened and bewildered, she headed up the hill. Seeing where she was going, Anna and the boys ran to catch up to her. Florence and Bill were left alone beside the house.

"Where are they going?" he asked.

"Anna Taylor is buried under that tree. They go there when they need help."

"Did you ever meet Anna?"

"No," she said.

"I only met her a few times. Her daughter looks just like her. Acts like her too. If she says you're Anna Taylor, then I'll go along for her mother's sake. Anybody who knew her would do the same."

Florence was near to tears. "I don't want to leave here. If I could stay and people said I was Anna, then no one could take this farm away from them. They work so hard Bill. You should see them."

"People that knew Anna ain't a problem. The problem is people who know you."

Florence was startled to realize that that was true. She belonged to the WCTU and the WKKK. Neither of those organizations actually did anything violent, but they made recommendations to the KKK, and those men definitely carried out violent acts. She clasped her hands in front of her and hung her head in shame.

"I hate my life. Did you know the ladies at the WCTU keep a list of suspected Papists and sympathizers? Sally Ingram gives it to her father to make certain none of those people can get a loan. Did you know the ladies in the WKKK had a tea party when we got the news that Sacred Heart burned down in Corydon?"

The tears began to flow. She lifted a corner of Anna's apron to wipe her eyes and said, "I've been a horrid person. I want to make up for all that. I want to be Anna Taylor!"

Florence's tears became a torrent, and she ran up the hill to join the children. Bill watched her go and smiled. Florence was a sweet, beautiful woman, but she was no Anna Taylor. She always tried to be what people wanted her to be, and as a result, she never quite grew up. Even now, the wants and wishes of children were molding her. He wished her well in her efforts to become a better person. If she wanted to be Anna Taylor, then he would do what he could for Florence and the children living at Yellowwood Farm. He got into his car and left.

When Florence reached the grave, gasping and clutching her side, she wailed through tears, "I won't leave! I promise!"

The children were already kneeling around the grave, straightening the stones. They looked up at her and smiled. Florence got down on her knees at the foot of the grave. It was perfectly tended, but she placed her hands on it anyway, leaving her handprints among the hundreds of others already there. She closed her eyes and prayed for the strength and purity of the woman whose life she would try to live.

Emma pressed her hands together and bowed her head. The other children did the same.

She closed her eyes and said, "Momma, I am lost."

A memory came, of a day long ago. She stood with her mother just outside their church. The day was cold and gray. Her mother reached down and took her hand. She looked through the doors of the church and saw her father, standing with a group of men speaking softly to Pastor Williams. Jack Hansen turned to look over her father's shoulder at her, and she could feel the goodness in him, but his eyes smoldered with barely restrained anger.

Then it was gone. She had no idea what it meant. Instead of love and comfort, it left her with a feeling of foreboding.

Anna said a quiet prayer, "O my good Angel, appointed by God to be my guardian, enlighten and protect me, direct and govern me this day. Amen."

Emma turned to Anna with a look of surprise. Her mother's answer made sense now.

Anna smiled sweetly. "God gives everybody a guardian angel."

When they walked down the hill, the boys clustered around Florence, until they came nearer to the barn. Tommy took off at a run, followed by Chris and the twins. He stopped outside the chicken coop, and the other boys joined him. They held on to the wire, looking in at a big hole in the henhouse, lined with feathers.

Tommy said, "Emma ain't gonna like this."

Claude said, "Damn stupid chickens."

Chapter Twenty-Three

Cecil Hammond sat in the second row at the movie theater, listening to the Exalted Cyclops speak from the stage. The Klan owned this theater now and was quickly purchasing others in every small Midwestern town. D. W. Griffith's 1915 film, *The Birth of a Nation* was playing again this week to sold-out crowds.

The film was wildly popular in the Midwest, but in the Deep South, it's portrayal of Klansmen as heroic figures and Southern blacks as violent rapists, was met with eye-rolling and head-shaking. Where the issues touched upon by the film existed in real life, it was a flop.

Cecil fluffed up his robes and sighed. The Exalted Cyclops was repeating the rhetoric about Catholics, Jews, and blacks he used to open with every meeting. In Indiana, it was illegal for whites to marry blacks. The Klan was intent upon enacting something similar to the Louisiana law that forbade Protestants from marrying Catholics, although those unions were not so readily apparent.

Things were not going well for Cecil. He had lost his car, his gun, and his sheriff's badge. He paid his ten-dollar Klan dues, although he had no savings to speak of. His Klan brothers would readily find him a job, but he was unaccustomed to doing anything more strenuous than slinging a bullwhip. He sighed again. His beloved whip was washed away when Florence crashed his car in the river. He longed for the days when she would plead with him to crack his whip out in the back yard. She would shiver with delight and clap for him.

When the Exalted Cyclops said, "What new business do we have?" Cecil stood up.

"I found Florence. She's up at the Taylor farm. The

widow Taylor is letting her stay there and she has that Papist girl and her brother too! Florence is dallying with some fella by the name of Jack Hansen."

The Exalted Cyclops was actually Jim Henderson, the owner of the hardware store. News travels fast in a small town. He knew Cecil had lost his job yesterday, and was also aware of Florence's infidelity with a farmer by the name of Jack Hansen. Florence's own mother had confirmed the rumors.

He said, "If there are Papists on that farm, then there must be liquor to supply their rites. The Taylor farm butts up against the Pearson place. It's common knowledge that Ike Pearson is a drunk, yet you found no evidence to support an arrest."

Cecil heard his cue and responded appropriately. "I believe there is a still on the Taylor property. Without a man to operate that farm, it's the only way to explain how they keep it up the way they do."

Jim nodded. "I'll approve an investigation. Did Bill give you back your gun?"

Cecil shook with righteous anger. "That bastard stuck my own gun in my face! No, he didn't give it back. If he had, I'd have shot him!"

Jim chuckled. "Yeah, I heard about that. Bill had his chance to join up, that alien ain't interested. You stop by the store and I'll loan you a shotgun. Keep your nose clean and maybe we'll make you sheriff when elections come around next year."

Jim waved Cecil forward. He walked down the aisle and climbed up onto the stage. The Exalted Cyclops sat in a big padded chair, carried in from the lobby.

Jim said quietly, "Take the Terrors over there tonight. You need to find some sort of alcohol and make some arrests. I don't care what you do with Florence. Just don't make a stink about it."

Cecil nodded and walked back to his seat with a smile on his face. Things were looking up.

***

Most Klan members in Indiana were issued badges, given powers to conduct investigations, and make arrests by Indiana's Attorney General. The force of law came from an archaic piece of legislation called the Horse Thief Detection Association.

In the early 1800s, a rash of horse thievery resulted in the abandonment of some of Indiana's most productive cropland. In those days, the loss of a horse significantly affected a family's ability to survive. The HTDA was intended as a means of organizing and empowering the citizenry to enforce the law in areas where no other form of law enforcement existed.

When the state government realized the enormous cost of trying to enforce Prohibition, the Klan was welcomed into law enforcement. They actually paid for the privilege, in the form of HTDA dues, collected by the state.

***

Ike had come to enjoy his nightly vigils on the wagon trail at Yellowwood Farm. He sat under his favorite tree, chewing a piece of hardtack. A mother raccoon came down the trail followed by three kits. He tossed them a piece of hardtack. The mother shied away, but one of the kits stopped to pick it up and ran to catch up to his mother.

It was a nice night. A few low clouds moved over the landscape, driven by a stiff breeze. Ike could feel the rain coming in his bones, so he brought a rain slicker.

Ike had been sober for nearly a week. He felt better than he had in years. Just in case, he had a couple of bottles hidden under the floor of the barn, but he has stopped thinking about them. His thoughts remained focused on a man whose face he had never seen.

A yellow glow appeared on the road, and soon he heard an engine. Ike had no idea what time it was, but he knew from the call of a whippoorwill that it was close to dawn. A car pulled to the side of the road just down from the wagon trail and two more pulled up behind it. Ike stood up and rocked back the hammers on his double-barreled shotgun.

A dozen men climbed out of those cars, wearing white robes, their faces hidden beneath white hoods. Ike scowled and felt his pockets, counting his ammunition. He had two in the breech and two in each pocket—only half what he needed. He could only hope the carnage frightened the rest away.

It was time. In the long, lonely hours sitting beside the wagon trail, Ike made his peace with God and begged forgiveness for what he was about to do.

Voices drifted up from the road.

"Where are the torches?"

"I got a lantern."

"A lantern! Lanterns ain't exactly awe-inspiring."

"Here they are. Wait until we get up there to light 'em."

Ike slipped quietly behind an ancient oak just beside the trail. He held his shotgun at the ready. It was loaded with slugs, and there was another in his pocket. The other three shells held double-ought.

After a long delay, the men beside the road finally began walking up the wagon trail. Ike felt a pang of fear, not for himself, but for the children on this farm. He had underestimated the number of men he would be facing on this night.

The robed men stumbled up the trail in the dim light of a single lantern. When they came abreast of Ike, he picked out one of the men carrying a shotgun and gently pulled the first trigger. BOOM, and a white flash illuminated the scene in brilliant light. The man he aimed at toppled into the trees.

The Klansmen shouted and ran in every direction. Another shot rang out, followed by a scream. Ike smiled— they were doing his work for him. He targeted another man carrying a shotgun and put a slug in his chest. His feet came off the ground and he landed flat on his back. A dark stain spread out from a black hole in his white robes.

Ike ducked back behind the tree and quickly reloaded. When he peeked out at the trail, he heard a shot. Buckshot raked his arm and face. He was surprised to find that it did not hurt nearly as much as a whip. He put his last slug through the head of the man who shot him. His white hood puffed up like a balloon and he dropped to the ground.

Another shot went off, but it was wild. The trees behind him rattled and shook. One of the men ran up the wagon trail toward the house, the rest ran toward the road. Ike took careful aim at the one running up the trail and placed the entire spread in his back. The man went face first into the ground and didn't move.

Stepping out from behind the tree, Ike walked carefully down the trail while he loaded his last two shells. He tasted blood. He stooped down to retrieve a shotgun and broke it open. A spent shell popped out, so he left it there.

The sound of an engine made him quicken his pace. He reached the end of the trail just as the first car pulled away from the side of the road. He couldn't see past the headlights, so he stepped out into the road and sent a blast through the windshield on the driver's side. The car continued past him and went nose down into the ditch.

A fusillade of shots rang out, and Ike felt his body dance in the loose gravel. He swung his shotgun up one-handed and fired his last shell. Then the sky opened up to him, and he left his body lying face down in the road.

***

Nearly an hour later, Cecil Hammond crawled out of the back of the wrecked car—weeping. He had never been so frightened in his life. He was covered with blood, but not his own. Clark Patrick was slumped over the steering wheel, missing a good portion of his face.

Cecil had huddled in the back of the car, until the darkness began to recede. Dawn was near. The eastern sky was pale gray. He stood beside the wrecked car in a light rain and saw Ike's body lying in the road. Warm liquid ran down his leg. Even dead, that old man was terrifying.

Whimpering in fear, he quickly shed his white robes and tossed them into the car. That old man might have friends. He plodded down the road, trying to look in all directions at once. For the second time this week, he was going to have to walk all the way back to town. A clap of thunder sent him scurrying.

***

Jack Hansen rode in the rain with Joe beside him. Bill Robertson had paid him a visit two days ago and described what had taken place at Yellowwood Farm—in front of Mary. Bill didn't know Mary was unaware of what was going on, and he had to caution her that if she actually did kill her husband, she would spend a night in jail. She used words Jack was surprised she knew.

Yesterday, she had insisted that Jack drive her to Yellowwood Farm in the buggy. She spent most of the morning fawning over the children and doctoring Florence.

When the children led Mary up to Anna's grave and begged her to promise not to tell, she wept and made her promise. She also forgave her husband.

The rain came down steadily. Jack was lost in thought, rocking in the familiar rhythm of riding on horseback.

Joe sat up straight on his horse, peering off into the distance. "Pa."

Jack looked over at his son. Joe pointed ahead. There was a car in the ditch, and a body was lying in the road. Jack urged his horse into a gallop and Joe rode after him. Jack knew it was Ike Pearson before he jumped down out of the saddle. He rolled him onto his back. Buckshot riddled Ike's body. A double-barreled twelve-gauge shotgun was still in his hand.

Joe ran to the car and called out, "Pa! There's a dead guy in here!"

Jack looked up from Ike's body and shouted, "Stay here, Joey!"

He leapt into the saddle and galloped up the wagon trail. Bodies littered the trail, wrapped in white robes stained with blood. Jack was frantic. He should have known! He should have stayed here!

A lone figure stood at the top of the wagon trail, dressed in a yellow rain slicker three sizes too big for her. Jack reined in his horse and he slid in the mud, stumbling to a stop. Jack jumped down and grabbed Anna by the shoulders.

She held a finger to her lips. "Shhhh. Emma does na need to see this."

Jack picked her up. "Are you okay? Is everybody okay?"

Anna squirmed. "Careful of my eggs! We're fine! I

thought I heard shooting. Emma was asleep. I snuck out here when I went to get the eggs. Don't let her see this, Mister Hansen."

Jack placed Anna on her feet and sank down to the ground, relieved to hear that the children were unharmed.

Anna peeked over his shoulder. "It's a right awful mess. Ike protected us. He was our guardian angel."

She placed a hand on his shoulder. "Come to breakfast but keep quiet about this until we can clean it up. Emma is a gentle angel, she would na understand."

Jack looked up into her sweet face, framed by strands of wet auburn hair. The way this slip of a girl calmly coped with catastrophe was a little bit terrifying.

"Go back to the house. Tell Emma I had to send Joey into town. I'll take care of this."

Anna turned and walked back toward the house, carefully cradling her wicker basket containing two precious eggs.

***

Less than an hour later, Bill Robertson's patrol car roared down the road and slid to a stop at the entrance to the wagon trail. He was unshaved and in a surly mood. Jack dragged Ike's body out of the road and covered him with a bloody sheet he found in the car.

Bill jumped out of his car and ran up to Jack, standing beside Ike's body. "What the hell happened here?"

Jack said, "Florence and the kids are fine."

Bill turned in a circle, surveying the scene. "Sorry, Jack. Anybody been here? Anybody drive past?"

"It's early yet. Ain't much traffic hereabouts anyway."

"How many? Dead I mean."

"One in the car, five up on the trail, and Ike here was

lying in the road. I ain't checked the woods yet. They're all Klan, except for Ike."

Bill rubbed the stubble on his chin. "Good God! Seven men dead! This is bad, Jack."

Jack had already thought this through. "Remember the Parker boys?"

Bill stopped looking around and focused on Jack. "It's a shame about that girl. There are still warrants out. They disappeared years ago."

Jack said, "That's right, they just disappeared. When people just disappear, it's no big deal. When they turn up dead, all sorts of nasty things start to happen. Those kids up there will lose the farm if this gets out."

"Seven men, Jack! Seven men do not disappear! Not in my county!"

Jack got angry. "What do you mean your county? Who do you think takes care of business out here while you're off serving summons!"

Bill waved his hands in a placating gesture and said, "I know this job is bullshit, Jack. I always looked the other way when Regulators was involved, but things are changing. We got electricity in town now and a telephone!"

Jack calmed. "Look, Bill, I know you ain't Klan. I know you're inclined to do the right thing. What's the Klan gonna say if these men just disappear? They were out here in the middle of the night with shotguns, ready to face down a woman and six children! They don't want nobody saying that out loud."

Bill looked up into the rain and groaned loudly. "You know this will cost me the election."

"You ain't Klan, Bill. You're gonna lose that election anyway. You might as well stick a burr under their saddle while you can. Besides, it's only six. Old Ike here deserves a proper burial, died of natural causes."

***

By the time Joe galloped down the road from town, splashing through the rain, Ike's truck was parked beside the road with a heavy load, covered with a tarp. His father and Bill Robertson were kneeling down, washing the blood from their hands in a puddle.

He jumped down from his horse and ran up to his father, his eyes wide with fear. Rain poured from the brim of his hat.

Jack stood up and put his arm over his son's shoulders. "You alright, boy?"

Joe nodded, but he was far from alright.

"Look, son, this is a hard thing. You're too young to see so much death, but these men had it coming."

"I know, Pa. It ain't right what that man done to Florence, or to Emma."

"I'm proud of you, boy. You've done a fine job looking out for Emma and those kids. Bill is gonna help us out here. These men are gonna disappear. Ike deserves to be buried proper. He died in his sleep. You understand?"

"Yes, Pa. I won't say different."

"Good. Now go and get Ike's draft horse and pull that car out of the ditch."

Joe ran back to Verne and jumped up into the saddle. He whirled him around and galloped up the muddy road into Ike's barn. He was not the least bit surprised to find his father's horse, brushed and dry, contentedly munching on a bucket of oats.

Chapter Twenty-Four

Emma stood at the sink, looking out the window at the rain. Joe only stopped by today to tell Anna he had to go into town. Everything that could be done on a rainy day was done, but she still missed having him around.

Florence was slowly recovering. She looked much better, baking a raspberry pie to have with dinner. Emma watched her put a few small logs of white oak in the woodstove and open the dampers. She stood up and brushed a wisp of dark hair back behind her ear. She was an excellent cook, and she knew how to bake a pie.

She could hear Anna in the parlor, furiously sewing away. She had lit a lamp to add to the dim light from the cloudy sky. Emma walked into the room and watched her for a moment until she finished a seam and snipped the thread. She jumped up and held a small shirt up against her, judging the size. She was an exceptional seamstress. She knew how to sew.

Emma turned to the lamp table and picked up her parent's wedding picture. She had not touched it in weeks, and now, it brought feelings of loss. Something was amiss. What else needed to be done? All the little things that needed doing had absorbed her for so long, perhaps she felt lost because she had nothing to do. She turned a circle in the parlor. Everything was as it should be, yet she felt that something was left undone.

She heard a knock on the door and went into the kitchen. Jack Hansen was visible through the window. She ran to throw open the door, and Jack stepped inside, followed by Joe. They shook off the rain and removed their hats.

Emma could see they were troubled. "What's wrong?"

Florence came around the table with a concerned look on her face. "What is it, Jack?"

Anna peeked into the kitchen and came to stand beside Emma.

Jack took Emma by the arm and sat her down at the table. He sat down beside her and said, "I'm sorry to say that Ike died last night."

Emma's lips trembled and she began to cry—softly, quietly. "I knew something was wrong," she said.

Jack put his arm around her. "He died peacefully, Emma. He didn't suffer."

Emma nodded through her tears. "I'm glad for that. I have to tell the boys."

Florence stood on the other side of Emma and used the corner of her mother's apron to wipe away Emma's tears. "I'm sorry, Emma. I only met Ike that one time, but he saved me. He was a good man."

Emma looked up at her in surprise and said, "He was. He tried really hard to be a good man. Joe, would you go and get the boys for me?"

Joe put his hat back on and stepped out into the rain. On days like this, he knew he would find them in the barn.

Florence carried a kettle over to the sink and filled it with water from the pump. "I'll make some tea."

Joe was back in less than a minute. The boys had picked up from his demeanor that something serious was happening. He herded them inside, wide-eyed, wet and dripping.

Florence held out her arms to them, but they ran past her to cluster around Emma. They could see she was hurt.

She pulled Clyde and Claude close to her and said, "Your grampa died, boys. He died in his sleep, he didn't suffer."

The twins began to cry and clung to Emma. She held them close. "Shush now. Everything will be alright. I'll take care of you."

Jack stood up. "I'm sorry, boys. Your grampa was a good man. Emma, I've got something to take care of. You watch over the boys, and when I get back, we'll have a proper service. Ike is buried beside his wife, like he wanted."

Joe stood up with a look of concern. "Pa, I'm going with you."

Jack roughly hugged his son with one arm. "Not today, Joey. You stay here and keep an eye on things."

Joe had looked into the faces of each of the dead men in the back of Ike's truck—a hard thing for a fourteen-year-old boy. Cecil Hammond was not among them.

***

Jack rode slowly in the rain, hunched over in the saddle. He had never done anything like this in town. Regulators watched over their own—farmers. People in town lived entirely different lives. The Klan never caught on among farmers, they were too busy and too widely separated for such nonsense.

The majority of Klan members were middle-class men, living in small towns. Prosperity came in the wake of the war, and those men found amusement in fraternal societies. Farmers, on the other hand, suffered from the post-war isolationist policies that shut them out of European markets.

Ike's shotgun was wrapped in an old rain slicker, tied to his saddle. Jack collected three others, left abandoned on the trail, and scavenged two twelve-gauge shells. He thought he would only need one, if any.

He and Bill drove Ike's truck over to the Blue Hole, an abandoned quarry, filled with water now—rumored to be a hundred feet deep. The bodies would never be found. Jack hoped they suffered in their deep, cold Hell—next to the Parker boys. He planned to drop Cecil Hammond down beside them.

When he reached the switchback that led up into town, he felt a moment of fear. He had never ridden into town with a shotgun strapped to his saddle before. Town people were different from those he normally associated with. They lived so close together that nothing went unnoticed, and they talked and talked and talked. His fear was not for himself, it was for his family, but his mind was made up. He planned to ride out of town with an unidentifiable something wrapped in a blanket over the front of his saddle.

A flash of lightning and a crash of thunder was followed by pouring rain. He removed his hat, tilted back his head, and took a cool drink from the sky.

When he asked Joe where Cecil lived, Joe said, "No, Pa." Eventually, he gave him the address. It was better than making him ask in town.

Jack turned left, up the last street in town, avoiding Main Street. The rain had cleared the streets of people, although he did see a few, sitting on their front porches.

When Jack reached Cecil's house, he sat on his horse beside a big maple tree, considering how to proceed. He might not be home. More likely he was in bed. It was two o'clock in the afternoon, or thereabouts, but Cecil had been busy all night.

Jack swung down out of the saddle and was un-strapping the shotgun when a car roared past him and swerved up into the grass of Cecil's front yard. Four men dressed in white robes jumped out and ran into the house. Jack took the reins and backed his horse up behind the tree.

Surely those men saw him, but apparently it didn't matter.

Less than a minute later, they crashed through the front door, leaving the screen door hanging by a single hinge. They carried a struggling little man wearing only his undershorts with a sock in his mouth. Each man held an arm or a leg.

He watched Cecil Hammond struggle and squirm until he slipped loose and fell into the grass. One of the men pulled a shotgun out from under his robes and brought the butt down squarely between Cecil's eyes. He went still, and they picked him up again without any trouble. Tossing him into the back of the car, they climbed in to put their feet in his back. Then they drove away.

Jack laughed. His horse nuzzled him, and he put his arm around his neck. "What do you say about that, Hank, old boy?"

An elderly lady came out onto the front porch of the house next door and timidly looked around. Jack tipped his hat to her.

She took a step toward her door and then hesitated. She peered through the rain at Jack and shouted, "Good riddance!"

Jack shouted back, "God's will be done!"

He swung up into the saddle and rode slowly out of town in the pouring rain—laughing.

***

By late afternoon, the sky cleared. Emma wore her best dress, as did Anna and Florence. They had scrubbed and dressed the boys as best they could. They sat at the table, listlessly picking at pieces of raspberry pie. Mary Hansen pulled up beside the house with her son, John, driving the buggy. Joe and Jack came out of the barn to meet her.

Emma said, "It's time, boys."

They all rose from the table and met Mary at the door. She gathered up Clyde and Claude in her arms.

"Your grampa was a brave man," she said.

Jack gave her a look, and she covered her mouth with her hand.

Jack led the procession, still carrying Ike's shotgun. They walked down the wagon trail in a long line with the boys lined up behind Emma. The rain had washed away the blood.

When they came within sight of Ike's farm, Emma held out her hands. Clyde and Claude stepped up on either side of her, and each placed one of their hands in hers, wiping away tears with the other. Emma allowed her own tears to fall.

The grave was on a low hill surrounded by a low iron fence. One gravestone stood there, with the name, *Martha Pearson*, and below that, *Beloved Wife and Mother*. Two unmarked graves were to the left, and to the right was a fresh mound of earth.

Christopher and Tommy held on to Florence. She took their hands and led them to the side of the grave. Emma walked the twins up to the other side, and Anna joined them. They all knelt down in the mud. Jack and his family stood behind them.

Emma said, "O Jesus, by your resurrection, death no longer has dominion over those who die. So we ask, take Mister Pearson into Heaven. Shine your warm light upon him. Tell him we are well and all together and we are thinking of him. Let our love for him bind us together. Amen."

They all stood up and walked away toward the road. Mary turned to her husband with a puzzled look and he put his arm around her.

They searched through the gravel, selecting the whitest stones they could find. Then they returned to the grave, knelt down to smooth the earth, and arranged the stones to spell out Ike Pearson. Small handprints and those of a woman, who finally found somebody she could love, covered the grave.

Anna stepped around to the other side of Jack and tugged at his sleeve with a muddy hand. He looked down at her, and she motioned for him to come closer.

When he leaned over, she kissed him on the cheek and whispered in his ear, "You were very brave."

www.ingramcontent.com/pod-product-compliance
Lightning Source LLC
Chambersburg PA
CBHW051635180726
48284CB00006B/1736